Received On

ry

Limelight

ALSO BY AMY POEPPEL

Small Admissions

Limelight

a novel

AMY POEPPEL

EMILY BESTLER BOOKS

—

ATRIA

New York   London   Toronto   Sydney   New Delhi

EMILY
BESTLER
BOOKS

ATRIA

An Imprint of Simon & Schuster, Inc.
1230 Avenue of the Americas
New York, NY 10020

First Emily Bestler Books/Atria Books hardcover edition May 2018

EMILY BESTLER BOOKS / ATRIA BOOKS and colophon are trademarks of Simon & Schuster, Inc.

For information about special discounts for bulk purchases, please contact Simon & Schuster Special Sales at 1-866-506-1949 or business@simonandschuster.com.

The Simon & Schuster Speakers Bureau can bring authors to your live event. For more information or to book an event, contact the Simon & Schuster Speakers Bureau at 1-866-248-3049 or visit our website at www.simonspeakers.com.

Interior design by Amy Trombat

Manufactured in the United States of America

10 9 8 7 6 5 4 3 2 1

Library of Congress Cataloging-in-Publication Data

Names: Poeppel, Amy, author.
Title: Limelight : a novel / Amy Poeppel.
Description: First Emily Bestler Books/Atria Books hardcover edition. | New
    York : Emily Bestler Books/Atria, 2018.
Identifiers: LCCN 2017052475 (print) | LCCN 2017055058 (ebook)
Subjects: LCSH: Celebrities—Fiction. | Mothers—Fiction. | Domestic fiction.
    | BISAC: FICTION / Contemporary Women. | FICTION / Family Life. | FICTION / Literary.
Classification: LCC PS3616.O345 (ebook) | LCC PS3616.O345 L56 2018 (print) |
    DDC 813/.6—dc23
LC record available at https://lccn.loc.gov/2017052475

ISBN 978-1-5011-7637-1
ISBN 978-1-5011-7639-5 (ebook)

To our moms:
Pamela and Christiane
Rena and Susan

Thereza: "I thought you hated the theater."
Calvero: "I do. I also hate the sight of blood,
but it's in my veins."

Charlie Chaplin
Limelight

Part One

NEW YORK MOVES

"I can't imagine living anywhere else . . .
It's amazing: I'm a New Yorker . . . I never thought I would be."

David Bowie
In Other Words: Artists Talk About Life and Work by Anthony DeCurtis

one

OUR FIRST MORNING IN NEW YORK CITY, before anyone else in the family had shown signs of life, I was up, surveying the situation. In bare feet and pajamas, mug of coffee in hand, I stood in the open doorway of our new apartment, wondering if you even use a doormat in a carpeted hallway. When I heard a creak down the hall, I ducked back inside before a man heading out with a pug under one arm and a newspaper under the other could spot me in my sleepwear.

The left side of the small living room, opposite the north-facing windows that overlooked a beige brick building, was a wall of boxes. I found one that was especially well labeled ("**OPEN FIRST**") and began unpacking towels, stuffed animals, lamps, school supplies, and toilet paper so we would have the essentials right from the start. Before going to bed the night before, I had unpacked the coffee maker, mugs, and cereal bowls. I had a hammer and nails handy so that I could hang pictures, along with a baggie of magnets to clutter up the refrigerator. The Jawbone speaker was on the kitchen counter, ready to play pop music to get my kids in a chipper mood for their first day as New Yorkers. Above all, I wanted everyone to feel at home, in spite of the upheaval. One needs a doormat, for example. Or so I thought. Standing in the living room that morning, with the doormat still rolled up, I had a suspicion that the universe was scoffing at me and my futile attempts to settle in. But I didn't let that dampen my mood; I was finally getting the chance to live in Manhattan.

As soon as I heard voices coming from the kids' rooms, I went old-school and turned on the Beastie Boys' "Body Movin'." But before we could *get some action from the back section*, the doorman called up with a noise complaint. The new refrigerator was wood-paneled and non-magnetic, a barren expanse, and the box I'd carefully labeled "FRAG-ILE! WINEGLASSES!" made a sound like a package of Legos when I went to open it. Our furniture seemed confused and uneasy to be sitting thirteen stories in the air. I couldn't shake the worry that it was all too heavy and eventually the floors would give way, sending couches, beds, book boxes, and the upright piano through the ceilings until finally all of our possessions landed in the lobby. Our cat, Jasper, was hiding in a closet behind our GE Spacemaker stacked washer/dryer, my children were cranky and nervous about starting school the next week, and my husband was stressed about his new job.

I took a deep breath and continued unpacking.

⎯⎯

We had been living in New York for less than two weeks when we had our first, full-blown crisis. I didn't know how to handle it and almost called my mother for advice, but I stopped myself; she was still mad at me for moving away. I called Sara instead, my one and only friend in the city. As someone who had lived in New York for years, she was, in my mind, an expert.

"Is this bad?" I asked her.

"Honestly, I wasn't listening."

I closed the door to my bedroom and spoke clearly. "The principal says Jack offered a girl in his class a dollar to see her vagina."

"Ooooh."

"I know."

"That seems like a low offer to me."

"Not for a third grader."

"He obviously hasn't adjusted to Manhattan prices. Did he have a dollar?"

"I don't know," I said. "Maybe. Why?"

"It speaks to intent. Maybe he was asking hypothetically."

"But I'm asking—is this really bad? It's only his first week at this school, so can they kick him out? And does this point to something seriously wrong with him? Like is my son a sexual deviant?"

"He's *four*."

"He's eight."

"Whatever," she said.

"No—that's why the school is so mad. He's old enough to know better. Do you think he hates women?"

"To the contrary," Sara said. "So did she?"

"What?"

"Unveil the vag?"

"No! And she's very upset. Jack has to write an apology."

"You're blowing this way out of proportion."

"It's not *me*. The teacher asked him to write a letter. And she used the word 'troubling.' Like the act was a predictor of something worse to come. Like when young kids torture animals, it's considered 'troubling.'"

"Asking for pussy and lighting a cat on fire are not the same thing," Sara said bluntly. "He was probably testing limits. Or thinking entrepreneurially, like 'How can I turn a single dollar to my advantage in this shit economy?' That's not troubling. That's enterprising."

What I found most troubling, infuriating, actually, was that the girl's mother didn't call me directly. Or tell me to my face. I had seen her each day at pickup since school started, surrounded by her many friends, and we'd been added to the school directory already. She could have talked to me so we could smooth things over privately. But instead she went over my head and ratted Jack out.

"A written apology—"

"Why should he apologize?" Sara asked. "No money changed hands, so technically it's not even solicitation. It'll blow over. A week from now you'll be laughing about this. Did you start work yet?"

"Tomorrow," I said. "What if he grows up to be a regular customer at a strip club? Where all the dancers know him by name."

"Allison—"

"You're busy, I know. Sorry."

"No, but my boss just came in, and I can't wait to tell her about this."

"No! Don't . . . ," I begged, but I could hear her saying, "Hey, so my friend's male chauvinist piglet tried to pay for a peek of snatch . . . ," as she hung up.

That's the problem with Sara, other than being inappropriate and never available. She has no clue about discretion. Or about children. But she lives here, which makes her the only local friend I have. I need her.

I went back to the living room, past dozens of half-unpacked boxes, wondering how many people Brittney's mother had already told. Had she destroyed our reputation before we'd ever had a chance to build one? Jack would have to throw himself at everyone's mercy and hope for forgiveness. I wanted to shield him from further embarrassment, given what he would face at school the next day. As a teacher, I knew the staff would convene around the school secretary's desk and have a laugh at Jack's expense. And the only people who gossip more than teachers are elementary school children.

If this sort of misstep had happened back in Dallas, I would have met the moms for margaritas, and they would have made me feel better. *Oh, Allison, we love Jack, bless his heart.* I would have called up the girl's mother to talk; *Bygones,* she would have reassured me. We were known there. No moms knew me here.

I considered calling Lilly who was supposed to be my local mom friend. In college she had repeatedly made the case that New York City was the best—no, the *only* place on earth to live and had always urged me to move there. And then she'd promptly abandoned the place the moment I decided to take her advice. I put my phone back down; I was still, perhaps unreasonably, smarting from our last phone call in the summer.

"It took only twenty years," I had joked, "but I'm finally moving to New York!"

I waited for her exclamations of joy but heard nothing.

"Lilly? Bad connection?"

"Just bad timing, sweetie. We're moving to Montclair. Like, we're literally moving as we speak. I've got boxes all over the place."

"What?" Lilly leaving New York? Impossible. "Very funny."

"It was time," she said flatly and yelled instructions to the moving men who were in her apartment.

"Why? Time for what?" I asked. Lilly had been selling me on New York since the day we'd met. She was the one who had taught me that if I knew the inner workings of Manhattan, I could see a Broadway play for only ten dollars. She was the one who proved to me that the subway was indeed the fastest way to get around the city and that runway models, such as the dozens she worked with at her mother's agency, had acne in real life. "But you always said you could never imagine living anywhere else. That you loved the smell of concrete. That you were allergic to every other place on the—"

"I'll still see you all the time," she said. "I can hop on the train from New Jersey whenever I like. You, me, and Sara; we'll grab drinks anytime. But I've had it with the noise, the schools, just the whole . . . I don't know . . . *scene*. Montclair is amazing. You've *got* to come visit."

Her desertion, at the moment I was arriving, felt like a personal betrayal, and I didn't feel like calling her to commiserate over Jack's school incident. She would probably just tell me to move to Montclair.

—————

I checked the time; Charlotte would be heading home from cross-country practice at Van Cortlandt Park within the hour, and Michael would be getting out of the meeting he was holding with the entire staff at his firm. Meanwhile, Jack was in his room with the door closed, and my homesick fourteen-year-old was in hers. For some reason our new living room didn't seem to function as a family room, so the kids often retreated to their corners, and it was quieter than I was used to. I admit, I was homesick, too.

Since Jack and Megan were doing homework, I settled in to do mine: I continued the hunt for the many people we would need in our lives: a dentist, a veterinarian, a piano teacher, and a pediatrician. A math tutor, a hairdresser, a dry cleaner, and a handyman.

Dallas had been such a mellow, comfortable place to live. The streets are broad, the winters are mild, the air-conditioning has oomph, and parking is plentiful. But truth be told, I had grown a bit restless there.

Moving to Texas had been easy. I was welcomed. Literally. Instantly. On our first day in the Dallas house, a decade ago, as I unpacked my doormat and took it outside to the front steps, my neighbor Natalie walked up with her tanned, blond, preteen daughter and a heaping plate of homemade snickerdoodles. The recipe, calling for two pounds of butter, was taped to the Saran Wrap. "In case you want to give it a try," Natalie said.

We liked each other right off the bat. She became one of my walking friends, meeting me in our driveway twice a week at six thirty in the morning with her gooey-eyed cocker spaniel.

Over the years that our families lived side by side, Natalie's daughter Carrie, a fan of football, fast cars, and country music, grew up to be a partier, so Natalie confiscated booze whenever she or the cleaning lady found any half-empty bottles under her canopy bed. "You in need of some cheap rum?" Natalie would ask me. "I found a handle in the backseat of Carrie's car." Carrie got a coveted spot on the cheerleading squad once she got to high school and wore her short flouncy skirt to school every Friday; Megan's eyes would lock on those bouncy pom-poms and never blink, pupils turning into little cartoon hearts.

Charlotte, on the other hand, grew up to become decidedly antiparty and anticheerleader.

"What does it say about our society," she ranted one night at my mom's house for dinner, "when males get accolades for knocking each other down for sport and giving each other concussions with subsequent long-term brain damage, while the women dress up as sex symbols and chant inane rhymes in order to support some brutish, caveman rituals? Disgusting."

"I like her," Megan said.

"Popularity shouldn't be based on sex appeal," Charlotte said.

"She's popular because she's always sweet and *nice* to everyone. Unlike some people I know."

"I'd say that you're both one hundred percent right," my mother interjected, playing her role of keeper of the sibling peace.

When I told Natalie that the firm had made Michael an offer for a major promotion as long as he agreed to move to the East Coast office, she got teary and said, "Oh, how awful!" She caught herself and suddenly hugged me, saying, "What I mean is, awful for *me*. But hey! New York City! How exciting!"

"Yes, it is," I said. "I think it would be great."

"I mean, I would *never* want to live in New York, not ever in a million years, but how thrilling for *you*!" She looked away for a moment, imagining perhaps feminist demonstrations and political marches, and said, "Come to think of it, I can picture Charlotte fitting right in there."

My mother reacted to my news in a way that was far easier to interpret. "Have a nice life," she said when I told her. Neither one of us took that comment seriously, but I was starting to wonder how long she planned to punish me.

"You've got so many close friends here, so many people who love you and Michael and the kids. I don't see why you would want to throw that away," she had said.

I wasn't willing to admit to anyone that so far I wasn't feeling the love in New York. I was starting to get the feeling that no one cared how I was doing. New Yorkers have a way of looking at you as if to say, "Let's just see how long you last." I was up for that challenge. *Fine, I'll show you*, I thought.

Michael had initially been on the fence about moving to New York, even after I was all in. As soon as I'd landed a teaching job, I couldn't be dissuaded by anyone. I got a perfect long-term sub position: I would be replacing an English teacher who'd abruptly decided to get married and was taking a one-year leave of absence to move to Boston with her husband-to-be. It was the perfect combination of serendipity and connections: a teacher friend of a friend had recommended me, and I took the job right away, knowing it might very well lead to a long-term position.

The more I thought about it, the more I was convinced that an adventure and change would be good for all of us, while Michael continued to worry about uprooting the kids. We went out for dinner one night to make our decision, one way or the other.

"We'd be crazy to turn this opportunity down," I said.

"Three kids and no backyard?"

"Who needs a backyard when we have Central Park, and our kids will never drink and drive."

"I read that sixteen thousand pedestrians get hit by a car every month in New York. That's more than five hundred a day."

"Michael."

"What?"

"You've been offered your dream job. It's an honor; it's what you've worked for your whole life."

"But if it's bad for the kids—"

"It'll be great for the kids. When I was visiting New York in college, I remember looking at all the faces on the subway and thinking, '*This* is real life.' Dallas isn't real life."

"It's real to me," Michael said, looking around the restaurant. He waved at someone across the room. I turned to see who it was and waved to the couple as well; I'd taught both of their children.

"But New York would be so much . . . realer. I have such a good feeling about it, like this is exactly what we need."

"What do we need that we don't already have? I'd miss the guys. Where am I going to play golf?"

"Lawyers in New York play golf somewhere."

"What about Dorothy? Do you really expect your mom to move again because of us? We've all got a good thing going here. Why not stay put?" he asked.

I couldn't put my finger on it, but I think it had to do with my urge to stir the pot, to keep things interesting, to stop aging. "Adventure," I said, picking up my glass and swirling the wine in the bottom. "Stimulation. It'll keep us young and edgy. It's so sexy to live in a big city."

Michael perked up. "Go on," he said.

"At our age, we're on the very brink of becoming frumpy and dull. Do you want that? Or do you want a new lease on life?"

"What did you mean by 'sexy'?"

"It's a turn-on, don't you think? I picture a big night out, a party with interesting, smart, quirky people. High heels and a low-cut, hot wrap dress." I touched my toe to his calf. Men were so easy.

"That sounds fun," he said.

"It would be a jolt, in a good way. Invigorating."

"Your cheeks are pink," Michael said.

I felt it, too, my reaction to the prospect of change.

"But I don't know," Michael said, shaking off my fantasy. "Yanking Charlotte out of school before her senior year?"

"Every single college on Charlotte's list is on the East Coast, so if we move to New York, we'll be so much closer. She could come home for Thanksgiving or maybe even a weekend or two."

"Yeah, that's true, but—"

"Our kids," I said with a confidence I was beginning to feel, "will become more interesting, independent, open-minded people."

But here we were, a week-and-a-half in, and, so far, life in Manhattan was making one kid a pervert, one a depressive, and the other an asshole. Megan was lost and couldn't get the hang of things academically. She wore her misery all over her body like an ugly outfit. Her skin had broken out, and her shoulders slumped inward until I thought they might touch in the middle. Even her hair was limp.

"Where's that chipper face?" I'd ask.

She would shrug. "How should I know?"

Charlotte, meanwhile, was sulky and rude, which wasn't entirely surprising given that she was seventeen, but she hadn't so much as smiled once in the time we'd been here. She had been cautiously optimistic about the move when we first discussed it last spring, but bam!—did she ever go sour on the idea after she started dating her very first boyfriend. The timing was a bitch: She and Theo got together at the end of the school year and spent the summer falling in love. The goodbye scene with her robotics-club beau was tearful and tragic for both of them, and the only way we got her on the plane to LaGuardia was by promising a family trip back to Dallas over the winter break.

"You'll see each other in four short months," I said, handing her a tissue across the aisle. She gave me a mean look and blew her nose. By the time we landed, she added a new feature to express her anger and resentment: she went mute. She now huffed around and wouldn't speak to us, even when we asked a direct question. "Who wants dim sum? Hellooo?" Nothing.

My mother was never one to be swayed by teenaged drama, but I knew perfectly well what she would say: *I told you so.*

I checked the time and realized I needed to give some thought to dinner. I looked up from my computer and into the kitchen. Our apartment wasn't what I'd hoped. In Dallas I'd had a granite island, two sinks, a six-burner stainless-steel Viking, and a Sub-Zero. A wine refrigerator and a butler's pantry.

"Why in God's name would you abandon this glorious kitchen?" my mother had asked. "Trading this house for a New York apartment"— she pointed at me—"will in every conceivable way be like going from an Escalade to a Vespa."

"Vespas happen to be extremely cool," I said, "so now I know we're doing the right thing." It was the kind of logical fallacy a student would make in a losing argument.

"Well, don't expect me to follow you this time. I'm not downgrading from my beautiful boxed garden to some Chia Pet on a windowsill."

I figured that once Michael and I found a wonderful place to live, she'd change her mind. Unfortunately, the real estate broker assigned to us by the relocation company said that we should forget those tree-lined streets in the Village, and we couldn't get into any of the uptown co-ops that were known as "A+" or even "A" buildings. We were too disconnected, he said, and our financials weren't in line with what those co-op boards required.

"What do you mean?" Michael had asked.

"The kind of apartment you have in mind," the broker had explained and then looked down at the notes he'd taken from the hour he'd spent on the phone with me, shaking his head, "four bedrooms, plus a study-slash-playroom-slash-guestroom, living room, dining room, we're talking at least double the budget you set. Maybe more."

Michael whistled. "That much?" he asked.

"It's New York," the broker said, as if that explained everything.

I nodded, agreeing with him completely.

"What?" Michael asked me. "This is absurd."

"We're moving to the capital of the world," I said. "Of course, that comes at a price. It's not all about hearth and home, you know."

"It's a little about hearth and home," Michael argued.

"We'll get a perfectly nice place," I said. "We just have to be flexible."

"Now that I think about it," the broker said, "'B' buildings aren't really going to work for you either. Let's forget all this co-op and brownstone talk. Let's take a look at some nice, high-rise condo buildings. No application process, closer to your price range. Quick and easy. In fact," he said, looking up at us suddenly, "have you considered renting?"

So we looked at Upper East Side and Upper West Side condos, all lacking in charm and personality. We finally found an apartment north and west of Columbus Circle on the thirteenth floor of a twenty-story building. It wasn't one of those classic New York prewar architectural wonders like I'd seen in so many movies. And it wasn't like the brownstone Lilly had lived in when I'd gone home with her during college. It was built in 1983. Boring, boring, Marriott-like. It had no views to speak of, but if I leaned out the living room window and craned my neck to the right, I could catch a tiny sliver of Central

Park. It had a slightly depressing vibe; our lobby felt like a doctor's office. And Jack's "bedroom" was eight feet by ten feet. It held a twin bed, a tiny desk, and that was it; his clothes were in a closet in the hallway.

Worst of all: the girls had to share a room. Charlotte heard that news, and her attitude about the move swung from heartbroken about leaving her new boyfriend to disgusted by her terrible parents. From slightly apprehensive to utterly horrified.

"We can't *share* a room," she'd said.

"Sure you can," Michael said.

I nodded. "It'll be like a slumber party every night of the week!"

Charlotte actually stomped her foot. "If New York is so absurdly expensive," she'd asked, "then why are we even moving?"

"Because it's *New York*," I said. "We're going to love it."

"And no one, I mean *no one*, moves for their senior year in high school."

"I'm sure someone has," Michael said, "somewhere." He looked at me.

"Name one," Charlotte said. "My college counselor says this is the dumbest thing ever."

"That's *not* what she said," I reminded her. "She said it's *unusual*, but that you can spin it to your advantage with the right attitude. You can write your essay about how swimmingly you handled change."

"Why can't you guys just wait and move next year?"

"I told you. Dad's promotion—"

"Well, I want to stay here," she said, "and live with Gram."

I raised an eyebrow. "You mean with Theo?"

"No way," Michael said.

"All I'm saying," Charlotte said, "is that we should leave the option on the table in case I don't get into a decent high school."

Call me naive, but I wasn't too worried about schools.

Jack was easy: he got a spot at the neighborhood public school. It was a short walk from our apartment and known to be excellent, according to every online forum I consulted.

The situation for the girls was totally different. The deadlines for the public middle and high schools had passed, so we had to go private or face having them placed randomly in whatever schools happened to have room for them. So we started the off-season private school application process, and they promptly got rejected by seven schools. Only one place took them: a brand-new, shiny, for-profit school called Orbis Academy, not far from Gramercy Park, a school that had branches—actual franchises—in other cities in the world.

"Well, isn't that just fucking fabulous," Charlotte had remarked when the email acceptance came. "Megan and I will be attending the McDonald's of private school education."

"Don't say fucking," I said. "And it's only for a year."

"Thank God."

Orbis was bright and beautiful, and the science facilities, even Charlotte had to admit, were state-of-the-art, but getting there from the new apartment involved a lengthy subway commute. Charlotte did a search on Google Maps and announced that she hated me. "This is seriously going to suck," she said. "*Please* can I just stay here with Gram and graduate with my class?"

It was out of the question, of course, and by that time, the momentum was unstoppable: I'd accepted my new job, put the house on the market, and paid the tuition at Orbis.

———

I saw something moving in the corner of the living room and spotted fat, old, matted Jasper, who had finally ventured out from behind the washing machine after a week of hiding, and was now slinking around behind the couch. I went to pat him, and he jumped out of a half-empty box of books and rubbed up against my leg. I was relieved by this first show of affection since we'd moved and stroked the top of his head. "Hey there, Jasper, you like it here?" I asked, rubbing his ears.

He hissed at me and clawed my hand.

"Oww, you little shit!" I hissed back. Apartment living, with our thin walls and floors, was teaching me to mind my volume, so I kept my cursing level permanently set to low.

I ran my hand under the kitchen faucet, wrapped a paper towel around the scratch, and then texted Charlotte to get her ETA. The message didn't deliver, which I hoped meant that she was on the subway. I decided to treat myself to a glass of wine, to toast what had been a rather difficult day: my offspring had risked expulsion, my hand was bleeding, and I had a growing sense of doom that was killing my New York buzz. Above all, I wanted to raise a glass to my final evening of summer vacation, the last night before I would be back in the classroom teaching full-time again, plunged into the day-to-day work that would consume me for the entire academic year.

Since my wineglasses had shattered into tiny crumbs of stemware in the move, I filled up a coffee mug with red wine and started cooking dinner. I opened the little kitchen cabinet that held the small amount of food I'd bought and took out a box of pasta and a jar of sauce. From a box in the hallway, I found the large spaghetti pot and a pan for garlic and ground beef. I took out the red pepper flakes, the salt, and the olive oil. In these few small acts, I had used up every square inch of the counter space in the kitchen. I realized that with an arm outstretched I could touch the counters on all sides without taking a step.

Cooking suddenly seemed too hard. The oak cabinets felt weighty and out-of-date. I couldn't remember where I'd packed the colander and hated the idea of cleaning up the mess I was about to make.

"Maybe we've made a mistake," I said to Jasper.

Doing domestic chores wasn't the way I wanted to spend my last evening before my school year started, so I went back to my laptop and ordered Chinese. While I waited for the takeout to arrive, I called my former neighbor Natalie and left a message. And then I remembered: tonight was book club. They were all going to—whose house was it this month? Sue's?—to drink Chardonnay and talk about novels, their husbands and exes, their jobs, their kids, or whatever TV show everyone was hooked on. I sent a group text message to the girls: *Miss you lovely ladies!* I added a frowny face, deleted it, and added a smiley face instead.

———

The front door opened, and I heard Michael calling my name before he'd even come inside.

"Hey," I said. "How was—?"

"Guess what happened?" He was flushed and breathless, briefcase in hand, suit jacket over his arm. He looked at me expectantly, actually waiting for me to guess.

"Umm . . ." I threw my hands up randomly. "You got us theater tickets to *Hamilton*?"

"No, but I like your thinking. Guess again."

"You're the employee of the month."

"I just got interviewed"—he paused—"by Humans of New York. Where are the kids? I want to tell them everything."

"They're doing homework, but Charlotte's not back yet. I have news, too. Here," I said and got another mug from the kitchen. "Have some wine. You'll need it."

"Why?"

"I'll tell you after you've finished it."

"I hope it's not that bad," he said, "because I've had such a fantastic day."

I felt a twinge of jealously, thinking of him working side by side with the beautiful lawyer who'd followed him from Dallas to Manhattan. I'd confronted him already, and we regularly went round and round about her.

"Oh, great. So you and Cassandra had a fun time together?"

Michael smiled at me and shook his head.

"What?" I said. I narrowed my eyes at him. "I know what I know."

"Is that like 'It is what it is'?"

"Don't mock me."

He kissed the top of my head. "For the one hundredth time, I'm not sleeping with Cassandra. I'm not attracted to Cassandra."

"Who the hell has a name like Cassandra anyway?" I asked. "She's just calling attention to herself with a name like that. And why do you always pronounce it like that—Cass-*ahn*-dra? Why not Cassandra, like a normal person?"

"You say tomato—"

"And you know perfectly well I have proof of . . . something."

"It's flimsy. It's not even about anything. Any judge worth his salt would throw you out of court."

My proof: Michael brought her along from the Dallas office as part of his "team," and then she'd posted on Facebook: "Check out my hot NYC pad!" and tagged Michael in the picture of her new bedroom. It was disgusting.

"And besides," Michael said, "I've got counterevidence now: she apparently got a serious boyfriend who's into mixed martial arts. I even saw a picture; he looks like John Cena."

I turned this new piece of information over in my mind. "Did John Cena move here with her?" I asked.

"Not yet, but—"

"Ah-ha," I said. "See?"

"See what? When are you going to come check out my new office? And let's go out for dinner this weekend. Have you noticed how many terrific restaurants there are in our neighborhood? I've been bookmarking the heck out of Yelp."

"Food is expensive here," I said. "I bought a gallon of milk today for seven dollars."

"We can afford dinner."

"Maybe. But you can't afford me *and* a mistress, that's all I'm saying."

He clapped his hands together. "I'm a bona fide *Human of New York*! Can you believe it? I wonder if I'll make it into a book."

I decided not to tell him about Jack quite yet. Why ruin his mood?

"I'm going to change into jeans. Want to take a walk later?" he asked and went back to our room.

I heard Charlotte's key in the door and sighed with relief. She didn't say anything or even look at me as she came in, but I thought for a second—incorrectly, as it turned out—that she'd smiled as she dropped her bags and kicked off her shoes.

"Everyone's home," I called out to Megan and Jack.

Jack came into the living room, looking sulky and tired, followed by Megan, who looked unhappy and frustrated. She was holding a paperback of *Romeo and Juliet*. For once it would be nice to see my children *not* completely miserable at the same time.

"Ah! Here we are," I said, forcing myself to keep up my good spirits in the face of gloom. "The band's back together!"

"What's for dinner?" Jack asked.

"Chinese," I told him. "It's on the way."

"Did you get dumplings?"

"No."

"*Great.*"

"How was school?" I asked Charlotte.

She pulled off her baseball cap; her hair was in a messy braid down her back. "Awful."

"Awful how?" I should have left well enough alone.

She didn't answer. I started to ask if she'd heard from Theo, but I thought I'd better not bring him up, lest she burst into tears.

"Were your classes okay?" I asked instead.

"No."

"How was running?"

She rolled her eyes and took off her socks.

"Was it fun? Honey? What'd you do?"

"I *ran*. Duh."

"Do you like the coach?"

She turned her back on me and pulled out the elastic holding the bottom of her braid.

"Hungry?"

She sighed like she couldn't believe anyone could be so irritating.

"I am," Megan said. "When's dinner?" She had showered and changed into pajama bottoms and a T-shirt. She was standing with the weight on her heels, her toenails wet with pink polish.

"I ordered about twenty minutes ago."

"I *hate* the subway," Charlotte said on her way to her room. "I'm covered in Ebola. It fucking sucks here!"

Three sentences? This was progress! I made a quick calculation with my fingers. "That was a haiku, Charlotte!" I called after her. "Like an ode to Manhattan."

"Leave me *alone*!" she yelled. "And nobody bug me while I'm facetiming Theo," and she slammed the bedroom door.

"She seems pretty good," I said to Jack and Megan. We heard music turn on.

"She's turning into a serious bitch," Megan said. "I don't even like her anymore."

"Don't call your sister a bitch."

"Well, it's true. And you don't like her, either," Megan said.

"Your dad's home," I said in order to change the subject, "and he says he just got interviewed by the *Humans of New York* guy."

"Wait, *what*? For real?!" Megan said and ran on her heels to find him in our room.

Jack kicked the side of the couch.

"Five-seven-five," I said.

"What?"

"A haiku. Do you have homework?" I asked.

"My teacher hates me. She looks like she's mad at me all the time."

"Like she scowls at you?"

Jack made a face to show me.

"I'm sure she likes you just fine." How to broach the subject? I lowered my voice. "So about what happened today . . ."

"I wrote the letter already."

"Oh. Shouldn't we talk about it first?"

"I don't feel good. Can I stay home tomorrow?"

"Nope," was all I said. I had a very high bar for my kids when it came to missing school, like fever or uncontrolled bleeding. "Is your homework done?"

"I have to do a reading response in my journal."

"Can I see the apology you wrote?"

"No."

"Really, I think I should take a look."

"It's private."

So's her hooha, I thought, *and that didn't stop you*. "I feel like I should help make sure the tone is right."

"The only help I need is getting some food in my face." He walked to his room and slammed the door. It was a wonder any of our doors were still on their hinges.

I went to pick up Charlotte's backpack off the floor and saw her physics test sticking out of the top. I stopped short of pulling it out all the way to find out how she did; it felt like something that would get me into trouble, but peering in, I could see "13" scrawled on the top. Thirteen? *Thirteen?* How does a straight-A student even get a thirteen on a test? I heard the buzzer, dropped the backpack on top of a box marked "KITCHEN—random," and opened the door to meet the Chinese food delivery guy. *Jesus*. Is she going to have to rethink her college list? How could she go from As all the way to Fs? From ninety-eights to thirteens? And why thirteen? I'm not superstitious, but that seemed like a bad omen.

I HAVE A STRATEGIC OUTFIT THAT I WEAR for the first day of the school year that I like to think projects to the students my serious, down-to-business, no-nonsense attitude. It says *Don't mess with me*. It says *I'm experienced*. It even says *Books are cool*. Slim J.Crew khakis, a fitted white blouse, and a navy blazer; it works every time. I wear a pin on my lapel that my father gave me before my very first day of teaching about fifteen years ago: an enamel stack of four colorful books.

My new school was on Seventy-Fourth Street, and I walked there with my heavy book bag digging into my shoulder. I had my files with the class rosters, my summer reading lesson plans, my fine-tip purple pens (grading in red is perceived as hostile scolding, while grading in purple is a friendly critique), copies of *Lord of the Flies* and *Great Expectations*, and the new Dell laptop the school had given me. I walked into my first class of tenth graders that morning and got things off on the right foot: I maintained a stern face and talked very fast but very clearly. I started by going over class procedures on the SMART Board and then hit them with an engaging poetry assignment they had to complete within the period. My philosophy: make the students earn a smile, eventually, but not before October 15. I always seat the kids in alphabetical order by first names, so I knew that it was Abby in the front row on the left who raised her hand to use the bathroom and William in the back row on the right who was acting up. During third period, a group of girls gave me attitude about the assigned seating; I used the name of the queen bee of the group and got them in line before they even knew what hit them.

"Our teacher last year let us sit wherever we want," she said.

"Well, Samantha," I said, "that was last year. In tenth-grade English we have assigned seats."

She muttered something, and the girl next to her stifled a laugh.

That girl came up to my desk after class and apologized.

"Thank you, Olivia," I said, while I stacked the poetry assignments and put them in a folder. "You did a nice job speaking for your group today."

She smiled at the compliment.

When the bell rang at the end of the fifth period class that day, the kids filed out into the hallway, and I heard some girls squealing. I gathered my things and followed them out of the classroom, where they were jumping up and down, embracing an attractive young woman who glanced up at me for a second and then went back to talking to the kids.

While I was reviewing my rosters at the end of the day, Joan, the headmaster, called me into her office and told me that the teacher whose classes I'd taken over had broken off her engagement and wanted her job back, effective immediately. "Poor girl," Joan said, leaning toward me with her elbows on the desk. "He cheated on her," she whispered.

"So . . ." I tried to formulate the right question. "How does this—?"

"We're like a family here," she said. "And when one of is hurting, we circle those wagons."

"Right," I said, drumming my fingers on her desk, wondering where this was going. "It's lovely that you're all so supportive."

"You can understand that we think it would be best—given that the kids adore her—to bring her back into the fold. Full-time."

I didn't mean to divert attention from the broken-hearted bride, but I was clearly being pushed outside the wagon circle and off a cliff.

"But we'd love to keep you on," Joan said.

"Oh, wonderful," I said, exhaling in relief. "How, exactly?"

"We'll welcome you here as a sub, anytime we need one. You'll be the first person we call. Flu season is right around the corner."

I shook my head. I'd subbed right out of college, and there was no way I was going back to spending a year babysitting other people's students. I would sooner agree to clean the boys' bathroom every day. "No, thank you," I said, adjusting my lapel pin. "That's not what I—No, I need to have my own classes."

"I understand completely," she said, just as a kickball smacked the window behind her, making her jump. She spun around in her swivel chair to identify the culprit. "And I'm so sorry to leave you in the lurch like this," she said, swiveling back. "I can certainly make a few calls. See if there's anything else out there? I know someone at NYU who's looking for writing tutors. That's probably not what you have in mind either, but it might get you through until another long-term position comes up; and one will come up, of course. People get pregnant all the time," she said cheerfully. "You'll be the first to know."

I had been concerned when I got up that morning about being late to pick up Jack. As it turned out, I got to his school ten minutes early, the work bag on my shoulder a whole lot lighter now that I'd turned in the Dell laptop.

———

I had to rethink everything. I had no lesson planning to do for the next day. I had no student names to memorize, no assignments to grade. No paycheck coming in either. Nothing on the calendar for tomorrow. I had no job. Other than my summer vacations, I had *never* not worked before.

That night, Joan, my boss for one day, sent me the contact information of a guy named Rick at the New York University writing center; I emailed him my résumé immediately. "I am available to come in at your earliest convenience," I wrote him. "In fact, I happen to be free tomorrow morning, if that works for you."

"Too desperate?" I asked Michael, after I'd hit "send." We were in bed and didn't have cable set up in our room yet, so we were both sitting up with our computers on our laps.

"Just eager."

"Somebody at the school will get knocked up," I said. "And then they'll come crawling back to me."

"Of course they will," Michael said. "Enjoy the break while it lasts. You'll be back in a classroom in no time."

"Yeah, maybe this will be good," I said. "In the meantime, I'll have all this extra time to help Charlotte with her college applications. I can read books. I can . . . ," but I couldn't think of other ways I would fill my time. What was I going to do?

I checked my email again to see if Rick had responded already. He hadn't. Instead I got an email from Jack's teacher.

Dear Mr. and Mrs. Brinkley,

    I really appreciate that Jack wrote a note to the student he upset in class yesterday. It was short but sweet.

    Meanwhile, there's another private matter that I need to discuss with you. Could you arrive fifteen minutes early tomorrow for a brief meeting?

Sincerely,
Carolyn Hendrick

I showed the email to Michael.

"Well, at least you're free in the morning," he said. "Silver lining."

I gave him a look. "This can't be good. 'Private matter.' What does that mean?"

"I'm sure it's nothing. Jack's not a troublemaker. I'd go with you, but my morning's packed. And you've got the dates for my big trip, right? I feel bad leaving before we've gotten properly settled."

"We'll manage," I said. "What are you smiling about?"

Michael turned his laptop to show me the Humans of New York page on Facebook. He was still gloating about being featured.

"I've got way more likes than this guy they interviewed today. *Me*, you know?" he said. "Who would have ever thought I'd be basically a celebrity?"

I restrained my eyeballs from rolling back and smiled at him instead. "Well, I wouldn't get *too* carried away."

"Megan told me over six million people probably saw that picture. And that quote they got from me? I don't even know where that came from, but it was really good, right? Profound?"

Michael's quote, beneath a picture of him in his suit, briefcase in hand, looking handsomely into the distance with the Wall Street Charging Bull blurred in the background, was: "I was reluctant to move here, I admit. You hear things, you form opinions about a place based on what? On movies, on false ideas, on opinions. But New York City, as it turns out, is *real*. It's sexy. Invigorating. It is surprising me every day, delighting me, actually." He had grown fond of quoting himself. "Sexy," I wanted to remind him, was *my* word and not one that was panning out in real life.

"We hit seventy-seven thousand likes!" he said.

"Yay," I said. It came out flat.

I reached for my phone and typed a message: *Hi there. I'm giving you till tomorrow to call me, or I'm going to have to find a new mother. Lost my job today. Feeling a tad rudderless. Miss you.*

———

Ms. Hendrick was a short, compact woman who wore dresses that looked like they came from June Cleaver's closet. She was far too young to own outfits that were so dated and conservative; I assumed her look was supposed to be retro, but it just made her look stodgy.

"Hello, Jack," she said with a cool reserve. "I'd like you to wait out here in the hallway for a moment so I can talk to your mother alone."

"See you in a minute, Jack." I waved at him and then walked in the classroom, taking a little chair at the round table where Ms. Hendrick had folders with names of all the children in her class. I would be busy shredding my student rosters at some point soon.

Behind me there was a cage, and the hamster who lived in it was running maniacally on his wheel. On the wall there were self-portraits, all quite impressive, and I looked all around the room to find Jack's. When I turned back to the table, I saw his picture lying there in front of me. Cute round face, little oval eyes, triangular nose, rectangular torso, and a well-depicted cylindrical penis, sticking straight out. Spherical balls. He had the perspective well rendered, but that was hardly the point. I wanted to die as Ms. Hendrick took her seat next to me.

"Jack's picture isn't on display," she said. "And I thought you should see why. I can't hang this up with the others. You understand."

I certainly did. "Yes, of course."

"I just have to tell you," she said, and I braced myself for an onslaught of criticism; maybe they'd decided to expel him already. *Where would he go?* She leaned in and smiled. "Jack is really a creative, bright, hilarious kid. I mean, look at this!" She held up the portrait and laughed. "He's trying so hard to make inroads, make friends, make a big impression. Swinging and missing, but hey, hats off for trying, right?"

"I take it he's the only one who went pornographic with the assignment?" I said, smiling faintly.

"I'd love to see him get on track. I've been so strict with him, probably too strict, but I want to make sure he doesn't get in trouble again, like *real* trouble. I watch him like a hawk. That whole thing with Brittney . . ."

"I still can't believe he did that," I said quickly. "It's totally out of character."

"No, no, it's just that the incident was brought to the principal, so the school had to address it and show that we were taking it really seriously."

"Of course."

"The trick now," she said, looking at his portrait, "is to get Jack on the straight and narrow. One more big misstep, one more student taking offense like that, and . . . you know." She looked up at me suddenly. "I'm not trying to scare you—"

"No, you're right, and believe me, I'm concerned. And very confused," I said. "I just don't understand what's going on with him."

"And this is just between us, but this isn't the only work that I can't display or let him share with his classmates." She handed me a piece of paper that read, "Haiku: An ode to boobies" as the title. Jack's handwriting. *Oh God*, I thought.

> Round, flat, or floppy,
> Big or small, they make me LOL.
> Why do girls have boobs?

"How about we banish him to an island," I said.

"On the bright side," she said, "he got the meter right."

"I swear my girls never went through a phase like this." I was starting to get a headache. "I don't know what this is about, but I'll talk to him."

"Any thoughts on what I can do?" she asked. "What's worked well with him in the past?"

"I'm feeling a little out of my parenting depth at the moment," I admitted.

"You're a teacher too, right?"

I smiled at her. "He's maybe feeling insecure, so you could try giving him some extra responsibility, like ask him to help you with some task in the classroom. Give him a special job, as a show of confidence? And maybe—if you can, that is—find some reason to compliment him?"

"That won't be hard. Aside from this, he's doing great."

I could see now that her dress wasn't June Cleaver at all; it was Mindy Kaling as all hell, and she was adorable in it.

I thanked her profusely and waved, and then I swung the classroom door open, smack into Brittney's mother, who must have been standing with her ear pressed against it.

"Sorry, Beth," I said. I'd knocked her Goyard bag off her shoulder. "Have a terrific day."

I said goodbye to Jack, imploring him to be extra-well behaved, and gave him a kiss on the top of his head when no one was looking. As I walked out into the sunshine, wondering about Jack's newfound interest in human anatomy, I saw the usual cohort of elementary school moms as they chatted conspiratorially, deciding to go grab a cup of coffee together before Pilates or work or wherever it was they all went off to. I knew—as I told my own kids regularly—that I would have to make an effort and actually introduce myself if I wanted to make friends. I put on my dark glasses and watched the women. One, her blond hair pulled back in a ponytail, was laughing while she showed another something on her cell phone. They looked friendly.

I had nowhere to be, so I mustered up the courage to break into their circle. I opened my mouth to say hello just as my phone rang—a loud Rihanna song that Megan had set as my ringtone. The women turned to look at me.

I spun around to silence the call when I saw that it was my mom's picture that had popped up on my screen. I answered right away.

"Hi?" I asked, walking away from the group and sticking my left finger in my ear so I could hear her, wondering if she'd butt-dialed me. "Mom?"

"I only have a few minutes," she said. "But I'm very sorry you lost your job. What happened?"

"The teacher I was replacing got dumped by her fiancé and came back."

"Sorry for her, but sorrier for you."

"And I'm worried about Jack. He's going through . . . something." I didn't want the moms to overhear me discussing that particular issue, so I didn't elaborate.

"Carve out some one-on-one time with him," she said. "And give him a hug."

That was often her solution to any problems with my kids. "How are you? Are things going okay?"

"I have a favor to ask, something I want you to do today."

"Mom—"

"There's an open house. Not that I'm moving, because I'm not, but I thought you could take a look."

"Today?" I stepped back to let a woman go by with a stroller.

"It's a place I saw on Zillow and it looks nice and possibly even affordable."

"Mom, are you actually considering—?"

"I doubt it, but since you're free—"

"How's Dallas?" I asked.

"Hot," she said. "I went to your book club last night."

"Mine?" I asked. "With *my* friends?"

"They invited me. We drank wine, gossiped a bit, and then discussed Anna Quindlen. Was I supposed to say no?"

I looked up and saw that the cool moms were all walking away together down the sidewalk.

"So you'll go?" she asked.

She seemed pretty eager for someone who wasn't sure about moving. I smiled. "Where's the apartment?" I asked.

"It's a house, actually."

"A house—?"

"Katonah."

"What's that?"

"It's in Katonah. You can be there in a little over an hour."

"Wait." I rubbed my forehead. "It's not in New York?"

"It certainly is," my mother said defensively. "New York *State*."

This time *I* didn't answer.

"I've told you, Manhattan is out of the question for me."

"You want me to get my car, drive upstate for over an hour to look at a house in a town I've never heard of? I can't just take off for the day. I have to pick up Jack, in addition to figuring out how to salvage my career." My phone pinged.

I heard her make a *tsk* sound. "It's not that far away; you'll be back in a few hours. I just texted the listing."

"Mom, I'm not—"

"I've gotta run," she said. "A friend of mine set me up on a date with a retired professor, and we're meeting for coffee. Drive safely and try to enjoy yourself."

And she hung up.

This was absurd. I started to call her back, but I admit there was one small thing that appealed to me in this idiotic plan: in that moment I actually liked the idea of getting in my car and driving. Leaving town. It sounded freeing. I called Michael and asked if he could pick up Jack after school in the event that I got a flat tire or something and didn't make it back in time.

"Is she actually considering moving?" he asked.

"I'm not sure I see the point of her moving to some random place an hour away. But I'll check it out anyway."

"Where is this?"

"I have no idea, north somewhere. But if the traffic's really bad, you could pick up Jack, in theory?"

"Sure."

"And remind me," I said, "where did we leave the car?"

———

I called the garage. The privilege of parking a car in New York was costing us $750 a month, another expense that seemed crazy, especially since this particular day, about two weeks after our arrival, was the first time I'd laid eyes on our Ford Explorer since we'd had it shipped from Dallas. I walked quickly from our apartment, where I'd stopped to use the bathroom and fill a water bottle for the road, three blocks to the parking garage, and when I saw the car pulled up and waiting for me, my heart jumped like I was seeing an old boyfriend. I climbed in and got a mad wave of nostalgia from the smell of McDonald's chicken nuggets and leather. I turned on the CD that Charlotte had in the player, a Beyoncé album I'd always found cheering, adjusted the mirror, and took a minute to enjoy the familiar, empowering feeling of taking the wheel and being in charge. I inched out onto Broadway carefully, like a first-time driver.

I got stuck on a one-way street and ended up heading east across Central Park, which was not my intention. Cabs swerved around me and honked, offended by my cautious driving, and I tried to stay calm as I made my way to the FDR, which I soon realized was the worst, craziest highway in North America: potholes that could swallow a car, huge stretches of road with no dividing lines between the lanes, sudden bouts of traffic that would ease up for no particular reason. I had to concentrate and be on the lookout for unannounced lane changes, confusing forks, and unmarked exits. I got over some bridge with help from Siri and headed north on 684. The traffic became less congested, and the scenery improved dramatically. And then it turned beautiful.

It was after eleven o'clock when I drove up the driveway of a white farmhouse off a tree-lined street in Katonah. There was an ancient, low stone wall that ran the length of the gravel drive, and I sighed as I pulled in, past the *For Sale* sign, to the front of the classic but peeling clapboard home. I turned off the engine, collected my purse and phone, and stepped out of the car, noticing the faint smell of a fire and appreciating the hush over it all: there was no honking, no sirens, no construction. I heard nothing but wind and birdsong and caught a glimpse of a chipmunk scampering over the stone wall. So much more aesthetically pleasing than rats climbing out of sewer grates. I felt an urge to lie down in the grass. I stretched instead, leaned against the car, and took a deep breath of country air.

Made it, I texted Michael. And then, *Wow, really nice here.*

He sent me a thumbs-up emoji and a heart. *Have fun!*

With a spring in my step, I went up the flagstone walk and rang the bell. There were pumpkins and potted mums on the front porch. It brought Halloween to mind, and I suddenly wondered, *How the heck does one trick-or-treat in a high-rise?*

The door opened, and a woman greeted me.

"Leigh Miller," she said, shaking my hand and giving me her business card and a flyer about the house. She was wearing elastic-waist pants and bathroom slippers. "Would you mind taking off your shoes?" and she pointed to a row of sneakers, crocs, and loafers. "The owner's a little particular about her floors. They're the original hardwoods."

I stepped out of my low suede boots and followed her in socks down the hallway, past the kitchen, and into the living room. We passed a long, low bookshelf filled with dusty hardcovers, the top of the shelf covered with magazines, bills, and coupons. There were greeting cards and loose photographs in stacks and propped up in a long row; kids, dogs, and families posing. I wondered if the pictures would be packed up or thrown away.

"Feel free to look around," Leigh said. "The owner wasn't able to tidy much." There was a sprawling lawn out the back windows behind her, and past the sweep of grass, an old red barn. The yard was by far the nicest part of the property; everything inside was dark and a little grimy. I noticed a stain on the living room ceiling and a vague smell of cat pee.

"I've never been out here before," I said, making small talk. "I live in New York City."

"Ah," she said. "And you're ready to make the move to the suburbs? You've got kids?"

A clock on the wall was ticking. "Yes, but—"

"Wait, are you Allison?"

I was taken aback.

"A woman called me from Texas this morning and said her daughter lost her job out of the blue and was driving up from the city and feeling 'rudderless,' she said. Is that you?"

Matricide, I thought. *Is that what it's called?*

"You're a teacher, right?" Leigh said.

I nodded.

"Or you *were*, I guess. Are you okay? Your mom's worried about you."

"I'm fine, thanks." I looked up at the moldings on the ceiling and then wandered into the dining room. Leigh followed me.

"She told me she moved to Maryland to be closer to you after her husband died. And then she followed you all the way out to Houston after that."

"Dallas," I said, wondering why I bothered.

"And now you've moved again, and she's house hunting already. She must be very devoted. You're one lucky daughter."

"Yes, I know," I said, feeling defensive. Instead of entering into a discussion about my mother, I studied the dining room and its hideous brass light fixture that was hanging slightly off-kilter. One of the bulbs had burned out. I tried to picture the room with recessed lights instead. Pinpoints on the table, maybe.

"From what she told me, it didn't sound like there's much keeping her there with you and your family gone."

"There is, actually. She's on a date with a professor as we speak," I said, deciding I could be indiscreet, too. "She's got a whole life there. She has friends, her music students, her garden club." *And my book club, apparently.* I looked down at my socks; they were Megan's from Urban Outfitters and had kitten faces on them. "And she recently put in some really nice custom book shelves in her den, and she enjoys reading there."

Leigh was also looking at my socks. "Custom bookshelves don't keep a person away from family, though, do they? I couldn't stand to be away from mine. Are you in the city . . . for good?" she asked.

"May I go upstairs?" I said.

She stepped to the side to let me through the doorway and gestured politely. "Of course, take a look all around," she called after me. "I can even show you the chickens out in the coop. The owner plays music for them in the barn. Apparently they adore Debussy."

I heard her footsteps behind me on the stairs.

"Are chickens a lot of work?" I asked.

"Not compared to children," she said, "but I hear they've got just as much personality."

I went through the bedrooms. The windows all needed replacing, and the bathrooms were terribly dated with ugly medicine cabinets and flowered wallpaper peeling in the corners. The ceilings were low. We went back downstairs and I took a quick look at the fifties-style kitchen. Out the window, over the chipped ceramic sink, there was a vegetable garden, surrounded by chicken-wire fencing.

This house would be perfect for a young family with the energy to do major renovations, but not the right place for a widowed, semiretired piano teacher.

I thanked Leigh for her time and put my boots back on.

As soon as I was in the car, I called my mom; she didn't pick up, so I left a message: "Hey, so are you actually looking at houses out here, as in for real? It's really pretty, but I'm worried we'll never see you. Call me."

I drove through the town, past the train station, and looped around the quiet streets and little shops. Was it the feel of a quaint town that had drawn Lilly away from Manhattan? I decided to park the car and take a little walk. Katonah was charming, wholesome, and neverthe-less sophisticated. There were numerous little boutiques with designer clothing and handmade pottery. I passed Squires Family Clothing and Footwear, looked in the windows of three or four real estate offices, and noted that Katonah had everything else one could possibly need in life: stores selling eyeglasses, toys, and antiques, and even a barbershop and a big liquor store, all in close proximity to the train station, where one could hop on the commuter rail that went right to Grand Central. I stopped at a place called Tazza Café to get a latte before my drive back. I asked for a double shot to keep me peppy, but instead of going back to the car, I stalled a little longer, taking my cup to a table out on the side-walk. I checked my email. In addition to a notice from Megan's teacher to the class about violations of the school dress code (". . . so remind your children NO bare Bs, please! That means no exposed bottoms, breasts, or bellies!"), there was an answer from Rick at NYU:

Hey there,
Thanks for reaching out. Yeah, I'm hiring tutors.
Can you come in tomorrow at ten?
~R

I accepted Rick's invitation, and texted Michael right away: *Got an in-terview at NYU for tomorrow! On my way home. Not the right house for Mom, but wow, SO nice out here.* I added emojis of a tree, an acorn, a house.

A boy about Megan's age walked by me with two golden retrievers on a leash; I wondered why he wasn't in school.

It was suddenly hard to imagine that Jack and Megan would spend the remainder of their childhoods cooped up in an airless apartment, when life had *this* to offer just an hour away. My mother had put New

York's polar opposite squarely in my line of vision, and I wondered if she was really looking for a way to be closer to us or if she was trying to make me question my decision to move to New York in the first place. Or maybe I was doing that part all on my own.

———

As I got closer to the city, I hit terrible traffic, and as I kept checking the time, I finally accepted the fact that I would be too late to get the car parked back in the garage by the time I had to be at the school to get Jack. I had no other option than to pick Jack up in the car, and I wasn't sure exactly how one did that. First I missed the street because it went one way in the wrong direction. I circled around and then pulled up right in front of the school, hoping to wait, just as if I were in Dallas. Except that this wasn't Dallas, and fifteen seconds after I got there, someone was behind me, honking, unable to maneuver around my big car. I had to circle the block again. Twice. By the third time around, I saw that the kids were being let out. I rolled down the passenger window, searching for Jack, as another car pulled right up behind me and started flashing his lights at me.

I spotted him. "Jack," I yelled. Nothing. "Hey, Jack! Over here!" Most of the moms and nannies turned to look at me, as I waved wildly, but Jack still didn't hear me over the street noises. He was looking off down the sidewalk, probably wondering where I was. The guy in the car behind me lost patience and started honking, and I yelled again, "Jack!"

Everything turned hectic very quickly. The guy kept honking (short, short, loooong). Ms. Hendrick, whose lipstick had faded considerably since I'd seen her that morning, spotted me as Jack suddenly ran toward the car. One mother took her kid's hand and ran after Jack. There was angry yelling: "Yo, move your fucking car, lady!" But I couldn't drive off now that Jack had seen me. I inched over toward the cars parallel parked on the right, trying to give the guy behind me enough space to go around. In a moment of panic, I stepped on the gas a little too quickly, the car jerked forward, and suddenly I heard a deep, crunching sound: right there in front of the school, in front of a large, attentive audience, I had sideswiped the mirror off the door of a BMW, my fat fender denting in the black car's shiny side.

"*Mom!*" Jack yelled, looking horrified, as kids flocked over to see the wreckage. "Shit, mom, seriously?"

"Don't say 'shit,'" I told him, unbuckling my seat belt.

There was nothing to do except to get out of the car and see the damage for myself. The guy in the car behind me was waving his arms at me.

"Nice," I said and waved back to him, beauty queen style. There was a gash near the sports car's front wheel; red paint had rubbed off, giving the impression that the BMW was actually bleeding. I stood next to the flock of moms and shook my head.

"It was like he came out of nowhere!" I joked to mask my mortification.

"Are you okay?" one of them asked.

"Yes, a hundred percent," I said. "I just didn't realize how close I'd gotten." I smiled. "Whoops," I said and shrugged innocently.

"I'm Lauren," she said, "Ben's mom. Can I make a call for you or something?"

"We're fine," I said, "but it's nice to meet you."

I heard another mom whisper, "A little too much wine at lunch?"

The traffic behind my car was piling up, and more cars joined in the honking.

"Hop in the car," I said to Jack, getting down to business. "Do you have something I can write on?" I asked him. Jack reached into his backpack and ripped a sheet of lined paper out of his spiral notebook.

"Hurry up," he said.

"Do you have something I can write *with*?" I'd never felt less equipped. He handed me a marker, and, using the hood of my car as a desk, I scrawled, "Sorry about this. I have insurance. Please call to discuss."

I folded the note and started to put it on the windshield. "What about your phone number?" Jack yell-whispered out the window. "How's anyone supposed to call you without a phone number?"

"Jeesh, where's my head?" I asked. He handed me the pen again, and when I was done, I carefully placed the note under the wiper blade. I used a deep voice, like a cop, and said, "Show's over, folks. Nothing to see here." No one laughed. Jack slumped down in his seat and put his hands over his face.

One of the moms, I noticed, took a picture.

A cute, young nanny, wearing a short skirt and boots halfway up her thighs, called out to me, "Bummer, right? You okay?"

"Yeah," I said.

She looked about twenty years old and she was pushing a toddler in a stroller and gripping the hand of a rowdy seven-year old boy; she pulled her ward's backpack onto her shoulder and said, "Shit like this happens all the time," and she smiled. "Seriously, no big deal."

It wasn't true. I knew that wasn't true, but in that moment I loved her, whoever she was.

Jack was less generous. "This is *the* most embarrassing thing that's ever happened to anyone *ever*."

"Oh, come on," I said. "No one even got hurt." I started the car and pulled away from the banged-up BMW, feeling like once again, New York had me beat.

three

FOR MY JOB INTERVIEW WITH RICK I dressed in a suede skirt and boots, a pea jacket, and shades; I was attempting to look upscale collegiate. I slung a cross-body bag over my chest, opened my new iTrans NYC app, and walked to Columbus Circle with the intention of taking the downtown B train to Broadway-Lafayette. However, it had been years since I'd taken the subway in New York, and the ticket machine completely intimidated me with questions about one-way tickets and monthly passes, and a line of impatient commuters and German-speaking tourists was growing behind me while I tried to figure it all out. Feeling overwhelmed and rushed, I abandoned the purchase and climbed back up the stairs to take a taxi. As soon as I got in the cab, I realized I had taken the fall fashion thing way too far: I was sweating from head to toe.

I got out at Astor Place and walked south on Lafayette, counting off the building numbers along the way. Lilly had lived downtown after college, and I remembered the charm of her neighborhood, but there was no charm here. Here I saw ugly parking lots with cars stacked, literally stacked, one on top of the other on rusted steel platforms, next to construction barriers that closed off swaths of sidewalks, detouring pedestrians into corrals going down the street. The billboards were close and big and in my face; a model's eyes, under her bushy three-foot-long eyebrows, stared me down. And it was indescribably loud, sirens, honking, yelling, and jackhammers. Even the pigeons added to the chaos in their jerky way. Dog poop was smudged on the sidewalk from poorly executed pickup efforts. There was no green anywhere.

Rick was the director of the Writing Resource Center at NYU, and he was looking for support teachers for students who needed extra instruction. He was younger than I was expecting him to be, and he had a big tattoo of an orange chameleon on his left arm. It sat on a tropical leaf and had googly eyes that looked off in two different directions. He wore long cargo shorts and had the words "Whatever works, works" tattooed in a ring around his calf. We shook hands and walked through the writing center, past students and tutors working side by side. Something about the collegiate scene, something about Rick's tattoo and outfit made me feel out of place. And overdressed.

We went into Rick's tiny office, and I got ready to sell myself.

"Your résumé came like a gift from the gods," he said.

"It did? Wow. That's nice."

"We get so many applications from kids who just graduated from college and need a part-time job while they write their masterpiece or wait to be called in for a *Wicked* audition. I need some older people working here. I need people who teach for a living, who have real experience. Especially for our continuing ed students. They just don't want a tutor who's a third their age, and I get that."

"You're hiring me because I'm old?"

"I just mean that your age happens to be an asset for us at the moment."

He filled me in on the job, which sounded like a big change from teaching in a high school classroom. Here I would be assigned mostly to adult students, many of them staff members at NYU who were going back to school to get a degree. Occasionally I would get a college student or two, but "old people" would be my specialty. "Old people," I discovered, meant anyone over the age of thirty. He went over the rules: no editing papers, no assessing the validity of grades that were received on assignments, no coming up with ideas for the students, and no teaching them the subject matter.

"It's not your job to be a Nietzsche scholar. Just guide them through the writing process."

"Guide them."

"Yes, help them develop a thesis, go over their outlines, and read their completed drafts. Guide them."

"Got it."

"We'll get you some regulars along with the walk-ins. I'll call your references, and assuming that goes okay, we'll get started in a week or so."

In case he'd missed this on my résumé, I reminded him, "I'm used to working with high school kids."

"Then this'll be really easy."

That went well, I thought. I took a walk through the neighborhood and checked out an antique store, celebrating my forthcoming employment by buying wineglasses to replace the shards that had been trucked in from Dallas. These glasses were etched and beautiful, eight of them, and, doing the math in my head, I figured out they were only about thirteen dollars apiece. I love a good deal. I chatted with the saleswoman and watched while she carefully wrapped each one, first in tissue, then in Bubble Wrap. Then she layered pieces of cardboard in between them as she put them, gently, into a box, and the box into a large handled paper bag. It took forever, and I admired her efforts. When she was finally finished, she handed me the sales slip to sign. I did a double take and studied the receipt. It wasn't $100 for the set of eight. My total bill was over $800. As in $100 per glass. Plus tax. *Fuck.*

There was nothing to do but sign. I couldn't possibly have her unpack the glasses all over again, not after all the trouble she went to pad them, to keep them from breaking each other.

I took the subway home from Broadway-Lafayette, which was easier to navigate than I'd expected, and on the way, I decided that as penance, I would make myself empty two boxes before picking up Jack, a punishment for my accidental splurge; after all, if I unpacked enough to be able to cook, we could cut back on food-delivery costs. I knew when we moved to New York that I would have to manage our money more carefully, that life here would be expensive. Everyone said so. Spending close to $1,000 on some glasses was not the kind of fiscal discipline I'd committed myself to.

I was so preoccupied thinking about which boxes I would open and, the more difficult problem, where I would put my All-Clad pots and pans, that I missed the Columbus Circle stop. I stood at the doors, waiting for the next one, but we sailed past it.

"Excuse me," I said to a couple, but then noticed a Russian NYC tourist guidebook the husband was clutching in his hand. "Never mind."

"It's going express," a man said.

"Ah, thanks. Meaning . . . ?"

"It's not stopping."

"Ever?"

"Until 125th."

"Oh, shit."

"Take a load off," he said. But there weren't any seats.

—

After I walked back into our quiet apartment, I changed into jeans and unpacked a box of cooking spoons and spatulas, mixing bowls, and baking pans. I wasn't much of a baker, so that exercise seemed a little pointless. I moved on to a book box, pulling my favorite novels out and arranging them alphabetically on the living room bookshelf. In another box marked "living room random," I found framed photos of the kids as babies, a wooden pencil box my dad had made for me, and Michael's and my college diplomas. A stack of birthday cards from my mom, audiobook CDs, piano sheet music for beginners, and tangled extension cords. A Tiffany vase and a ceramic bowl Jack had made in an art class. I put some of the objects on the shelf, the vase on the dining room table, and the sheet music on the upright piano. A realization began to settle in: we were going to have to give away or pay to store a ton of our stuff. There was simply no way it would all fit in the space we had, and I wondered how I would choose what to keep and what to sacrifice.

After a few hours, when I needed a break from all the newsprint and cardboard, I wrote Rick a thank-you email, practically begging for the job, after which I unpacked the pricey wineglasses. I washed them each by hand, carefully. Then I took the last one and poured myself a nice Pinot Noir. I frowned at the glass. A hundred dollars. A hundred fucking dollars.

"You were an accident," I said to the glass. Hmm. That seemed mean. "But that doesn't mean I didn't want you."

———

When the kids were all home, they each made comments on the steps I'd taken that day to settle us in, and fortunately, none of them noticed that I'd moved several of their boxes of "Random" into the front hall closet. Michael had a meeting that night and said to eat dinner without him, so the kids and I had pizza together at the dining room table on the special square plates I'd unearthed, after which they went to their rooms to do homework. I put the plates in the dishwasher and checked my email: Rick had offered me the NYU writing tutor job. I would be making fifteen dollars an hour.

My friend Sara was a spontaneous woman, always had been, so it wasn't unusual when she texted that night to say she was on her way over. When Michael and I got married, she never RSVP'd to the wedding, but then showed up, having flown in from Argentina in a long black tiered skirt, tank top, and numerous beaded necklaces, surprised that I was surprised to see her. All the groomsmen lined up to meet the gorgeous dark-haired hippie who was wearing a thin ankle bracelet and no bra.

She came into our apartment that night, an enormous satchel over her shoulder, wearing tight black skinny jeans, Doc Martens, and a ripped graphic T with a picture of Blondie on it: PETITE INGENUE. Not that it mattered to her, but she had a runway model body.

She said hi to Jack who was sitting on the floor with his iPad, big headphones covering his ears, and then she looked out the living room windows with her hands on her hips. She marched down the hallway leading to the bedrooms, and finally dropped her bag on the couch, saying, "Are you fucking kidding me with this shit? A doorman? *Three* bedrooms? This place is huge! I can't be your friend anymore."

"You have to be my friend. You're the only one I have here," I said.

"What about that girl who went to Middlebury with us, Lilly? You guys were always pretty chummy."

"She moved to Montclair."

"Gross," Sara said, looking disgusted. "Why would she do that? Is she still in publishing or something?"

"She commutes now," I said.

Sara shook her head and then held out a box of wine that had a pink sticky slapped on it: "Welcome to Gotham, babe."

"Thank you," I said.

"It's much more environmentally friendly than a bottle. And non-GMO, in case you were wondering."

"Great, let's open it."

"Only a sip for me," she said. "I gotta run to a thing in twenty minutes. Just thought I'd swing by for a quick check-in."

"You can't stay?" I asked, twisting off the plastic cap and pouring the Shiraz into two of my new glasses.

"Not today." She eyed the glass before drinking. "Fancy." It wasn't a compliment. "Cheers," she said. "We're going to have a blast together. We'll go to raves. I'll teach you to hate this West Side bullshit as soon as you spend some weekends with me in Brooklyn."

Jack looked up at me from the floor and raised his eyebrows.

"I don't know about going away for a whole weekend," I said. "I have kids."

"So abandon the little fuckers. He looks old enough to take care of himself anyway. It would be good for them. Besides, can't what's-his-name take care of them?"

It was clear she just didn't grasp the nature of my life.

"They need me for all kinds of—"

"Hey, you," Sara said to Charlotte, who was walking in on her way to the kitchen, "you don't care if your mom takes off from time to time, do you?"

Charlotte gave me a snarky look. "Please. You can keep her," she said.

"See! Permission granted. I'll make some plans. Your mom needs a break, know what I mean?"

Charlotte shook her head. "A break from *what*?" Her voice was disdainful.

"Ex*cuse* me?" I asked.

"She needs a chance to find herself," Sara said, "after being managed her whole childhood by tyrants."

"My parents were not tyrants," I said.

"They smothered you. 'Call me, come home, where are you?' Hugging you every five seconds. They kept you on a tight leash."

"They kept track of me."

"Well, you're on your own now. You're all grown up, and Dorothy's off doing her Dallas thing. Your kids don't want you around bugging them. So now, you can break out and go a little wild."

"Good riddance," Charlotte said. "And pardon me while I go vomit," and she walked out.

The idea of going wild didn't really appeal at this point in my life, and, in fact, Sara had always been more edgy than me. We had gone to the same middle and high schools, played on the same soccer team, dated the same boys, went to the same parties, and slept over at each other's houses. We even went to Middlebury together freshman year, living on the same hall with Lilly. But during our first college summer, Sara took off with a radical environmental group, and, even though we'd always kept in touch, our lives were never really in sync again after that. She traveled to a string of third world countries, identified as bisexual, embraced sexual fluidity and polyamory, and moved to New York to work for Foundation Center, a nonprofit that from what I understood educates wealthy people about nonprofits. They met with philanthropists and ran seminars, wrote articles and advised charities. As Sara had explained it: "We're like Robin Hood, except instead of stealing from wealthy assholes, we just talk them into giving their money away."

My life, in comparison to Sara's, was admittedly dull and traditional: I finished college, got married, and had children. In the years right after college, while I was teaching in the same high school we'd gone to, Sara was living in Williamsburg, growing out her armpit hair, sleeping with a slew of men and women, and committing to causes she believed in. Then we moved to Maryland and later to Dallas, and I continued my life in the same job with the same husband, while Sara reinvented herself over and over again with new jobs, new relationships, new causes, new ways of looking unintentionally gorgeous. She had barely aged at all in the face of all that change.

She kicked off her shoes, raising doubt in my mind about her claim to be leaving soon, and we sat on the couch together.

"What's with your hair?" she asked.

"What? What's wrong with my hair?"

"You look like John Lennon when he was parting his down the

middle." She reached over and tried to make my hair cover my forehead. "What is this? You looked better with bangs."

"Ow, stop. They're all grown out right now, and I don't know where to go to get a haircut. If I brush them down, I can't see anything."

"So find a place. Jesus, Allison. Ask around. How hard can it be to get a bang trim in Manhattan?"

"Fine," I said.

"So how's Dorothy taking the abandonment?"

"Not well."

"So what's stopping her from tagging along after you? I'll bet you"—she stopped to think for a second—"I'll bet a box of wine she moves here by January."

"I hope so, but she doesn't want to move to the city," I said. "I think she's starting to consider Westchester County or something. She's gotten very into gardening in her old age."

"People garden here, you know. There are over six hundred community gardens in the city. I'll send her a link to the GrowNYC site. I hope she doesn't believe all the stuff outsiders hear about New York, shit that was maybe true in the seventies but isn't anymore. She may have bought into a false, racist narrative."

"How's work?" I asked.

Before she could answer, Jack got up from the floor and tapped me on the shoulder. "I need help with my math," he mumbled.

"Sure," I said. He walked out of the room looking glum. "I'll come help in a minute," I called after him.

"I take it the little perv isn't doing too great," Sara said.

I shushed her.

"What?" she asked.

I waited to make sure Jack was out of hearing range. "He's just going through a phase where he's especially . . . curious or something. I don't know. Things are turning out harder than I expected."

Sara looked at me, clearly not getting it. "Your Manhattan upper-class life is *hard*?" she asked flatly.

"No, I just mean the adjustment is tricky." I spoke quietly. "Jack's having trouble fitting in. And Charlotte's doing badly in school, which is a total shock, and she hates me for taking her away from her boyfriend.

And Megan seems so flattened. Meanwhile, all five of us *and* the cat are squished into this tiny little apartment—"

"*Tiny* apartment?" There was an edge to her voice. "You live in the biggest sprawl I've ever seen. Honestly, do you even hear yourself?" She took a big sip of her wine. "Did you know that one-point-seven million New Yorkers live below the poverty line?"

"I'm not saying we're starving to death. I'm just saying that it's a big production, you know, to start over from scratch."

"I guess so." Sara took a minute to study me, fiddling with her long necklace that had a little skull pendant attached. I could tell she was trying to dig deep to find a scrap of empathy for my situation. "Your perspective seems off to me, but maybe," she said finally, "you're feeling a little . . . displaced. Not like homeless displaced or Syrian refugee displaced or victim of human trafficking displaced, but still, I guess I can sort of imagine . . ." She stopped. "No, I can't, actually. I don't understand. You have a roof over your head and a family. Health insurance. You're living large in one of the most exciting, relevant cities in the world, a city where you've always wanted to be. I'm telling you: there's a cure for self-pity, and it's called 'good deeds.' I can hook you up, any cause you like."

"I'm not feeling sorry for myself. I'm just dealing with change. Moving," I said defensively, "is one of the top five most stressful events in life."

"Says who?"

"Says . . . Oprah."

"I'm going to try to say this nicely, but you have a tendency to be closed off. Like in a Republican way. Like you're someone who doesn't ever have sex. You're never going to like it here or anywhere if you walk around in this smog of negativity." She used her hands to give a sense of my smog's reach.

"I have sex," I whispered. "And I'm not being negative. I have every intention of making new connections here. But it's going to take a while, so be nice."

"Fine," she said and smacked my knee. "But you should at least consider the possibility that you've outgrown your husband. You've been with what's-his-name for way too long."

"Not at all," I said. "Michael and I are fine."

"Monogamy is so unnatural," she said.

I didn't bother answering.

"Do you remember when I came to see you that year you were studying in London," she said, "and that friend of yours . . . What was his name?"

"Who? Gustavo?"

"Gustavo, yes. He came over to your awesome flat and asked us to drop acid with him, and you didn't want to, remember?"

"That flat had mice and a broken toilet."

"And then he suggested you skip a week of classes so that we could all go to the Algarve together and hang out on the beach."

"I had a Beckett paper due."

"You said you 'couldn't possibly.' And then he—very sweetly, I might add—asked us to have sex with him. And what did you say?"

"I said no."

"You said no."

"And?"

"You didn't even consider it."

"Sara," I said, "these are not decisions I regret."

"Well, I said yes to Gustavo, all three times, and I never regretted those decisions either. The sex was great. So were the beach and the acid, but you wouldn't know about any of those things because you shunned each and every opportunity."

"I don't see it that way."

"When was the last time you said 'yes' to anything?" she asked.

"As a matter of fact, I said yes to a brand-new job today. After I lost the teaching position I'd lined up."

"Oh, babe," she said sadly. Unemployment was an issue Sara could get behind. "I'm so sorry. What happened?"

"It's fine, I bounced back already and got something temporary."

"Good for you. It's a tough job market out there. Do you need contacts? There's a great educational foundation we work with that's chucking everything we know about experimental charters out the window. I can hook you up."

"I'll let you know. For now I'll be tutoring NYU students."

"Shaping minds. That's wonderful." She took my hand and squeezed it, her stack of silver bracelets clinking against each other. "I'm so glad you moved. And I want you to embrace the myriad of opportunities out there," she said, and she pointed to the world out my living room windows. "Take this moment as your chance to say 'yes' to every experience that comes your way."

"I'm a mom. I can't drop acid."

"It doesn't matter what it is. It can be tame enough to fit even your conservative lifestyle—but take advantage of what New York has to offer."

"I was thinking of getting tickets to *Book of Mormon*. I hear *Hamilton* is imposs—"

"Ughh, I fucking *hate* Broadway," she said. "I'd rather go anywhere on the planet than Times Square." She looked at me like I was some kind of lost cause after all. "So when's your mom visiting? I'd like to see her."

"I don't know," I said. "She hasn't planned a trip yet. We're going back to Dallas for Christmas."

"Nice. I'll be in Ghana then. Anyway," Sara said and drank the rest of her wine in one swig. She stood up, handed me the glass, stepped back into her Doc Martens, and laced them up. "Sorry I can't stick around and get loaded with you tonight. But seriously, hon?" She took me by the shoulders and looked me straight in the eyes. "You need to be fierce to live here; let New York pull some crazy ass shit on you, and then meet that shit on the playing field. Know what I mean?"

I had no idea what she meant. I just nodded and walked her to the door, opening it just as Michael was coming off the elevator, once again looking bright-eyed and energetic.

He gave Sara a bear hug. "So good to see you," he said. "You have to go?"

"You certainly look chipper," she said.

"Well, you'll never believe what just happened," Michael said, putting his briefcase on the floor as if to free up his arms to tell the story better. "I just saw Kevin Kline near Columbus Circle. He was sitting by the entrance to the park, like a regular person, just reading a magazine. Look," he said and held out his phone. "I got a selfie!"

Sara didn't seem as excited by the news as I was.

"An actor in New York City?" she said flatly. "Shocker."

Michael's enthusiasm wasn't dampened in the least. "He was just so approachable. And when you talk to him, he's, like . . . a nice guy."

"I've loved Kevin Kline since forever," I said, taking his phone and studying the picture more closely. Kevin looked so youthful for his age and thoroughly handsome, wearing a black sweater over a white T-shirt. Michael was smiling with his mouth wide open, his face uncomfortably close to Kevin's. "I'm impressed," I said, handing the phone back. "I would have been too star-struck to speak."

"Get used to it," Sara said. "This city is infested with celebrities."

"I know, right?" Michael said. "It's like you never know what's going to happen here." He smiled, zooming in on the picture. "Kevin!"

four

THREE CHILDREN, ONE BATHROOM.

First thing every morning, Jack, bare-chested in Star Wars pajama pants, would run into our room, saying, "I gotta pee so bad, and Megan's hogging the bathroom."

"I gotta pee so bad*ly*," I would say. "And don't forget to lift the seat."

The fights over the bathroom were getting brutal, so I made a schedule and taped it to the door. No one followed it, but my hope was that the existence of rules would make my kids somewhat more considerate of each other. So far, it wasn't working.

I woke up extra early on the day that I had my first appointment at the NYU writing center. I was already out of the shower and getting dressed when Jack ran in to use our bathroom, as usual.

"I gotta go," he said.

"Lift the seat," I yelled before he slammed the door.

"Excited?" Michael asked.

"Nervous. I've never taught anyone over eighteen before."

"I'm sure they can smell fear just like the younger ones. Use your bag of tricks."

"Not sure I'll need tricks anymore. These people are coming to see me *voluntarily*. How weird is that?"

I put on my first day teacher clothes, swapping dark jeans for the J.Crew khakis. I put on my blazer with the enamel pin on the lapel, put a thesaurus in my bag, and threw in a worksheet I'd developed on structuring essays, just in case.

The girls and Michael all left for the subway together, and I quickly stacked up the cereal bowls and put them in the sink.

"Ready?" I asked Jack. "You've got toothpaste on your chin."

He touched his chin and then wiped his hand on his jeans. "Maybe you could get a job at my school."

"Yeah," I said, "maybe. Let's see how it goes today."

When we got to his school, Jack ran into the building, and I saw the cool moms, standing together in a herd and laughing. One of them, a brunette with a boy in Jack's class, caught my eye and waved. I waved back. *But not today, ladies*, I thought and turned quickly to walk to the subway; no way was I going to be late.

I was in an upbeat mood, excited that one mom at the school had actually noticed me, and I paid it forward when I got on the C train, smiling at a nice twentysomething girl whose eye I caught by accident; she looked at me as if I'd grabbed her ass.

Once I reached my stop, I checked the time and stopped to buy a latte at Think Coffee. When I got to the NYU building, I took a beat to smooth my hair and check the buttons on my shirt before walking in to meet my new student.

Rick pointed me to Howard, a college campus security guard, dressed in his uniform, having just come off the night shift. He was waiting for me with a book of poetry and a binder, sitting up straight and clearly on the lookout. His police hat was placed on the table next to him.

He stood up when I approached and shook my hand. I tried to reduce the formality, given that I was pretty sure we were about the same age. High school kids need boundaries, right from the get-go. They need structure and rules, but I assumed, looking at the man across from me, that we could be more collegial. We sat down, and I asked him to tell me a bit about himself. He looked confused. And then he yawned.

"I should have brought *you* a coffee," I said.

"I have my own." He reached under the desk and brought up a thermos. "But I try to stop drinking it at five a.m.," he explained. "Otherwise I have trouble sleeping when I get home."

"So you'll go to bed after this?" I asked.

"I sleep during the day and get up when my kids come home after school," he said, no self-pity whatsoever. "My wife gets back from her shift at the hospital in the evening, so we have family dinner together, unless it's a night when I have class. Otherwise I leave at ten to go back to work."

"Wow, sounds exhausting."

"I take three classes a year. This semester I'm taking poetry."

Howard handed me his anthology with his finger holding the page open to a Wordsworth poem, the stupid one about the daffodils. I happen to hate this poem, but I didn't say so, not to Howard, not to anyone. It's like saying you hate the Beatles: everyone's just going to think you're an asshole.

"The problem with poems is I always get to the end and even though I understand all the words, I still don't get what it means," he said.

I knew exactly what he meant. So we went over the poem line by line and eventually we got to the part about how the memory of something pretty can kick in long after you've seen it and make you feel better.

"Okay," Howard said.

"Okay?" I asked.

"I get it," he said, and then he yawned again.

"Tired?"

"It's late."

"Let's draft a quick outline for the essay before you go," I suggested.

"That's okay."

"It won't take long."

"I got this," he said.

"So you know what you'll say about it? What idea you'll argue?"

"I can say what it's about; I understand it now."

"The assignment requires analysis, so you'll need to go beyond re-telling what it says. We could come up with a thesis quickly."

Howard wasn't grumpy, but he was done; I could tell he was. He was also an adult, so there was no keeping him. As he packed up his book and notes, I quickly tossed some ideas at him, things to consider: loneliness, memory, the mind, the senses, nature, a barrage of relevant words to use when analyzing the poem. "And what about structure?" I asked him. "Remember to organize the paper in a way that helps you make the argument."

Howard shook my hand. "I'll see you next week," he said. "And thank you." He put his police hat on and left.

I smiled, spun on my heel, and headed back to the table where we'd been working, when Rick came over abruptly and sat down next to me, shaking his head.

"No," he said.

"No?"

"You have to spend your time with him working on writing; you're not here to teach poetry."

"Sorry," I said. I had apparently managed to screw up my first appointment. "But how can we write a paper—?"

"How can *he* write a paper . . ."

"How can *he* write a paper about a poem if he doesn't understand the poem?"

"He has a professor for that," Rick told me. "We're only here to address writing skills. The next time someone comes in with questions about the material, send him to his teacher."

"That seems kind of, I don't know, unnecessary," I said. "I *am* a teacher, and Howard works full-time."

"That's not my problem. You're a writing instructor. Instruct writing. Got it?"

"Got it," I said. "Anyone else today?"

"No, I think we'll start slow."

"I'm really hoping to have a full schedule," I explained. "I actually like this one-on-one thing. And frankly, I could use the money. Do you think—?"

"We'll see, but let's just take it one session at a time until you get the hang of it."

———

I had assumed I'd be there for a few hours and had no idea what to do with the rest of my day. As I walked out to the sidewalk, I figured it out: I decided to go to Michael's office. He had asked me to come so many times, and I figured today made perfect sense since he was about to go away on a business trip. I had nowhere to be until pickup, and, checking the iTrans app on my phone, I realized that I was more than halfway there already.

I found my way to the R train on Prince Street. Once it came, it was a straight shot all the way to Rector, and I was relieved that I wouldn't even need to make a change. At Canal Street the train emptied out somewhat, and a woman got on and asked for our attention. She told a sad story about how her husband had abused her, and her daughter had epilepsy, and they all got kicked out of their homeless shelter. I gave her five dollars. The scraggly-bearded guy standing next to me, in a cardigan and Clarks, carrying a satchel and an extra cloth bag that said BROOK-LYN FARMERS' MARKET CO-OP shook his head at me.

"You shouldn't do that," he said.

"No?"

"No."

I wanted to follow up, but we stopped at City Hall, and he got off. I found a seat, and for the rest of the trip kept to myself, tracking my progress on the subway map while an empty beer bottle rolled around at my feet.

———

Michael's building was straight out of *Mad Men*. His office in downtown Dallas, with its views past Klyde Warren Park all the way to Fort Worth thirty miles away, had been impressive, but this was grand on a completely different scale. I stopped at the security guard's desk in the lobby and was asked if I had an appointment.

"Oh, I'm just saying hi to my husband," I said. "Just dropping in, you know."

The guard, unimpressed by spontaneity, called up to the office, asked for my ID, took my picture, and asked me to sign the book.

The ornately designed brass elevator was also dated, and it dinged quaintly to mark the passing floors as we headed up. But when the doors opened to Michael's floor, I was in the twenty-first century again: There was a large backlit sign saying ITC for International Tax Consulting. There were sleek glass partitions and recessed lighting, bleached hardwoods, and outrageous views. Michael had been buzzed by the guard in the lobby, so he was waiting as I stepped off the elevator. He looked harried and surprised to see me. He kissed me quickly and led me down the hall.

"Is this a terrible time?"

"No, just unexpected." He glanced at me and checked his watch. "There's a lot to do before my trip tomorrow, and I've got a call in ten minutes, but if you're willing to wait, we can get coffee after."

"It's okay. I just wanted to see your new digs." He was so business-like and at home here, and I noted, he looked quite handsome. He led me briskly down the hall, leaving me a step behind. "I can come back another time," I said.

"You're here now," he said. "Stick around."

Michael quickly introduced me to people here and there along the way. Ann, a secretary. Sam, a CPA. Susan, a consultant. They all matched the tone of the building, orderly and conservative.

At the end of the hall we came to his office. It was smaller than I expected, about half the size of his Dallas office. I walked in, and he kissed me again, this time like he meant it. He had something weird happening with his hair that I fixed by brushing my hand over his head.

"Look at this view," he said, walking over and pressing his forehead up to the glass. "If you stand over here and lean to the left, you can see the Brooklyn Bridge."

"So we're facing east?" I said.

And then I heard it, a familiar "Yoo-hoo!" along with the rapping of fingernails on the wall. Ugh. There she was.

"Cassandra," I said. "Hi."

"Allison! It's *so* good to see you!" Her accent was true Texan, and she was intense with her eye contact, focusing on my face in a way that made me want to take a giant step back, like she was studying me for signs of melanoma.

Cassandra looked amazing, in a tight pencil skirt and a ruffly blouse with a bow that I never could have pulled off; on me it would have looked matronly, on her it looked feminine and hot. She had her hair twisted up in a complicated way that looked like it came from YouTube video instructions or from an actual hairdresser. She hugged me. "How's it going, girl?"

Girl? *Girl?* "Fine, thanks. Getting adjusted, I suppose."

"I *love* it here!" she said. "Don't you just love New York? The people, the food, the fashion. Delivery! I love taxis. I love shopping. I just love everything. People say I've got the makings of a real New Yorker. Right, Michael? What did you tell me yesterday?"

"I don't remember. Was it—?"

"He said I should give tours to people who move here. Of course, he's the New York City celebrity, though. I told everyone I know to check out his Humans of New York post. Did you tell Allison about that restaurant we found the other day?"

"You mean the one on the pier?" he asked.

"No, silly," she said, "I mean the poke bowl place."

Michael pointed at her. "*That* was amazing," he said.

"Poke bowl?" I asked.

"Delish," Cassandra said. "It was Michael's find. Brilliant."

"Ohhhh," Michael said, in a revoltingly bashful manner, "it was only a tip I got from this New York food blogger on Instagram."

Their rapport was making me want to stab somebody, specifically the sexy woman standing a foot away from me with the pussy bow blouse.

"So?" she asked me. "Isn't it wonderful to see your husband so happy?" She playfully punched him on the arm.

"Sure is," I said.

"And you?" she asked. "How's it going?"

"I may need another week to settle," I said. "Or two. Maybe more. It's me versus a mountain of unpacked boxes, and it kind of seems like the boxes are winning, you know?"

Cassandra looked like she felt sorry for me, or maybe sorry for Michael. "Well, I'll let you two talk," she said.

"Good to see you," I said, as sincerely as I could manage.

"You, too! Don't be a stranger!" and she clicked down the hall in her stilettos.

I looked at Michael, and he put his finger up to his lips.

"I wasn't going to say anything," I said, holding my hands up.

"Sure you weren't." He shut the door. "You like it?" he asked, looking around his office.

"Of course. It's beautiful."

"What's wrong?"

"Nothing."

"Cassandra's situation is simpler than ours," he said, walking over to me. "She came here with a job lined up, no kids to worry about, it's totally different for her. We're doing great, don't you think? Why don't you make plans with Sara? Go out for dinner?"

"Why don't *you* just spend every day having lunch dates with your hot, young girlfriend?"

"Allison," Michael said, rubbing my back, "you're being crazy."

I felt my whole body stiffen.

"What?" he asked.

"Forget it," I said, worried I might start shouting if we got into it. "My brand-new boss reprimanded me today. I'm totally overqualified, but he was treating me like I don't know what I'm doing. And I'm just saying that seeing that Westchester neighborhood the other day, the chickens and the chipmunks, and . . . the grass, and it all made me wonder if maybe . . ." I exhaled. "Never mind."

"Wonder if maybe what?"

"If maybe we should have done something less drastic. Like moved *near* the city, not *to* the city."

"You can't be serious," he said. "We just got here, and it's great. And I mean, who cares about *chickens*?"

"It's not about chickens, per se. I just started thinking about Halloween and Jack riding a bicycle. Like when is that boy ever going to get to ride a bike around like a normal kid again, you know?"

Michael looked concerned.

"It's all fine. I'm just having some doubts."

"Maybe your mom will move to the suburbs and solve all of our problems," he said. "We can store our stuff in her attic. How were your students today?"

"Student, singular. He was great," I said. "Very nice man, polite and concentrated. But I hope this job picks up. It was a pretty long trip downtown just for—"

Michael's desk phone rang. "Do you want to wait for me? We'll grab a coffee?"

"Forget it," I huffed. "I'll see you at home."

He gave me a quick kiss and turned his back on me to take the call.

On the subway home, I was feeling sick about Cassandra and tried to reason with myself about their relationship. *It's nothing*, I thought. But I hated their banter. I hated their shared stories. I hated their chumminess. I hated her. *But Michael's not an asshole, he's not the kind of guy who would dump his wife and kids.* An image of the two of them together flashed through my mind. *Is he?*

I pushed the sickening thought away and checked my phone. I'd gotten a voice mail from "Unknown." As soon as I got off the subway, I stopped on the sidewalk, phone to one ear and hand covering the other, and listened to the message:

Yeah, so I'm calling for the asshole who smashed into my BMW. Call back or even better just get your insurance information over here, so I can deal with it. Fifteen Central Park West. ASAP, got it?

MICHAEL WAS PACKING HIS SUITCASE before leaving for work; he was planning to take a cab straight from his office to JFK to leave for his first business trip since the move. I was used to Michael traveling and to his systematic method of packing (from the feet up), but somehow being left in New York for the first time was making me feel unglued.

"Do you *have* to go?"

"Since when do you mind if I travel?" he asked.

"Since now. What if there's a terrorist attack? Where do we go? And how do we get there?"

"Are you actually asking?"

"Yes. Terrorism is a real thing."

"Okay. How about Dallas?"

"On foot?"

"Okay, hunker down in the basement. Or on the roof, whichever seems safest in the moment."

"What if the building collapses?"

He snapped his fingers. "Drop, cover, and hold on. Right? That's from some disaster movie we watched." He'd packed his shoes and socks and now started folding his boxers.

Jack rushed into the room and went into our bathroom. He didn't even bother closing the door.

"I've been thinking," I said quietly, over the sound of peeing, "that we should really keep an open mind about whether high-rise living is right for us, you know? Because it's feeling like the wrong fit. I think New York is trying to chew me up and spit me out onto its filthy, poop-covered sidewalks."

"Can we talk about this after I get back in town?"

"I'm just giving you something to think about on the flight."

"I'll be in Frankfurt and then Geneva," he said, heading into the closet and returning with his pants still on their hangers. "And we'll be back in a week, and then you can explain this drastic change of—"

"We? Who's *we*?"

"The team."

"Meaning?"

"Meaning the team."

I felt my blood pressure spike.

The toilet flushed, and Jack came out of our bathroom. "Is there time for pancakes?" he asked.

"Not today, buddy," Michael said. "But I'll make you some as soon as I'm back in town."

"I'm bored with Cheerios," Jack said and went to get dressed.

I stared at Michael in disbelief. "You're telling me that you're going on a European vacation with Cassandra?"

"It's certainly not a *vacation*," Michael said, folding the slacks and coiling a belt.

"No wife would be okay with this. She's beautiful, young, and you spend more time with her than you do with me, eating your poke-bowl-aphrodisiac lunches. It's obscene."

"There's nothing going on with her. The whole team is going, so it's not like we'll be alone."

"She's too young for you."

"She's a coworker, that's it. You're being ridiculous."

"You're going to be one of those embarrassing, decrepit fathers, tottering around at high school graduation on a walker. Your bastard child will be ashamed of you."

"And now I've *impregnated* her. That was fast." He put in shirts, folded in plastic from the dry cleaner, and neckties, and then he went to the bathroom to fill his leather dopp kit with travel-size shaving cream and razors.

"If we decide to move again, I don't want her following us this time."

"We can't possibly move. We just—"

"You know what? Have a lovely honeymoon in *Switzerland*."

"Jeesh," Michael said.

He went down the hallway and said goodbye to the kids. I heard him opening and closing cabinets in the kitchen.

When he came back, he handed me a cup of coffee and kissed me.

"Tell you what," he said, zipping up his suitcase, "I'll be back in a little over a week, and we'll see how things are going. If you still want to move, say, after the holidays, we'll figure something out," he said, "even though I happen to really like it here so far, and if we moved to Westchester, I'd be spending almost three hours commuting every day, round-trip. Metro North to Grand Central, and then the subway down-town. I'd see a lot less of you and the kids."

"You looked up the commute?" Call me desperate, but I was touched.

"Your bicycle comment got to me," he said, shrugging. "But I'm not even close to ready to give up on this yet. Everything you said about New York? You were right about it. It's the capital of the world, remember? The heart of the country. And so we moved. We're here now, and I love it. It's going to be great." He kissed me again, took his bag, and left.

———

After the girls left for school, I got dressed to take Jack. I went in the bathroom and picked a towel up off the floor. Under it there was a book I'd given Megan a few years ago, an American Girl publication called *The Care and Keeping of You 2: The Body Book for Older Girls*. I didn't know how it had ended up there, but I took it back to Megan's room and put it on her bookshelf.

I knocked on Jack's door and opened it. "Did you eat breakfast?" I asked. "We've only got fifteen minutes." His tiny room was a mess, crammed full of toys, and his clothes were strewn all over the floor.

"How about we clean this disaster area after school today?" I said.

"I don't have anywhere to put anything."

It was true.

"We've got to start by getting these boxes out. There's no room to maneuver." I slid an empty laundry basket to the side and lifted the flap of a box to see what still needed unpacking. It was full of books.

"Those aren't even mine," Jack said.

"Yay," I said, "then that's the first thing to go," and I picked up the heavy box and put it in Megan and Charlotte's room. I started to unpack the books, realizing, for one thing, that there was no room on their bookshelves, and for another, Megan had already read and likely outgrown all of them: *Holes*, *Wonder*, and *Matilda*. She'd probably stuck the box in Jack's room because she was done with them and figured Jack would want them eventually. Where in the world could I stash them in the meantime?

A thought popped into my head, and I grabbed the American Girl book back off the shelf, flipping through it. Things started to make sense. The book, filled with advice about puberty and growing up, illustrations about girls' changing bodies, and discussions about everything from peer pressure to periods, had been in my bathroom, and Jack was the only one of the kids to use it regularly. I smiled, realizing that Jack must have found the book when Megan put the box in his room. *That* was why he was suddenly so interested in breasts and every other part of the human body. I was flooded with relief: Jack wasn't a perv at all. He was just overinformed, freshly exposed to some fairly accurate depictions of lady parts. I put the book back in the box and moved it into the hallway, to neutral territory. I couldn't wait to tell Michael. I texted him: *Sorry for being such a bitch this morning. Going to miss you.*

He texted back: *Wish you were coming along.*

I dropped Jack off at school, giving him a smile and his hand a little extra squeeze when I said goodbye. I didn't even bother with the moms that morning; I had a plan. I decided to take a long walk around the neighborhood, to get to know it a little better. I strolled up Columbus Avenue to Joe's for coffee and then continued on past the Museum of Natural History. Once I got to Ninetieth, I crossed the street and walked south again, staying alert, hoping to spot Hugh Jackman or Kyra Sedgwick or some celebrity so that I, too, could have a cool New York story to tell. But all I saw were busy, hurried people, a homeless man sleeping on the sidewalk, and a young woman wearing an apron, yelling at someone on her phone. "No," she said, "no, no. *You're* the asshole, asshole," and she shoved the phone in her apron pocket and lit a cigarette.

She was standing directly in front of a hair salon. On a whim I walked in and asked for an appointment. The girl in the apron channeled her anger into the best shampoo and head massage I'd ever had, and the stylist gave me highlights, lowlights, and a kickass cut. The whole to-do cost a fortune and took over two hours. I felt great afterward. Sara was right, the hairdresser told me; I do look better with bangs.

Back out on the sidewalk, I ran my hands through my hair and put on my leather jacket. A man in jeans and aviators smiled at me.

I walked down Columbus until I got to Book Culture where I bought the new Zadie Smith novel. Then I went on to Jonathan Adler and browsed for a while. I decided to grab some lunch and stopped at a sandwich place.

When I couldn't put it off any longer, about forty-five minutes before it was time to pick up Jack, I set off to do the one important errand on my to-do list: dropping off my insurance information for the owner of the BMW. I walked past the guard outside the revolving door at an extremely fancy apartment building: 15 Central Park West. There was a large, private courtyard that gave the place a sense of elitism and glamour.

The envelope in my hand, I went inside to the lobby to check in with the doorman at his desk. He smiled at me as I approached.

"I have something for the person living in apartment"—I said, checking the piece of paper where I'd written down the address—"PHB?"

He stopped smiling. "Is this about the incident?" he asked.

Mortifying. Even the doorman knew.

"Yes, but it was just an accident."

"Sure it was," he said. "Sign here," and he offered me a pen. I signed my name in the book beneath some of the sloppiest handwriting I'd ever seen.

"Come with me," he said. He started walking toward the elevator.

"Really? I thought—"

"You expect *him* to come down from the penthouse to see *you*?"

"Sorry, no. I just thought you could, you know, pass this along to him whenever you see him."

"That could be today or sometime next week. So if you want him to get it—"

"Sure, fine," I said.

Leaning into the elevator, he put a key in the slot next to the top-floor button and turned it. "Good luck," he said, looking disgusted. He pulled the key out, and left me in there alone as the doors closed.

It seemed unnecessary and punitive to have to face the owner of the BMW I'd hit. I cleared my throat and arranged my new hair, preparing myself for a cool apology and a quick retreat. *No big deal*, like the nanny had said. *Shit happens.*

The elevator, wood-paneled with inset mirrors, opened directly into an apartment with a spacious foyer. The first thing I saw was a headless and armless royal-blue sculpture of Venus, standing on a pedestal. She was taller than me and sturdy, posing in front of a breathtaking view of New York. From the entry, which alone was big enough to waltz in, I could see an expansive living room with huge windows, sleek, modern furniture, and an animal-skin rug. There was a strong smell of cleaning products mixed with smoke and cologne, but no one was waiting for me.

"Helloooo?" I called out.

Nothing. No one. Under a massive mirror there was a glass semicircular table with a tacky gold base, and I carefully placed the envelope on it. "Okay, then," I said out loud. "Here's my insurance information; it's all right here. And my cell phone and email address, too. Hello?"

There was a loud noise—slam—and a woman, around sixty years old, walked angrily toward me, waved her arms around, and started yelling at me. In Spanish. I only heard about four recognizable words (*estúpido, coño, mierda, animal*). I couldn't believe how much she hated me. "It was an accident," I said, taking a few steps backward. "I'll pay for it."

"Pay for it?" she asked, taking a step closer. "*Pay* for it?"

"Of course."

She spat on the floor. "There's not enough money in the world."

"Look, these things happen."

She took a key off of her keychain and put it in my hand. "I'm sorry?" I asked. "What is this?"

She pushed the elevator button, threw a plastic CVS bag into the closet, and took her coat and purse out. "Tell him I quit."

As soon as the elevator doors closed behind her, I pushed the button again, hoping to exit as quickly as she had. I looked at the key in my hand and put it on the table next to my envelope. "Hurry," I whispered, pushing the elevator button ten more times in a row, fast.

"Fucking mother*fucker*," I heard from the depths of the massive apartment. "Are you still here? Come *on!*"

"Hello," I said. I was trying to keep my composure.

"Don't leave," the voice called, getting closer. "I didn't even *do* anything. Just give me my pills."

It was a man in shorts. No, it was a boy. It was a boy limping through the living room, in bare feet across the rug, past an artsy photograph of a woman's boobs, five times larger than life-size. He stopped several feet away from me, leaning on one crutch.

"Who the fuck are you?" he asked. He had a swollen, black eye, and his arm was in a sling, fastened tight across his chest.

"I'm the woman about the car."

"Where's Loida?"

"I really wouldn't know. I . . . I put my contact and insurance information on the table," and I pointed to it. I thought about mentioning the key and the screaming lady but decided not to overcomplicate the transaction.

"Look, I'm dying here," he said. "I need a lot more than fucking *information*."

I panicked for a second until I remembered the reality of what had happened: "You weren't *in* the car when I hit it," I said, stating the obvious. "There were witnesses, dozens of them, in fact. So if you're trying to—"

"I seriously don't give a fuck," he said. His knee was encased in a bulky Velcro brace, and the bruising around his eye looked brand-new.

"Okay," I answered. "Well, in case someone else in the household decides they *do* care, and I think someone will, you know how to reach me." He was wearing a white tank top, and he had a raised, red, irritated tattoo with the words

FUCK
YOU
LIE

on his bicep. *I'll kill my kids if they ever get tattoos*, I thought. *Fuck you lie? That makes no grammatical sense whatsoever.* Was it simply missing a comma? *Fuck, you lie* was at least a sentence.

The kid swayed a little, leaning on his crutch. He looked like hell.

"Are you okay?" I asked.

"The cleaning lady hid my pain pills 'cause she's a cunt."

I bristled. "I think she may have quit," I told him, "but you probably knew that already."

"I hurt like a motherfucker."

I stepped closer and saw that his eyes were watering. I could also see that he had nice features, once I looked past the split lip and the puffy, purple left side of his face. He was wearing a watch that probably cost a full year of Michael's salary. The teenaged offspring of a CEO. Hedge fund brat. Limitless allowance. Parents out of town somewhere decadent, Turks and Caicos, maybe, and who knows what kind of trouble their kid had gotten himself into. He looked about seventeen or eighteen, and was probably still in high school. He could have gone to school with Charlotte, for all I knew.

"It's none of my business," I said, "but you look like you should be in bed."

He turned awkwardly and limped away from me, revealing a pot leaf tattoo on his shoulder blade.

"Do you need me to contact someone?" I called after him.

"If you see my pain meds around, I need them. Fucking Advil isn't going to cut it." He went down a hall and out of sight. I waited for the inevitable slamming of a door but never heard it; I was so accustomed to my own children slamming doors, that this almost seemed like a friendly gesture.

He may have been a rich, spoiled brat, but he didn't seem to have anyone looking after him. The apartment was sprawling and quiet; I wondered who, other than the blue, headless Venus, was around. I checked my phone to make sure I wasn't late for Jack, and then looked into the living room, marveling at the extravagance (and garishness) of the decor and the absurdly stunning views. What were these people like? Did they convene for family meals in formal wear, kiss each other on the cheek before discussing homework and basketball practice?

On a hunch I quietly opened the closet where the woman had gotten her coat and saw the plastic CVS bag she'd tossed in on the floor: in it was a full bottle of OxyContin. I couldn't in good conscience give that child the whole bottle; I knew better than that. I wouldn't entrust my own kids with something so lethal, especially after whatever this boy had been through. I walked past the living room and into the kitchen, which was easily ten times the size of mine. It had floor-to-ceiling windows along one side and was sleek and modern: a built-in cappuccino maker, glass-fronted refrigerator, and white lacquered cabinets. I tried to picture the kid's mother in here cooking macaroni and cheese. No, this was a caterer's kitchen. The counter was for lining up flutes of champagne, not sippy cups of milk. It was too beautiful to mess up with everyday food. This was a canapé kitchen, a shrimp cocktail and caviar kitchen.

I opened drawers until I found a pen and took out four bottles of Fiji water from the fridge. I checked the instructions on the pill bottle and spread out four paper towels on the center island. On each paper towel I put a bottle of water and one pill. I checked the time again, and wrote "Take at 4:00" on the first, "Take at 8:00" on the second, "12:00" on the third. He should really sleep after that, I reasoned, so I wrote "Wait until 5:00 a.m." on the last one. On a fifth paper towel I wrote the words "Drink ALL water to stay hydrated. NO ALCOHOL!" It was time to get Jack, and I buttoned up my coat to go. I added a P.S.—"Hope you feel better" with a smiley face.

I hid the pill bottle back in the front hall closet, and, before I walked out of the apartment, for some strange reason, I took the cleaning woman's key from the table and put it in my pocket.

———

Lining up wasteful, plastic water bottles for a foul-mouthed rich kid who'd gotten himself into some kind of trouble was hardly the kind of philanthropic cause Sara believed in. But as I emerged from the courtyard of the apartment building, things felt different. I waved to the clique of moms at the school, like we were friends, and said hello to Lauren. I introduced myself to the nanny who'd been so nice to me after I'd crunched the car.

When Jack came out of the school building a few minutes later, Ms. Hendrick caught my eye, pointed to him, and gave me a thumbs-up.

I smiled at her and mouthed the words, "Thank you."

"You look different," Jack said as we walked toward home. I noticed he had a spring in his step.

"I got a haircut. You like it?"

"It's okay." He sniffed. "It smells funny."

I leaned over and said, "Do you have any idea how terrific you are?"

"I practically got kicked out of school already."

"Yeah, well, people make mistakes. Just learn something and move ahead. How's it going with Ms. Hendrick?" I asked.

"She's pretty nice."

I stopped walking. "She is?"

"She gave me a job. It's really important."

"What job?"

"I'm in charge of taking care of Arthur."

"Who's Arthur?"

"The class hamster."

"Wow, that's a big deal. She must think pretty highly of you. We should celebrate," I said.

"Celebrate how?"

"Let's make a feast tonight."

"You mean, like, *cooking*?"

On the way home, we stopped at the grocery store and bought a big organic chicken, a head of garlic, lemons, baby potatoes, and salad for a meal that used to be a weekday staple. I told Jack he was responsible for dessert, and he kept putting things in the cart that I wouldn't let him keep (a bag of Starbursts, a package of Oreos, marshmallows) until finally he picked something I could go along with: a frozen apple pie and vanilla ice cream.

While Jack was cleaning his room and I was cooking, Michael called from the airplane to say goodbye. He had to shut his phone off for take-off, so I couldn't tell him about my weird encounter with the boy.

"Hope you can sleep," I said, trying not to picture Cassandra in the business class seat beside him.

"*Auf Wiedersehen*," he said. "Love you."

Megan came home from school, smelled the chicken roasting in the oven, and said, "Did dinner already come?"

"I'm cooking," I told her.

Her jaw dropped.

"What?" I asked.

"Nothing," she said. "Your hair looks really pretty."

"Thanks, I found a place not far from here."

"Can you make an appointment for me?"

"Sure," I said, happy that this was something concrete I could actually do for her. "How was your day?"

She handed me a math test with a red C circled on the top. "I don't understand what we're doing in class. My teacher never explains anything."

"Your teacher's a tough grader, huh?" I asked.

Megan had never gotten Cs before. I looked over the test. There were red marks, crossing through wrong answers, but no explanations, no corrections.

Megan shrugged. "Or I'm a bad student."

I looked up at her, wondering if I should start doing research into other schools for the next year, just in case.

"You're a very good student," I said. I could help manage Charlotte's college process while also taking on Megan's high school one. And that reminded me: I needed to ask Charlotte how her final college list was coming along, a conversation I'd been postponing until she was a little less mad at me. The last time we'd discussed it, she had Johns Hopkins at the top of the list.

About an hour later, I heard Charlotte's key in the lock, and she came into the apartment, sweaty from cross country, loaded down with her sports bag and backpack. She looked around the apartment and asked, "What's that smell? Is that . . . Did you *cook*?"

"I'll call you when it's ready," I told her.

"What did you do to your hair?" she asked.

"I went to a salon," I said, prepared for a harsh critique.

She took my hair between her fingers and fluffed it. "Looks really good, Mom."

I tried to mask my astonishment. "Thanks. How was your day?"

"Fine." She walked away, and I heard the door to her and Megan's bedroom close with a gentle click. It was music to my ears.

Music, I remembered. I played pop songs off my iPhone through the Jawbone speaker (Beyoncé, Sia, and Madonna). I took out the silver

Chilewich placemats. I set the table with our nice plates, after washing off the visible newspaper print. I lit candles and saw that everything looked perfect. Like a home.

Charlotte, Megan, and Jack walked in to the room, eyes wide open, like it was Christmas day.

six

THE NEXT MORNING, I showered before the kids were even up and had breakfast ready on the table. It was a fresh fall day, and as I got dressed in jeans, a black sweater, and boots, my phone pinged with a text from Michael: *Landed in Frankfurt, off to a meeting and fyi I love you.*

The kids and I went through the usual morning routine of packing backpacks, remembering subway cards and school IDs, and finding the right weight jackets. When Jack and I headed out and I was locking the door behind us, the neighbor came out of his apartment from the other end of the hall with his pug, and the four of us waited awkwardly for the elevator together.

"Can I pat him?" Jack asked.

"You can have him," the man said. He was around sixty, I guessed, with a grumpy expression, and he picked up the dog and handed him to Jack. "I won him in the divorce. Lucky me," he said dryly.

"Ah," I said. "Sounds complicated."

"I take care of our class hamster," Jack said, holding the flat-faced dog and patting him on the top of his head. "I'm pretty good with animals. We have a cat."

"We moved in a month ago," I said as we stepped into the elevator. "I'm Allison, this is Jack."

The man shook my hand. "Yes, the door slammers," he said. "Welcome to the building." He turned to Jack. "If you ever want to walk Pancake, just let me know. I pay ten dollars a walk with a bonus if you can lose him."

"His name's *Pancake*?" Jack said, delighted. "I'm a great dog walker." The dog snorted unattractively. Jack was clearly falling for him, but I wasn't. I had other matters on my mind anyway. The key to the guy's apartment felt hot in my hand, shoved deep in my jacket pocket. If the kid's parents were back, I would talk to them about damaging their car and simply leave their key somewhere in the apartment. If they weren't back, I would do what any mom would do: check on the boy, make sure he was okay.

We said goodbye to our neighbor, who was pulling a poop bag out of his pocket, and headed off to school. After dropping Jack off, I walked quickly toward Central Park West, wondering what sort of accident could have caused that young man so much bodily damage. A fall down a flight of stairs? A fight at school? A cabdriver taking a fast right-hand turn? An image of Jack with his face bruised and battered popped into my head, and I wished I'd given him an extra hug before saying goodbye to him.

As I passed a deli, I decided to buy the kid a scrambled egg and sausage sandwich with a side of grilled potatoes. An orange juice for vitamin C. He'd looked so bad; I figured a good deed was an appropriate act. While I waited for my order, I picked out magazines for myself as well, *People* for fun, the *New Yorker* for substance.

When I got to the apartment building, weaving past a crowd on the busy sidewalk and nodding to the security guard, I said hello to the doorman, the same one from the day before.

"Is he home?" I asked. "Because I'm still resolving that incident," and I made a face like I was exasperated.

"He's up there," he said.

"So is his family here?"

"As far as I know, the kid's alone."

"He gave me a key," I said, and I showed it to him. "I can let myself in."

"Sign," he said and handed me the pen. "I've never known him to sit around on his own for so long," the doorman said. "Always got a whole gang of derelicts with him. He's a frickin' lowlife. I don't care who he is, you don't piss all over the lobby of your own building. And from what I heard that was just the beginning of his night."

"Disgusting," I said. *Good grief, he peed in the lobby?*

"Tell me about it. So are you his lawyer, or what?"

"I'm with Brinkley," I said. My husband was a lawyer, and technically I was *with* him. "So you don't think anyone is up there?" I asked again.

"Only him, as far as I know."

"Wow," I said. "That's pitiful."

"*Pitiful?*" he said loudly enough to startle me. "I don't feel sorry for him. The guy's a prick. Don't let him manipulate you."

"No."

"'Cause he's good at that. Orders everyone around like he's king of the world. He's a real shithead, I'm telling you."

"Got it."

"Good," he said. "Turn the key while you hold down the button."

As I stepped in the elevator, I tried to think of exactly what I would say to him, how I would explain my return. Would I have to tell him where I got the key? I put my sunglasses in their case, thinking I should have brought Neosporin for the cut on his face.

The doors opened, and I was greeted again by silence and the large, headless Venus in the entry. I went to the kitchen, noticing that the pills on the counter had all been taken. Not all at once, I hoped. The sun was shining in the windows, lighting up a glass shelf in the living room of what I guessed was a collection of Steuben glass. Steuben glass and just to the right of it, a row of souvenir shot glasses from various beach resorts. Nothing here went together.

From the front hall closet, I retrieved the pill bottle and took it to the kitchen. I poured the bottle of orange juice into a glass and went down the hall to his room. The door was open, so I tapped my nails on it.

"Hellooo?" I whispered. His TV was on, but he was lying in bed with his back to it. The blackout shades were down. "Morning."

"What?" he asked, rolling over and squinting to see me. "The fuck are you?"

"It's me, the lady who crashed into your car, remember? We met yesterday?"

"You 'crashed' what?"

"Well, crash is a little strong. I scraped it. Dented it a little. Knocked off your side mirror. You called me about resolving everything."

"No I didn't."

"Yes, I brought a copy of my insurance card yesterday, left it on your hall table." He didn't say anything. "You don't remember any of this?"

"I'm a little out of it."

"How're you feeling now?"

"Like complete shit. My head hurts."

"Here," I said and handed him a pill.

"Is that my Oxy?" He sat up carefully and took the orange juice I offered. There were empty water bottles on the floor near him, and a pair of boxers. It occurred to me that he might well be naked. His tattoo, still red and painful-looking, was hurting my sensibilities.

"Why don't you get up for a bit," I suggested, "walk around a little. Do you want something to eat? I got you an egg sandwich."

"Sandwich? Did Lyle send you? How'd you get in?"

"I bumped into your car a few blocks from here," I said, skirting the question. "I made a scene and embarrassed my kid in front of about fifty people. I'm a good driver, actually; I don't know how I could have done something so careless. Sorry, by the way." He didn't say anything but by the looks of him, I could tell he wasn't thinking about the car. "I'll be in the kitchen," I said. "Are you hungry?" He didn't answer. "I can recycle these empty water bottles for you."

I found white dinner plates in the cabinet above the dishwasher and put the sandwich on one, dumping out the Styrofoam container of potatoes next to it. Not exactly Martha Stewart, but it would do. About five minutes later he came hobbling into the kitchen and sat on a barstool. I put the plate in front of him, along with a napkin and a fork. "I can leave if you want. Totally up to you. I just wanted to make sure you're okay and that you found the envelope I left yesterday."

He held the fork the wrong way; it was jutting sideways out of his closed fist, and he brought his mouth to the food, not the food to his mouth. I blamed his parents for his shocking lack of table manners. "Is there someone I should call or email?" I asked. "Are you expected to be somewhere? School, maybe?"

"The fuck are you talking about?" he said with his mouth full.

"You're in pretty sorry shape, and I figured you might need me to contact someone or call—"

He dropped the fork. "Don't bust my balls, lady. There's no calling anyone or going anywhere, or doing anything. I'm fucked and everything's fucked, so who would you even call? That asshole Lyle? That backstabbing piece of shit Simon? Who? Give me another Oxy. My knee is fucking killing me."

Even Charlotte would never talk to me like that, no matter how angry she was. In fact, no one had ever talked to me like this before, and I wasn't having it. I used my calm, stern mom voice. "Let the pill you just took kick in—you can't take another for four hours. I'll leave today's pills for you as long as you take them on a schedule. Those meds are very strong," I said, wagging my finger, "and quite addictive."

"*Who the fuck are you?*"

"Allison. We met yesterday. Now why don't you tell me who Lyle is. Is he a friend of yours? Did he do that to your face?"

"Fuck you is who Lyle is."

"Excuse me, but don't talk to me like that." I shook my head at him. "You're being *so* rude."

If I'd hoped to talk him into being polite, I failed. Instead, he got up and intentionally dropped his plate on the floor, smashing it, bits of egg and china scattering everywhere.

"Why—?"

"What do you want from me, lady?" he asked. "I know you want *something*, so why don't you come out with it and stop with this bullshit concern? Just tell me what it is. Some shitty old T-shirt? Want me to sign your tits? You want a stupid fucking selfie? What?"

"You are . . ." I got my purse and started to leave. "Does your mother know you talk like that? You are the most conceited, angry boy I have ever met, and I taught high school, so that's saying a lot. I don't know who you think you are, but you are shooting yourself in the foot acting like this. You looked like you could use a little TLC, I felt like I should check on you and bring you something to eat, and you behave like an ungrateful two-year-old. Shame on you. What's your name anyway?"

He looked at me like I was crazy.

"I need it for my insurance report."

"Jose Cuervo."

"Your *name.*"

"Fuck the report. And fuck you, and fuck your . . . car."

"Oh, okay," I said. "Fine." He was, in fact, a shithead, just as the doorman had said. And definitely not worth one more second of my time. I picked up the bag that had my magazines in it, and in my moment of anger, I handed him the bottle of OxyContin. "Take *one* pill every four hours. No more than that, mister, or you're putting your health at great risk. Good luck."

On the way to the elevator, I turned back. "I'll tell you something else—public urination is revolting, unacceptable behavior. And you should have talked to someone with a brain before you got that tattoo because it doesn't even *mean* anything. *And* it looks like it's getting infected, so . . . so . . . so go to a doctor!" *Ha*, I thought, straightening my jacket and fixing my hair. *I really told him.*

I was halfway home when I realized I still had his key in my pocket.

———

What if he overdoses? What if he overdoses? What if he's lying on the kitchen floor, choking on his own vomit? It was past midnight, and I was sitting on the living room couch with the magazines I'd bought. I flipped through the *New Yorker*, looking only at the cartoons, trying to distract myself since I'd completely given up on the idea of sleep. I paced the floor. I checked on the kids. At 1:00 a.m. I still couldn't sleep, so I decided to call Michael, figuring that with the time change, he would be awake already. He picked up on the first ring.

"What are you doing up so late?" he said. "I miss you."

"You do?"

"Of course. I have a nice room and the most amazing bed with one of those European comforters. You should be here with me. Everything okay there?"

"Sort of. Not exactly. I thought I found a good cause, but then it didn't exactly work out. It's a long story. I think my cause might be overdosing on OxyContin as we speak."

"What?"

"Never mind." I picked up the *People* magazine. "How's it going there?" *Sexy boots for winter. Fave bags for a night on the town.*

"I have gossip," Michael said.

"What gossip?" *Katy Perry's hair. Justin Timberlake's tuxedo. A Hollywood divorce.*

"Cassandra's engaged."

I looked up. "Really? To the mixed martial arts guy? For real?"

"Yes. I thought you'd like that."

"Wow. Phew. That's great news. Are you heartbroken?" I asked.

"I'm thrilled," he said. "We took her out for a drink to celebrate."

"I'm sorry for acting pathologically jealous for no reason."

"It's okay. But don't do that. Ever. It's totally unnecessary."

Gwyneth Paltrow said something classist. Alec Baldwin said something offensive. Miss Florida said something stupid. They all apologized on Twitter. "Well good," I said.

"I'm not interested in anyone else," Michael said. "What are you wearing right now?" *A new blockbuster movie with Jennifer Aniston had its premiere in Berlin.*

"Ugly sweatpants and your T-shirt."

"Hot."

"Not really." *A star-studded musical is coming to Broadway, starring Kevin Kline! Also on the marquee: a TV/film actress and a big-time pop singer.*

"I think you're sexy," he said, "especially if you take off the sweatpants."

"Really?" I asked. "You do?" *Selling out fast, so grab tickets to Limelight before it's too late!* The article had a picture of Kevin Kline with the two young stars in the cast. *She has her own sitcom, but who knew she could sing?! And he can sing, but who knew he could act?!*

"Wait," I said. "Hold it. Oh my god!"

"Hold it?"

"Oh my God!" I squinted and looked more closely. "Is that—?"

I grabbed my laptop, searching for a better picture of the actors.

"Allison?"

There he was, smiling his adorable smile, waving to a crowd of fans, looking nothing like the boy with the black eye and bad attitude. "Holy shit," I said. "Holy *shit*! Oh my god oh my god oh my god!"

"Wow. What's happening over there?"

"I've got to go. Oh my god! I'll explain later. Tell Cassandra I say congratulations. I love you," I said and hung up before he could answer.

I ripped a sheet of paper out of Jack's notebook that was on the dining room table and wrote a quick note to the kids. I stepped into Charlotte's UGGs by the front door, and hurried out of the apartment.

It was raining. I ran the whole nine blocks and was completely winded and soaked when I got to the building. I went inside and saw the night-shift doorman; we hadn't met.

"Would you believe," I said to him, trying to catch my breath, "I just got a call from you-know-who on the top floor. Middle of the night. I'm sound asleep, and he calls because he suddenly remembers some 'details' about that incident the other night. The peeing in the lobby and all the rest of it. You know. Legal stuff." I shook some of the water out of my hair. "He asked me to come right over, you know how he is. So here I am, getting 'details.' "

"Sure, I'll buzz him," he said, turning to the switchboard.

"No!"

He turned back. "No?"

"I was here twice already. I'm in the book. I have a key." I showed it to him. "No need to buzz him. He just wants me to come up to discuss the matter, and I'll be on my way."

"You the one Jeffrey mentioned? He said something about a lawyer was here."

"That's me, yes."

He crossed his arms and widened his stance, bouncer style. "Pretty late for a lawyer visit, wouldn't you say?" He raised his eyebrows.

I looked at him, wondering what exactly he was implying. I hadn't anticipated having an issue getting in and wondered if I should just level with him.

"Believe me, I don't want to be here. But it's my job, you know. He said to come, so I came. But you know what, forget it," I bluffed. "I'll just go home. Let him know I tried, okay?"

He took a closer look at me and relaxed, handing me the sign-in book and a pen. I guess my ripped sweatpants, Michael's shirt, and Charlotte's soggy UGGS in no way resembled a hooker outfit, and I simply didn't look like someone who was here to party or cause trouble.

"I'm just doing my job," he said. "I let the wrong guest in, I get fired."

"I understand," I said.

"Buzz me if he's out of control up there, and I'll call the police. It wouldn't be the first time."

In the elevator, I turned the key, pressed the button, and closed my eyes. *Don't be dead. Don't be dead. Please don't be dead.* I was picturing the news stories: *Megastar found unresponsive in NYC apartment . . . History of drug abuse . . . A life cut short . . . Housewife saw him last and gave him lethal dose of prescription meds . . . Did middle-aged woman cause gifted celeb to overdose?* There would be a picture of me, holding my hands up to hide my face. Millions of teenagers would hate me. I would have the worst fifteen minutes of fame *ever*.

The apartment was silent when I walked in, and it occurred to me that if he wasn't dead, I could get arrested or even shot for trespassing. Maybe the doorman would lose his job after all for letting me up.

Don't people like him have a security team? An entourage? Where is everybody?

"Hello?" Silence. "Hi there," I whispered to no one, "it's just me again, Allison, the lady who crashed into your car? Please don't kill me." Nothing. I looked around the darkened entry and then slowly tiptoed to the kitchen. The broken plate and scrambled eggs were still on the floor. There were crackers on the counter and a frozen pizza that had never made it into the oven. *How does CPR go?* I wondered. *Is it five compressions and a breath? Or ten compressions?* I turned to walk back to his room, holding my phone out, ready to dial 911. But then on the counter, on the right-hand side of the kitchen, I saw my setup from earlier, crudely re-created: four paper towels lined up, each marked, in terrible handwriting, with the proper times, four hours apart, each with a single pill and a Fiji. The pill bottle was there as well, and I gave it a shake; still pretty much full.

I exhaled. He was alive, and I was both relieved and ecstatic. I put my phone away, took a second to take a deep breath, and then walked silently to the elevator, remembering this time to leave the apartment key on the table in the entry.

"He's sound asleep," I said to the doorman. "Can you believe it?"

"So he calls you in the *middle* of the night and then goes to bed before you even get here?" I couldn't tell if he was doubting my story or feeling sorry for me. Either way, I felt like I should get the hell out of there.

He shook his head. "Too bad you made the trip. What did you say your name was?"

"Allison," I said, offering my hand.

"Bernard. I'll see you again soon, I guess."

"Nope, I'm done here," I answered.

"I wish I could say the same. We've got paparazzi showing up out front at all hours, and on a bad shift, vomit to clean up in the elevator. Consider yourself lucky."

The rain had slowed to a drizzle, and I pulled my hood up as I walked home in the dark. The streets were far from deserted, and I took my time, walking past closed shops and a few open bars. I wasn't sick with worry anymore, but I couldn't stop thinking about him. I didn't know if he was okay. The kid might be a huge celebrity, but he was clearly in rough shape.

I was trying to decide if I would tell my children in the morning that I'd met a Grammy-winning pop star, a boy who was famous at twelve, yet totally unrecognizable to me, even though his poster had been on Charlotte's wall for at least a year, maybe two. I hadn't recognized him, but it wasn't just the puffy eye; I'm just not "with it" that way. But now that I knew who he was, I could recall all sorts of things about him, his adorable face when he was a preteen, a dimple-cheeked boy with the voice of an angel, singing songs about girls before he was old enough to know anything about them. And then years of being *the* teenaged heartthrob. And more recently he'd gone rogue. There were all kinds of rumors about fights in bars, DUIs, and a pregnant girlfriend or two, one of whom had refused to take a paternity test; he swore it wasn't his kid. I also remember his irresistible smile, his charisma, his magnetic personality. He was a celebrity idol. Worshipped even after he started disappointing his original fans; in fact, some felt his wild antics were succeeding in making him seem edgy and tough, and were helping him attract a new fan base.

And then I came along: I'd smashed up Carter Reid's car. I'd stood in Carter Reid's kitchen and lectured him on polite behavior. I'd reprimanded him for getting a tattoo. I'd scolded him and stormed out in a huff, without a clue who he was.

By the time I got home, it had stopped raining, and I had decided it would probably be best to keep my celebrity encounter fail to myself. But as I flipped through the *People* magazine after I'd crawled into bed, I couldn't stop wondering, *Why is Carter Reid all alone?*

Part Two

TURN IT AROUND

"I had reached a point in my life and in my career where everything seemed to be going downhill. I just kept getting worse and worse and worse . . . It was like I had to challenge myself, because all my life, you see, I'd told myself that I was the greatest thing that ever lived."

Anne Bancroft
Actors Talk About Acting

seven

IS THERE ANY FOOD IN HIS APARTMENT? *Has he gone to a doctor? Who's helping him? An agent? A manager? Some Broadway producer?*

I couldn't stop thinking about Carter. Whether I was shopping at CVS, loading the dishwasher, or running in Central Park, I was preoccupied by the questions piling up in my mind: *Who gave him that black eye and busted knee? Will he recover in time for his musical? Is he icing his face? Who is Lyle?* I felt uneasy, like there was unfinished business. And I hadn't told a soul about it.

Michael was in Vienna, the kids were at school, and I had a day with nothing on my calendar other than the usual to-do list, which involved grocery shopping, paying bills, and doing endless laundry. Instead of tackling any of those chores, I tried to call my mom. As usual she didn't pick up. She'd been so busy lately. Every time I called, she was running off to meet someone for lunch or she had a piano student ringing the doorbell or she was simply "in the middle of something." I was starting to think that she was avoiding me, that her idea of moving to the New York suburbs had been nothing but a passing thought, and that she was too settled in in Dallas, too happy to consider uprooting her life again because of me, and she was postponing the act of telling me. Meanwhile, the more I imagined her living nearby, of taking the kids up to spend a weekend with her in the country, the more I liked the idea. But my mother seemed to have lost interest.

Since my mom was unavailable, I filled up my coffee mug and watched *Entertainment Weekly*, hoping for news about Carter. I Googled him to learn exactly how he was discovered as a nine-year-old in Oklahoma through a Nickelodeon casting call his school music teacher brought him to, back when his name was still Roy Carter. How his teenaged mother taught him country songs as a child, in between periods of being out-of-her-mind drunk, and began to self-destruct after her son was remade and branded as "Carter Reid" by a talent scout who'd seen his Nickelodeon audition tape. How his first manager paid her to put him in charge of all decision-making; she agreed. How she died of cervical cancer when Carter was thirteen because she hadn't been to a doctor since he was born. Carter became rebellious, unstable, and dumped the manager, shifting his image from sweet preteen child to teenaged badass. He eventually signed with a new manager who kept his career going strong, but either couldn't control him or was happy to let him make a complete ass of himself. If it weren't for Carter's actual talent as a musician, he would have been a washed-up former child star years ago.

It was all so cliché, and I wished I could shake him, tell him to stop misbehaving, to figure out who he really was. I had imaginary conversations with him: *Come on now, Carter!* I might say to him firmly but kindly. *Britney tried this, and look how that turned out! And what about Justin Bieber? Does anyone take him seriously anymore? Stop trying to be something you're not!* I fantasized about giving him a square meal, good, motherly advice, and some tough love. I would set limits and make sure he slept well. I would make him see that if only he would stick to what he did well—singing—he would forever be a success, and I would help him find a manager who appreciated him and had his best interests at heart. We would discuss his image and reputation. I would remind him that while, yes, he was seen by some as a boy toy, singing fairly trivial, four-chord love songs, he was talented. Truly talented. "Roller Coaster Love" was one of Megan and Charlotte's favorite songs of all time to sing to in the car. I would keep singing it after I'd dropped them at school, tapping my hands on the steering wheel. *Sure the last few years have been shaky for you,* I wanted to tell him, *but you can turn it around! And this Broadway musical is the ticket to put you back on track.*

I jotted down some information about his show, the dates it was running, and clicked on the page for tickets. Why was Broadway so damned expensive? Just for fun I looked up tickets to *Hamilton*; many dates I entered had seats available, but the starting price was $550 a ticket, often it was more. I looked up information on how to enter the lottery for tickets and on a whim signed up for that night. The limit was two tickets. So which child would I bring if I actually won? I could only imagine the fight my kids would have over this.

I was mulling over this trivial version of *Sophie's Choice* when I got a text message from my mother: *What are your plans for Thanksgiving?*

I picked up the phone to facetime her and was relieved when she actually answered.

"Now wait, hang on a sec, would you?" she asked, while propping her phone up against something in front of her. The she scooched her chair back, fixed her short hair, sat up straight, and said, "Okay, I'm here."

"You were here the whole time," I said.

She clapped her hands. "Well, I'm ready now."

Everyone always described my mom as youthful. She volunteered for the Dallas Bach Society and had limitless energy, a slew of young piano students coming and going, and a garden that was the envy of her neighborhood. I certainly didn't want her to abandon the life she'd built, but I had assumed, wrongly, as it turned out, that she would jump at the chance to move with us to Manhattan. I hated the thought of her living alone, without any family in the area.

She was wearing a pink-and-white-striped button-down with the sleeves rolled up and her short string of pearls. She'd always kept a preppy, New England style in spite of the fact that she'd lived in Dallas for a decade.

"You got a haircut," she said and leaned in toward the screen.

"Finally. You like it?"

"Looks chic. You could go even shorter. How are the kids?" she asked. "Seems like they're getting used to things there." She looked at herself on her computer and applied ChapStick.

"Did you talk to them?"

"I follow them on Facebook and Instagram," she said. "I take it there's trouble in paradise with Charlotte and Theo. Not surprising, though, is it?"

"It's a surprise to me." I shook my head. "What makes you think there's trouble?"

"I saw that a girl named Chelsea has been tagging Theo in an awful lot of Facebook photos," she said. "And he posted a cat meme on her page, and then she commented with a heart emoji. Doesn't look good."

"What? No, Chelsea's one of Charlotte's friends." I thought of Cassandra's engagement and my irrational worry. "I'm sure it's nothing. Charlotte seems to be happier recently anyway. She's excited about our trip this winter. Like, she made an actual days-to-Dallas countdown calendar."

"Did you find Jack a piano teacher?"

"Not yet."

"Allison."

"How can he have lessons or practice here with all of us in the apartment? We'll have to hide in our rooms, and if Charlotte comes home midlesson . . ."

"There's a school I've heard about called Lucy Moses. Call them. And don't wait too long. It's not good for him to take a break. He's very good, you know. And Megan's developing quite a bosom."

"*Mom.*"

"She is."

"What does that have to do with piano?"

"Nothing, but I saw some posts and noticed that she's growing up very fast. You need to keep her steady through the onslaught of hormones. You give her a great big hug from me."

"She's still sweet and little."

"Sweet, yes," my mother said. She left the rest of the sentence hanging.

"So what's this about Thanksgiving?"

Thanksgiving happens to be one of my favorite holidays. No gifts to buy, and the only real expectation is to provide lots of food and a halfway decent turkey. Add gravy and gratitude, and it's a complete success.

"I spoke to Leigh Miller, that realtor you met, and she's going to show me some houses."

"That's great. But you're not going to look at apartments here at all?" I tried to keep the disappointment out of my voice. "What about the New York Philharmonic? The opera? The thousands of piano students who would be lining up at your door."

"I just can't see it," she said, "living in an apartment? In a city that crowded? Not at this point in my life, anyway."

"So fly to New York, and we'll go look at houses together. We should look in New Jersey, too. My friend Lilly loves Montclair."

"I'm thinking of staying in Westchester for a few days actually, just to get the feel of the area. I'll rent a car."

That sounded promising. "And you'll come here for Thanksgiving?"

"But I can't be away too long," she warned. "I've got a million things going on here. My students have a recital coming up, and the garden club is bringing in a botanist for our winter lecture series."

"So a short visit," I said. I wasn't getting the feeling that giving up her life in Dallas was truly on the table. And given that she was happy there, I felt selfish for wishing for it at all.

"Is that the piano?" she asked, looking past me at the living room. "I thought it was going in the den?"

"There is no den, remember? That's part of the problem."

"Get it tuned," she reminded me, another chore on my list.

"We were lucky to fit it in the apartment at all. Want a quick tour?" I said, flipping my camera around to show her the living room.

When Jack and I got home that afternoon, Megan was already at the apartment, looking at a TMZ page I'd left open on my laptop.

Jack went into the kitchen and got a bowl of cereal.

"Why are you obsessing about Carter Reid?" Megan asked me, looking through my notes. "You're, like, Google-stalking him, and you used a highlighter in *People* magazine. You're being so weird."

"I was just reading up about his show on Broadway," I said, shooing her off my chair. "I was wondering if it'll be any good." It was unfortunate that his publicist had been unable to control any of the recent press about him; there was gossip all over the Internet with pictures of him, drunk and unruly, during his recent, terrible night out. There was even a video clip of him sticking his hand down his pants, yelling, "Hey, assholes, want a pic of my cock?" just as his bodyguard was shoving him into a car.

"Can we see it?" Megan asked.

"See what?"

"His show? Please?"

The tickets for *Limelight* weren't nearly as expensive as *Hamilton*, but they were still a fortune. Multiplied by five, plus the handling fees and taxes, would come to over $1,500, a total splurge, and not something I felt like I could do while I was basically unemployed.

"We'll see," I said.

Megan hugged me. And yes, her changing form, which was perfectly normal, was noticeable. I got a pang of nostalgia for her elementary school years, for the days when she would climb into the car at the end of the day, holding a construction-paper collage and a new library book.

"School okay?" I asked.

"Meh. There're some mean girls."

Every school seemed to have them. "I was thinking," I said nonchalantly, "we should consider some other places for high school. It would make perfect sense to make a change after this year, and we've got plenty of time to see what's out there."

"I just got here," Megan said.

"I know, but we should consider all the possibilities. It'll be fun, actually."

"I don't think I want to start all over again. And I've made a couple friends."

"Want to invite someone over?"

"Maybe. Some girls were talking about going to a movie this weekend."

A bunch of young girls going to a movie together in New York City? I suddenly felt terrified for her. My mom had advised I find something to steady Megan, but I wasn't sure what that something should be.

Jack, sitting at the dining room table with a mouth full of cereal asked, "When's Dad coming home?"

"Tomorrow," I said.

"Can I walk Pancake today?"

"Not by yourself."

"Who's Pancake?" Megan asked.

"The dog that lives down the hall," I said. "He's a pug."

"I'll go with you," Megan said.

I smiled. "After you've both done your homework."

"He's gonna pay ten dollars," Jack told her.

"Seriously?" she asked. "Are you going to split it with me?"

"Sure," Jack said, and they shook on it.

While the kids were in their rooms studying, I started reading the Zadie Smith novel I'd bought, thinking how strange and sort of wonderful it felt not to be grading a thick stack of papers on *To Kill a Mockingbird* (or as one former student had called it, *How To Kill a Mockingbird*). I didn't miss that part of the job. I read for an hour and then got up to deal with dinner.

I checked my email and found that I had not, in fact, won the *Hamilton* lottery. Crisis averted.

———

"You're an old dog and all," Rick said the next time I walked into the writing center, "but I want to make sure you remember the new trick."

"*Dog?*" I asked. "Old?"

I hated him.

"Remember to stick to writing," he said. "You're here to go over the work the student has prepared for the meeting."

"I remember," I said.

"And Allison, come to work on time. Your security guy is waiting for you."

"I'm on time," I said, checking my phone. "He's early."

"Hey, it's just a gentle reminder. Don't get defensive."

"I'm not." I was. "But I'm just saying, I'm on time."

"Chop-chop," he said.

Howard was sitting with his thermos, hat, and poetry anthology beside him on the table. He stood up and shook my hand.

"So what are we working on today? Your essay?"

"Essay?" he said.

"Or outline. On the Wordsworth poem?"

"I turned that in already. But we got a new one I don't understand at all. I don't know why poetry always seems like secret code to me."

I looked over my shoulder to find out if Rick was listening and saw him, sitting at his desk in his office with the door open, watching me. "What's the poem?" I asked quietly.

"It's about some lady," he said, leafing through his anthology. "Something about her painting a wall."

"'My Last Duchess'?"

Rick sniffed, and I noted how well I could hear him.

"One thing I should clarify," I said. "I can't actually teach you the material. I mean, it turns out I'm not allowed to explain the poem itself to you."

"Why not?"

"I'm restricted to talking about writing."

"Doesn't a poem count as writing?" he asked.

"Of course. I mean *your* writing. I can only go over what you're writing about the poem."

"I haven't written anything yet."

"Right."

"I just need help with the poetry." He found the page with the Browning poem. "I'm a pretty good writer, actually."

"I'm sure you are. It's just that your professor needs to teach the content. I'm only allowed to help with your essays."

"Why?"

"I don't know. It's pretty stupid, if you ask me," I whispered. "Maybe you could get help from your professor first, and then come see me after."

"I can't," he said. "Her office hours are during the afternoon when I'm home sleeping."

"Ah, right. That's a problem."

"This is the one," he said, pointing to the poem.

It was one of my favorites, one I'd taught every year to high school students. I wondered if there was a way to discuss the poem while simultaneously writing an outline for a paper. Two birds.

Rick got up and walked out of his office, past the table where we were sitting, and out of the room. I seized the opportunity and talked fast, taking Howard line by line through the poem: the painting of the duchess, Fra Pandolph's hands, the look on her face, that spot of joy, her heart too soon made glad, the bough of cherries, white mule, you disgust me, I choose never to stoop, commands given, smiles stopped. Now about that dowry. Off we go, but check out Neptune taming a seahorse. Jealousy! Possessiveness! Murder! Howard was riveted. I took a breath, glanced over, and discovered that Rick was standing right next to me.

"So the husband had her *killed*?" Howard asked.

Rick looked pissed, and he asked Howard to excuse us for a moment, escorting me into his office and closing the door.

Five minutes later I came back out and sat down with Howard again. I held my hands clasped together in front of me on the table and said robotically, "If you write an opening paragraph, I can help you hone your thesis."

"What?"

"We'll make sure that you're setting up a good argument."

"Argument?"

"But like I said before: I can't talk about the poem."

Howard looked past me into Rick's office. "He's tough, huh?"

"Nightmare," I mouthed.

"Sorry if I got you in trouble."

"Not at all. Let's brainstorm on a thesis statement."

"I'd rather work on my essay at home," he said. "I like doing the writing part. I don't know why poetry always seems so hard. I look at the words and just freeze up. It helps to talk it through with you."

"We could meet tomorrow if you want."

"Next week is okay." He stood up, shook my hand, and put on his hat. "I'll see you then."

As soon as he left, Rick came over to tell me I wouldn't be meeting with Howard anymore.

"I didn't intentionally violate the rules," I told him, "but it's hard to understand why it's so forbidden to make sure he understands the material before he writes about it."

"Because I need you to stick to what you've been hired to do."

"I can, I will, but it's not like I was showing him porn. I just don't see the crime in discussing a poem with a student of poetry. And we seem to have a good rapport."

"You could teach it wrong."

"It was 'My Last Duchess.' Not *Finnegans Wake*." I may have been smirking.

"We've had professors get angry about this in the past; tutors have tried to teach material and have said things that are flat-out incorrect to their students. This rule isn't up for discussion. And I thought I'd already explained it pretty clearly."

"Okay, okay. We 'guide' writing." I know I sounded obnoxious. "I get it."

"Let's just call it a day for now, all right? Let this all sink in."

"It's a pretty big trip down here for one session," I said. "I mean, it's not just my time, you know. I'm paying over five dollars to get here and back on the subway and making about ten after taxes. Any chance I could work with two students next week? Or several would be even better."

"No, for real," he said and slid his hands in his pockets. "Let's take a break. I'll give a shout in a couple months if I want to give this another try."

"You're *firing* me?"

"It doesn't seem like a good match," he said. "You seem to see yourself as too experienced for this job."

"I thought that's why you hired me," I said. "I'm old, and I'm experienced."

"I didn't expect it to backfire like this."

I had lasted two sessions in my new job. Just like in "My Last Duchess," Rick gave commands and all smiles stopped. The door hit me in the butt on the way out.

Out on the street, my phone dinged. I had missed a text from an unknown number while I was getting canned:

Since u came by before, I was thinking u could bring some food over here, like one of those sandwiches. If ur busy, fine, nbd. I was just thinking eggs. Or literly anythg.

I answered immediately:

Sure thing. I'll come tomorrow 9am.

eight

HERE ARE THE FACTS I EVENTUALLY PIECED TOGETHER on the recent scandal involving Carter Reid:

Carter went on a twenty-four-hour, drug-infused party binge with his entourage (as reported by TMZ, *Us Weekly*, and Carter himself). The day I drove into the parked BMW, he was seriously wound up on coke and drunk on Jim Beam and had booked a well-known club in Harlem to have a big private party. His personal assistant, Lyle, had been busting Carter's balls all night, and on the way there, he made a crack about Carter's super-expensive designer T-shirt that had a picture of a woman and the words JESSIE'S GIRL.

"Shit, you're not even old enough to get that reference," Lyle said in the limo that had about ten people in it. Several of the girls laughed with him although they likely didn't get the reference either, since none was older than twenty.

"I get it," Carter said.

"So? What's it from?" Lyle asked.

Carter didn't know, so he punched Lyle in the face, opened the door of the slowly moving limo, and, as the driver slammed on the brakes, attempted to throw Lyle out. Lyle didn't press charges, but he walked away and never came back.

At the club that night, Carter accused one of his security detail of trying to pick up girls he wanted for himself, while also calling the guard a "fucking faggot," which was not only offensive, but also illogical. He then attempted to punch the guard, injuring his own hand in the process. The security guard wasn't injured, but he was pissed off and threw Carter into a wall, popping his shoulder out of joint. Instead of taking Carter to the hospital, the guard quit his job on the spot and left. The remaining partiers in the group decided to go back to Carter's apartment. Paparazzi intercepted them outside the club, got in Carter's face, and Carter lunged for a camera, missing and slamming his own face against the lens. A picture of that particular moment, of Carter's cheek pressing into the chest of the camera's owner, mouth agape, eyes half-mast, was especially unattractive. Then, captured on cell-phone video, was his attempt to offer up his penis for a portrait before his remaining bodyguard shoved him in the car.

Once they made it back to the apartment, Carter pissed in the lobby of his building. Security footage showed him stumbling and shouting while purposefully aiming the urine at his only remaining security guard, who punched him three times (face, stomach, and arm), and then quit his job. Carter, his face a bloody mess and his pants soaked with urine, threw up repeatedly in the elevator. Bernard the night doorman, who didn't have the luxury of quitting, much as he might have liked to, called the cleaning staff to deal with elevator disinfection duty. The party raged on with an assortment of random people coming and going all night. Two of Carter's so-called "friends" stole a case of Dom Pérignon, an Xbox, and his drugs, and took off.

At Carter's request, a tattoo artist from the renowned parlor Needles to Say made a house call.

Carter got the guy high, and they passed a bottle of tequila back and forth between them.

"My PA is such a fucking liar-ass dickface," Carter told him. "I want a tattoo that, you know, like . . . comemberates how much I hate his guts. 'Fuck you, Lyle,' right here," and he pointed to his arm.

"'Fuck you, Liar'?"

"Fuck you, Lyle," Carter slurred.

"Oh, I get it," the tattoo artist said, taking another shot of tequila and nodding enthusiastically. "Like fuck you and fuck your lies."

"Damn straight!" They high-fived.

Halfway through the tattoo, Carter wanted to take a break to meet the two maybe-of-age party crashers who were dancing topless on his coffee table. He later had sex with both of them in the shower, where he slipped and twisted his knee. (The girls later sold their story to TMZ for $20,000 and got an invite to the Playboy mansion.) Finally, in the morning, his cleaning woman, Loida, arrived and found him passed out naked on the bathroom floor, his leg swollen and his eye bruised. She called a doctor, a man whose house she cleaned, who came over and patched Carter up, strongly medicated him, and charged $30,000 for his trouble. Loida worked hard all day, cleaning up the filthy apartment. She washed Carter's pants, scrubbed the puke-covered rug, and threw out the pink thongs she found in the shower. He rewarded her loyal service by asking if she would call up that hot babe she had brought with her the day before to come over and hook up with him. The girl he referenced was Loida's fifteen-year-old niece, so Loida, of course, also quit.

And then I showed up.

It took me a while to piece this information together. All I knew the day he texted me was that there was a badly injured, wildly famous teenager who was completely unsupervised and alone. Notoriously spoiled, emotionally immature, ill-mannered, cocky, horny, and sexist. Irresistible. Out of Control. Hated. Worshipped. Everyone knew all that.

What I wanted to know was why wasn't anyone looking after him.

———

Michael finally came home, bearing boxes of Lindt chocolates for the kids and a gorgeous Hanro nightgown for me. After the kids went to bed, I slipped it on, and we stayed up late in spite of his jet lag. I could finally, for the first time, whisper the events that had happened while he was away. I told him about Megan's body book ending up in Jack's room and my mom's Thanksgiving plans. I told him about how I got fired. And, of course, most importantly, I told him everything about Carter Reid.

I told the story of Carter so well, a play-by-play with all the details, and Michael's stunned reaction made the long wait to talk about it worth it.

The next morning we were up early. I was busy getting ready for the day and had that same feeling I normally had when I was going to work: I had a purpose. Bringing food to Carter that day was a no-brainer; he was hungry, and I was a mother.

"Are you sure about this?" Michael asked. He was unpacking his suitcase.

"I'm dying to know *what* is going on over there," I told him. "Are the eggs still on the floor? Is some doctor killing him with pain meds? Where is everybody? I mean, who the hell looks after this kid? Why is he asking *me* for food?"

"Interesting questions, but I don't like it."

"Are you jealous?" I asked.

"Of an eighteen-year-old druggie who urinates in public and gets in bar fights? No."

"Jealous that I'm hanging out with a famous pop star. Jealous that I'm finally as cool as you are with your regular brushes with celebrity. Did I tell you he's in the show with your BFF Kevin Kline?"

"No way. Kevin didn't even mention it."

I made a mock sad face. "Sorry, babe."

"You're cooler than me, I grant you that. But I'm still worried. What if Carter's on heroin and does something to you?"

"Then we'll sue him for a billion dollars."

"What if he kills you?"

"All the more for you and the kids. You can buy a brownstone and live happily ever after."

It's not like Michael could stop me; we didn't have that kind of marriage. "I promise to leave if he acts weird or belligerent or nasty."

"Make sure your phone is charged in case there's an emergency. And you're not telling the kids about any of this?" Michael asked.

"That I'm going to the penthouse of a bratty teenage heartthrob to bring him food? No, I don't want to tell them."

"And remind me again, given what an asshole he was, why you're going over there?"

"Free Broadway tickets?" That obviously wasn't the reason.

I was going because I wanted to, I was curious, and I wondered if I might have something to offer.

———

I was so eager to get the day started that Jack and I left the house about ten minutes earlier than usual. As we walked up the sidewalk, a bus drove past us, and I saw, for the first time, a huge ad on the side with Kevin Kline's face right next to Carter's and the word *Limelight* arching over their heads. My stomach did a little flip.

At the school, Jack ran inside, waving to me over his shoulder, and I saw Beth and the other moms standing in their tight circle. I suddenly missed the suburban carpool routine. I had a feeling that this New York method, convening on foot in front of the school, standing in a crowd made up of cliquey subgroups, was never going to feel normal to me. I checked the time on my phone; I had forty-five minutes before I was supposed to be at Carter's, so in spite of my discomfort, I took a deep breath and walked right over to Beth and her posse.

"I'm Allison," I said to all of them at once. "I'm the one who drove into the parked car the other day."

"*Jack's* mom," Beth told them, eyebrows raised.

"Ohhh," the women said.

"We're new here," I said.

"Too bad about that fender bender," Beth said.

"Yeah, that was pretty dumb," I admitted.

"How's Jack doing?" one woman asked, as though he'd been diagnosed with something incurable.

"Pretty well," I said. "Bit of a rough start, but it's not easy being the new kid, not knowing anyone. He's starting to settle in."

"We've met already," Lauren said. "Jack and my son Ben are reading buddies."

"Yes, of course. Jack's mentioned him."

"I'm Lindsey's mom, Diana," the other one said. "Lindsey doesn't play with boys, so you wouldn't have heard about her."

"I have, actually," I answered. "You have a dog, right? A little schnauzer? Spiffy? Sparky? Jack's crazy about dogs."

"Skippy, yes! I had no idea our kids even talked to each other. Lindsey never tells me what she does all day."

Beth was looking irritated. The other moms, all except Lauren and Diana, were trying not to make eye contact with me.

"I guess you all heard that a few weeks ago Jack had an inappropriate conversation with Brittney." They looked at their feet. "I just want to say, he's a really sweet kid. I think he just lost his bearings temporarily in the move," I said. "I've been a fish out of water myself these days." No one smiled; tough crowd. "Anyhoo."

"You're settling in?" Lauren asked. "A little?"

"Absolutely."

"Do you live nearby?" Beth asked, not like she actually cared, but more like she wanted to know if a sexual predator was living in her area.

"We're five blocks north."

"So are we!" Diana said. "Maybe you and Jack want to come by after school?"

"Sure! Yes." I pictured drinking coffee and gossiping while the kids played with the dog. "You mean today?"

"Oh, no, we can't today. But sometime."

"Great! When's good for you?"

"Mondays I can't because I have a nanny in the afternoon, and Tuesdays are no good because of dance class. Wednesdays are sometimes okay but not for the next two or three weeks because we're having a slew of visitors. And Thursdays are iffy."

"Friday?" I suggested.

"We go to our place in the Hamptons on the weekends. But we'll figure it out at some point."

I could see that New Yorkers were more capable of an empty "y'all come" than Texans.

"Ben would love to have Jack over sometime," Lauren said.

"Thanks," I said. "That would be great."

The group started to break up and the ladies headed off in pairs or triplets in different directions.

I gave Lauren my email address and then went to the grocery store.

Half an hour later I arrived at Fifteen Central Park West. I walked through the door, saying a bright and cheerful "Good morning!" to the security guard in passing. Setting my grocery bags on the floor, I un-wound my scarf and said hello to Jeffrey, the doorman.

"You're back?" he asked.

"Apparently I'm here to cook some food for the kid," I said.

"Are you out of your freaking mind?"

"Quite possibly."

He let me in the elevator, and I rode up to the penthouse, humming Carter's "Roller Coaster Love" on the way.

⎯⎯⎯

The apartment smelled bad. Carter had left the broken plate and bits of eggs on the floor, and the trash hadn't been taken out for days.

"Have you never heard of a sponge?" I said. "This is disgusting."

"I don't clean."

"You don't *clean*? Even when you've got a health hazard on your kitchen floor? You could end up with a roach infestation." I was on my hands and knees, scooping up parts of the plate and wiping down the floor, while Carter sat on a barstool, scarfing down food like he hadn't eaten in days, which apparently he hadn't. He was shoveling it in at a pace that was impolite and, frankly, gross. I had cooked pancakes, fried eggs, and bacon, and I'd bought a big container of cut fruit. I was also planning to make macaroni and cheese, enough to last for a few days. And because I associated feeling under the weather with milkshakes, I'd bought a big tub of chocolate ice cream. I'd clearly gotten carried away in the grocery store, but I was motivated; I could cook in a big kitchen like this, just the way I used to for my own kids: lasagna, chili, beef stew, penne pesto, spaghetti and meatballs.

"But I guess you're not really in the best shape to be crawling around on the floor. How's your knee feeling? Any better?"

He was slamming down a glass of orange juice and didn't answer me.

I finished sponging down the floor. "There, you see? Easy as pie."

"Can you not?" he said, putting the glass down.

"Not what?"

"Talk."

I stood up. "Sure, but first let me say that I think you're going to need a new cleaning person." I rinsed the sponge in his deep stainless steel sink. "It doesn't look like that last one is coming back any time soon. I could maybe help you hire one."

"Find a babe," he said. "That last one was an old bitch."

"Seriously?"

He was chewing with his mouth open. "Nah, don't bother," he said. "I'm taking off anyway. I'm over New York. I fucking hate it here."

"Really? You're the first person I've met who doesn't swear they love it."

"New York is shit."

I unpacked the remaining groceries, leaving the ingredients for a cheese sauce out on the counter. "Do you happen to have a food processor?"

"What?"

"One of those things that chops—"

"How the fuck would I know?" he said.

I started opening cabinets. "So where are you going anyway?"

"L.A."

"When?"

"Don't know. When I'm better."

"Sorry to pry, but aren't you starting rehearsals pretty soon? I read that your show's opening in March."

He stood up, and I thought for a second that he might smash another plate.

"You done with that?" I asked. I took it from him, gently placing it in the sink.

He started to limp through the kitchen, and I figured there was no time like the present to offer sound advice if I could.

"Listen," I said, handing him his pill and trying unsuccessfully to get him to look me in the eye, "you're down to your last few days of OxyContin. You might want to think about weaning yourself off the stuff. Downgrading to something safe like Tylenol. I can bring you some if you don't have any. Are you feeling okay?"

He adjusted his crutch. "I'm fine."

"You shouldn't take those prescription pills any longer than you have to."

"Jesus, I'm sorry I sent you that stupid fucking text. I must have been delirious from starvation."

"Why didn't you order some food in?"

"I don't know."

"Should we talk about the car?" I asked.

"What car?"

I figured he was loopy from the meds. "Later," I said. "Go take a rest. If it's okay, I was thinking I could stay to make lunch."

He didn't answer.

"Or should I leave?"

"Whatever," he said.

He reminded me of Charlotte, how grumpy she would get after a bad running competition, when she felt wiped out and defeated.

Carter went to bed, and I wandered around his apartment, looking at the art and guessing how much work and money was needed to maintain this place. In the living room, which the cleaning woman had left in perfect order, I stopped to look at Carter's coffee-table books. They were so incongruent: a world atlas, a book of Tiffany lamps, a catalogue of Audubon etchings, and a survey of the world's most scenic golf courses, all clearly bought by a decorator. And then there was also a bong on top of a book of photographs of naked women posing on cars. These I figured were Carter's contributions to the decor. The apartment was weird. Full of expensive things, some tasteful and some tacky. One item would offend, like the gold twelve-inch-tall grinning circus elephant with a jeweled headdress, holding its trunk aloft, and the next would impress, like the blue Venus in the entry; she was a commentary of some kind, I supposed. Made recently but without her arms, without a head, even. She stood there, looking regal and calm. Dignified in spite of her predicament. She was a modern woman, a fresh take on ancient Rome, or ancient Greece, maybe, a gaudy blue depiction of a classic. She was kind of bold and fabulous. I read the little plaque attached to her pedestal: Jim Dine. *Good God! A real Jim Dine! Or is it a copy? What in the world does a Jim Dine cost anyway?*

On the left side of the apartment, I opened a door to a wood-paneled study that didn't look like a room Carter would use; the desk was cluttered with bills and papers, and, under a box of cigars that I carefully moved to the side, I spotted a bound copy of *Limelight*. I quickly put the cigar box back and continued scoping out the condo.

I counted three more bedroom suites, each with its own spacious marble bathroom.

And Sara thought my *apartment was big?* I wondered what she would say if she saw this sprawl.

Back near the entry, there was a staircase leading up to a lovely loft space, white slip-covered couches, an oversize ottoman, views looking all the way downtown. It was a tasteful and light refuge, high-ceilinged, perfect for escaping, for reading in the afternoon with a glass of Chardonnay. I thought back to our conversations with the real estate broker; this place was probably worth over $40 million.

I went back downstairs to the office and took the copy of *Limelight* from under the cigar box. I opened the script at random, somewhere near the beginning:

Calvero	There are cures for that, you know? Let's get you to a doctor.
Thereza	No, no, it's not what you think.
Calvero	I'm an old sinner, so I wouldn't judge.
Thereza	It's true I've been sick. And I can't work anymore.
Calvero	What do you do, Thereza?
Thereza	People call me Terry. I'm a singer.
Calvero	A singer? Really?
Thereza	Why?
Calvero	Because, Terry, I'm a performer, too. Maybe you've heard of me?
Thereza	Who are you?
Calvero	Calvero.
Thereza	[*Laughing*] No, are you—? You're not The Great Calvero?
Calvero	[*Tips his hat.*]
Thereza	Are you really?

I flipped through the pages, seeing the music scores throughout along with the lyrics to songs such as "Washed Up and Weary," "Fickle Fans," and "You Feel It, Too." Then I went back to the title page: "Based on *Limelight.*" Underneath, in fine print, it said: "A thoroughly modern, pop-music reimagining of the 1952 classic Charles Chaplin film."

No kidding, I thought. I had never seen the movie but remembered that my parents had always liked the music. And I was intrigued by the idea of a classic remake. I made myself comfortable on the leather couch and started reading. At the end of act 1, I took the script with me to the kitchen, cleaned up breakfast, and started cooking the elbow noodles and making cheese sauce. I placed cut-up broccoli on a shallow pan in the oven, and then sat on a barstool and kept reading while everything was in the oven.

By the time I called Carter to lunch, I had finished the play and read the lyrics to all the songs. Catchy rhymes. And funny lines throughout the script. I assumed this modern version was sexier and dirtier compared to the original, but it was still very much a period piece. The opening scene called for lighting and costumes that would make the whole stage appear as though it were in black-and-white. And yet the crux of the show applied to the present: show business and the downsides of celebrity, the allure of the stage, and the pressure on stars to always keep their fans delighted. It was at turns very philosophical, even touching on the need to have a reason to live.

Carter scowled when he limped in and saw the script in my hands.

"You can toss that," he said.

"Don't be silly."

He abruptly took the script from my hands and threw it in the garbage. I was half surprised that he knew where the trash can was.

"Hang on a sec—" I said.

"It's not happening."

"The show? In that case I won't have to shell out the money for tickets," I said. "Wait, the show's not happening or you're not doing it?"

"I'm not doing it."

I took the script out of the garbage and wiped off the pancake syrup. "Do you mind if I keep this?" I asked. "Is it classified or something? I won't leak it."

"Take it. Burn it. Use it to wipe your ass. I seriously don't give a shit. I told you, I'm going to L.A."

"When?"

"Soon."

I was confused, thinking of the bus that had driven by me that morning with Carter's face plastered on the side. "What happened with the show?"

"Nothing. The show can blow me."

"Well, as a matter of fact, there are a couple amusing oral sex jokes in here, as I'm sure you already know."

He shrugged. "Is there any beer?"

"No. How old are you? It's the middle of the day."

He opened the fridge and, after looking around, drank out of the milk carton. I went to get him a glass.

"So you're not doing the show," I said, "and instead you're going to L.A. Do you need a housekeeper, then, just to keep the place clean when you're not here? Is that a real Jim Dine sculpture in your entry?"

"Lyle handles everything for this place."

"And where's Lyle?" I filled a glass with milk and handed it to him.

"How the fuck would I know where Lyle is? What am I, a fucking detective? Lyle's not working for me anymore, so he can blow me."

"Him, too?"

"That car you hit," he asked, "was it a BMW?"

"Yeah."

"That's awesome." He smiled for the first time since we'd met, a gorgeous smile in spite of his cracked lip and bruised face. "I hope you fucking trashed it. Lyle is such a little bitch about his car."

"I hit *Lyle's* car?" I asked.

"I don't drive in New York," he said. "Why would I have a car?"

"Can you give me his number?"

"Fuck no," he said and slammed the milk glass on the granite counter. "Forget about it. You won't hear from him, and neither will I, which means I don't know how to get to L.A."

"Do you have a plane ticket? Or, wait, do you have a *plane*?"

"Lyle gets me a plane from somewhere." He sat on a barstool, letting his crutch clatter to the floor.

"Like a private, charter plane, probably. You want me to look into it?" I picked up the crutch and leaned it against the counter. "But wait, I don't get why you're not doing the show."

He didn't answer. I opened the script to the cast list in the front and saw his name printed, directly under Kevin's.

"It would be pretty cool, right? And you might not care, but the money's probably not bad. And it's, you know, *Broadway*." I did jazz hands to make my point; Carter looked at me as if I'd belched. "What?"

"Don't ask me about the fucking show again," he said. "It's shit."

"I don't know that I'd say 'shit,' but, hey, if it's not your taste, I get it. To each his own." I got a plate and began to scoop up the macaroni and cheese for him. He was looking at his phone and didn't look up.

"So why did you take the role, then? I mean originally?"

Nothing.

"They know you're not doing it, though, right? I mean, you broke up with them or you canceled or whatever it was you were supposed to do?"

Silence. He was good. Better than Charlotte, maybe.

"Well, of *course* they know," I said, answering my own question. "What am I even saying? Of course you did what you had to to avoid burning bridges." I broke up a slice of crispy bacon over the mac and cheese. "You don't think it would be pretty cool, though? To be a Broadway star?" I said. "Broadway is one of New York's most spectacular institutions. Everybody loves Broadway." *Except Sara*, I thought, but she was most certainly an outlier. "Don't you just love a good musical?"

He looked up from his phone with his eyes closed and then said, "Can you stop? 'Cause the sound of your voice is fucking killing me."

I mimed zipping my lips shut. But then I unzipped them and added, with a little wag of my finger, "Maybe you're getting mad because you know I'm onto something?"

"Maybe I'm getting mad because you won't stop talking."

"Fine. I get it."

"Good."

"But one last thing—"

He sighed.

"I suppose I could come back tomorrow if you want. Pick up some Tylenol for you, cook some more food. Figure out flights to California. I don't want to presume, but it seems like you could really use some help around here."

He didn't say anything.

"In any case, I'll leave the leftovers on the stove for later."

His face was one inch from the screen.

"Well," I said, putting his lunch in front of him, "bon appetit." It didn't get him to talk, but it got him to put his phone down.

After cleaning the kitchen, I put on my coat, wrapped my scarf around my neck, and walked up Broadway to the school to get Jack.

On the way I passed a bus stop that had another advertisement for *Limelight*, similar to the one I'd seen on the side of the bus. There was Kevin's handsome face, and on the bottom half of the poster, next to photos of Annabella Hatter and Carter, were the words MAKING THEIR BROADWAY DEBUT! I stood in front of the poster and touched the spot on Carter's eye that was bruised. He looked great next to Annabella, and I could definitely picture her as the sensitive, lovestruck singer. But Carter? It was hard to imagine him playing the polite, restrained, clean-cut Neville from the script, a young up-and-coming singer-songwriter who falls in love with Terry but never quite wins her heart. Or does he? The ending of the play was somewhat inconclusive on that, but one would hope so, probably. Carter as a spurned, earnest, lovestruck suitor? He certainly hadn't been typecast.

Moreover, it struck me as odd, worrying, even, as I walked down the street with the script under my arm, that these expensive advertisements had come out all over town in spite of Carter's decision not to take the role. Who was replacing him? Was there a stand-in taking the role? Another big-name pop singer? I got my phone out and Googled the show; on the *Limelight* website, tickets were available and Carter's name appeared, alongside Kevin's and Annabella's. And a new actor I hadn't seen before on the cast list: Melissa McCarthy playing the comedic role of the landlady; I almost dropped my phone on the sidewalk. I bookmarked the tab and kept walking.

Lauren and the clique of third-grade moms were in front of the school, huddled together in their trench coats and Burberry boots, waiting for the kids to come out. I took a spot in their circle.

"Hi again," I said. "Allison," I added, as a reminder.

"How's your day going?" Lauren asked.

I was tempted, of course I was tempted, to blab all the details, but instead, I changed the subject entirely. "So I was just wondering, do any of you have the name of a really outstanding housekeeper? A quiet, discreet, experienced person?" I thought about Carter's request for someone hot, and then added, "Preferably a man?" They all started talking at once:

"A *man*?" Beth asked.

"Sidney's dad has a valet," Diana said.

"Does a valet clean," said Lauren, "or just take care of someone? Like, what's the difference between a valet and a butler?"

Beth scoffed. "Haven't you watched *Downton?*"

"What about that company that screens nannies and housekeepers?" Lauren said. "I think they find all kinds of people."

"Grapevine," Beth said.

"No," said Lauren, "the other one."

"Sutton Personal Services?" Diana asked.

"That's the one." Lauren touched my arm. "We found our driver through them. I would go through an agency. They'll do the legwork for you. You get a criminal background check, fingerprints, mailing address," Lauren said. "It's a great service."

Beth leaned in closer. "Did you hear that Nancy's cleaning lady robbed them blind, and when the police came, she realized she didn't even know the woman's last name?"

I had clearly come to the best possible source. "Thanks, you guys are amazing. Sutton Personal Services," I said, typing the name into my phone. And then looked up again. "What about chartering private planes?" I said. "Just hypothetically." They must have thought I was one of them.

"NetJets," Diana said. "We flew them to Santa Fe last spring. It was fabulous."

"We've flown Jet Suite before," Lauren said.

"What about Luxury Wings?" Beth asked.

"I hear it's going under," Lauren said. "NetJets is really good."

The kids started to file out of the building. "Can you arrange flights last minute or do you have to book way ahead?" I asked.

"You can do whatever you like, but be prepared for some serious sticker shock," Beth said.

"Oh, that's not a problem," I said.

Well, it wasn't *my* problem. In fact, this sounded like fun. I would spend the afternoon making inquiries about planes and butlers. Maybe I would get a glimpse of what life was really like for rich and famous celebrities. Or at least I could learn a little more about Carter's life, which as far as I could see was completely lacking responsible adult guidance.

THE ABSENCE OF ESSAY GRADING as a major part of my life was something I was appreciating more and more with each passing day into the semester. Sure I missed the daily lessons and, even more, the relationships that would start to feel rewarding right about now if I were actually in a classroom. But as it turned out, I had no desire to get out my purple pens to tackle a stack of sixty four-page *Lord of the Flies* essays. I knew I should be looking into getting a new teaching job, certainly for the following academic year, but my evenings were my own again, my family's, and for the time being, I was enjoying every moment.

Here was something completely impossible in my life before this particular fall: Me sitting on the couch with Michael on a weeknight, deciding which TV series to start watching together. I'd already helped Jack with a book report, I'd called Lilly to try to organize a night out for drinks with Sara, I'd cleaned up after dinner, and it was only eight o'clock. It was like summer every single night.

Jack and Megan were reading in their rooms, and Charlotte was sitting on the bathroom floor, talking to Theo on the phone.

"Latest season of *House of Cards* or start a show, like *Orange Is the New Black*?"

"What about *Veep*?"

He looked away from the television to see what I was doing on my laptop: an intense Google search of private planes, learning the difference between buying a fractional jet ownership and simply booking a flight. "I swear I'll put this away the second you hit 'play,' " I said.

"The kid doesn't deserve you. And I hate to sound judgmental, but why is he slouching around his apartment doing nothing? He can certainly plan a trip home at his age, can't he?"

"Well first of all, he's slouching around because he got beat up. He hasn't even gone to a proper doctor. I mean, should he? Does a guy like this even *have* health insurance? Or does he just pay?"

"And second of all?"

I wrote a reminder to myself: *doctor appt for Carter?* "And second of all . . . I forgot what second of all was."

"Something about slouching around, doing nothing?" Michael said.

"He may be slouching right now, but he's not on tour or recording or whatever it is he normally does, which is probably a lot of work. But do you know what else? I don't think he knows *how* to do anything. Aside from Snapchatting and playing games on his phone, I don't think he knows how things work. Has he ever purchased toilet paper or paid his electric bill?"

"Should we get Snapchat?"

"We're too old."

I'd been pondering Carter's lack of life skills; he'd asked me what he should do about a burned-out light in his bathroom.

"I'll just buy a new bulb for you," I told him.

"Oh," he said, visibly relieved. "You can do that?"

Michael pointed to the television. "What about *The Crown*?" he said.

"Thematically perfect," I said. "Carter's like the American version of royalty. If you've never had to do anything . . . If everything has always been taken care of for you . . ."

"There are certain basic tasks in life that we should all be able to do, no matter who we are. Like cook pasta, write a check, change a flat tire."

"I can't change a flat tire."

"Neither can I," Michael admitted, "but I acknowledge that as a personal failure."

"I don't think he knows how to do anything practical. I wish I could teach him a few life skills. He's so dependent on people, and they're untrustworthy and sleazy, and he probably has no idea how his money is budgeted."

"We should make sure that Charlotte knows how to do those things before she graduates. I wouldn't get your hopes up too much about teaching Carter anything. He doesn't sound like a very willing student. He may take off to L.A. without even telling you."

"Please. He wouldn't have the first clue how to get there."

There was a crashing noise coming from the girls' bathroom, followed by cussing, stomping, and a slam of the bedroom door.

Michael and I ran.

"What happened?" I asked.

Jack was standing in the hallway while Megan went into the bathroom and came out with Charlotte's phone and handed it to me; the screen was cracked.

I knocked on the bedroom door. "Charlotte?"

I could hear crying.

"Honey? What happened?"

"Leave me alone," she said between sobs.

Michael took Megan and Jack to the living room, and I heard him say cheerfully, "Who wants ice cream?"

I knocked again. "Open the door, okay?"

I pressed my ear to the door. "Charlotte? Charlotte, please? Are you okay?"

"No," she said. She blew her nose.

"Can you tell me what happened?"

"Can I have a few fucking minutes to myself, *please*?" she yelled.

"Don't say—" *Not the battle to pick.* "I need to know that you're okay."

I heard the lock click, and she opened the door. Her nose was red and her face splotchy. "Theo dumped me, okay? He dumped me."

I was shocked. Based on how often they spoke on the phone, I had assumed things were fine. I couldn't believe my mom had seen this coming, had given me a heads-up, and yet I was completely taken by surprise and didn't have any advice on breakups prepared.

"Oh no, I'm so sorry." I went to hug her, but she stepped back.

"Can you tell Megan to leave me alone tonight?"

"What happened exactly?" I saw her days-to-Dallas calendar ripped to pieces on the floor behind her. "I mean, what did he say?"

Charlotte started crying again. "Yeah, because that's what I want to do right now. I want to talk through the shitty details with my *mother*." She slammed the door.

Megan and Jack were staring wide-eyed at me when I came back in the living room.

"It's all okay," I said. "Charlotte's very sad right now, but she'll be fine."

"What happened?" Jack asked.

"She and Theo are calling it a day," I said.

"What's that mean?"

"Means they broke up," Megan said.

"Oh," Jack said.

"I'll say good night to her," Michael said, walking to her room and rapping gently on the door.

I took Jack back to his room to read to him. That night, Megan, in an attempt to give Charlotte the space she'd requested, slept on the couch.

———

In the morning, Charlotte didn't talk to any of us, but it wasn't like before. She wasn't angry and sulking; she was heartbroken. Eyes swollen, she drank a sip of coffee, put her laptop in her bag, and went to the door. I followed her and Megan to the elevator, and we waited together.

"I know how hard this is," I said, rubbing her back, "but I promise you one thing: it gets better."

With her head still down and a tissue balled up in her hand, she glanced up at me. "Don't appropriate slogans," she said. "You're better than that." The elevator came and she got on without giving me a chance to give her a hug. I leaned in to give Megan a kiss on the cheek and got smacked by the elevator as the doors closed; I looked over and saw that Charlotte was pressing the button.

I quickly cooked Jack some eggs and went to get dressed while he ate.

"Charlotte's in bad shape," I said to Michael. He was brushing his teeth with his tie over his shoulder. "I think she blames us."

"This is our fault?"

"We made her leave Dallas," I said. "It's fine; she'll recover. But she's going to treat me like shit for the foreseeable future."

———

The moms were warming up to me, and I started to lose that nervous twinge I always felt when I rounded the corner and saw them standing together on the sidewalk. Every time I arrived at school that week, they would greet me, engage me, even.

"How'd the reservation for the jet work out? Simple to book, right? And so posh, you'll just love it."

"Oh, and you asked about hairdressers? You should call Antonio at Zinnia's; he does Jake Gyllenhaal's hair. I'll text you his number."

"Most respectable physical therapists will make house calls. I'll ask my trainer for a name. And I'll email you about that concierge physician service."

I was, slowly but surely, beginning to feel connected to the group. My email inbox was filling up with helpful tips and flat-out kindness:

Hey Allison, don't know if you still need this—I'm passing along the name of a chef who comes highly recommended: Fabio. He is terrific. And by the way, he's offering a kids' class called "From Pastry to Pies." My daughter Sabrina is going to take it. Did you say your daughter is in 8th grade, too? Would she be interested in a baking class? Let me know!

Also are you going through the public high school process? It's killing me.

- Lauren

Oh and yes, Ben would love to go to the Nat. Hist. Museum with you and Jack. Does Thursday work?

Hi Lauren!

Awesome and thanks. Yes to the baking class (Megan is thrilled) and to Thursday! I'll do pickup and will bring Ben to your place after the museum. (Does he have allergies or anything? - let me know.)

-A

I had told the moms I was a private tutor for high school and college students. It was the closest thing to the truth I could think of without telling them how I actually spent my days. One of them had asked for my card, asking if I did coaching for college essays.

"It's just so hard to work with your *own* kid on something like that, you know?"

Oh, yeah, I knew. Charlotte was barely speaking to me at all, and she would shut me down every time I mentioned her applications. I was trying to be patient, to give her the space she was asking for, but it wasn't easy.

———

Carter was feeling somewhat better, looking better, and, as a result, he was growing restless. It was early October, and he was bored and, I suspected, lonely. He didn't read books, he never wanted to leave the apartment, and I wasn't sure how to recommend he fill his days while he recuperated. He had a few ideas of his own, and I wasn't going to let them happen. I'm a grown-up, a mother, and I have no problem whatsoever saying no to a child. You just say no.

"No."

"Come *on*," Carter said.

"No."

"What's the big deal? It's medicinal anyway."

"No."

"Just enough for a couple hits? It's basically legal now."

"No."

I was making a chicken-breast marinade in a big plastic baggie, and

Carter was sitting on a barstool in shorts, giving me a hard time for refusing to buy him pot.

"Lyle kept me happy."

"I'm not Lyle."

"It's not like I can't get it on my own."

"Well, you shouldn't. It's bad for you."

"I'll get it anyway."

"Not with my assistance."

"You're such a bitch, you know that? Do you have kids?"

"Yes, as a matter of fact I have—"

"I feel sorry for them. Their lives must suck."

"That may be, but I'm still not going to help you damage your nice brain."

"Fine. Jesus. Then bring me a bottle of Patrón."

I got the chicken out of the fridge and closed the door. "You're underage."

He slammed his hand on the counter. "Are you *shitting* me right now?"

"No. I am absolutely in zero ways shitting you."

"It's like I'm in prison."

"Well, you've been cooped up here too long. How about we go out for a bit, take a walk, maybe."

"Now I know you're shitting me."

"What?"

"Take a *walk*?"

"It might be good for your knee to put some weight on it. And you need oxygen."

"Holy shit."

I sighed. "What now?"

"You seriously don't get it, do you? I'm famous as fuck. I can't take a *walk*. I wouldn't make it half a block without getting attacked."

"Oh. Right," I said. "Sorry, I forgot. Is there a roof deck or something? It's not healthy to be stuck inside all the time."

"That's why I need weed."

I offered the only distraction I could think of: "Would you like to have dinner at my apartment tonight? My kids might get worked up, but I think they can handle it."

"Sounds lame," he said.

"My children are not lame."

"How old are they?"

"Charlotte's seventeen, and she's going through—"

"So she could buy me pot," he said.

I scoffed. "Oh please," I said, "she wouldn't have the first idea how to get it."

"Yeah, sure." He laughed. "If you say so."

"She wouldn't."

"Right."

I dropped the pieces of chicken in the baggie, sealed, and shook it around. "You like potatoes?"

"Sure." He sighed and rubbed his hand along his injured shoulder.

I felt sorry for him, even if he was a "poor little rich boy." He was trapped in a city he hated. And as if he were reading my mind, he said, "I feel pretty much good enough to go back to L.A. now. Did you book me a flight?"

I handed him a cookie in hopes of softening him up. "I wanted to ask you something about the show," I said. "I keep seeing these ads everywhere and—"

"Don't talk about the fucking play." The cookie crumbled all over the counter and with a flick of his hand, he swept the crumbs onto the floor.

"No, it's not about the play, exactly. It's just that your picture is on the ads still." I got my phone out. "And when you go on the website, see? There you are."

"So?"

"So, I was wondering," I said, trying to sound casual, "do they know? I mean, who's replacing you."

"What do I care?"

"Have they told you?"

"It's not my problem, so just drop it. And I need worms."

"Oh god," I said with a loud sigh, "*worms?* What is that? Some new drug?"

Carter smiled. Or smirked, maybe. "No, like real worms."

"Like floating in the bottom of a tequila bottle?"

He got up and left the room, coming back with a small, clear plastic container that he set gently on the kitchen island.

"I need worms. Or some kind of food."

I leaned over and looked into the tank. There was a greenish-brown turtle, no bigger than my pinky, floating on the surface. "When'd you get that?"

"A few weeks ago, just before . . ." He pointed to his black eye.

"Well, it's cute," I said. I stepped around and looked at the tiny critter from a different angle; the tank was filled with murky water, and the turtle was doing a perfect dead man's float.

"Is it okay? I mean, is it . . . alive?"

"Sure. Hey there," Carter said, tapping his finger on the plastic. It didn't budge. "I think turtles sleep during the day."

"Does the tank need to be cleaned?" I asked. "It's a little filmy. Doesn't smell so great, either."

Carter shrugged.

"How big will he get?"

"It's a her."

I wondered how he knew that.

"They were selling a bunch of them in Chinatown, and I picked her out."

"Nice." I was not a fan of reptiles, amphibians, or fish as pets. I just don't understand the point of keeping an animal that doesn't show any affection. This particular creature was just floating there and appeared to be lifeless. "Does she have a name?"

"Skittle."

"Like the candy?"

"Yeah, and like when I got her, she was skittling around, you know." Carter was watching her bob in the water. "Hey, Skittle, hey, girl, you asleep?" I was in equal measure shocked by his attentiveness to something other than himself and worried that Skittle was, in fact, dead. Just then, she craned her head around and looked up with what seemed a doleful expression and paddled her little feet.

"She's adorable."

"Yeah, but she needs food. I ran out."

I was about to bring up the topic of reimbursement for groceries when the buzzer by the elevator rang abrasively. I went to answer it, and Jeffrey's voice came through the intercom, saying what sounded like, "Mr. Bric-a-Brac here to see you."

"Thanks," I said. "Send him up."

"Who?" Carter asked.

"A housekeeper you're interviewing. His name's Owen something. You ready to meet him?"

"He's a guy?"

"Yeah. So? He comes highly recommended."

"A *guy?*"

"Just talk to him, okay? I don't know what you want done around here. And what happens after you leave for L.A.?"

"I really don't care." He picked up the little tank to take it back to his room. "Let's go, little Skittle," he said. He was using a voice I'd never heard, higher and more playful. And then it dropped to the usual, dismissive tone: "And I need a new Xbox. Today."

"You want *me* to—"

"I'm bored shitless. Can't you just call one of those stores and order it? I don't care what it costs."

"You've been having an awful lot of screen time," I said. "Maybe you could read something? Or try writing some music?" *Too far?*

"I can't write songs without drugs."

"Oh, come on now. With your talent and your bright, young mind—"

"Fuck this *noise*," he yelled from the hallway to his room. "I need you to stop with the lectures, seriously. Don't talk to me for the rest of the day."

It might have been funny if he had been kidding.

CARTER'S LIP HAD SCABBED OVER and the bruising on his face had faded. His shoulder and knee still seemed to be causing him pain, and I started researching orthopedists, in the event that I could convince Carter to see one. The only thing he really wanted was to get well enough to go back to L.A. and never come back, and he kept asking me about flights.

I was stalling.

Every time I saw posters for *Limelight* on the subway, or ads in the *New York Times*, or even the flyer in my mailbox, I got a little jolt of anxiety. It made no sense that tickets were being sold on sites that loudly announced his name as a star in the cast. It seemed like false advertising, and I even wondered if there was someone at the theater I could ask since Carter refused to talk about it.

I often thought about how quiet that huge apartment must be at night and wondered how he spent his time, alone with nothing but a lethargic baby turtle for company. I worried about him. Part of me wanted to get him on a plane to L.A. as quickly as possible, assuming that he must have had a better life there with work, friends, and sunshine. But every time I thought about *Limelight*, about the play with his name stamped on it, I was certain that Carter hadn't dealt with it correctly, hadn't officially withdrawn or canceled or whatever it was he was supposed to do.

———

I took Skittle to an exotic pet hospital because she was clearly not well, and even Carter had remarked on her listlessness with concern.

"Be careful with her," Carter had said as he handed me the small plastic container.

I got an earful from the vet on how to set up a proper habitat, what she needed to eat, and why she was an illegal pet to begin with. "These red-eared sliders have to be at least four inches or stores aren't allowed to sell them."

"I found her," I said, worried that I was going to get in some kind of trouble, "in Central Park. Under a bench."

"Riiiight," the doctor said unconvincingly. "They carry salmonella, you know, so be sure to tell anyone handling him to wash their hands with warm water and soap."

"It's a boy?"

"And I assume you know you'll have him for the next fifty years or so."

"Seriously?" I did the math. "I'll be dead by then."

"And please don't get the idea you can just put him back where you 'found' him in some park or pond or something."

"No, of course not. We're quite attached to each other, actually."

Skittle turned away and tried to walk off the edge of the stainless steel table.

The room was sterile and predictable, except for a large, garish portrait covering one entire wall of an iguana eating a cantaloupe.

"Although," I added, "she may be moving to California. Can she do that?" I asked suddenly. "Fly, I mean. On a private plane?"

"Is he going into showbiz?"

"Something like that, yes."

"If you clean out this little tank for travel, and treat the water like I said, he'll be fine. But get him set up properly as soon as you get there and find a herpetologist. The antibiotics will help, but he won't make it much longer if he isn't in a better habitat. You've got to keep the tank clean and the water fresh."

"But you think she's going to be okay? Can she handle a big trip?"

"It could go either way. Try to get him healthy before you go."

"At least she's going to travel in style."

"I know a man who chartered a plane for his hedgehog," the vet said. "Some of these pets live fancier lives than I do."

With a long sheet of instructions that he'd printed out for me, I went to Petco, determined to nurse Skittle back to better health. I bought a special UVB heat-and-lighting kit, a larger aquarium, a water filter, an attractive island structure, nutrition pellets, gravel, and a bag of live crickets. I put the receipt in an envelope I'd labeled "C owes me"; I was racking up serious rewards points on my credit card.

Carter talked to Skittle more than he talked to me, and I wanted her to stay alive. That afternoon, I fed her a mealworm by hand.

As empty and dull as Carter's life in New York was, my life was getting busier and more complicated. Jack often brought the neighbor's pug over in the afternoons to keep him company while the man was at work, and Jasper and Pancake would chase each other around the living room, knocking over framed photographs and scattering papers. Megan was working on a big history project in which each student in the class was assigned a decade to research. Megan got the 1950s, and she had poster boards and library books all over the dining room table. Charlotte was prepping for the math and physics SAT subject tests, while still taking breaks to cry about Theo, and I was going back and forth between looking for schools to work at in the following year, in spite of my ambivalence, and bookmarking ones that I thought might be a good fit for Megan to attend.

And life was only going to get crazier moving forward: Jack was starting piano lessons at Lucy Moses, Megan was signed up for baking class with Sabrina (thanks to Lauren), college deadlines were looming, and Michael had splurged, buying us a subscription to the Public Theater, the very place where *Hamilton* had gotten its start.

On one particularly stormy, bleak day, I was home with Jack after school when he looked in my tote bag for a pen and found a plastic container of frozen turtle food.

"Eww!" Jack said. "What's 'Herp diet'?"

I still hadn't told my kids anything about Carter, so I certainly hadn't mentioned the new turtle in my life. I stood there, looking at the drippy package of worms and brine shrimp and said, "It's a wrinkle treatment. For my skin."

He sniffed the package and instantly jerked his head away. "Yuck. You're rubbing this on your face?"

I took it from him and put it in the freezer. "Unless you'd rather have it for dinner."

A few minutes later Charlotte and Megan came home from school together. Cross-country practice had been canceled.

Charlotte walked in, kicked off her wet shoes, and said, "This city is even more disgusting in the rain. Oh, and I'm failing history." She went to her room and slammed her door.

Megan opened her backpack. "Look what I got." She pulled three assignments out and handed them to me: C, C+, and B-.

"An upward trajectory," I said. "This shows improvement."

"Still not good," and she put the papers back in her backpack.

"So did Charlotte say anything to you about Theo?" I still didn't know what had prompted the breakup.

"Oh sure," Megan said sarcastically, "we linked arms on the way home, and she opened up to me and shared all of her feelings."

I smiled. "Right," I said.

Megan went to the kitchen to get a snack, and Jack came in, found the sheet music for the last piece he'd been working on with my mom, Bach Minuet in G, and started playing it, badly.

After about two minutes, Charlotte came in and told Jack to knock it off.

"But I have to practice," he argued. "Right, Mom?"

"Well, I have to study," Charlotte said, "and standardized testing takes priority. Tell him, Mom."

Megan walked out of the kitchen. "Can we go to the grocery store?

There's no food in the house." She plopped down in a chair by the window with her book.

How exactly was this going to work?

"Okay, Jack and I will go to Whole Foods now," I said. "Charlotte and Megan will have at least forty-five minutes of complete silence, and then after dinner Jack gets to play piano for a half hour."

Charlotte made a sound of disgust. "You better buy me noise-canceling headphones while you're out because I'll go crazy if I have to listen to that hideous noise." She stormed out of the room.

Jack didn't look even remotely hurt, but I still didn't think a comment like that should stand.

"She's just in a bad mood," I said.

"I know."

"Put your shoes on; we'll leave in a couple minutes."

I knocked on Charlotte's door and opened it.

"I'll apologize," she said. She was crying again.

"I know heartbreak is miserable," I said. "And I'm not going to tell you to feel better because I get it that being happy isn't something you can just turn on."

She blew her nose. "Well, what, then?"

"The only cure I know is distraction, taking your mind off him, looking forward. Take your focus and energy off Theo and commit your time to the activities you love, to your goals—"

"Is this just another way to tell me to do my college applications?"

"No, but thinking about college might help, now that you mention it. I'd love to go over your essay with you. And what's this about failing history? I can't imagine you failing anything."

"I'll deal with it," she said. "Bye."

"I'm trying to talk—"

"Isn't Jack waiting for you?" she said.

I sighed. "Try not to take your anger out on your family, okay? Apologize to him later."

"Fine."

I put on my Hunter boots, got my umbrella, and Jack and I headed out into the deluge. From my raincoat pocket, I heard my phone ringing, and I pulled Jack under an awning on the sidewalk. It was an unknown number, and a woman introduced herself to me as the dean of student affairs for the continuing education program at NYU. Howard, it seemed, had lodged a formal complaint against the writing center, claiming he was being discriminated against for being an employee of the school. Specifically, he accused Rick of unfairly depriving him of his tutor, of firing the person who had been assigned to support his academic efforts. The poetry professor was called into administration, and she told them that, given that she could not possibly rearrange her office hours to meet him early in the mornings, Howard should be reassigned to the tutor who had been helping him with the poetry class, at an hour that accommodated his schedule. The administration had deliberated and ultimately decided I should be rehired.

I heard her out, thinking it was crazy that I'd been the unwitting subject of a minor university controversy.

"Really?" I said. "Rick's not going to like this."

"You won't be working for the writing center anymore," she told me. "The continuing ed program would like to contract your services independently. We'll email time sheets for you to fill out, and we'll pay the same twenty dollars an hour."

Call me dishonest, but I didn't correct the error in my going rate. "Are there restrictions?" I asked.

"What do you mean?"

"Am I actually allowed to talk about content? To go over the poems he's learning in class?"

She was quiet for a moment. "Isn't that what you do?"

I smiled. "Of course."

"Can you start tomorrow morning?" she asked and gave me Howard's cell number to confirm the appointment.

Standing there in my rain boots and coat, with Jack tugging on my hand and water running off my umbrella, I felt excited and vindicated. I hung up and squealed.

"What happened?" Jack asked.

"I got a job," I said.

———

I walked into Carter's apartment right after my tutoring session with Howard the next morning and found Carter in the living room with a slick-looking guy in a pinstripe suit. I had never seen a visitor in the apartment before. Carter was ranting: "You tricked me into this bullshit, motherfucker, so get me out of it." He jabbed one crutch in the air for emphasis.

I stayed in the entry and watched them from a safe distance. The man, I noticed, was flustered but keeping his cool, unlike Carter.

"You need to hear me out because you clearly don't get it," the man stated. He had a pen behind his ear and a thick stack of stapled pages in his hand. "No one tricked you; you just weren't listening. You can't just decide that . . . that . . . this isn't the way you want to spend your time. This isn't a health-club membership, it's an Equity contract."

"Whatever, just fucking get me out of it."

"That's what I'm telling you: there's no getting out. You signed. We sat there together, going over it with a lawyer who walked you through every section in it. You remember this? You signed it. Look!" And he held up the contract to show him his own signature.

"You all tried to pull one over on me. *I* decide, Simon. *I* decide what tours I go on, what music I sing. I'm in charge. And I'm not doing some faggoty-ass musical with a bunch of losers."

Simon sighed, looked up at the ceiling in exasperation, and then spoke slowly. "You agreed, Carter. You wanted to work with Max again, and he'd like to work with you—this is a good thing. We talked through it, and we agreed that it's an excellent opportunity, a way for you to get the respect you want and need, for you to be taken seriously again. You need to transition to a new phase, and this is the way to do it."

"Who the fuck doesn't take *me* seriously? I'm Carter fucking Reid." He was now having a full-blown tantrum, a solid, red-faced, tight-fisted fit. "Everyone takes me seriously! And I've made so much money for you, asshole, you'd be a nobody if it wasn't for me, and now I want you to *fix* something, and you're pulling this shit. Just undo it. Call them, write them, go blow them, I don't give a shit. But just so you know, so you get what I'm saying: No. Fucking. Way am I doing this thing, and you can't make me."

Simon cleared his throat. "Your latest publicity move involved puking on James Corden during *Carpool Karaoke*."

"So? I got carsick."

"Bullshit, 'carsick.' You were drunk and high and being a complete prick. You're burning bridges, everywhere, with everyone. What are you doing, Carter? James Corden, for Christ's sake."

"Who gives a shit about Corden anyway?"

"He buried the clip for you. He was unbelievably decent to do that. You should be beyond grateful that millions of YouTube viewers didn't get to see Carter Reid barfing all over the famed Range Rover." Simon paused for a second, flipped through the papers he was holding, and shrugged. "Look," he said with renewed calm and a slight smile, "you don't have a choice here. You're *obligated*. The sooner you face that fact, and start working on the script I gave you, the sooner you get with the program, the smoother this is going to go. They're expecting you to show up for the first rehearsal in January. You've got plenty of time to get comfortable with the lines between now and then. It's just a table read to start with, nothing more. Just a chance to sit down with the cast and read through the whole thing. Show up to that, and you'll see this is the best career choice you've made in a long time."

"No."

"Carter—"

"Fuck you."

"You—"

"If you think I'm playing some asshole named *Neville*—"

"You have to—"

"I don't *have* to do anything! You're a fucking liar, always have been."

"Well, I give up, then," Simon said, dropping the contract on the coffee table. "If you don't do this show, then we're done. And I'll be screwed; I'll have zero credibility after this." The pen fell on the floor from behind his ear; neither of them bothered to pick it up. "I went to bat for you so hard on this. They wanted you for a year, and I talked them down to six months, with the two-month option, just like we said. I negotiated this *palace* for you to stay in. I got you every goddamn thing you asked for."

"Worst fucking manager ever," Carter said. "You suck."

"I just told you I— How . . . In what possible way do I suck? They're paying you forty-five thousand dollars a week, for fuck's sake. That's more than they paid Hugh Jackman."

I put my hand out and touched the wall to steady myself.

"So what," Carter said. "I hate him, and I hate you."

I shook my head, wishing he would stop sounding so embarrassingly childish.

"You're making a monumental mistake," Simon said quietly. "I wish you at least knew that I'm genuinely trying to help you. Give me a call when you finally understand that." He picked up the contract and held it out to Carter.

"Get that shit out of my face."

Simon shook his head and picked his pen up off the floor. "Sure thing, Carter. Whatever you say. But do me a favor and call your lawyer. And good luck explaining this to the agency."

He put the contract on the table in the entry, and pushed the button for the elevator, noticing me for the first time.

"Who are you?" he asked.

"Allison. I'm his . . . I'm the new Lyle."

"I hope you can talk some sense into him. They'll sue him for every cent they invested in this project, and that's not the worst thing that's going to happen. He's in it for merchandizing and film rights. And if he screws over these people—"

"This is *your* fault, asshole. They'll sue *you*, not me." Carter yelled. "Maybe I'll sue you, too."

"If you bail on this show," Simon said, using one arm to hold the elevator door and pointing at Carter aggressively, "your career is dead. No more hit songs, no more tours. It would take a miracle to get you back where you were when you were thirteen. And get ready to give up your Hollywood Hills mansion. You'll be a has-been in a year."

As the elevator doors closed, Carter threw his phone in Simon's general direction, smashing it into pieces and leaving a dent in the wall. I went to pick it up.

"Fuck!" he yelled.

"Hi," I said.

"Where have you been?"

"I—"

"You just show up here whenever you feel like it—"

"Excuse me?"

"You know what?" he said. "Get the fuck out. I don't want you hanging around here anyway. Showing up whenever you fucking feel like it."

I hung my coat up, put my bag down in the living room, and went to the kitchen to get a plastic baggie for the phone. I ziplocked it and put it on the coffee table.

"Take a breath and pull yourself together," I said quietly, standing near him but not too close. "I'm not going anywhere."

He was getting sweaty. "Fuck you."

I didn't flinch.

"Don't tell me what to do in my house," he yelled. "I'm in charge here. So stop with all the how many pills I can take, or when I should get up or sit down or take a shit or eat or sleep, or break a plate or throw my phone . . . or . . . or . . ." He'd run out of examples.

"Are you done? Because I think you're scaring Skittle." I decided to go a little further: "The vet told me that this breed of turtle is very sensitive to noise and stress."

He glanced over at her new tank that I'd set up on a table; Skittle was sunning herself on a rock. "Bullshit," he said, but he'd lowered his voice.

"Your eye looks good," I told him. "You feeling okay today?"

"No."

"Need anything?"

"Yeah, a fucking *phone*."

It was so tempting to lecture him. "The same kind?" I asked instead. "Are you backed up?"

"I don't know."

"Do you have an account number?"

"I don't know."

"An old bill lying around? Who's your carrier?"

"How would I know *any* of this shit?"

In spite of his rudeness, my instinct was to pat him on the back, but I didn't.

"Where were you?" he asked.

"At work. So that guy, Simon . . ."

"Don't talk about him." He ran his hand over his head and through his hair; it looked like he hadn't washed it in days.

"Okay." I sat down on the couch, got a notebook out of my bag, and flipped it open to the right page. "I made a bunch of calls, but I need to know if you want a housekeeper just for a week or so until you leave, or if you'll still need someone to come after you go. I mean, whose apartment is this? That guy Simon was just saying that he—"

"I don't know, all right? I have no idea."

"Should I ask Simon?"

"No. Fuck him."

"Right. And you're one hundred percent sure about leaving New York? In spite of all that stuff he—"

"Yeah."

"Well, if you're leaving for sure, and the apartment isn't yours, maybe we just need some help cleaning for now and getting the place ready to vacate. I liked the guy the company sent, but he's more like a fancy butler when all you really need is a cleaning—"

"Fine. Did you book a plane?"

"I got the name of a good private charter."

"I want to go home."

I sighed. "When?"

"The second I feel good enough to get out of here. Next week, maybe."

"And return . . . ?"

"Never." He sat down across from me and pulled off the Velcro knee brace, wincing.

"Will you see a doctor before you go?"

"Nah," he said.

"Because I think it would be a good idea."

"Can a doctor come here?"

"You might need an X-ray or an MRI, and I want them to look at your shoulder, too."

"Forget it. I'm fine."

I decided not to push on that topic, but I was still thinking about what Simon had said. "Listen, do you want my husband to go over that theater contract?" I asked. "Find out if it's binding? If there's a loophole or something?"

"He knows about this stuff?"

"Sort of. Maybe enough to see if there's a way out."

"I'm not doing the show."

"Can I ask why not?"

"No."

"Can you give me a hint? You don't like it? Don't like the character? Because he's actually rather inter—"

"It wasn't a done deal, and I'm not fucking doing it."

"Okay," I said, closing my notebook. "So for now you want a phone."

"And clean stuff to wear."

I got my envelope of receipts out of my bag. "I need you to pay me for the expenses I'm out so far, like the vet bill and everything I bought for Skittle. And the Xbox. And frankly, I was thinking you could pay me some sort of salary; this is starting to feel like a job."

He reached in his shorts pocket and pulled out a stack of bills wrapped in a rubber band. "How much?"

"Holy. Cow," I said.

"How much do you need? Ten thousand? Fifteen thousand? What?"

"Wait—"

"How *much*?"

"Wait, let me show you what you're paying me back for."

"I don't give a shit."

"Carter. You're eighteen, right? You need to know where your money goes. You shouldn't just take my word for it. Why would you even trust me? You barely know me. I could walk out of here with that and never come back again."

"So? Wouldn't be the first time. I don't even know how much Lyle made off with."

"Did he keep records?" I asked.

He didn't answer.

"Carter—"

"I'll give you a thousand dollars to stop talking and go buy me a fucking phone. And get me a cleaning lady *today* because I don't know where anything is, like, anything . . . like my clothes."

For $1,000, I figured *I'd* be willing to do his laundry.

"A thousand dollars? Like for my time?" It beat what I made tutoring.

He dropped a stack of money on the seat next to me. "Take whatever."

I picked up the cash, took the time I needed to count out $4,000, and put it in the envelope with the receipts, handing him the rest. "I've got an itemized, running list of expenses, and I'll give you a full account-ing of everything I spend, and I'll keep a thousand for myself."

I was dying to ask him to reconsider the show, to discuss it with me, to talk through the problem. "One important question, Carter."

"*What?*" he snapped.

"Nothing. Never mind."

"I need a phone," he said, "like, half an hour ago."

I had an impossible time in the AT&T store. Impossible. I wasn't an authorized user on Carter's account, obviously. They wouldn't even tell me if there was an account in his name. So after a lot of arguing and refusing to tell the saleswoman "what he's *really* like" and whether or not the rumors were true that he'd gotten a girl pregnant, I got Carter a line on Michael's and my account and bought him the latest iPhone with the cash he'd given me.

A risk for sure, and I was anxious about it. The saleswoman calmed me down by putting an alert on the line in case Carter was in the habit of calling Hong Kong or downloading porn all day long. And she as-sured me I would get a message when the bill for his line exceeded $500. I could disconnect it at will. I thanked her, left the store with the new phone and brought it to Carter. He took it, turned it on, and smiled. "Is this a new number?" he asked.

"Yeah, they wouldn't let me—"

"That's fucking awesome. None of those pricks will know how to reach me."

Late that night I pulled the big stack of cash out of my purse and made a production of flipping through the bills in front of Michael. I took the rubber band off, made a fan, and waved it at my face. Then I threw it up in the air and onto the bed.

"Very impressive," Michael said. Then he started picking up the money, doing a cursory count. "My God."

"He must have an accountant somewhere, right?" I said, climbing on the bed and stacking the money back together. "Someone who pays his bills?" I asked. "A tax guy?"

"I certainly don't think he's doing his own taxes."

"There must paperwork somewhere in that office. I'm going to snoop around. Oh, and could you look at this for me?" I reached back in my bag and handed him a folder with the words Limelight CONTRACT across the front. "It sounds like Carter's going to be in big trouble, or maybe he's getting screwed over, I don't know." I handed Michael the Equity contract Carter had signed for the production.

"Where'd you get this?"

"From his manager. Former manager. Or maybe he's an agent."

"I'm not a contract lawyer. And I'm certainly not an entertainment lawyer." Michael turned off the overhead light and got in bed.

"No, but you're a lawyer. Can you just read it over? Let me know what it means?"

"Sure, but it'll take some time."

"I'll pay you. Say, three hours of legal counsel at three fifty an hour. Is three fifty okay with you?"

"He doesn't have to pay me."

"Why shouldn't he? This is work, and we need the money."

"We're not as bad off as you think," he said.

"With these private school bills? We're worse off than *you* think." I looked at him to make sure he took that remark seriously. The sides of his hair were graying, and I imagined running my mascara brush through them. "I got the name of a really high-end men's hair stylist," I said. "A guy named Antonio who makes house calls. Maybe your pal Kevin Kline goes to him."

"I wonder how Kevin feels about doing a play with a pop star. It's a little undignified for him, isn't it?"

"But what pop star?" I asked. "Who's replacing Carter?"

eleven

LAUREN HAD BECOME my first real New York friend.

Ben and Jack were at her house with a sitter, Megan and Sabrina were at their first baking class in SoHo, and Lauren and I were waiting for them at Ladurée, a total treat. I was drinking the prettiest cappuccino I'd ever seen, and we were sharing an assortment of macarons while sitting in the back of the restaurant, overlooking a beautiful courtyard. It felt like heaven.

"I'm obsessed with the high school thing," Lauren said, stirring agave syrup in her tea. "You're so lucky Megan can stay where she is. The rest of us are losing our minds over the public school process."

"Well, she *could* stay at Orbis," I said, disappointed that such a stressful topic of conversation was invading the serene setting. "But I'm not sure she should. I don't have much confidence in the school so far."

"What's wrong with it?"

"I'm paying about a million dollars for my daughter to be perpetually confused by the teacher's expectations. And there's no community as far as I can tell. I haven't met any of the parents or kids."

"Let me know if you decide to look around. The public schools are super competitive and the process is confusing, but I can help you narrow it down. Is she a STEM girl?"

"She's more into English, history, writing." As someone who was allergic to bragging parents, I didn't mention that Megan had won a poetry contest at her school the year before or that she frequently wrote long, well-developed stories that she would edit for hours.

"Same as Sabrina. She plays clarinet, so she's auditioning at LaGuardia and Special Music School, but I think we'll end up somewhere more humanities-based. What's Megan into? Would she want a big school? A small school?"

I put my cup down. "If it's really competitive, I'm not sure Megan can get in. Her grades at Orbis aren't very good so far."

Lauren smiled at me. "But how were her report cards for seventh?"

"Fine. Great, actually."

"You're in luck, then, because the Department of Ed. doesn't even look at eighth-grade report cards, so no one will see her transcript from Orbis. Each school has its own requirements, a portfolio or a writing sample. You should at least look into it. I can help."

By the time Lauren and I left Ladurée to pick up the girls, I had a list of five schools to research: Beacon, Eleanor Roosevelt, Art and Design, Frank McCourt, and Baruch. And by the next day I had gone online and registered for open houses at each of them. I admit, I was motivated in part by a fantasy of tearing up the next pricey tuition bill from Orbis to shreds.

———

Michael had a new favorite hobby: finding excellent restaurants in neighborhoods other than our own to get us to seek out new parts of the city while enjoying a fantastic meal. One night we went out to dinner at a lovely place he'd read about in the *New York Times*, I Sodi in the West Village, and he suggested we meet there after work. Charlotte said she would babysit as long as she could pick what they ordered in for delivery.

"Deal," I said and handed her my laptop with the Seamless.com page open.

I put on a skirt and boots and took the subway to Christopher Street. The restaurant was understated and tiny, only about ten tables, and we sat along the bare wall in the back, sharing steak tartare, *cacio e pepe*, and grilled branzino. It was perhaps the best meal I'd ever had.

The waiter came and refilled my wineglass.

"I know that Carter can't wait to leave New York," Michael said, "but he's got a problem on his hands. He's in denial if he doesn't see that." Michael had read over Carter's contract at work that day, and he was confirming what I suspected: Carter would be in big trouble, professionally and legally, if he quit the show.

"Well, I'm going to have to make him see it," I said. "So what's my argument?"

"The argument is that there's no *out*. It's just too late. Even if they think they've made a massive mistake hiring him, they'll hang on to him. They've got investors who want this thing to pay off, and he's the draw."

"But what do I say to him? He's supposed to go into rehearsals in early January, and he plans to be sitting by the swimming pool at his L.A. villa."

"The good news is he's only committed to a six-month run."

"That's an eternity to him."

"There's an option in the contract for a two-month extension if he and the producers want it, but he's not obligated to go past the initial six months."

"So you're saying he has to do the show."

"Well, he doesn't *have* to, no, but they'll sue him unless he can make a case for a serious illness or something along those lines. A life-threatening, incurable health condition. A brain tumor. A broken spine."

"Jeez."

"He really doesn't have a choice here. The contract's airtight."

He passed me the plate of sautéed spinach to go with the fish.

"Maybe I'll take him to see a musical," I said, "just to expose him to some theater. Something like *Dear Evan Hansen*?"

"What makes you think he'd go with you? No offense, but doesn't he have younger people to hang out with?"

"He doesn't have anyone."

"And what about you?" Michael asked.

"What about me?"

"Are you and New York getting along any better?"

I had to think for a moment. "Yes," I said, "we're getting along fairly well, actually. But I think it's only sensible to keep an open mind about next year. I want to keep the option of the suburbs on the table, depending on how things are going with the kids."

"Fair enough," he said. "But I'd miss date nights like this one. Something tells me no suburb can offer food like this."

I had just taken a bite of the sublime pasta as he said this and nodded in agreement, closing my eyes; there was no way I could argue with that.

———

When we got home that night, I searched all the Broadway plays and musicals that were running, trying to find something cool and edgy, yet classic and broadly appealing. As I looked through the list, I thought of someone else who would benefit from seeing emotion and action played out onstage, of words brought to life.

I picked up the phone and called Howard.

———

After all her big talk of making plans and getting together, I found that pinning Sara down for an actual night out or coffee date was difficult. And to find a night when both she and Lilly could get together was near impossible.

"I can't Saturday," Sara would say. "I'm helping a friend sell his raw goat cheese at a farmer's market in the East Village."

"Not Wednesday," Lilly would explain, "I've been invited to join the Montclair Conservation Committee."

"Sorry, babe," Sara would say. "That whole week I'm going to the Adirondacks to an LGBTQ conference-slash-meditation retreat with the guy I'm fucking who's a totally subtle genius."

"Not any night next week," Lilly would tell me. "We've got a major young-adult book festival we're organizing."

They were always sorry.

"You never have time for me," Sara said when I'd called the week before.

"You're kidding, right?" I asked, laughing. "*You're* the one who never has time."

"You're all tied up with your family, your kids, husband, blah blah. Just call me when you have a window," she said.

"I have a window! I have a window right this minute. Or tomorrow. Or any night next week. I've got tons of windows."

So finally the three of us were meeting for drinks together on an unusually warm night in the end of October. I arrived at the bar first and found a table. I watched as the two of them walked in one right after the other, without noticing each other. As they both scanned the bar looking for me, Sara in super-tight, mile-long, artfully torn jeans and a leather jacket, and Lilly in a blazer with a Chanel handbag over her shoulder, I wondered what—other than one year at Middlebury—these two women could possibly have in common. What was I thinking to insist we get together as a threesome?

I waved, and they headed over to the table, finally seeing each other once they were standing right in front of me.

Sara had chosen the bar, one of those loud Lower East Side pub-by-type places I hated. We had a tiny table that wobbled until Sara stuck a folded coaster under one of the legs. There was no table service; I asked what they each wanted to drink and then had to push my way up to the dark wood bar, which was sticky with God knows what. The bartenders had groupies, which made no sense to me, and it took forever to get their attention. I felt invisible. I got our drinks (draft beer for Sara, a lemon drop martini for Lilly, and a vodka tonic for me) and fought my way back to our table.

Sara spent the first twenty minutes lecturing us about local Brooklyn politics. I had been looking forward to having a more personal, lighthearted, relaxing conversation, but I listened politely and tried to follow her arguments.

"Anyway," Sara was saying, "I'd love to hear what you guys think about the rise of crowd-based capitalism in the city, especially after you have a chance to read Arun Sundararajan's book. I'd lend it to you, but I got mine from the library."

"How're you liking New York?" Lilly asked in a brutal change of subject.

I surprised myself when I said with all sincerity, "I like it."

"Good for you," Sara said. "For a while there, I was worried you were going to be one of those people who ends up in the suburbs. I would have had to kill you."

"*I* ended up in the suburbs," Lilly said curtly.

"Well, that's different," Sara said. "You grew up here. You probably have all kinds of issues to work out, reasons to want to rebel against your childhood."

"What? There's no 'issue.' I love New York. We'll probably move back here once my kids are grown. I just wanted them to have more freedom."

Sara laughed. "Since when does New Jersey corner the market on freedom?"

Lilly then launched into her own twenty-minute speech on all the benefits of life in Montclair, covering everything from the passion and the education level of its residents to the history of Essex County to the enduring character of the township. She boasted about the ease of her commute into the publishing house where she worked four days a week.

"I felt the weight of the world lifting when I moved to Montclair. Like this calm settled over me. It was beautiful. I'm completely off Xanax."

"I'm so glad you're happy there," I said, hoping to diffuse the tension. "I mean, New York is terrific," I said with a nod to Sara, "but it can be tricky here with kids. So, really, you're both completely right."

"Last year," Lilly said, leaning in to express her horror, "I had five friends with eighth graders, and none of their kids got into a single public school they applied to. And at that point I decided, who needs it? And started house hunting."

Sara looked confused. "That's so strange," she said, "because I have a friend whose kid goes to Stuyvesant. She said it was really easy to get in. There's just one test you take, and you go."

"Ha," Lilly said. "Easy? You have *got* to be kidding."

"I'm just telling you what she said."

"And I'm just telling you," said Lilly, "that's totally ridiculous. Nothing about raising kids in New York is easy."

Oh dear. I took a swig of my drink.

"A lot of parents do it successfully, so it can't be that hard," Sara said.

"Well," I said, poking my ice cubes with my straw, "we're going to take the plunge and apply to public. I want to have a choice next year, something aside from this for-profit, overpriced school I—"

"Your kids' school is *for-profit*?" Sara asked. The look she gave me was as if I'd told her I spent my free time murdering puppies for sport. "Come *on*, Allison."

"Look, we parents just do the best we can, okay?" Lilly said. "Sometimes, for the good of our kids, we have to make compromises. Life gets a little complicated when you're not thinking only of yourself all the time."

"I hardly think anyone can accuse *me* of acting out of selfish interest. I literally work for the greater good."

I didn't know how to get the nasty edge out of the conversation and could plainly see that this reunion had been a total lapse in judgment. Was there any topic that didn't lead to conflict?

"So, Sara," Lilly said, "are you seeing anyone?"

Oh God.

"I'm single, actually."

"I'd be happy to fix you up," Lilly said. "I have tons of single friends in the city. Guys or girls?"

"Excuse me?" Sara asked.

"Are you dating guys these days, or girls?"

"See, I hate that sort of binary thinking. Gender means nothing to me. I like who I like, and the rest is just details, like eye color." She sighed with disgust. "Never mind, you're so entrenched in the heteronormative culture, it would be futile for me to try to explain it to you."

Lilly held her hands up confused. "Then isn't the answer just 'either'? You don't have to make your sex life more complicated than it already is."

At this point I worried that one of them would storm off in a huff. I had no need to ever repeat this exercise of getting the three of us together again, but on their own, these were two women I wanted to keep in my life.

"I'm Carter Reid's personal assistant," I blurted out.

They both put their drinks down and stared at me, eyes wide.

"You're *what*?" Lilly said.

"Not officially or anything. I mean, I don't have a title. And please don't tell anyone. I haven't even said a word about it to my kids. But that's what I've been up to recently."

"How did *that* happen?" Sara asked.

"Long story. It's temporary, just while he's in town."

"My girls are dying to see him on Broadway," Lilly said. "Can you get us backstage?"

I decided not to disappoint her by telling her that Carter had no intention of doing the show. "Maybe," I said.

Sara was still looking at me with disbelief. "Are we talking about *the* Carter Reid?"

"Yep," I said, feeling a vague sense of pride.

"The pop singer?"

"He's the one."

"Isn't he a total misogynist?"

"Sure," Lilly said, "they all are. But if he's got Allison in his life now, think of how good she could be for him."

I didn't feel like explaining my lack of influence, so I simply nodded and sipped my drink.

"This is so cool," Lilly said, her voice suddenly high-pitched.

Sara seemed to be less convinced of my coolness. "True," she said warily. "You could try to teach that kid to show some respect for women."

"You could tell him to keep it in his pants," Lilly agreed.

I laughed. "That's maybe a little outside my job description."

"So what *do* you do for him, exactly?" Sara asked.

"I cook. I clean." I didn't like how this was sounding. "I buy stuff for him. Make appointments to get his hair cut, organize his travel, pay his phone bill."

Lilly smiled. "So basically you're his mother."

"No, not at all," I said, not sure how to convey Carter's and my dynamic. "He kind of hates me, actually."

"Exactly," Lilly said.

"How's it going with rehearsals?" Sara asked.

"They haven't started yet. He hurt his knee recently . . . going over some dance moves. I'm concerned that it's not getting better."

"Oh, I know the best doctor," Lilly said. "He's at the Hospital for Special Surgery. He did my daughter's medial patellofemoral ligament reconstruction."

"Her what?"

"Knee surgery—ballet injury. I'll send you his information."

"And while we're worrying about his health and well-being, here," Sara said, opening her canvas tote bag and putting handfuls of condoms on the table.

"Sara!" I said.

"These are official New York City condoms, part of the campaign to stop the spread of STDs. Seriously, Allison. Give these to him; don't be a prude."

"I can't give him—"

"Yes you can," said Lilly, "and you should. Good thinking, Sara. You should certainly educate him about safe sex."

"I'm sure he already—" I opened my purse and put them in, shaking my head. "And we really don't have that kind of relationship."

"Well, excuse me, *teacher*," Sara said. "Why don't you try to school him on a thing or two. You've got his ear, right?"

"That may be overstating my role."

"This is such an opportunity," Lilly said. "You can civilize him. Get him on the right track."

"Help him discover his inner feminist," Sara added.

"So tell us," Lilly said, "what's he really like?"

Somehow Carter had brought peace to my Girls' Night Out.

And while I appreciated their interest, their enthusiasm, even their curiosity, no way was I going to betray his confidence.

"He's a great kid," I said.

twelve

"SO ARE YOU SAYING there *is* a way out of the contract?" Carter asked me. We were sitting in the living room across from the big naked boob picture, and I was trying to break the news to him while he was feeding Skittle a piece of lettuce.

"Not exactly," I said. "I guess it depends on what the definition of *is* is." Carter just stared at me; he never picked up on references to anything that happened earlier than the previous week.

He was starting to look like the boy from the poster that had hung on Charlotte's wall.

"Your face is healing up nicely."

"So?"

"No, nothing, it's just that you're a pretty good-looking guy when you're not scowling," I said.

"Good-looking? Me?" he said flatly. "Wow, I never heard that before."

"Ah, see, now *that* is what people in the theater world would call a 'deadpan' delivery."

"Just tell me what the lawyer said. Your husband or whatever."

I was surprised he was willing to talk about it at all. I cleared my throat. "It comes down to this: you *want* to do the show."

"No I don't."

"You just think you don't."

"I *know* I don't." He leaned back on the couch cushions and closed his eyes.

"Why don't you want to?"

"None of your fucking business."

"Right."

"I'm not doing it," he said.

"It's just that if there were a reason, a really good one, then we might have something to work with."

He opened his eyes again. "What kind of reason?"

"A life-threatening illness."

"Fine. I'm ill."

"Are you?"

"Dying, sure, whatever."

I decided to humor him. "What do you have?"

"None of your business."

"See, that's not how the producers will feel. They'll need a concrete reason, an indisputable diagnosis, something so serious it would make it impossible for you to do the job, to even go to rehearsals. And you'll have to prove it."

"Just say I have a stomachache."

"A life-threatening stomachache?" I asked. "I don't think so."

"What do they want from me?" he asked, sounding like a true victim.

"They'll want a diagnosis from a doctor. And it can't be discomfort. It has to be a diagnosis of something irreversible like multiple sclerosis. Or severe IBS."

"What's that?"

"Irritable bowel syndrome."

"Meaning?"

"Meaning," I said, "you have bouts of intractable diarrhea."

He sat up. "The fuck are you talking about? I have an *image*. I can't have diarrhea."

"When Jeremy Piven quit his Broadway show, he said he had a health issue and got sued by the producers anyway because they didn't believe it."

"Who?" he asked.

"Jeremy Piven? Ari Gold?"

He shook his head.

"*Entourage*? He played Vince's agent."

"You know him?"

"No, but I read up about it."

"How much did he get sued for?"

"A lot."

"How much?"

"Well, he happens to have won his lawsuit—"

"See? See?! He won? So I'll say I have whatever he had. If he got away with it. . . ."

"You can't have the same thing as Jeremy Piven; that would look fishy." I got nothing for that joke.

"What if I try to kill myself?"

"Diarrhea's unacceptable, but suicide's okay?"

"Sure."

"Right," I said. "How are you going to do it?"

"Pills."

"So now you're dead?" Humoring him may have been a mistake.

"No, you call nine-one-one, and they'll revive me."

"Oh my god," I said, standing up and facing him. "What if they can't revive you?"

"They can. They can totally bring people back."

"Except for when they can't."

"They can."

An article I'd once read about the pointlessness of arguing with a toddler popped into my head.

"I have a better idea," I said, "why don't you focus your energy on the script instead of on feigning an illness. I think it would be a lot less trouble to honor the contract you signed, and do the job you agreed to do."

He stood up and faced me, careful not to put too much weight on his bad leg. "You're worse than Simon." He went to put Skittle back in her tank and replaced the top.

"How? I'm on your side, completely," I said. "And go wash your hands."

He spun around. "What if I got sick from Skittle? What if she gave me salamander or whatever? You said it's really serious."

"Salmonella." I shook my head. "You'd need a doctor to prove it."

He threw up his hands. "I'm not doing the show."

"Why not?"

"Because," he said.

"I'm trying to help you here. Because *why*?"

"Because!" he yelled. "Because Simon took me to some meeting, and he and that producer bitch and some other asshole had totally pulled one over on me. First they told me I'm working on some new music with Max, and I said, 'Fine,' and they're like, 'You can stay in this great New York apartment and party,' and I'm all 'Sure,' but then we walk into the next meeting, and they hand me the thing, not just songs, but this whole fucking . . ." He searched for the word. ". . . *book*. So I looked at it, the . . . script, and it's complete bullshit, and I said to Simon, 'Fuck no, I didn't sign up for this shit.'"

I was trying to keep up. "Who's Max?" I asked.

"Max!" he yelled, as though my hearing was the problem. "His shit's great. But this—what?—I'm supposed to *be* some stupid 'guy'? Act like some jackoff named Neville who talks like a loser and says boring shit? Those fucking *words*? No way. I don't talk like that."

This was by far the longest speech I'd ever heard him give. "Okay," I said, taking a step toward him just as he took a step away from me. He always made me feel like I had bad breath. "You feel tricked, I get it, but I can't help you fake your suicide."

"This is bullshit. All I want is out of this thing. You're fucking useless, you know that? Everyone's useless." He limped to the kitchen, opening the refrigerator violently.

I followed him. "You're mad because I'm trying to keep you from taking a handful of pills. Seriously?"

"Where's my Fiji?" he asked.

"Your what?"

"My bottled water."

"I can get you a glass from the tap," I said and went to fill one up.

"I don't drink fucking tap water. What am I, *poor*?"

"New York water is very good, actually, renowned for its quality—"

"I want bottled fucking Fiji in here," he said, "all the time. Got it? *All* the time."

"Plastic bottles? They're so bad for the environment—"

He stared at me like he wished me dead. "Is this too much for you? Stock my fucking fridge with bottled Fiji. Or get the fuck out. Got it?"

"Sure. Yup. Bottled water."

"*Fiji.*"

"Got it."

"Jesus. Is that so hard?"

"I don't know, is it so hard to remember to wash your damn hands after you play with the turtle? Or do you *want* intractable diarrhea?"

"Fine," he said, turning on the sink.

"Fine," I said, handing him the soap.

"God, you're bossy as fuck."

"Yeah, well," I said, "maybe we should go with your near-death plan, and I'll run you over with my car."

"Okay." He sounded serious. "I'll do it," he said.

I handed him a glass of water; he poured it down the drain.

"Before we put you in the ER," I said, "or more likely the morgue, I want you to do one final thing for me. Like a last wish."

"What?" He walked away from me and sat on a barstool.

"Okay, hear me out. I want you to go see a show with me tonight."

"No."

"I already got the tickets," I said.

"Not interested."

"Just come with me, and as soon as the curtain comes down at the end of the show, we'll stand you in the street somewhere, and I'll run you down with my car. Just please go see this thing with me, okay? You're leaving New York soon, you'll never see me again, so I'm asking you to do just one thing for me." Guilt often worked with my kids. "And then I can die happy."

He sighed. "What is it?"

"It's a Broadway musical."

He looked at me like I was punishing him. "Will it bore me to *death*?"

"If you're lucky. But keep an open mind," I said. "You may like it.

And in the meantime, you're getting a haircut here at four thirty this afternoon. Highly recommended guy, the best of the best."

"Sure," he said.

Since he seemed to have agreed to both attending the musical and getting a haircut, I decided to ask for one more thing. "And I'd like to take you to see an orthopedist before you go."

"What's that?"

"Remember I was saying someone should look at your knee because I'm worried that you're still in so much pain. And your shoulder should probably be X-rayed while we're at it."

"Yeah?" he said, an idea formulating in his head. "My knee's pretty bad, actually." He brightened up and looked at me. "I can barely walk on it. No way I can dance."

I could see his mind working. "Please don't tell me you're *hoping* to have a severely damaged knee? Your whole career would suffer; you gotta think long-term here."

"I'm just saying—"

"I know what you're saying, but come on, Carter. Never, *ever* wish for poor health; it's bad luck. All I was suggesting is that we make sure you're healing up properly so that you can get completely back to normal."

"Yeah, okay," he said, latching on to the idea of a busted knee. "Make me an appointment."

"Fine. And I'll see you tonight for the play."

"Whatever."

———

I put on a black wrap dress, tights, and heeled boots and said goodbye to Michael and the kids as they were finishing dinner.

"Where are you going anyway?" Charlotte asked as I was putting on my coat and grabbing my keys.

I drew a total blank.

Michael cleared his throat. "Mom has a . . . work thing."

Charlotte looked confused. "Since when do tutors dress like *that*?"

"It's a fund-raising event for adult students. Gotta run," I said. "See you all later. Love you!"

"She looks really pretty," I heard Megan say as I was closing the door.

"That's because she puts frozen herp diet on her face," Jack said confidently.

I closed the door as Charlotte started to argue with him. "What are you even talking about, you weirdo?"

———

I met Howard in the lobby of Carter's building. Howard, too, had dressed up for the occasion in a dark suit with a tie. We sat down to wait for Carter.

"Who is he again?"

"He's a pop singer," I said. "You know him."

"I don't know him."

I looked at him skeptically. "Everyone knows him."

"I sleep all day."

"*Yolo, baby, so kiss me twice?*" I sang. "That was his big hit, like, three years ago."

"Huh?"

"At least I don't have to worry about you getting starstruck."

Howard straightened up. "Is he the kid with the video where he's standing up on a moving roller coaster?"

"'Roller Coaster Love'! You *do* know him."

"It's not safe. You'd die if you did that in real life."

"Don't take it so literally," I said, laughing. "It's a catchy song."

"I don't like it. And just so you know, I've never done protective services detail."

"That's not why you're here. I thought you'd enjoy the play."

"I'm just letting you know this is outside my skill set."

I looked at him, nervous that I'd screwed up this outing. "I really don't think we'll need security. I mean, we're just going in and out of the theater. We're not walking anywhere."

Howard shrugged.

I looked over and saw Carter coming off the elevator. He looked fabulous—dark glasses, dark jacket, dark fedora. He was still limping, but he'd left his crutch upstairs and his bruises were barely visible. His hair was perfect.

"Wow," I said.

"What?"

"Nice haircut."

"Yeah?" he asked, running his hands through the longer section that fell across his face. "Let's get this shit over with." He didn't even look at Howard. It was as if he didn't see him. I blocked his path when he headed out to the SUV.

"Carter," I said, "this is Howard."

"Hey," Carter said, keeping his hands in his pockets.

Howard nodded at him.

"You security?" Carter asked. "There's more than just you, right?"

"Just us," I answered. "And Howard's coming as our guest be-cause—"

Carter looked incredulous and threw his hands up.

"What? We'll be okay," I said. "Won't we?"

Carter shook his head. "You so don't get it. I'm out," and he turned around to go back to the elevator.

"Wait!" I said.

"I've been working security for over twenty years," Howard called after him. "I know what I'm doing."

Carter stopped, while Howard raised his eyebrows and mouthed the words to me, "I don't know what I'm doing."

"So did you hire a driver?" Carter said, turning back to us, "or are you planning to take me on the fucking subway?"

—

Our driver, Eddie, an eager young man in a boxy suit, who came highly recommended by Lauren, was waiting out front, and as soon as he saw us coming, he jumped out and held the doors open. Carter and I sat in the back, and Howard sat up front with Eddie. Carter bitched about my lack of foresight the whole way to the theater, mumbling about how we would create a mob. When Eddie pulled up to the front entrance on Forty-Fifth Street, we saw the crowd milling in front of the theater entrance, and Howard suggested we drive around until a couple of min-utes before showtime. As I saw the number of people and realized how much Carter looked like The Carter, I wondered if we should abort the whole mission. But after one slow trip around the block, Eddie stopped the car and got us out very quickly. Howard and Carter walked straight to the door of the theater, but I was stopped. A man with a flashlight asked to see the contents of my purse, which I quickly opened, forgetting that it contained the fifty or so condoms I'd gotten from Sara. The guard smiled at me; I smiled back and shrugged. He winked.

Mortified, I caught up with the guys and was relieved that no one seemed to notice Carter until we were walking to our seats down the carpeted right center aisle.

"Right here," I told them. "Row F."

And that was how I found myself in a beautiful, iconic Broadway theater, sitting with a famous pop star on one side of me and a middle-aged poetry student on the other.

The theater felt surprisingly small and wonderfully old-fashioned with its gold painted motifs on the walls and creaky red brocade flip seats, vaulted ceilings, and brass light fixtures. The heavy red curtain kept the set a secret for the time being.

"This is so exciting," I said to Carter. "Right?"

"What is?"

I didn't bother answering. While we waited for the show to start, a woman about my age came up to us, shyly waving her fingers.

"Excuse me," she said to Carter, "but would you mind signing my program for my daughter? She's a huge fan." She had a pen ready, and her husband stood nervously behind her, pretending to be examining the lights on the ceiling.

"Sure," Carter said. "What's her name?" He was so appealing when he smiled like that, engaged someone, laughed. It was a face I rarely saw, but when I did, I was reminded of why this disagreeable, bratty teenager had die-hard fans.

"She's so excited about your musical," the woman went on. "We bought our tickets three months ago. She'll just faint when she finds out I saw you."

Carter took the pen and signed the Playbill, right across the faces of the five young actors in the show.

The theater was filling up, and more people were noticing Carter. There was a buzz growing, attention shifting in our direction, fingers pointing. I started to get anxious when a man got up out of his middle row seat and tried to come over, but we were saved by the dimming of the house lights.

"You may want to take your sunglasses off now," I whispered, "and turn your phone off."

"Hey," Howard said, nudging me. "Isn't that Glenn Close sitting over there?"

"Oh my god!" I whispered. I tapped Carter's arm and pointed. "Look: two rows up on the left. That's Glenn Close in the audience!"

He looked where I was pointing and shook his head. "Who?" he asked, as the theater went dark and the audience burst into applause.

The Breakfast Club musical starred Hailee Steinfeld as the basket case, Zendaya as the princess, Ansel Elgort as the jock, Whoopi Goldberg as the detention supervisor, Matthew Broderick as the janitor, and two actors I didn't know as the brain and the criminal.

Right away there was the familiar, fabulous song by Simple Minds blaring through the sound system: "Hey, hey, hey, he-ey, Oooooh-ooooh-ooooh-oh." With the music playing, the exterior of the school building appeared and we could see the kids showing up, one at a time, walking past us down the aisle, and the audience clapped as each actor went up the steps to the stage and through the big double doors into the school. The criminal, a ringer for Judd Nelson, overdid the walk a bit as the last one to enter the school. And then Matthew Broderick made his big entrance with a rolling trash can and a broom, sweeping the stage, and the audience went crazy.

"What the fuck?" Carter whispered.

"It's Matthew Broderick," I said.

"So?"

The backdrop went up and behind it was the set, somewhat re-imagined, but nevertheless recognizable as the library, complete with a staircase that wound up to a gallery.

The show was a wonderful send-up of the eighties and a perfect tribute to the original movie while being a parody of itself at the same time with references to Molly Ringwald and the Brat Pack. I kept looking over to see Carter's face and couldn't quite tell if he was enjoying it or not. He never laughed.

The curtain dropped at the end of act 1 and the lights came up.

"Wow," Howard said.

I didn't know if he was referring to the show or the fact that the people all around us seemed to be much more focused on Carter now that news of his attendance had rippled through the audience.

"Whoopi Goldberg," I said, trying to keep my growing worry of a mob situation to myself, "don't you think she's good? And," I said, checking my program, "I love that other guy, the nerd. He has great presence. What'd you think?" I asked Carter.

"I gotta take a leak," Carter said.

"Charming." I turned and looked around for a sign to the bathroom.

He put his sunglasses on and stood up.

"You're coming back, though, right?" I asked.

Howard got up as well and accompanied Carter up the aisle, jostling him through the crowd of people who gasped and leaned with their hands outstretched, trying to get his attention, taking his picture.

And then I heard whispering (*pssst*) and felt a tap on my shoulder.

"Are you his mother?"

"Excuse me?"

"That's Carter Reid," she said. She had her hands on the back of my seat, and she leaned forward to get a better look at me. She was wearing thick foundation that had settled into the creases of her face, and her red lipstick ran in little slivers above her lip. "I was wondering if you're his mom."

"No," I said, pulling my hair out from under her hand.

"His aunt?"

"Nope."

"Who are you?"

I had to think for a minute. I wasn't his friend; that was obvious. I wasn't anything, really. "His . . . helper," I said.

"I heard all about him," she said. "He's a mess, right? Mint?"

"Sorry?"

She shoved a tin of Altoids in my face. "I read that he once had sex with a minor in a restaurant bathroom."

"No, that's just . . . no," I said.

"I saw it on the Internet," she said and rattled the Altoid tin.

"No, thank you," I told her. "And don't believe everything you read."

"I heard he got several girls pregnant and that—"

I spun around and stopped her. "He's not like what you heard. He's a good kid, much maligned."

"They say he did so much hallucinatory drugs and such, he's gotten a little dumbed down."

"Are you from the South?" I asked, trying to change the subject.

"Oklahoma, same as him."

"I moved here from Texas."

"My goodness," she said, "you left Texas to live here? Well, at least you can see theater whenever you want. I make Lester take me to New York twice a year just to see something on Broad*way*."

Lester apparently heard his cue and leaned over the other side of my seat, chewing gum with his mouth open. "Nell here says he's some kind of deadbeat dad."

"No," I said again, feeling my cheeks turn red. "Gosh," and I put on a touch of Southern accent, "when you're famous like him, people can make up whatever all they want about you, and then he has to either decide he's too dignified to address the rumors or he tries to defend himself, and no one believes him anyway. I know him: he's a good person." Whether or not I believed what I was saying, I couldn't sit there and not defend him against baseless tabloid rumors. "He's just a boy," I added. "A motherless boy."

This comment brought a sad look to their faces. "He's doing a show soon, I hear," she said. "A musical. We'll come see it, won't we?" She elbowed Lester.

Carter was standing in the aisle, waiting for me to move so that he could get past me. Both he and Howard took their seats again as the buzzing about Carter's presence continued to grow.

The lights dimmed again, the curtain went up, and the second act started. It was very quiet, so quiet I could hear the gum in Lester's mouth. Carter's stomach grumbled, and he shifted in his seat. I wondered if he'd eaten the dinner I'd left.

Onstage, the kids were sleeping in their chairs, and everything was silent. People in the audience started to notice that above them all, the Judd Nelson character was crawling along in an air duct over their heads, and the music started up again, playing the rhythmic dream montage from the movie. The other kids kept dozing until suddenly, the air duct gave way, and the actor fell from fifteen feet or so behind the sculpture in the middle of the room. The audience gasped, and when he bounced up, brushing off his pants and taking a seat next to the brain, you could feel the collective relief. Carter, who was used to all kinds of stage tricks and fancy set changes, appeared completely unimpressed. I was holding out hope that his coolness was just an affect and that he was actually enjoying himself. *Maybe*, I thought, *just maybe Carter will see the appeal.*

When the show ended and the lights went out, we did something that was previously unthinkable to me: we left before the applause. Howard took charge and at his prompting, we were out of our seats and up the aisle before the lights had even come back up for the actors' curtain call. At the back of the theater, I stopped Carter and had him take about three seconds to watch the audience burst into applause as the actors took their bows, smiling and looking radiant, pleased with themselves; they held hands and acknowledged each other generously.

Howard put a hand on both of our backs and hurried us out while the audience was in mid–standing ovation.

As we exited the theater, I was shocked to see the throng of photographers swarming the entrance. Thankfully, Eddie was right there, exactly where he'd said he'd be, waiting with the car doors open, ready to go. Girls screamed and the photographers yelled to get Carter's attention. Dozens of cell phones were held up, catching every moment, and although there was a barricade up, it didn't look very official, and the theater's security did their best to hold the crowd back.

"Carter! Carter!" yelled a man with two huge cameras around his neck and another he was currently using: *click click click*. "How'd you like the show?"

Carter took off his glasses and smiled at him. "Kicked ass," he said. I wondered if he meant it.

I had never seen anyone get surrounded like this before, and from such close proximity, I found the scene both thrilling and terrifying.

"Hey, Carter," yelled another man. He was wearing a leather jacket and leaned way over the railing, shoving his camera right up in Carter's face. "Since when do you like theater? Hey, why are you limping?"

Carter held one hand up, slightly blocking his face from the flash. Howard stepped in between, giving Carter more distance from the cameras.

"Who are you sleeping with these days, Carter?" the first guy yelled. The girls screamed louder.

"You gonna be any good onstage?" the leather jacket asked. "Or are you gonna bomb on Broadway, huh, Carter? What's with the limp? Over here, Carter!"

Howard took my hand and gestured for me to get in the car.

Carter was totally calm; he gave one wave to the crowd, still smiling as he got in the SUV after me. Howard closed the door and walked around to get in on the other side.

Eddie started the car and pressed the button to lock the doors.

"Unbelievable!" I said. "They're so rude!" My adrenaline had kicked in, and my heart was pounding. "That was unreal."

"Please," Carter said. "It gets way worse than that."

"I drive celebrities pretty regular," Eddie said, pulling away from the curb and into the row of stopped traffic. "I've been in car chases with those assholes before."

"Why aren't they outside your apartment?" I asked. "Where have they been this whole time?"

"I haven't done anything lately," Carter said. "I haven't gone anywhere. Lyle usually leaks a tip to someone."

"You mean he would tell the photographers where you'd be?"

"We got one behind us now," Eddie said. I turned around and saw the leather jacket guy on a moped, pulling right up to the side of the car. "I can't lose him if we're not moving."

"Doesn't matter," Carter said, leaning forward on his elbows, chin on his fists.

I tapped his shoulder. "What did you think of the play? Did you like it?"

Carter shrugged.

"What? What's that mean?" I asked. I imitated his shrugging. "You didn't enjoy it?"

"It was all right," Carter said.

"Only *all right*?"

Eddie took a hard left turn up Sixth Avenue right through a yellow light, trying to lose the guy on the moped.

"I liked it," Howard said. "The way they worked the music in. And they kept it close to the movie without it being too close. It was good."

"Zendaya is hot as fuck," Carter said.

"Okay," I said, "that's, like, totally offensive. I'm asking, what did you think of the acting? Of the show as a whole? The way they incorporated the essay into a song at the end?"

"Jesus," Carter said, turning toward me. "Who cares?"

"I do," I said, feeling myself shifting from hopeful to upset. "And you should care, too, because plays are important; and even when they're absurd and funny, they take parts of life and they stick them in front of your face and say, 'Look at that.' A good play makes you forget where you are and think about your life, about humanity." I felt myself getting teary. Maybe it was the stress of getting Carter to the theater and back without incident. Maybe it was just my disappointment that the evening hadn't had the effect on him that I'd hoped for. Maybe it was the fact that I was realizing that I knew of no way that I could get him to stay and do the show. I looked through my purse for a tissue. Howard handed me his handkerchief.

"God, you take this shit way too serious," Carter said.

"I do take it seriously," I said, wiping my eyes, "and so should you. It matters. Art matters."

Carter rolled his eyes. "Why are you yelling?" He looked at Howard. "Art? The fuck is she even talking about?"

"I'm trying to tell you," I said calmly, "that theater, like poetry, like literature, like *music*, has a purpose. To be a part of a play is to do a valuable community service; it's doing your part to document the human condition. *You* actually have a chance to be part of that. And you want to throw it away. I don't get that."

Howard hadn't said much since we got in the car, but I saw now that he was looking confused.

"Carter has been cast in a Broadway musical," I told him. "It's called *Limelight*."

"Yeah?" Howard said. "I've seen the signs for it on the subway."

"Well," I said, throwing up my hands to show my hopelessness, "he's not doing it."

"No?"

"No. But the problem is, he already committed to it, and he'll damage his reputation in the entertainment industry if he quits," I said, getting worked up again.

"But he doesn't want to do it," Howard said, very matter-of-fact.

"Right," I said.

"I understand."

"See," Carter said. "He gets it."

"Why?" I asked. "What do you understand? Because I don't understand."

"When I got deployed for the third time," Howard said, "I didn't want do that, either. And everyone kept saying, 'You don't have a choice, you can't quit,' and I said, 'Watch me.'"

This wasn't exactly the lesson I'd wanted Carter to hear.

"See," Carter said. "That's what I'm talking about." And he reached his hand up to give Howard a high-five.

Howard's hands stayed in his lap. "I went anyway."

Carter dropped his hand.

"I said I'd serve," Howard said. "I signed on the dotted line, and I knew I had to do what I had to do. It wasn't easy, either; I got shot in the head. Three times."

"Jesus. Are you serious?"

Howard smiled suddenly. "No," he said, "I'm just messing with you."

Carter turned away to look out the window. "Dick," he mumbled.

"Maybe," Howard said, "but if you can't handle a little Broadway song and dance, you're the one being a dick, if you don't mind me saying. Talk about a first world pain: 'I don't want to make a ton of money singing and dancing onstage'? Seriously, this city is full of unemployed actors who would murder you in cold blood for that job and wouldn't even think twice about it."

I held my breath and waited for Carter to start yelling; he was clearly fuming. But Howard, undeterred, kept talking. "It's not like you're being expected to do something dangerous, or strenuous, like trash collection or construction. It's not like you have to take on my wife's job working as a nurse in an ER. *That's* a tough job. What's your problem anyway?"

"Who asked you?"

"Never turn down a good job, that's all I'm saying."

Eddie took a left on Fifty-Ninth and we drove past a row of horse-drawn carriages that were parked along Central Park. My phone buzzed with a text from Michael: *How was the show? Check Twitter & Instagram. #BreakfastClub*

As soon as I opened the app, I saw that the feed had pictures, some blurry, some impressively clear, of Carter in dark glasses sitting in the theater, all with captions like *This week's sexiest sighting on Broadway!* And *Check out New York's hottest young thespian!* and *A smarter Carter attends Broadway's star-studded play.* One was a retweeted selfie of Glenn Close with Carter in the background. She'd captioned it: *#CloseEncounters.* In that picture, half of my face was showing, and, wouldn't you know it, my one visible eye was closed. TMZ had posted a picture of him outside the theater, hand up shading his eyes, with the headline, CARTER'S CRASH COURSE ON BROADWAY. And there I was, making a mad face in the background.

"You're getting some interesting press," I said to Carter.

I waited for the retort: *Well, fuck you* or *Mind your own fucking business.* Maybe he felt we were ganging up on him, maybe he was too angry to talk, but he didn't say anything.

Eddie drove around Columbus Circle and onto Broadway, as we sat side by side, all staring straight ahead. For a split second, I saw the three of us as some kind of dysfunctional family unit. And then I remembered there was nothing whatsoever binding us together. And as if to make that clearer, Eddie pulled into the courtyard off Sixty-First and stopped the car. We all got out to go our separate ways.

The moped pulled into the driveway behind us, and the building security guard walked over to shoo him back out to the sidewalk with the others. Leather jacket didn't put up a fight; he was busy on his phone, tipping off whoever it was he needed to contact.

"Thanks for coming along," I said to Howard.

"It was interesting. Sorry if I was hard on you, Carter."

Carter didn't answer and turned to go inside.

I waved to Howard and followed Carter into the lobby. "Do you want to talk about it?" I said. He acted like he didn't hear me. "So . . . I'll just see you tomorrow, then."

I watched while he walked away, shoulders slumped and hands in his pockets.

I felt of surge of anxiety and ran after him, all the way to the elevator.

"Hey, Carter," I called, catching up to him. He stopped but didn't turn to look at me. "I don't need to worry about you, do I? I mean, promise you won't do anything stupid, okay?"

Carter stepped in the elevator and turned around. "I don't have anything to off myself with, even if I wanted to."

It wasn't quite the reassurance I was looking for, but it was better than nothing. "You'll text if you need me?" I said.

"What for?" he asked. "You're not on my side."

The elevator doors closed.

I walked back outside to the car. "Can you take me the rest of the way home?" I asked Eddie. "I'm too demoralized to walk."

thirteen

THE NEXT FEW DAYS, as Carter and I went about our business, he ignored me as much as possible.

We had one important task remaining: an appointment with the orthopedist Lilly had recommended. Carter had taken to limping in a more pronounced way around me and complaining about pain in his shoulder, and I knew he was exaggerating, holding out hope that this appointment would get him out of the theater contract. I, on the other hand, was hoping for a clean bill of health. I understood Carter's thinking: a diagnosis from a renowned knee surgeon would surely be enough to prevent a lawsuit and the destruction of his professional reputation, but I couldn't sit there and hope to hear that Carter's knee was severely and possibly permanently damaged.

Eddie picked us up and drove us through Central Park and all the way to the East River to the Hospital for Special Surgery. Sitting with me in the backseat, Carter kept his body angled away, looking either at his phone or out the window at the shops and bars along First Avenue, baseball cap low over his eyes. I wondered if he was worried, but I didn't dare ask.

After seeing how nerve-racking and unsettling it was to be out in public with Carter, I'd called ahead and explained to the hospital's patient advocacy service that I needed help with a high-profile patient. They assured me they could handle it, and they did: there were four security guards waiting for us in the drop-off area with a wheelchair for Carter. They escorted us inside and took us to the correct department.

I took a seat in the waiting area and got out the book I'd brought along. About two hours later, a nurse called my name, and I was brought into the examining room. *Did he ask for me?* I wondered. I walked in and saw Carter sitting in his paper hospital gown and felt, irrationally, I suppose, a wave of protective impulses. I stood by his side as the doctor, who acted as though Carter was just another normal, teenaged patient and I was just another mom, told us that both his knee and shoulder would fully recover over time. He needed physical therapy, but was healing well. No surgery was needed, and he would be dancing again after another month or so. With tremendous relief, I said something like, "That's great news. Thank you so much."

I had been in many doctors' offices with my own kids over the years and was so familiar with the underlying anxiety and fear of pain, that before I could even think to stop myself, I put my hand on Carter's back.

He looked disgusted and jerked away as though my hand had been full of poop specimens from the hospital lab. He glared at me. "Great news?" he yelled. "Are you stupid? If my knee were fucked, I'd be done with this whole thing."

I'm not sure which insult hurt my feelings more: his physical revulsion toward me or his calling me stupid. For a second I thought I might cry. I squeezed my eyes shut and inhaled deeply, refusing to let myself get upset in a hospital examining room just because this boy was wishing for a reverse miracle. "I'm not going to feel bad for celebrating your good health," I said, "so get over it."

The doctor made notes in his computer, acting as though nothing had happened. We waited silently while he finished and handed me referrals for physical therapy.

Security escorted us back to our car, and Eddie closed us into the backseat.

"The second we get to the apartment," Carter said, "book my fucking flight out of here."

"And how do you want me to pay for it? Charge it on my American

Express?" I started to laugh at my own joke, until I suddenly pictured all the rewards points I would get by charging what was close to a full year's tuition at Orbis. "I mean, if you give me cash, I'd be happy to put it on my credit card."

"Just book it."

Back at his apartment, I sat on the floor and counted out stacks of one-hundred-dollar bills until they added up to $34,000. Just to be safe, I took a cab home that night.

Two days later Carter was leaving. I went to his apartment and found him playing a video game in his room.

"Eddie's picking you up at two," I told him. "That's early, but traffic will be bad."

He didn't answer.

"Carter, just nod so I know you're hearing me."

"I hear you," he said. "I can't wait to get out of this piece of shit condo."

My keys were in my hand, and I felt like chucking them at his head. He had no idea how badly I would have loved to move my family right into this "piece of shit condo" as soon as he got on the plane.

"Any chance you'll let me book a return flight?" I asked.

"Don't bother."

I tapped my foot on the floor. "Carter—"

"No."

"But—"

"Don't bitch."

I wondered if he meant "Don't bitch" or "Don't, bitch," as I went to the office and got out my computer. I called to confirm the flight from Teterboro to Van Nuys airport at four o'clock. "No, no return," I told the woman. I texted Eddie to double-check the time he would pick Carter up and drive him to the airfield in New Jersey, and then I booked a car service in California to meet him when he landed. I called Owen, the housekeeper I'd interviewed, to let him know we wouldn't be needing his services after all. Owen was a man of low affect, so I couldn't tell if he was thrilled or disappointed to be out of this particular job.

I picked up my bag and keys and knocked on Carter's open door, where he was standing in his boxer briefs with ESPN blaring. He was trying to cram into his suitcase a huge pair of Nike high-top sneakers; they were named after him, his signature stamped across the soles.

"You're all set," I said. "Do you want me to go with you to—?"

"Fucking *fuck*," he yelled. I stepped over to help him. Jack had more life skills in his pinky than this kid.

"Roll the socks up first and stuff them in your shoes," I told him. "And . . . here." I took out a pile of shirts that he'd shoved in and started folding them one at a time on the bed: Cucinelli, Tom Ford, Zegna. "Jeesh, who buys your clothes for you anyway?" I asked. "I mean, do you *need* stuff this pricey? Haven't you ever heard of Urban Outfitters?"

"People give me shit all the time," he said.

"Seriously? That's cool." I wondered what they expected in return. An Instagram post? An endorsement?

I emptied the rest of the suitcase and made neat piles of his things, just like I did when I helped my kids pack for camp.

I put the Carter-edition Nikes in a plastic bag in the bottom of the suitcase, followed by Rag and Bone jeans and Balmain cargo pants. Then I layered the designer shirts and Calvin Ts on top. Rolled up his boxers and popped them into the corners. Dsquared² asymmetrical leather jacket folded carefully on top. There was room to spare; I'm an efficient packer.

I reached in my purse, still filled with condoms, and pulled out the cash I had left over from the stack of bills he'd given me. I held out my spreadsheet that showed all expenses I'd incurred.

"What's that?"

"An accounting of exactly how much money I spent. And the three hundred twenty-seven dollars leftover."

"Keep it," he said.

"What for? I already took the thousand you said you'd pay me."

He didn't answer.

"Aren't you going to look at my spreadsheet?"

"No."

"It's very accurate. And I organized it by specific categories of expenses. Maybe your tax guy will want to see it for deductions?"

I held the papers out, but he wouldn't take them; my Excel skills were clearly not impressing him. "How about you just bring it along?"

"When's my flight?" he asked, typing in his phone.

"Eddie's picking you up at two," I told him again. "And a driver will meet your plane in L.A. to take you home. I've got Skittle's smaller container ready for the trip, and you'll have to get her set up in a real one as soon as you get her home. I called a pet store and told them what you need. They're delivering everything tomorrow at noon. I wrote out a list so you'll know exactly what's coming and stapled it to the spreadsheet. And I found the name of a vet not far from where you live."

He never looked up from his phone but mumbled, "Thanks."

Thanks? *Thanks?* That was a first.

"And this?" I asked, holding out the money again.

"I said to keep it."

"Thank you," I said. I saw an opening and figured I may as well try one last time: "So you're an adult and can do whatever you like. Obviously."

"Yeah."

"Please call a physical therapist when you get home. Promise?"

He didn't say anything.

"For the record," I said, "if you were to change your mind, I think you'd be really great in that musical, and I think you should go home, catch your breath, have some fun—not too much fun, of course, but a little—check in with your agency and your lawyer, and then come back to start rehearsals in January. Just text me, and I'll book a flight for you. I can help, you know." He didn't say anything. "It could be fun."

"I'm not coming back here," he said, "so hop off my dick, all right?"

I sighed. "Is that supposed to *mean* something?"

"Means back off."

"Sure, okay," I said, "but just allow me to—" and at that, he got up and walked out of the room. "For what it's worth," I said, following him, "I think you could play the part brilliantly. You'd be terrific!" I stopped in the hallway and then raised my voice a little louder, saying, "I think you could wow everybody." I knew he wasn't listening, and I was sorry that that glimpse of his back was the last I would ever see of him.

As a last-ditch effort, I went back to his room, reached in my bag, and took out the copy of the script I had made and bound for him. I re-opened the Porsche suitcase and placed it neatly on the top of his leather jacket before zipping the bag shut again. Then, as an afterthought, I took all the condoms Sara had given me and zipped them in a side pocket.

When I walked into the kitchen and through the living room, Carter was nowhere to be seen. I called out "Goodbye" and waited, hoping for some kind of closure. Not a hug, obviously, but something. Anything. In the entry I reached up to give Venus a pat on the knee, took a last look around the apartment, and left.

Part Three

FAMILY

"So you thought you wanted to observe life? Motherhood shakes her head, clenches her fist, and demands, No, you must live it."

Sarah Ruhl
100 Essays I Don't Have Time to Write

fourteen

THE TEMPERATURE AND MY MOOD took a steep nosedive after Carter left. Through the rest of October and into November, I had a tough time feeling positive. The subway smelled like pee. The wind became icy and brutal, and the entry of our apartment turned into a mudroom, piled high with boots, hats, single gloves, and backpacks, an assortment of things to trip over on our way in and out. Our tight quarters and high-rise living in general were making me feel claustrophobic. Since my mom was planning her house-hunting trip, I checked out Westchester County houses on Zillow for her the way some guys look at porn: as a fantasy, an escape from my current restrictive situation, something fun to look at that I couldn't really have.

Carter was still on my mind, and I sometimes surfed the Internet to find pictures or news of him. It seemed he'd practically gone off the grid, and I wondered who he was with, how he was spending his time. I texted him once *Hope all is well* but he never answered. I set up a Google Alert to email me if his name was in the news, but the only notifications I got about him were related to *Limelight*. His name, with Kevin Kline's and Annabella Hatter's, remained on every promotional poster, article, and magazine ad I saw.

I didn't limit my online stalking to Carter. I checked out all the members of the cast. There were pictures of Kevin with Phoebe Cates at the World Trade Center Memorial. And hundreds of Annabella in Los Angeles, heading into a Bar Method class in exercise tights, walking down the street with a green juice and a rescue dog, or wearing an adorable minidress to a film premiere. In every picture, she looked healthy and energetic. She drove a white Tesla and insisted that Supercharger stations were "super-convenient." She had landed the December cover of *Cosmopolitan* and a campaign for Maybelline, ads that showed off her dewy, flawless skin. And, I learned from *People* magazine, she had recently broken off a two-year relationship with a British film director. They had grown apart, she said, and she felt a need to focus on her career, wellness, positivity, and self-actualization. She was looking forward to spending time in New York and performing in live theater.

Just as Annabella was working on being positive, and just as I had counseled Charlotte during the Theo debacle, I finally decided to take my mind off Carter completely by looking forward—by committing to my family and to my life in New York. The holidays were approaching, and I wanted to make the best of them.

I called my mom to discuss her plans for Thanksgiving: she said she was flying to a little airport in Westchester County and staying at a bed-and-breakfast for four days, after which she would take Metro North to Grand Central and spend the whole week with us through Thanksgiving.

"How about I meet you up there for the last day, and we'll drive back to New York together?" I said. "You can have Jack's room while you're here."

"I'm not putting anyone out," she said. "I already got an Airbnb, not far from your apartment."

"You're not staying with us?"

"Houseguests are difficult, and I'm not coming to add complications. Honey, are you following Megan on Facebook?"

"Yeah, why?"

"Because some of her new friends seem a little fast."

"Are you stalking my kids on social media?" I teased.

"I'm keeping in touch with my grandchildren through a very convenient medium. And I think Megan's getting influenced by some girls who maybe aren't the best characters. Have you met any of them? Like this girl Lizzie?"

"No, but she mentioned Mason," I said, feeling guilty that I wasn't better informed.

"Is that her first name or her last?"

"First."

"Haven't heard about her yet. Anyway, you should keep tabs on these girls: like Lizzie, and there's another one—"

"It's hard enough trying to keep tabs on my *own* girls," I said. "I don't see how I can police the whole class."

"You're right," she said. "But I can help."

—

Waking kids up for school is by far the most heinous part of parenting. I'm not a morning person, and I discovered soon after I had kids that being a morning person is the single best quality a parent can possibly have. I wake up every day feeling like I've been run over by a slow-moving truck. Michael has always been better at mornings. He's able to pull off basic responsibilities that are hard for me, like hearing the alarm, getting out of bed, making coffee.

This particular morning, I woke up to the sound of Michael singing the Rolling Stones' "Beast of Burden" in the shower, and I sat up sluggishly, trying to get ready to face the day. Charlotte was still refusing to show me her personal essay for her college applications, and I was wondering how much her list would have to change given her current grades, what safety schools she would need to add. Megan was doing better in school but still needed a tutor in math. She had her first sleepover party at a classmate's coming up. And Jack was consumed with starting a dog-walking service in our building, and since he couldn't walk dogs alone at his age, I was his default business partner.

"Let's go see some jazz this weekend in Greenwich Village," Michael said from the bathroom, way too cheerfully for this early in the morning. "Let's do something fun."

I flopped back on the pillows.

He came in, rubbing his hair with a towel. "Up and at 'em."

"Can you wake up the beasts?" I asked.

He went out of our room, and I heard him in the hallway rousing the kids. He never woke them up in a sunny, silly way, like dads do in the movies. No singing songs or tickling anyone. He would knock on the first door, crack it open, and say, "Hey, time to get up, let's go, let's go," and on down the line.

He made coffee and came back to find me in the exactly the same position I was in when he left.

"Don't be too pokey this morning," he said. "What time's our appointment?"

I didn't tell Michael, but until he mentioned it, family conferences had slipped my mind completely.

"Not until nine o'clock. I'll be ready." I got out of bed, stretched, and said, "This oughta be fun."

"I'm detecting sarcasm," he said.

Megan wandered in in her pajamas. "I have a headache," she said.

"No you don't," Michael said, kissing her on the top of her head.

Megan turned to me. "Can I stay home?" she asked. "I have a stomachache."

"Come here," I said. Megan was always willing to be hugged.

"Don't make me go," she said. "Let's just blow it off."

"Sweetie." I've never gotten over how wonderful my kids can be when they want something from me. "There's nothing to be worried about."

"We can stay home instead, and I'll keep you company all day," she said. "We'll bake cookies."

"Megan."

"Please? Please, don't make me. I'm too nervous."

"You've been working so hard. What could you possibly be nervous about?"

She shrugged. "No reason."

———

We called an Uber, dropped Jack at school, and then went to Orbis with the girls. While we waited in the modern, sterile lobby, I noted once again the lack of art on the walls, of any sign of creativity or joy of learning. I shuddered. The first time we saw the school, I had thought the barrenness and lack of character was due to a massive summer cleaning effort, but here we were in mid-fall, and the only decor was an engraved plaque of donor names.

"Prepare yourselves for mediocrity," Charlotte said and walked toward the stairs.

"It still reminds me of a bank," I whispered.

"Or an insurance firm," Michael said. He was dressed for work, carrying his briefcase, and he fit into the surroundings better than Charlotte did in her jeans and Everlane 100% HUMAN sweatshirt.

Charlotte's appointment was first, so Megan took a book out of her bag and sat in a sleek leather chair in the lobby, where other families were milling around. Michael, Charlotte, and I climbed the stairs silently in single file.

"Hey, Charlotte," a girl said as she came up behind us with her parents. "Is that your little sister in the lobby? She's so cute."

"Not really," Charlotte said.

"She's not really your sister?" the girl asked, laughing.

"Right," Charlotte said. "I wish."

The girl and her parents went through the door to the third floor.

"Who was that?" I asked.

"No one."

"That wasn't very nice to say about Megan," I said.

"It's called *humor*," Charlotte said. Several more kids passed us and said hi to her.

"I thought you said no one likes you here," I said.

She shrugged and led us to the classroom. Before we walked in she turned to us, with her hand on the doorknob. "Don't say *anything* unless you absolutely have to."

Charlotte's advisor was a heavyset physics teacher named Mr. Callahan who greeted us warmly, which surprised me, given Charlotte's chronic foul temper.

"Come in, come in! Welcome Brinkley clan!" His bow tie was pointed up and down instead of side to side, and his upper lip was sweaty. He arranged us around a lab table and took a seat on a stool. He and/or the room had a chemical smell that made me queasy.

"Let's jump in," he said.

"I just want to say," I started, "that we know this move has presented a tremendous challenge for Charlotte."

"*Mom*," Charlotte hissed.

She didn't deter me: "Any difficulty she's having adapting is really our fault."

"Texas, huh?" Mr. Callahan asked us. "The ol' Lone Star State? Home of Bonnie and Clyde. Pow-pow," and he pretended to shoot Charlotte with his finger. "Remember the Alamo! Charlotte tells me the fam's going back over the winter break. How about I come along? Eh, Charlotte?" He waited for her to laugh.

"Ha," Michael said awkwardly. "Right."

Mr. Callahan smiled. "The students love my bad jokes. The dumber, the better."

What a dolt, I thought.

"Anyway," Charlotte said, straightening her glasses.

He slapped his hands on his thighs. "I'll kick things off by saying how happy I am Charlotte's joined us. What a terrific young lady. She's doing so good. She's caught on to things very quick, learned how to use the online homework portal, how to make appointments with her teachers. Really, she's doing super. Smart as heck."

"Okay," I said, shaking my head. "But . . ."

"No, it's all good. Her teachers say that she's participating in class, getting very comfortable with her peers. Her homework's always perfect. Here," he said, handing me her progress report. "I assume she showed you this already."

Michael and I each took a side of the piece of paper he gave us and scanned it. I saw a long row of numbers: "11/11, 24/24, 13/13, 35/35 . . ." "What? What is this?" I said. "I don't understand."

"Quiz scores, test scores, class participation, all that fun stuff," Mr. Callahan said. He turned to Charlotte. "Didn't you show your parents your grades?"

Charlotte shrugged.

"Thirteen out of thirteen?" I asked. "You mean, like, one hundred percent?"

"It's all really easy," Charlotte said. "I've done most of it before."

"She could pretty much teach here," Mr. Callahan said. "I'm keeping the old fingers crossed for college placement."

Nothing that came out of this man's mouth was making me feel any better about the school, and I was feeling baffled and frustrated by Charlotte.

"This isn't surprising," Michael said. "She got straight As at her last school. She's always been an excellent student."

"This *is* surprising," I said, correcting him and handing the paper back to the teacher. "Charlotte told me everything's going terribly."

"Excuse me?" said Charlotte.

"Your transcript is a 'mess,' you said. You're 'failing.' This move is the worst thing that ever happened to you, right? That's what you've been telling me."

"I never said I was *failing*," Charlotte said. "You weren't listening."

"I was too," I shot back. "You said you—"

"Whatever," Charlotte said. I thought I detected a slightly guilty look pass over her face as she fiddled with the end of her braid.

Mr. Callahan looked uncomfortable on his stool. "Anyhow," he said, "like I was saying, she's really been a terrific addition to the class. She's starting a, um"—he looked at his notes—"'robotics and coding club' for the underclassmen for her community service project, and the kids are just thrilled about it. I don't know much about coding or any of that, so Charlotte's really leading the charge, signing the group up for competitions already. We should put her on the payroll."

"I don't understand," I said, hoping Charlotte would jump in with an explanation. "This doesn't jibe with what she's been saying, how she's been acting at home."

"*Jibe?*" Charlotte asked.

"But this is wonderful to hear," Michael said, picking up the sheet of grades again, focusing on outcomes rather than attitudes, which I couldn't seem to do at the moment. "Wonderful. Outstanding. A surprise, sure," he added, as a way of acknowledging my feelings, "but great news. All's well that ends well."

"What?" I asked him. "Whose side are you on?"

"Oh, no need for sides!" Mr. Callahan said. "We're just having a chitchat."

"Apparently I'm in trouble for getting straight As," Charlotte said smugly.

"You're in trouble for being manipulative," I said, "and dishonest."

"*Mom!*"

"Allison," Michael said, putting his hand on my knee.

"Mrs.—"

"She's been saying she was miserable ever since we moved," I told the teacher. I turned to Charlotte again. "Did I miss something? I get that you're not challenged, but you told me that moving here had ruined your life. How do you think that made me feel?"

"Oh my god," Charlotte said, crossing her arms across her chest. Her sweatshirt now read 0 HUM. "Let's just make *my* school conference all about you."

"It just would have been nice to know that you're doing okay," I said. "That you're thriving."

"Well, then, all to the good because she's doing great!" Mr. Callahan said. "This is all good. Like I said, she's a super-duper addition."

"Okay, Allison?" Michael asked. "This is good. She's doing super. Duper."

I looked at all three of them and clenched my jaw. "Just so you know," I said to the teacher, "I'm a very supportive parent."

Charlotte smirked. "That statement doesn't exactly *jibe* with your behavior today, just saying."

———

After that fiasco, which left me simultaneously relieved and upset, Charlotte took the subway home by herself, without even saying goodbye. We got Megan from the lobby and went with her to the middle school floor.

Her teacher was slow-moving and distracted, with a permanent look of boredom on her face. She spoke in a dull monotone.

"Megan's trying hard," she said vaguely. "And there's been a big improvement in her grades." She looked through a stack of papers in her file but couldn't find what she was looking for. She found another file and rifled through it. "I know it's here somewhere," she said, walking over to her desk. "Ah!" she said finally and handed us a report for English class: "10/20, 12/18, 3/5, 8/10, 17/20."

"So she really is improving," I said. "That's great. Can you show me the rubrics for some of these assignments?"

"The what?" she asked.

I glanced at Michael. "The expectations for the assignments," I said, trying not to sound condescending.

"Well," she said, shuffling the papers around on her desk again, "I'll have to email you." Her phone rang. She looked at us and said, "Do you mind?"

We shook our heads and watched while the teacher took a call, listening for a moment and then saying, "I'm actually with some parents right now, so I can't really talk."

Michael looked at me, his eyes asking, *WTF?*

I watched the teacher in disbelief, waiting for her to say something that indicated an emergency at home, a house fire, maybe, or a sick child in need of medical attention. Instead—

"Oh my *god*, I can't wait to hear the whole story. Yeah, I'll call you back in a few minutes," she said to the caller. "Uh-huh, yeah, no, I know, right? I want to go over the invites again. Okay, later."

She looked up at us. "Where were we?"

"You were saying—"

"I'm getting married, so my life is, like," she waved her hands around her face, "*aahh*, crazy right now."

"So you'll send me the rubrics?" I reminded her.

"An upward trajectory," Michael said, and patted Megan on the back. "This is great news."

Megan smiled faintly.

"Right, but there's something else we need to talk about," the teacher said and turned to Megan. "Did you tell your parents about the incident?"

"Not yet," Megan said, squirming in her chair. "I didn't really get a chance to."

"What incident?" Michael asked.

"Some of the girls at lunch pointed out, the, um, physical attributes of another girl, and that was the beginning of some very unkind conversations."

Megan was on the cusp of tears. Michael noticed as well and gave her a hug.

"What did they say to you?" I asked. I looked at Megan's newly but quickly developing breasts, her broken-out face, and felt my heart start to race in anger. "Oh, honey," I said.

"Megan, do you want to explain what happened?" the teacher asked.

Megan shook her head, tears now streaming down her face.

"What is it?" Michael asked her. "Someone was mean to you?"

"Sometimes eighth-grade girls," the teacher said, "for whatever reason, can be a little cruel."

"Well, let's not make excuses for them," I said. "If someone was bullying my daughter, they were bullying her, and there should be consequences. She's new here, for goodness' sake, which makes this even worse for—"

"Mom—"

"What was done about it? Were steps taken?" I turned to Megan. "I wish you'd told me, you poor baby—"

"Excuse me," the teacher said, cutting me off as I leaned over to hug Megan, "but Megan wasn't the one being bullied."

Michael looked up. I looked at Megan. Megan looked at the floor.

———

We walked to Union Square together in silence and sat side by side on a bench, Megan in the middle. It was too cold to be sitting outside, so the park was the perfect spot to process what had happened; we were all alone.

"Explain yourself," I said.

Megan started to cry again.

"This isn't like you," Michael said. "You don't have a mean bone in your body. Why would you gang up on another girl?"

"There's no excuse for this," I added. "And it's just so out of character."

"All these girls—" she started.

"I don't want to hear the rest of that sentence," I said. "I don't care what all the other girls were doing. Come on, Megan! This is *you*."

"This was about her *weight*?" Michael asked.

"I didn't even know what is was about at first. One of the girls said I should ask this other girl to put her arm up and wave, and I said okay. But I didn't know what it was for."

"But when you realized . . ."

"Her arms jiggled, and we started laughing," Megan said.

"You laughed at her?" Michael asked, horrified.

"And the girl you were picking on?" I asked. "I'll bet she wasn't laughing."

Megan shook her head and pulled her coat tighter around her.

"That poor girl," I said. "And then what?"

"And then we were talking about it to some other kids, because she gained— I mean, they were saying she's changed a lot since last year, and I guess she knew we were making fun of her."

"You're going to apologize. You're going to invite her over, and you're going to tell her how deeply sorry you are."

"I'll say sorry," Megan said, her teeth chattering, "but please don't make me have her over. We're not even friends. It would be so weird."

"I don't care how *weird* it feels; you have to make it up to her."

"Megan," Michael said. His disappointment was palpable. "*Never* pick on people, right? We've talked about this over dinner I don't know how many times: the cool kids are always the nice, smart ones, the ones who never need to make someone else feel bad."

"You, being *mean*?" I said. "That's not who you are."

Megan shrugged.

"I'm calling this girl's mom," I said. "What's her name?"

"No!" Megan argued. "Just let me do it. I'm almost in high school already. I can handle my own apologies."

"But this is really serious," Michael said. "You could have gotten suspended for bullying. *Suspended!*"

"We stopped as soon as she started crying," she said, as if that made this better.

Michael got up and picked up his briefcase. "You've got until seven o'clock tonight to think this over, Megan, and you need to have something more thoughtful than *that* to say by the time I get home."

———

Megan wasn't the only one who had a lot of thinking to do. I felt completely knocked off balance by both of my daughters, and I spent the day trying to figure out what I needed to do to get back on solid ground with them. Wasn't I supposed to know them better than anyone? Inside and out? So why did I feel as though I needed to be introduced?

Charlotte, Megan, and I had a somber, quiet day together, reflecting privately on our collective mistakes and, I hoped, on the value of knowing you belong to a family that loves you in spite of all of them.

fifteen

MY MOTHER CALLED AT EIGHT IN THE MORNING from Bedford, New York, to say that she was checking out of her bed-and-breakfast at ten and would be reading in the parlor until I arrived. "Don't rush," she said. "Drive safely, text me whenever you get here, and I'll come out."

She was a practical packer, so I wasn't surprised when the front door of the inn opened, and she appeared with a tote bag and a compact rollaboard. She was wearing a gray turtleneck and jeans tucked into sturdy boots.

"Hi, Mom," I said, hopping out of the car to hug her and putting her bags on the backseat. "Nice boots."

"I love a lug sole," she said. "They're indestructible," and she stomped one foot on the ground to demonstrate.

She got into the car, holding her wool coat on her lap. Okay, then," she said, smoothing her short hair and getting her phone out. "I've narrowed down the twelve places Leigh showed me to three houses I want you to see."

I started the car and turned on the heat as she entered the first address in her phone. "I have a favorite," she said, "but I won't tell you which one it is because I don't want to prejudice you one way or the other."

"So do you like it here? Are you taking this seriously?"

"Of course I'm taking it seriously. I didn't come up here to waste Leigh Miller's time."

"My realtor in Manhattan said he'd be happy to—"

"No, Allison," she said firmly, "it's a suburb of New York City, or I'm staying exactly where I am."

"I'm afraid we'll never see you."

"I'm seeing you now, aren't I?" she said. "And you'll be in Dallas in a few weeks, so that will be twice in four months. And that's with us living fifteen hundred miles apart. So one would think we could do better than that if there's nothing but a train involved. See, there's the little station. Take a right up there at the stop sign. How are the kids?"

"Well," I said, "Jack is doing well. We're taking care of the class hamster over Thanksgiving. But Megan and Charlotte . . . Those conferences were pretty rough."

"I had a feeling something was going on with Megan," she said. "I sound old-fashioned, I'm sure, but I don't like the way these girls put themselves out there online."

"It's not old-fashioned," I said as I drove toward the intersection. The leaves were completely gone and the area definitely had lost some of its appeal without them. "Some of the kids at her school are perfectly nice. There's a sleepover party tonight with one of them."

"Trust but verify," she warned, waving a finger in the air. "You need to talk to the mom who invited her. Take a left up here."

"I already called her," I said, "and she seems lovely. She's Italian, Francesca or Federica or something. I think maybe the girls were testing, like they're toughening themselves up for high school."

"I don't remember you going through a phase like this. Or Charlotte, either."

"Charlotte is going through her own awful stage. She barely speaks to me anymore. Everything I do annoys her."

"She's getting ready to fly the coop and probably wants to assert her independence. I'm not worried about Charlotte. How's the college thing going?"

"Fine, I guess. She doesn't tell me anything." I fumbled with the knob for the fan.

"Too hot or too cold?"

"Hot," I said.

"And what's happening with finding a new school for Megan?"

"We're almost done. She has two public school appointments this week, an interview at Beacon, and an observed group activity at McCourt. Then we wait to find out."

"I'll be keeping my fingers crossed. Right there," she said. "That's the driveway."

I saw Leigh Miller, bundled up in a lavender puffy coat, standing on the front stoop of a little bungalow. We got out of the car and went up the walkway to meet her. She was much peppier than the last time I'd seen her, sensing, I supposed, the real possibility of a sale. I decided I would play bad cop.

The first house she showed us was cute on the outside but very dark and way too cramped on the inside. The plus side for this one was the proximity to town, a five-minute walk.

My mother was standing stiffly, and I could tell from her body language that she wasn't at home and couldn't picture herself living there. Seeing her there, looking almost homesick, made me sad.

"I don't love it," I said. "It's a little gloomy, no?"

"Not much natural light," she said.

Leigh started explaining all the changes one could make to brighten up the house. "The trees could be trimmed outside, and this window here—"

But my mom interrupted, saying, "No, I agree with Allison. This one's not right."

We left my car there and went with Leigh to the second house, which I liked even less than the first. It was the most unattractive house on a street of gorgeous homes. "It's got a lot going for it," Leigh said.

"Yeah, like it's the last place in the neighborhood anyone would think to rob," I whispered.

"It's an ugly duckling," my mom said as we walked into the entry. "But there's potential, no? Come look at the family room. If you can look past the shag carpet and cottage cheese ceiling . . ." She led me into a room big enough for a grand piano and a reading corner.

"I see your point," I said, "but . . ."

"Your lack of enthusiasm speaks for itself," she said and pulled her handbag up on her shoulder.

"Have I hurt your feelings?" I asked. "Was this one your favorite?"

"I'm not telling you!" she said. "I want your honest opinion."

We got back in the car, and I sat in the backseat while my mother and Leigh chatted like old friends. Leigh was talking about her niece, who was about to have twins and had gone into false labor twice. "It's just Braxton Hicks," Leigh said, "but it can be hard to tell the difference."

"Twins," my mother said. "My goodness."

I didn't pay much attention to where we were going, preferring to look at the passing houses, churches, and schools out the window and enjoying the feeling of being taken along for a ride and not the one responsible for getting us anywhere.

A few minutes later we pulled up to a gorgeous shingled three-story home. My heart leapt, the way it does when one falls in love at first sight. What struck me most was the left side of the house, which had a rounded porch on the ground floor with a second level above it and then a turret crowning the top of the tower. There were massive twin oak trees in front of the house; one had a tire swing hanging from a branch. There were dormers in the attic.

"That's a whole lot of house for a single person," I said, "but wow, it's beautiful."

My mother turned around to the backseat and saw that I was looking out the right window. "Not that one," she said. "That one," and she pointed to the house on our left.

The home across the street was as charming as the large one was spectacular.

"I can understand the confusion," Leigh said. "They both happen to be for sale, but this one is much more in line with your mom's wish list. Mature landscaping in the front, a boxed vegetable garden in the back, three bedrooms plus a cozy study. Only a mile from the town center."

We got out of the car, and I looked at the handsome, symmetrical little house. The freshly painted blue front door was framed by wide bay windows. Leigh opened it, and we walked across the pale bleached hardwoods, past the living room and dining room, to the kitchen in the back. There was a downstairs master bedroom with French doors opening onto a porch. We went upstairs, and I saw that the brushed nickel hardware of every cabinet, every drawer, every door in the house matched. The wallpaper was tasteful and modern, and the whole house had a light, airy feel.

"What do you think?" my mother asked.

"I can see you here," I said, taking in the beautiful bathroom fixtures. "I can absolutely see you happy here."

Leigh smiled and said, "I can't even begin to tell you how pleased I am to hear it."

I followed my mom back down the stairs. Her shoulders were relaxed, and I half expected her to take me to the kitchen to make us tea.

"While we're at it," Leigh asked, "should I see if I can show you the house across the street?"

"Oh, no," my mother said, dismissing the idea. "The scale of this one is much more appropriate, and you've given me plenty to think over now."

"I meant for Allison," Leigh said. "Her family would need a home that size."

I could see the house out the living room window, spotted an orange soccer ball sticking out from underneath a hedge.

"I don't think so," my mother said. "She and her husband just settled in Manhattan, and they're quite fond of it."

"Yeah, it's not the time," I said, looking at the turret and the yard with longing.

"Well, don't wait too long," said Leigh. "Houses around here get snapped up pretty quickly."

———

That afternoon my mom and I drove into the city, talking through the pros and cons of the house she'd found, the town she'd discovered, and moving in general.

"And what have we got planned in New York?" she said.

"A long, touristy to-do list. I hope you've got good walking shoes."

By the time we'd parked the car, gone to her Airbnb (a tiny but darling apartment on Seventy-First), and then walked to our apartment, Megan was already at her sleepover. Michael had taken her to her new friend's enormous apartment and had spoken at length with the mom;

Benedetta had a lovely Italian accent, he said, seemed warm and friendly, and was "very attractive."

"Oh, really?" I said.

"She invited me to stay for a glass of prosecco, but I had to say no." He'd come home instead to take Jack over to Lauren's house. Charlotte, meanwhile, had gone to a science fair in Princeton, and the school van wouldn't bring her back until around ten.

My mother gave Michael a jar of honey she'd bought in Westchester. "Well now, Mr. Human of New York," she said, letting him know that she was very impressed, "I get the feeling that living here has exceeded your expectations."

Michael showed her around the apartment and then called an Uber to take us to a French bistro on Madison called Pascalou. The whole way there, he pointed out landmarks along the way.

"This isn't her first time in New York," I reminded him.

"I know," he said, "but it's her first time here with us."

I held his hand.

The hostess seated us in the quiet dining room upstairs. It was the first real meal my mother and I had eaten that day, and the food was divine. Michael wanted to hear about the houses we'd seen and asked the kind of questions that didn't interest me in the slightest, like "Does it have a slab foundation, then, or a crawl space?"

When he got to "How many gallons in the hot water heater?" I decided to change the subject, breaking the news of my experiences with Carter Reid and telling her everything there was to tell, from his bad attitude in general to his refusal to do the play.

"So *that's* what you've been up to. *Limelight*?" she said. "I remember beautiful music in that movie. What did you think of it?"

"I haven't seen it yet."

"Allison," she said, clearly disappointed. "You wouldn't teach a novel to high school students that you hadn't bothered to read."

"I don't see the point in watching it now," I said. "He's gone."

"You absolutely should because it's a wonderful film. Were you firm with him? Did you explain that he has to live up to his obligations?"

"She tried," Michael said. "Allison tried for weeks to convince him."

"And what did the kids think of him?"

"We never told them," I said. "He was recuperating, limping around, and in a grouchy mood all the time."

"Well, I feel very sorry for him," she said. "I think he needs tough love and a hug."

I laughed. "A hug? Would you hug a cat that's hissing at you?"

"Never," she said, "but that doesn't mean it's not what the cat needs."

———

We took a cab back to my mom's Airbnb, and then Michael and I walked home. The second we went in, I got my laptop and bought the movie *Limelight* on Amazon.

"Ready?" I asked.

Michael got into bed with me to watch it while we waited for Charlotte to come home. After fifteen minutes, he was sound asleep. I watched it on my own, imagining Kevin Kline as Charlie Chaplin sweeping Annabella Hatter off her feet. I was trying to picture Carter as the quiet, impoverished, sincere composer. It would have been a reach for him, to be sure.

Maybe Carter had been right after all. Maybe, I thought, he'd done the right thing to walk away from a part he wasn't suited for. Maybe things had turned out for the best.

I wondered what he was doing, how he was spending his time. I hoped he was happy.

———

One of the best parts of having my mom in New York was that it turned me into a tourist. I took her everywhere, to the Whitney, the New Museum, and the Guggenheim. We went on a frigid walk on the Highline, saw an art exhibit at a Chelsea gallery, and attended a New York Philharmonic concert at Lincoln Center. We went to Ground Zero.

The Tuesday before Thanksgiving, the kids had the day off, and my mom was thrilled to put the sightseeing on hold and stay home with them. She came over that morning with a sweater she was knitting, the novel she was reading, and a board game she'd bought on the way over. I had made plans for her to go with Charlotte and Jack to the Metropolitan Museum, but no one wanted to go. "We just want to chillax at home, don't we, kiddos?" she said.

Jack was already sitting on the floor by the coffee table, setting up *Monopoly*.

"Exactly," Charlotte said.

If I had used the words "chillax" or "kiddos" in front of Charlotte, I would have gotten the world's biggest eye roll. My mother was given a pass for such crimes.

Megan had her appointment at Beacon that day, so I took her to the school, ready to answer any questions and to support her in whatever way I could, which turned out to be in absolutely no way whatsoever. There was no role for the parents in this exercise at all. We went into the building and checked in, and Megan went off to the interview with another applicant. I was dismissed. I was told I was welcome to go to the cafeteria to wait, which I did, thinking I might strike up a conversation with some of the other parents, hoping to learn more about the school, and specifically, just how likely it would be to get accepted. But as soon as I found a place to sit down, my phone rang from a number in Los Angeles. I picked up my purse and stepped to the side of the room to take the call.

I heard a click and then, "Skip."

I switched ears. "Sorry?"

"It's Skip from CAA."

"From where?"

"CAA. Carter's agency. Do we have a bad connection?" he asked.

"What happened to Simon?"

"Simon's his manager," he said slowly. "I'm with CAA."

"I don't know what that is." There was a pause.

"Creative Artists Agency. We represent Carter." I didn't say anything. "Jesus," he said, "Google it."

"Sorry, but there're a lot of people involved in his life." I moved to the far corner of the room by the empty kitchen so I could hear better. "How is he?" I asked.

"Well, at least he's agreed to go back to New York," said Skip.

"He has? *Seriously?*" I said, louder than I'd intended. A woman at the table closest to me gave me a dirty look and then turned back to her conversation with some other parents. I lowered my voice. "Are you sure?"

He exhaled loudly. "Well, I assumed you knew already."

"He hasn't mentioned it exactly, no," I said. I leaned against the wall, a dozen questions popping into my head, and asked, "Would it be okay if I call you back in about"—I checked the time on the cafeteria clock—"half an hour?" There was a long pause. "You see, my daughter Megan is—"

"Look, just make sure you get Carter to every single rehearsal on time. And try to keep him sober, if you can."

"Yeah, okay, but that's not— I mean, he doesn't really . . . listen to me."

"Well," he said with a harsh laugh, "you're going to need to fix that or hand your job over to someone who has some control over him."

"My *job*?"

"He's going back to New York right after Christmas and his rehearsals start the first week of January. So can you handle this or not?" he asked.

"He's not very enthusias—"

"Because he has to be there. Period."

Carter had accused me of not being on his side, so I decided to make an argument on his behalf. "Can I just ask: If he doesn't do it, like, how bad would that really be?"

There was no answer.

"Or to ask another way, what if he's right and this particular show wasn't such a good idea? What if it's the wrong move, you know, career-wise for him?" Again, a pause. I wondered if he'd hung up on me.

"Exactly what kind of experience do you have?" he asked, like I was a plumber who had been selected to do his kidney transplant. "I mean, how long have you been a PA?"

"A what?"

"Did he find you through Grapevine?"

"Sorry?"

Silence. And then he sighed hard. "Oh my god. Listen, right move, wrong move, that's all completely beside the point now. He committed. I don't know what you *think* your role is, but your job is to get him where he needs to be. The decision's been made already by people who know more than you do about the stakes involved, so that conversation's over, nor, frankly, was it ever any of your goddamn business. Your business is to get him to show up for the first rehearsal. That's the deal. Get him there. And if you can't, you're gonna have an unbelievable shit storm on your hands. Got it?" And the line went dead.

———

That night the six of us went out to dinner at the Smith, an American bistro near Lincoln Center where I was sure everyone in the family could find something they wanted to eat. The restaurant was noisy, but we got a round booth in the back that made it possible to talk. Charlotte was especially sulky, Megan kept getting her phone out, and Jack knocked over a water glass within the first five minutes of sitting down together. My mother hugged him.

I was completely preoccupied with thoughts of Carter.

"Tell me all about your friends here," my mom said. "Any nice boys?" and she gave Charlotte a wink, an act that would have been deemed unforgivable had I done it.

"I hate them," Charlotte said. "New York guys are the worst."

"I'm sure there are a few good ones," Michael said.

"Maybe," she said. "The head of the math department is, like, twenty-five, and he's awesome."

"Awesome how?" I asked, not appreciating the sly smile on her face.

"He's a super-cool nerd. He has a model of DNA tattooed on his leg."

"How do you even know that?" Michael asked.

"Yeah," I said.

"All the teachers have tattoos," said Charlotte. "My PE teacher has this wavy vine that goes around her bicep, and the Spanish teacher has a bird on her ankle."

"I don't get the appeal," I said flatly.

"God, it's not a big deal," Charlotte said. "I might get a tattoo."

My mother looked up from her tomato soup.

Megan rolled her eyes. "Don't take the bait, Mom," she said. "She's trying to get under your skin."

"She's not getting under my skin. She's not eighteen. So it's illegal. It's a totally moot point."

"They don't even check. As long as you have some kind of ID, they won't ask questions. The music director has a treble clef on his wrist," Charlotte told my mom, "but he got it backwards. Idiot."

"I guess he'll have to live with it," my mom responded.

"You're not getting a tattoo," I repeated, taking the bait after all.

"Not today," she argued, "not this week, but I'm thinking about it."

"No you're not."

"Yes I am."

"You could contract hepatitis," Michael said. "Or HIV. It's not safe."

"I would go to a reputable place, obviously," she said.

"They all use sloppy methods, dirty needles," I said.

Charlotte looked alarmed. As someone who had spent a good deal of her free time looking through a microscope, she was a germophobe.

"Well," she said, shaking it off, "it's my body anyway so why do you even care?"

"Megan, put your phone away," Michael said.

"Obviously I care," I said to Charlotte and took a big sip of my wine.

"We care," Michael said quietly, "which is why you don't get to decide this yet. Later in life you can do whatever you like, but for now the law protects you from making a decision you're simply not equipped to make yet."

"Good times," Charlotte said flatly.

"Yes, cheers," my mom added, ignoring the obvious sarcasm and holding up her glass. "Here's to New York, everyone."

Jack picked up his Sprite and clinked it against her wineglass, just hard enough to break it.

The waitress came over and brought our entrées, more bread, and a pile of napkins to clean up the mess.

My phone buzzed, and I checked it under the table, in case it was Carter. There was a message I didn't understand, something about photo-streaming, iCloud, and an automatic download. And I saw that several new pictures had appeared. I clicked on them, and there was Megan with the Orbis girls at her overnight party. They were fully made up and leaning into the camera provocatively, showing their cleavage in tiny tank tops, and making that stupid duck face. Two were holding lit cigarettes and Megan was holding a beer. "Oh my god," I said.

"Mom, 'put your phone away,'" Charlotte said, mimicking a parental voice.

Michael looked at me. "What is it?" he asked.

I shook my head at him, turned off my phone, and looked up with a fake smile. "Nothing."

"Nothing?" my mom asked. "You've turned gray."

So far, Thanksgiving was getting off to a lousy start.

———

After dinner I took Michael back to our room to show him the pictures and figure out how we would address the problem with Megan.

"What's happening to her?" he said. He looked as traumatized as I felt to see these sexualized images of young girls, of our girl.

I asked Megan to come talk to us, and she sat nervously on our bed while I got my phone and handed it to her. She started crying right away, swearing that nothing was her fault and that the whole thing looked worse than it really was.

"How'd you find them?" she asked.

"Our Apple accounts are linked," I told her, "and you've got photo-streaming turned on. But that's hardly the point."

Michael started asking questions about how they got alcohol and lecturing her on the dangers of smoking and the problems with pictures on the Internet.

"I didn't want to be the only one who didn't go along with it," Megan said. "What was I supposed to do?"

"You could have called us to come to get you, and we would have been there in ten minutes," I said. "You could have told the mom, Francesca—"

"Benedetta," Michael said.

"—Benedetta that you didn't feel well. You could have made an excuse to remove yourself from the situation."

"Where on earth was she while you girls were doing all that?" Michael said.

"She went out."

"*Out?*" I asked.

"She was gone until after we went to sleep."

"Jesus," I said.

"But she was there when we woke up in the morning," Megan said defensively.

"Can you imagine?" Michael asked, looking at me.

"Leaving a group of eighth graders alone on a Saturday night?" I said, incredulous. "No, and Megan, you should have told us—"

"I know. I'm sorry," Megan said. "I'm really sorry."

"Anything else you need to tell us?" I asked. "This is a really good moment to come clean."

She shook her head. "No, nothing."

I wanted to believe her, but I realized we had entered a new phase, and I couldn't take her at her word anymore. And that realization made me as sad as the pictures themselves.

sixteen

I GAVE MYSELF A PEP TALK in the shower, deciding I would spend more time really listening to Megan, making sure she knew she could talk to me. I would consider Thanksgiving an opportunity to have constructive, positive conversations with my family.

At around ten, my mom came over. She played cards with Jack, while Arthur, the class hamster, tore up a cardboard toilet-paper roll and built a nest with it. Charlotte Instagrammed a picture of him surrounded by baby carrots with his cheeks completely filled up: *#HappyThxgiving #StuffYourFace*.

Megan, who was in a mopey mood, baked two pies she learned how to make in her class with Sabrina. I roasted the turkey and made mashed potatoes while Michael did his best to clean up behind us. The three of us did not easily fit in the kitchen.

As we all sat down at the table and passed the various dishes around, my mom said, "Well, I've made a decision that I'm ready to share with you all. I stayed up most of the night thinking it over, and I know what I want to do."

"That's exciting," I said and put my glass down, knowing I would feel guilty if she'd decided to stay in Dallas and guilty if she'd decided to move. And then I tried to correct my attitude: *No, I should feel happy for her if she likes Dallas so much that she wants to stay and happy if she's decided to be closer to us.*

"After a great deal of soul searching, I've decided to put my house on the market and move to Katonah."

"What's Katonah?" Jack said. "Can you pass the gravy?"

"Of course," she said, patting Jack on the back. "Now I know this may seem rushed, but the truth is: you were my home in Dallas. And with all of you gone it just doesn't feel right being there anymore."

"Ahhh, Gram," Megan said and leaned into her for a hug.

"You're giving up a lot for us," I said, feeling like I might start crying.

"Well worth it."

"I think that's great," Charlotte said. "Way to be bold, Gram. Moving all the way across the country? That's awesome."

"You're absolutely sure?" I asked.

"It feels right, what can I say?"

"I have an announcement as well," Michael said. "Trivial compared to Dorothy's, but I decided that for our trip to Dallas over the break, we're going to stay . . . at the Mansion."

Shit, I thought, realizing that Carter's supposed return to New York and our trip to Texas were exactly the same week.

Michael looked at us, waiting for our reaction.

"What mansion?" Jack asked.

"It's a very fancy hotel," Michael said, "with a spa and a great restaurant." He smiled at me. "It's a Christmas present for all of us, especially for you, Allison."

"Yay," I said weakly.

"Awesome," Charlotte said. "Do we have to share a room?"

"I don't mind sharing," Megan said.

Charlotte gave her a dirty look. "Kiss-ass."

Before I had a chance to say anything, Charlotte clinked her knife against her water glass. "And while we're all sitting around, sharing exciting and monumental news," Charlotte said, "I've got some, too."

"Please don't say you're getting a tattoo," I said.

"Not that," Charlotte said. "It's about college."

"Ah, wonderful," I said, passing the potatoes. "You want me to read your essay?"

"No."

"Charlotte," Michael said, filling my wineglass. "Your mom's a very good—"

"I decided to apply Early Action to Caltech," she said.

"Caltech?" I asked, dropping my fork, which clattered to the floor. "What happened to Hopkins?"

"I changed my mind," she said.

"But it's so far away! What about MIT?"

"Caltech," said Charlotte. "Early Action. That's what I decided. Not that I'm going to get in."

"You've got a very strong chance," Michael said. "If I were Caltech, I'd take you in a heartbeat."

"Thanks, Dad."

"*California?*" I asked.

"Yes, mom, California. Get over it."

"I love Southern California," my mom said. "Your grandfather and I honeymooned in Santa Barbara at the Biltmore."

I was still reeling and wondering how the West Coast had suddenly ended up at the top of Charlotte's list. It felt like a rejection. "But what about—?"

"I already made up my mind, Mom. And I'm scared shitless about it, so why can't you, for once in your life, just support me?"

"Fine," I said, picking up my glass of wine. "Caltech it is. So this weekend you can show me your essay. I'm happy to help edit."

"*Early Action,*" she said, like I was hard of hearing.

"I heard you."

"I sent my application in three weeks ago."

———

I spent the long weekend adjusting to the new normal: Megan was growing up way too fast, Charlotte was moving as far away as she could possibly get, and my mother was about to uproot her whole life again because of me. I was trying hard to see all three of these facts as positive developments, but it was hard not to feel anxious in the face of so much change.

———

Sunday morning, I did a very non–New Yorker thing: I took my mom to the airport in a cab. Jack came along for the ride. The traffic was terrible, and he played games on my phone the whole way there. I kept reminding him to look out the window, but he ignored me.

When we pulled up to the terminal, he helped with my mom's suitcase, and we made our way inside.

"How lovely that there's no need for drama," my mom said as we said goodbye. "I'll see you in Dallas in just a few weeks, and I'll schedule the move for the spring."

"You won't be mad at me?" I said and lowered my sunglasses.

"Why would I be mad?"

"Or resentful? For everything you're giving up there?"

"Every big step in life involves losses and gains," she said. "In this case, the gains far outweigh the losses."

"You're sure?"

She nodded. "But if you're planning to follow Charlotte to California, now would be a really good time to tell me. It seems to me that Michael is pretty set on staying right where he is."

"I keep thinking about that house across the street. Do you think we should—?"

"One thing at a time. For now, you should try to let your life take root. See you in a month, Jack," she said and gave him a big hug. "Let me know what you want for Christmas."

"I'm so glad you came," I told her. "Really, really glad."

She blew me a kiss as she went through security.

———

"I'm carsick," Jack said when we got back in a cab.

"Well, that's what you get for not looking out the window," I told him. I hated saying goodbye to my mom; it always made me feel homesick, like I was back in summer camp.

He handed me my phone. "Who's 'CR' anyway?" he asked. "Is this about our trip to Dallas?"

"What?"

"You got a message from CR."

I took my phone and saw the message: *Get plane. 12/26. Don't ask questions.*

seventeen

ON THE MONDAY AFTER THANKSGIVING, I found myself standing at the hostess podium of the restaurant in Bergdorf Goodman, handing over my heavy parka to coat check and arranging my hair.

"I'm meeting the Campbells," I said, trying to act as though I dined at five-star restaurants every day with New York fashion icons and business tycoons. I followed the hostess through the pale dining room and past tables overlooking a bleak Central Park. We stopped at the far corner in front of the Campbell siblings, Wilson and Kaye. Beautiful, blond, fit, and stylish, they stood up together to greet me. The couple at the next table was staring as I took my seat across from them.

I'd only had a day to prepare for this meeting, so I'd done some hasty research by reading a *Vanity Fair* article about them: the Campbells were glamorous, high-society entrepreneurs. They had built an empire with their massive inheritance, and no one could ever accuse them of being lazy or lacking ethics. Rather, they were involved in every level of their enterprise, from the designs of their outerwear line to the adherence to strict regulations in their factories. Now that their lifestyle company had made the Fortune 500 list, they were turning their attention to their other inheritance: their father and grandfather had been theater producers, and they'd grown up with the understanding that they would carry that torch forward.

I'd also learned that they didn't drink, they didn't smoke; their bodies were their temples. So while they were often in the tabloids, at galas and Broadway openings, they were always poised and elegant. Kaye was married to the CEO of a toy company, and Wilson had been named New York City's most eligible bachelor three years in a row.

They glowed with good health and fortune. As soon as I sat down, I noticed that Kaye was the more animated of the two, the more engaging. Wilson was cooler and harder to read; he had a habit of looking anywhere but at the person to whom he was speaking, even gazing out the window, giving the impression of being distracted although he was clearly paying attention. Kaye kept her eyes locked on me, leaving her diamond-studded phone on the table beside her. She was attentive and quick, making Wilson seem deliberate and steely in comparison. What struck me about them above all was their youth. *I could probably be their mother*, I thought.

"Great you could meet on such short notice," Kaye said. Wilson looked at me briefly and then turned his attention back to the Central Park trees he was watching out the window. "We were afraid it would have to wait until after the New Year," Kaye went on, "but given our mutual interest in the project, it seemed we might all feel some sense of urgency."

"I'm a fan," I said and instantly regretted it; I sounded provincial, pandering. "I mean, you're quite a team."

They didn't react.

"We try," Kaye said. "Our company is our baby, but producing new, exciting, first-rate musicals is what we're driven to *do*. It's in our blood."

"I don't know about driven," Wilson said coldly. "But we're in balls deep, regardless."

The menus came, and I reached for my purse to find my reading glasses. Wilson handed his menu back instantly. "We'll have the roasted cod," he said.

Kaye continued to look over her menu. "I don't know," she said. "I may want something different today. Maybe the ahi salad."

"You say that every time, and you always get the black cod."

"Just let me look. The scallops, maybe."

"Every time." He sighed.

"You're right," Kaye answered. "You're absolutely right. Allison? Black cod? It's light and comes on a bed of puréed parsnips."

I put my glasses back in their case. "Sure," I said. "Sounds great."

The waiter took our menus, filled our water glasses with Pellegrino, and left us alone. I noticed that the woman on my left was surreptitiously taking a picture.

"So," Kaye said. "How's the apartment working out? I assume Carter's happy with it? Our friend Steve really came through for us on that one."

"Steve?" I asked.

"It's been all over the tabloids," Wilson said. "I'm sure you know the background on this."

"I don't, actually."

"Steve Sloan," Kaye said.

"Oh," I said, recognizing the name. "That real estate guy?"

"As in the man who owns most of Manhattan," said Wilson. "He bought that penthouse for a so-called 'friend,' and it turned into a huge scandal. His wife found out about it, and her family threatened the mistress. They've got mob connections, so the girlfriend-slash-tenant packed up and fled home to Croatia, and the condo suddenly became vacant and available to us."

"Sounds like a Netflix show," I quipped.

"Steve agreed to rent the penthouse to the production for a reasonable fee in exchange for being named a producer on the musical," Kaye said. She leaned back and put her hands on the arms of her chair. "So. How did you end up working for Carter?"

I decided to interpret the phrase "working for" loosely.

"It's a long story," I said. "And it's pretty funny, actually. You see, I was driving—"

"Carter's very difficult," Wilson said, cutting me off abruptly.

"No," I said. "Well, yes, I suppose sometimes, sure, but not all the time. And, I mean, on some level, aren't we all?" *What?*

"He is," Wilson said. "He's difficult."

"What we'd like to know is," Kaye said, "what do you need from us? What kind of help or support can we provide?"

"Help with . . . ?"

"Handling him," Wilson said.

"Who have you worked for before?" Kaye asked.

"No one," I admitted. "I mean, no one like Carter, if that's what you mean."

"No celebrities?" Wilson asked.

"No."

Wilson, gazing out the window, followed up with, "So how did you become Carter's assistant?"

I shrugged, wishing I could say I'd interviewed well and beat out the competition, but I didn't see the point in lying. "Because I was . . . the only one there."

Kaye and Wilson looked at each other, and I could swear they were communicating telepathically: Wilson raised his eyebrows, and Kaye nodded.

"And the truth is Carter hasn't *officially* hired me. Yet."

"That's not what we were told," Kaye said, looking concerned.

"He needs a PA," Wilson said. "I assume you're planning to make it official soon."

"Of course she is," Kaye said condescendingly. "And we're here to support you, Allison, as you get him through this strenuous rehearsal period. You need to get him where he needs to be psychologically and physically. Keep him from where he shouldn't be socially and emotionally, avoid embarrassing scandals, promote positive exposure."

"Was the theater your idea?" Wilson asked.

I was lost. "You mean, doing the musical?"

"I mean attending *The Breakfast Club*," he said.

"That was brilliant," Kaye said. "So much good press came out of that. Put him in the best possible light. We were so pleased. I only wish we'd coordinated with Molly Ringwald's people. She went the very next night."

"I just thought it seemed like a good idea," I said, "to have him see what it's like."

"Exactly," said Kaye. "You showed him what it's like to get *good* publicity for once."

"No, I mean to know what Broadway is like," I said.

Kaye didn't seem to hear me; she checked her phone and put it down again. "In general, his social media presence is a disaster. His

Snapchat is nothing but drunken party clips, and his Twitter is a string of ignorant, uninformed, sexist, pathetic attempts at humor. Moving forward we want to promote the idea that Carter Reid actually has a brain, a life of the mind. That he reads books and subscribes to the *New Yorker*. That he's grown up, he's developed an appreciation for New York culture. That he donates to the Met. We've hired a publicist who will do all of his posts from now on. Carter isn't to interfere. Christ, you look confused."

Wilson smirked, and I tried to relax my face. I was completely baffled, and wanted to ask questions but worried I would sound as out of my depth as I felt. "You want to promote a new image."

"Obviously," Wilson said.

"I get that the whole out-of-control 'bad boy' thing is completely counterproductive," I said, "but what's wrong with a return to his pop-star image? Charming, magnetic, adorable?"

"He's too old to be 'adorable,' " Kaye said.

"He's *eighteen*," Wilson said, "and we know that he's not very bright, but he's playing a very smart, sophisticated character. So we have to do everything we can to make people see him differently. And we don't want him to say or do anything stupid—"

"Anything *more* stupid," Kaye corrected.

"—that embarrasses anyone involved in the production with him. Like us. Or Kevin."

I could understand Kevin Kline not wanting the reputation of the show brought down because of a night like Carter had in the fall, but I was offended by the idea of any child being labeled stupid. "Carter's actually very bright," I said, not sounding as confident as I wanted.

They looked at me, eyebrows raised, heads cocked, waiting for me to recant.

I was aware that of the three of us, I knew the least about business, marketing, branding, and social media, but their strategy seemed absurd and their opinion of him unfairly low. People, all people, it seemed, felt entitled to trash Carter's character in the harshest ways possible.

"This musical," said Kaye, "is a different world for Carter. It's a story full of emotion, with complex characters, not with 'types.' It's not just a theme strung together through a bunch of musical numbers. That's why we chose to produce it. We've meticulously managed every single element of this production, and we believe in it, deeply. Have you seen the film?" she asked me.

"Yes. And I've read the script."

"So you know the role of Neville is expanded somewhat in the musical. And Carter presumably realizes this is a reach for him, a serious challenge."

I didn't know what Carter realized, but I nodded.

"It's a moving story," she went on, "one that will have great popular appeal. Some members of the audience, the Chaplin fans, will come in with high and clear expectations. They'll expect to see a show as perfect as the classic film but brought back to life with a fresh perspective, one that honors his genius, and we can't disappoint them."

"Carter has to keep up with Kevin and Annabella," Wilson said. "They're both going to be excellent. And our concern is that as a defense, he'll self-destruct to shift the attention off of his lack of talent and onto his penchant for partying."

"He has talent," I said.

"But singing is *all* he can do," Wilson said.

"And dancing. Look, Carter can do this," I told them, even though I had absolutely no evidence whatsoever to back it up and didn't even know if he was planning to try. "You don't have to worry about him."

"It's our job to worry about him," Wilson said.

"We have a lot riding on this," Kaye added. "If it goes badly, our credibility on Broadway will be . . . You know what happened last year with *Dog Run*."

"That was yours?" I asked, as if I didn't know.

"Regrettably."

The *Vanity Fair* article had led me to a *New York Times* story that declared *Dog Run*, a Campbell Production, to be one of the fastest-closing musicals on Broadway, ever. It closed right after it opened and lost an enormous amount of money. Between PETA picketing outside the theater (due to the cast of dogs being forced to walk on their hind legs in restrictive costumes), the difficulty of training the dogs to do "dance" routines, and the awkward situation of having only four human cast members carry the romantic and corny story, the show was ultimately dubbed Broadway's biggest flop. It was a fiasco. One of the dogs took a messy poop onstage, giving the show the nickname "Dog Runs." I found one review in which the critic from the *New Yorker* begged, "For the love of God, someone euthanize this dog."

"It was an understandable miscalculation," Kaye said coolly. "Dogs are very popular in New York. We thought people would love it."

"I don't want to talk about it," Wilson said.

"The point is," Kaye went on, "this musical *will* be a success. It has TONY written all over it. We've chosen an iconic story, classic but still relevant. We commissioned songs from Max Martin." She waited for my reaction.

"Who?"

She glanced at Wilson and then spoke slowly. "Max Martin. He's *the* producer and songwriter for everyone from Katy Perry to Taylor Swift to, well, to Carter Reid. He writes hits. And with his help, we're going to have Broadway songs that are top singles."

"Aaron Sorkin adapted the film script," Wilson said. "It's modern while staying true to the original."

"And Edgar Sterling is directing. We've assembled an all-star A-list cast . . . and"—she sighed—"Carter. People will flock to see Kevin and Annabella onstage. And Carter, of course, has his own draw. He may not be an actor, but he'll appeal to a different demographic."

"But he has to show up," Wilson said.

"Every day. Every rehearsal. Every show. Every time," Kaye added.

"Of course," I said, grasping the seriousness of the task and the level to which they'd bankrolled this project. "I understand."

She leaned in and spoke seriously. "The character he plays, Neville, is a respectable man. He has manners, empathy, kindness, and intelligence. Old-fashioned dignity."

"Edgar has his work cut out for him," Wilson said smugly, "and he knows it."

"Carter needs the audience to be rooting for him. In spite of the circumstances, they should want him to get the girl in the end, to deserve her. So," she said, leaning toward me, "let's figure out what we need to get Carter to rise to the occasion. We'll hire as many people as you need. Handlers around the clock. Security to escort him to the theater, and home again. He'll need good food, lots of sleep."

"Absolutely," I said, hoping we were on the same side.

"Do you have children?" she asked.

"Yes, actually, I have—"

"Then you know what I'm talking about. He needs boundaries, sleep, and good, nutritious, raw foods. Is he a vegetarian?"

"I don't—"

"A pescatarian diet would be great for him," she went on. "Healthy body, healthy mind. Lots of omega-three. Flaxseed oil is essential; I'll send some over. And only small amounts of sushi," she said. "Not too much mercury."

"God, no," Wilson sighed.

"He should meditate and *tune in*," she said. "His frame of mind is everything. I have a guy who can work with him on quieting negative voices." She slid a business card across to me.

"He should drop gluten if he hasn't already," Wilson said.

"More tuning in," Kaye added, "and no partying. He's not to drink or smoke."

"Or fuck anything whatsoever," Wilson added. "No blow jobs. No hand jobs. No hookers, groupies, minors, or cougars." He looked at me without blinking. "No nothing."

I crossed my legs. "I'm supposed to keep him from having sex?"

"You're supposed to keep his hard-ons under control," he said.

I certainly wasn't expecting this professional meeting to get so embarrassingly intimate; the term "personal assistant" was taking on a whole new meaning.

Kaye placed her hands on the table in front of me. "We need you to ensure that for the next eight or nine months, our very expensive star is a goody-two-shoe, wholesome, mindful, meditating, kelp-eating, oxygen-breathing, nonsmoking, sober, celibate monk."

"After that," Wilson said, "I couldn't give a fuck what he does."

It was business for them, and Carter's long-term well-being clearly was not their concern. His short-term behavior was apparently all mine, and I was terrified by that assumption, knowing I had little to no control over him. I took a sip of my Pellegrino. "I've got this," I said confidently. "No problem at all." Maybe I was as good an actor as Kevin Kline because they simultaneously relaxed, as if they actually believed me.

"Who's getting him to Ripley-Grier every day for rehearsal?" said Wilson.

I had no idea what that meant. "Me?" I said, opening my purse, grabbing a pen and pad, and writing, "ribblygreer????" "And I'll talk to him about the rest, the rules and his behavior and image." And then I stated the obvious: "He's not going to like this."

"Of course he's not going to like it," Wilson said.

"He'll fight you every step of the way," Kaye said, "but I assume you're up for this or you wouldn't be taking the job. We get to run his life for him as long as he's in our production. Otherwise—to be clear—if he willfully ruins our show, we'll hold him accountable for every penny."

"He's contractually obligated to be our bitch," Wilson said.

"Have you heard our catchphrase?" Kaye said brightly. "On all the ads: 'And Carter Reid, like you've never seen him before.' It's intriguing, it implies that he's up to the challenge of live theater, that he's more than just a sexy pop star."

For the first time since I'd arrived, Wilson smiled at me. "Can you do this, Allison?"

The waiter approached and gently set down three gold-rimmed plates of black cod. I looked at my dish, knowing I wouldn't be able to eat.

Kaye smiled at me and raised her water glass. "Cheers."

eighteen

DURING THE SHORT STRETCH OF TIME between Thanksgiving and winter break, I felt like I was careening through an obstacle course in heavy fog.

Megan and I got her application and school materials submitted for the five public schools we'd chosen; the stakes felt especially high since I couldn't help but feel that Orbis was bringing out the absolute worst in Megan. In the thick of it, Michael took trips to Chicago and Atlanta for work, and Jack had a science project due involving walkie-talkies and huge amounts of tin foil that turned out to be massively time-consuming, environmentally irresponsible, and scientifically unsound. We started over from scratch with bean seeds.

Howard was in the final unit of his poetry class—a study of form, technique, and the terms used to talk about them—and was worried about his exam. We analyzed the poems he was assigned, and as the material got more difficult, he started showing me drafts of his essays to make sure he was structuring his arguments well. *If Rick could see me now*, I thought.

One day I asked Howard to read a sonnet out loud to me.

"Why?"

"It helps with comprehension," I said.

"I already understand it."

"Poetry is meant to be heard."

We were working on Shakespeare's "Sonnet 27," and when Howard started the first two lines, "Weary with toil, I haste me to my bed / The dear repose for limbs with travel tired," I was struck by his lovely voice.

"You read so beautifully," I said when he finished.

He smiled at me. "If there's one thing I understand, it's 'weary with toil,'" he said. "I can't wait to haste me to my damn bed."

"Try memorizing it," I said as we put on our coats.

"What for?"

"It's good exercise for your brain," I said.

He shook his head. "All right, teacher. You know best."

As he walked away I heard him mumbling the first line of the poem to himself.

Charlotte, meanwhile, was crazed, working on college application supplements in the event that Caltech rejected her. She was in a terrible mood all the time; I tiptoed around her and spoke only when necessary.

"Why are you always creeping around like that?" she said, when I quietly set a can of LaCroix water on her desk.

Even when I tried to stay invisible, I annoyed her.

"I'm truly looking forward to the day when you don't find it necessary to be so mean to me," I told her.

"Yeah? You and me both," she said.

I tried not to feel resentful as I went out to buy Christmas presents.

And then there was Carter. I'd reached out a few times, needing to know what was going on.

Finally, when I texted: *Got you a flight on 12/26 at 11:00 in the morning. PLEASE CONFIRM*, he answered: *Ya.*

That was the only response I got from him the entire time he was away. So it seemed he was, in fact, coming back, but I had no way of knowing if he was really planning to do the show.

When Michael returned from Chicago, I brought up the topic I'd been dreading: the trip to Dallas, the trip we'd planned almost six months before.

"Come on, Allison," he said, sounding exasperated, "the rehearsals—and that's only *if* he's going to rehearsals—don't start until January second. There's no conflict."

I didn't see it that way. I figured that if Carter came back, that week before rehearsals started might well be the most important week of the entire production.

"But he'll need to be practicing, working on his lines, getting into the right frame of mind."

"What are you saying?"

"I'm saying, I think maybe we should cancel the trip."

"But the kids, your mom—"

"I know. Literally everyone will be pissed at me."

"What about Natalie and Jim's big party?" he said. "And the Mansion?"

"You're right. And I feel terrible. So another possibility is we could partially stick with the plan."

"Meaning . . . ?" Michael said.

"Meaning . . . ," I said, "*you* guys could all take the trip to Dallas and have a wonderful time."

He looked as though I'd punched him. "Seriously? Without you? You're going to spend Christmas without your family?"

"We're spending Christmas here together anyway, and you'll be back before New Year's Eve. Don't be overly dramatic."

"It won't be fun to see our friends if you're not there. We're having drinks with them at the Mansion Bar. What about all our plans?"

That reminder smarted. "And I would love to be there with you, and I wish I could, but if Carter's coming back—"

"Let's just wait a few more days and see what happens. I bet you anything he'll cancel."

I checked my phone, but Carter was silent on this wager. And the producers were placing their bets squarely on the other side. After I sent a short thank-you email for the lunch with the Campbells, I got an email from the assistant stage manager that read:

For all cast and crew: Ripley-Grier 10am sharp Jan 3. Please note: This is their new facility. Enter on 38th - corner of 8th. 3rd floor. There will be breakfast before the read-through (not optional). Contact me with questions.

I had hundreds of questions, all of which I kept to myself.

———

The next hiccup came in the form of a classic first world problem: Lauren called to invite Megan to go with their family to Beaver Creek to ski for the week after Christmas.

"Sabrina is begging for her to come along," Lauren told me. "We've got a house right on the slopes, and we have a charter plane taking us there. I got a private ski instructor for the whole week. The girls would have such a wonderful time together."

"Wow," I said, blown away by such a generous invitation. "But I don't know. We're going to Dallas."

"Of course. I really should have asked you sooner—"

"Can I tell you in a day or two? Let me just see if I can make a change of plans."

I discussed it with Michael, and we both felt we owed it to Megan to let her go if she wanted to.

Michael looked disappointed. "I guess it's not every day you get invited to ski in Colorado for a week."

"She really likes Sabrina. And I trust Lauren completely."

When we talked to Megan about it, she dropped right down onto her knees, saying, "Please? Please? Please can I go?"

Michael sighed. "I guess she wants to go."

"Will Gram be disappointed?" she asked.

"She'll miss you," I said, "but Charlotte and Jack will distract her."

Megan ran off happily to her room just as Charlotte came home from school in tears. We went to the living room where she had dropped her bags on the floor and kicked off her shoes.

"I'm not going back to Dallas *ever* again," she said and collapsed on the couch, sobbing with her face planted in the pillows.

"What happened?" Michael asked.

She got her phone out and handed it to me: it was a picture of a group of students in tuxedos and formal dresses. And there was her ex-boyfriend Theo, his arms wrapped around the waist of Chelsea, one of Charlotte's best friends.

"I found out they've been together ever since I left town, and none of my friends had the decency to tell me."

I flipped through the pictures and saw that in one of them, Theo and Chelsea were making out. I closed Facebook and handed the phone back.

"I'm so sorry, sweetie."

"It's humiliating," she said. "I hate them all. I don't want to go back there."

"I get it," I said. "I do. But don't you think you should hold your head up and—"

"No! And if you make me go, I'll spend the whole week without leaving the hotel. I don't mind staying here by myself, and I'm old enough, and you should know that you can trust me by now—"

"Slow down," Michael said, and Charlotte started crying again.

"Dad and I are rethinking the trip anyway, and maybe I could stay here with you."

Michael shot me a look.

"What?" Charlotte said. "No, you're not missing the trip because of me."

"Just let us think about this, okay? Honestly, I'm considering staying anyway."

"Why?"

I looked at Michael, and he shrugged.

"Why would you want to stay here?" she asked again. "Why would you miss a family trip? I don't get it."

"I'm going to tell you something, but I don't want you sharing this with Megan and Jack, not yet, anyway."

"Oh my god. Is it cancer? Are you getting a divorce? What?"

"It's nothing like that." I took a deep breath, and for the first time, I told her absolutely everything about Carter.

The night before winter break began, I cooked a big dinner to celebrate the end of the first semester. After we ate, the kids went to their rooms, and Michael and I took our glasses of wine and sat on the couch, enjoying a moment of peace and quiet. There was no homework to be done, no alarm clock to set for the morning.

The moment of calm was interrupted by the sound of Charlotte screaming.

She was sitting on the floor of her room in sweatpants, cross-legged, looking at her laptop. All I could think was, *What has Theo done now?* But when she looked up at me, the expression on her face confused me: she was ecstatically happy.

"I got in!" she screamed. "I can't believe . . . Look, I actually got in!"

She turned her laptop around and there it was: her acceptance from Caltech.

"There's a form," Charlotte said, reading the letter more carefully. "I have to fill out a housing form."

"I'm . . . Holy cow," I babbled. "You're just . . . Wow, Charlotte!"

We hugged each other and kept rereading the email, awed at Charlotte's spectacular accomplishment, one she'd managed all by herself.

"Oh my god," she said, "I can feel my senioritis kicking in already."

"Sucks you have to keep going to high school," Megan said.

"I'm so proud of you," Michael said, hugging her again.

"I can't believe this! What are—? Mom, are you *crying*? Stop!"

"I'm happy for you, that's all," I said, shrugging and forcing myself to ignore the selfish part of me that was thinking only about how far away California was. "I'm just really happy."

***

After dinner that night, Michael climbed into bed and hugged me. I reached past him to grab another tissue.

"You know what I think would be really nice?" he asked.

"What?"

"You and Charlotte spending a mother-daughter week here together on your own. And Megan will go on her ski trip. And Jack and I will have some quality guy-time in Dallas . . . with your mother."

"Really?" I asked. "You'd be okay with that?"

"It's not the trip I had in mind, but sure."

I leaned over and kissed him.

"But you're the one who has to tell your mom," he said, kissing me back.

———

Christmas in our cramped apartment was not quite as magical as I might have hoped (no fireplace, no mantel), but with Megan giddy about her trip and obsessed with packing, Charlotte happy for the first time in months thanks to her college news, Jack excited to be taking a boys' trip with his dad, and me anxiously anticipating Carter's return, the collective mood was better than it had been since the first day we'd arrived in New York City.

Part Four

BAD BEHAVIOR

James: "You were wonderful tonight, Ms. Noyes, just wonderful. I was just telling the Coast how wonderful you were.

Virginia: "You got the Coast on there? Give me that thing. (*She takes the receiver.*) Hello, California, this is Virginia Noyes. I just opened on Broadway and you can all go fuck yourselves. (*She hands the phone back to James.*) Am I going to regret that?"

Terrence McNally
It's Only a Play

nineteen

ON THE MORNING OF DECEMBER 27, Michael, Jack, and Megan flew west on their trips to Texas and Colorado, while I marched east, heading to Central Park West. It was bright and bitter cold, and I had bundled for the walk to Carter's, leaving Charlotte to sleep in.

Eddie had texted to tell me he'd arrived in Teterboro. Remembering all the pictures I'd seen of fresh-faced, eager Annabella, I hoped Carter was feeling rested and ready to meet the cast and take on that fat script I'd packed in his bag. The first rehearsal was in a week, and since the Campbells had been perfectly clear with their instructions, I decided to operate as though the play was on and my job was to get Carter in shape for Broadway. Whatever that meant.

As soon as I got closer to his building my confidence began to flag: *What's my MO here, exactly?* I didn't want to spook him. I didn't want to piss him off. Or freak him out. After all, I didn't even know for sure what he was doing here.

Outside of his building, there was a throng of paparazzi, smoking and talking, cameras at the ready. Jeffrey opened the door for me and yelled to the men, "Stay back on the sidewalk, or we're gonna have a problem, got it?"

They laughed, and one said back, "Doing our job, just like you, buddy."

"You call that a job, asshole? That's not a job."

He ushered me in.

"Happy holidays," I said. "How's the star? Is he behaving?"

Jeffrey shook his head at me. "Haven't seen him yet. Today's my first day back. But if they're here"—and he pointed to the men outside—"they must have known he was back somehow."

I handed Jeffrey a box of Dean & DeLuca chocolates, the same ones I'd put in Michael's suitcase to give to friends in Dallas, and went to the elevator, leaving him to keep the paparazzi in their place.

The elevator doors opened, and it was as eerily quiet as the first time I'd walked in. It felt good to be back; I smiled at Venus, hung my coat in the hall closet, and acknowledged my feelings of anxiety to have the responsibility of Carter's Broadway debut on my shoulders.

Walking through the living room, I saw that Skittle was back in her big, bright tank, paddling around in the water. She looked lively. I turned on the filter and heat lamp and saw a small, tacky topless mermaid in the gravel at the bottom, an L.A. acquisition, I supposed. I had to hand it to Carter; Skittle had survived two cross-country trips and several weeks under his care, and she seemed perfectly healthy.

I went to the kitchen to make coffee and unpack the eggs, cheese, milk, and fruit I'd bought on the way over. There was music coming from Carter's room. Nice. Healthy body, healthy mind, just as the Campbells ordered. I was planning to make an omelet with tomatoes and cheddar cheese, oatmeal with sliced banana, and fresh-squeezed orange juice. There were only a few days to prepare him for the table read, and while I doubted we'd get very far in terms of the kind of transformation the Campbells were gunning for, I was hopeful that we could make a strong start. My biggest goal was to get him to open the script, and maybe even sit with me and read through it.

I finished cooking, banging a few pots around to alert Carter to my presence. When the flowers were arranged on the kitchen island and the fruit cut in a bowl, I heard the elevator open, and Owen the housekeeper walked in.

"Good morning," he said, setting down a briefcase and folding his coat neatly over his arm. "So here we are."

"Thank you for being so flexible. I'm not sure about his plans going forward, but he decided to come back after all."

"Indeed. And how is the golden child?"

"He flew in last night," I said. "That's all I know."

"I'd like to review the various needs and duties, after you've had a chance to assess the situation."

Owen Brichacek spoke in an affected manner that sounded something like Cary Grant. I'd hired him in part because I found him professional, snarky, and uptight, and the last guy you'd ever buy drugs from. I thought he could help me keep Carter in line.

"Of course," I said. "Is it all right if I call you Owen?"

"I'm glad you asked. It's traditionally pronounced ''wen.'"

"Really? You don't pronounce the O in Owen?"

"It's a pronunciation disorder in our family. An ancestral speech pathology. Some kind of littera-phagy in a primogenitor; he swallowed the O."

"So the O is silent? It's 'wen? Why can't you just add the O back on? Or take it out completely?"

"If this is too complicated for you, dear, I answer to Owen as well. I was simply giving you a piece of historical trivia, not an edict."

Owen wasn't a cleaning man, he had told me sternly when I'd interviewed him almost two months before. But he had a cleaning team who worked for him. He was a housekeeper, a butler, for the absurdly rich and famous. He kept refrigerators stocked, chandeliers dusted, pianos tuned, mirrors polished, and water filters changed; and he kept everything else, from remote-operated window blinds to heated bathroom floors, in perfect working order. He was an organizer. He was willing to cook, if Carter paid extra, but he would call a caterer for parties of six or more. I figured he was in his mid- to late sixties, but I knew nothing about his personal life, if he was straight or gay, single or married, pet owner or dog hater, and nothing about him encouraged any hunches on my part. Furthermore, something about him told me not to ask, that it wasn't any of my business.

"So," he asked, "what's the situation? Is he here to stay or is this another brief sojourn?"

"Well, he's back for the time being. Maybe doing the show, or at least I hope so. He must be considering it, anyway. And, according to the producers, I'm in charge of 'handling' him, but he hasn't actually confirmed that yet, either."

"Ah, so we know precisely nothing," Owen said. "Handle away," and he gestured down the hall toward the master bedroom.

"Thank you, I will. I'll go check on him, and I'll let him know that today is the first day of the rest of his—"

"—miserable, lonely life," he said dramatically.

"Yes, or maybe I can turn that around, you know? This could be a pivotal moment. The day we embark on a new way forward."

He looked at the breakfast I'd placed on a table mat. "That's an inordinate amount of pressure to place on one rather sad-looking omelet. But 'hope springs eternal in the human breast,'" he said. "Meanwhile, I have work to do." And he got started by pulling a leather folder out of his bag and clicking open a pen.

I loosened my shoulders, rolling them back a few times, and went down the hallway. *Pleased to see you, Carter. Hey there, how was L.A.? You ready for breakfast?*

I could still hear music playing. I knocked softly on the door. "Good morning," I called, "it's me." He didn't answer. "Carter?" I asked. "How was your flight?" I pushed the door open and was met with a revolting smell and an unusual, no, a disturbing scene. It was hard to know which hideousness to focus on first: Was that Carter? His top half was on the bed, but his bottom half was not. He was, in other words, kneeling, sort of. And he was completely naked. I couldn't quite make sense of his position until I saw that his left wrist was handcuffed to the bed, preventing him from slumping all the way onto the floor. That image (one I'd love to erase from my memory) was the first thing I saw.

And then there was the girl. Brown hair, one red stiletto, black fingernail polish. She was passed out on the far side of the California King, also naked, vomit and lipstick on the pillow next to her, and clothes (shiny, ropey-looking garments) strewn across the floor. The night table next to her had leftover coke smudges, a bong, and three condom wrappers.

My first impulse was to turn around and run. And then I remembered: I was responsible. This was my problem. I had to "handle" this miserable situation. But I was so disgusted, overwhelmed, and embarrassed, that I turned around and fled the room anyway.

Owen was at the sink, humming to himself.

"We have a . . . problem," I said, crossing my arms tightly, feeling my panic set in.

"Describe it." He had donned an apron and was washing my frittata pan.

"Vomit, nudity, drugs, and possible statutory rape."

"Did you check for a pulse?"

"No."

"I would start with that."

"I heard snoring."

"From everyone?"

"There's only two."

"How quaint," Owen said. "I can have a cleaning team here in under an hour. Let's try to have Carter conscious, and the other one, male? Female?"

"Female."

"Let's get her in a cab as quickly as possible, assuming she isn't comatose."

"So I should . . . ?"

"Get back to the barracks, dear. And rouse the troops."

"Right."

I went back to Carter's room, and just before I walked in, I thought of Natalie, who had had to deal with this kind of chaos a dozen times with her daughter Carrie. Well, maybe not exactly this situation, but still, I thought perhaps she could help. I stood in the hallway, got my phone out of my pocket, and gave her a call.

"*Allison?!*"

"Hi, Natalie."

"Oh my *god*! Where are you? I just heard you're not coming? What happened?"

"Yeah, I didn't make it, unfortunately. Long story."

"Is everything okay?"

"Yeah, of course. Listen, Natalie, I've got a kind of serious problem. Do you have a second?"

"Sure."

"When Carrie was in high school and you used to go in her room and find her drunk or passed out—"

"You mean like the time she got bombed and threw up on my nice Persian in the entry. Wait," she gasped. "Is Charlotte drinking *finally*? Lord, I thought this day would never come."

I started to tell her about Charlotte's acceptance to Caltech but decided this wasn't the best time. "No, but I was wondering—when you had to get Carrie up and functioning, like for school or church or just snap her out of it after a big night out, is there a trick to it?"

"You mean like when I had to get her to her high school graduation after she did a half dozen tequila shots the night before? All right, hon, here's what you're going to do: you march right in there, open the curtains, turn on the lights, and come in with the vacuum cleaner. Now listen, before you turn it on, take all the pillows, sheets, duvets, everything, off the bed. Just take it all away. Got it? Otherwise she'll just use the bedding to cover up her ears and then your tactics lose their power."

"Tactics?"

"You want to torture her."

"Okay, I guess. And that works?"

"Oh, hell no. Nothing works. That's just a little something I do for fun. No, what you need to do next is take her in the bathroom and tip her upside down over the toilet. You want to get her to throw up."

"Oh god. Really?" I pictured holding Carter's head while he puked, instantly triggering my own gag reflex.

"If that doesn't work, try to keep her on her feet, get her in the shower if you can, and if she starts yelling at you, smack her across the face; that'll give her a little rush of adrenaline that could be curative."

I heard coughing on the other side of the door, peeked in, and saw that the girl was throwing up again, this time on the floor. "I gotta go, Natalie. Thanks for the advice."

"Is that her retching? Don't slap her too hard, hon. You just want to get her attention; you don't want to start a brawl." She let out a little whoop. "I'm so glad Carrie's grown out of binge-drinking. And I'm so sorry you won't be here to see her at our party."

"Isn't she on her year abroad? Spain, right?"

"My pride and joy has returned home for something she's calling a 'gap semester,' but you and I know there's no such thing. Call me later when you've got time to talk."

We hung up, and I went back in the room, stepping over an empty bottle of Tito's. I approached the girl and put my hands on my hips. I would pretend, I decided, that she was Charlotte, hoping that would make me feel some sort of compassion to go along with the disgust. But before I got started, I decided to take a detour, grabbing a bath towel, which I threw over Carter's bare ass so I wouldn't have to look at *that* situation anymore. I opened the curtains and turned off the music, in an effort to shift the mood from late-night party to early-morning responsibility. Then I went to the other side of the bed, saying loudly, "Hello there, good morning, miss."

Nothing.

"Excuse me, you, honey, wake up."

She stirred slightly. I picked up her clothes and put them next to her. "Time to get dressed now. Let's go."

"Ughhh," she grumbled.

"Come on," I said. "Let's get some clothes on, okay?"

She started to throw up again, and I grabbed a trash can. When she was done, I managed to get her to her feet, wrap her in the bedsheet, and help her walk to the master bathroom. She didn't say anything, and unfortunately, I didn't anticipate her next move: as soon as she went into the bathroom, she shut the door and locked it behind her, leaving me there holding her clothes. I knocked, saying, "Hello?" Again, I got nothing. "Hey, are you okay in there?" After a few futile moments of banging on the door, I gave up. So much for "handling" anything; in my effort to take charge, I'd actually succeeded in making things worse.

I went to the kitchen and helped myself to the coffee I'd made earlier. Then, as a wave of nausea washed over me, I used a fork to scrape the omelet into the trash. It was cold anyway. I sipped my coffee and contemplated the entire unholy mess.

Owen came in from the living room. "Ah, taking a break already, are we?"

"I need a locksmith." I sighed, knowing I sounded defeated.

"Why would you possibly need one of those?"

"I've got a girl locked in the bathroom, and our employer is unconscious and handcuffed to the bed." I looked up at him. "I have no keys," I said for clarification.

Owen shook his head. "Have you never heard of discretion?" he asked. "We don't call a locksmith, *ever*." He went to the front hall closet and retrieved from his briefcase a small bag that appeared to be some variation on a toolkit. "Tricks of the trade," he said.

He went to the bedroom, with me trailing behind him, and stopped in the doorway, taking in the grotesque sights and smells, the aftermath of a raucous evening. "*Quelle horreur,*" he said. He put on rubber gloves before he walked up to Carter, fiddled for a count of three with the handcuffs and a thin nail, and deftly removed them. "Get rid of these," he told me.

"Really?"

"And wash your hands, for God's sake; use something antibacterial. I'll work on the bathroom door."

But before he could begin that challenge, the girl walked out on her own, one hand over her eyes, a towel around her waist, saying, "Has anyone seen my clothes?"

I handed her the whole glittery, spiky pile, and she went back into the bathroom to get dressed, or at least I hoped so. I heard the door lock again, the water turn on, and the sound of aggressive gargling.

"My, how attractive," Owen said. "I'll be in the kitchen," and he abandoned me.

Alone in the den of sin, I tapped on Carter's shoulder. "Hi there. Good morning. Carter?" I nudged him with my foot, and without the mooring of the handcuffs, he slumped over onto the floor. I repositioned the towel.

The girl came out of the bathroom completely naked. "I can't see."

"Excuse me?"

"My contacts musta fell out or something."

"You can't see at all?" I asked.

She squinted.

"How many fingers am I holding up?"

She swayed in the bathroom doorway. "Peace, baby," she said and smiled.

I smiled back, in spite of myself. "You're okay. Let's get you ready to go home."

"Do I know you?" she asked.

"I don't think so. What's your name?"

"What's *your* name?" she asked.

"I asked you first."

"Kimmie," she said.

"And how old are you, Kimmie?" I crossed my fingers.

"How old are *you*?"

"Seventy-three," I said.

"Seriously?"

"How old are you?" *Don't say seventeen, please don't say seventeen.*

"Twenty-two," she said, "and a half."

That was the first good news all day. "Seriously?"

"You look young for your age," she said.

"Thanks," I said. "You do, too."

"But I can't see for shit, so what do I know?"

I wanted to move things along and get her out, but I felt like this girl deserved a bit of dignity in this absurd situation. "How about, let's get you dressed in something a little more daytime, a little less nightclub?" I looked in Carter's open suitcase on the floor and found a clean, white, fitted T-shirt and a hoodie. I figured it was better than a metallic halter top. "Here," I told her. "Take a shower if you want. And then if you go to the kitchen, I can get you a little hangover cure."

"I'm not hungover," she told me. "I'm totally wasted." She closed the bathroom door. I wondered what the chances were that she would be dressed when she reappeared.

Meanwhile, Carter rolled over on the floor and groaned. "Carter," I said, shaking him on the shoulder. "Hey, Carter. Carter." I wondered where I might find a vacuum cleaner. "Carter!" Or I could smack him on the face, like Natalie suggested. But I was going to have to be more strategic than that; he was my boss after all. I got down on the floor and took him by both shoulders and hauled him up into a sitting position, with his back leaning against the bed. "Carter, we're going to get up, okay?"

"Zat you?"

"Yup, it's me," I said. And to think I'd wanted to spend the morning sitting in the living room with him, sipping tea and studying the lines of the play. Looking at Carter now, I almost laughed at the absurdity of that fantasy.

He said something incomprehensible: "Duff scran birds." His eyes were closed, his breath was terrible.

"What? What was that?"

"I don' understand," he said, slurring his speech. "Shit doesn't make any sense. It's too many words."

Another kid communicating in haiku format. "Yeah? What shit, Carter?"

"Words. *Blah blah blah blah*, shut th' fuck up. It's Chi*nese*." And then he made a series of politically incorrect sounds, caricaturing Mandarin: "Ching, chong, shing, shong."

"You're drunk, Carter," I said. "I know I talk a lot, but keep in mind I'm only trying to help you. Plus that's super-racist."

"Not *you*," Carter said, and he started laughing. "You're not *Chinese*."

"No, I know that," I said, trying to pull him up so that he could sit on the edge of his bed.

"No, you're just all . . . " and he did an unflattering impersonation of me by knitting his eyebrows, pursing his lips, and wagging his finger in my face repeatedly, saying "Rahr rahr rahr." I watched him; was that really what I looked and sounded like?

"Ha ha," I said quietly. "Hilarious." Once I got him seated on the bed, I put the towel across his lap and immediately went to his suitcase to get some boxers, thinking that if I got one more glimpse of his junk, I would definitely have to quit.

Carter was really cracking himself up now. "You think you're Chinese."

"*You* said Chinese, Carter, not me."

"Not *you*. I meant th' fucking words. The *play*," he said. "Ding bong, king kong, big-ass words no one fucking uses, love and shit, the *fuck* are they even talking about?"

I stopped looking for his boxers and turned around.

"What do I look like," he said with disdain, "a fucking *book* person? A fucking loser college guy?"

His bathrobe was on the floor, and I brought it over to him, helping him slide his arms into the sleeves. "I speak that, you know. I speak . . . loser. Those words? I can tell you what they mean."

"So thirsty."

"Let's go to the kitchen and get you something to drink. And you need clean sheets in here before you go back to bed."

"Did I bring someone . . . ?"

"Yes."

"Was she hot?"

"I guess so. Maybe. She threw up a lot."

"I didn't throw up."

"No," I said, looking around, "not that I know of."

"Did I hook up with her?"

"I . . . really wouldn't know," I said, "but I don't think you were playing chess."

"I need to take a leak." I helped him put one arm over my shoulder, and we stood up carefully; this time he tolerated physical contact with me.

"You can use the powder room," I said. "Kimmie's in your bathroom."

"Who?"

I walked with him down the hall and into the kitchen, where Owen was pouring a thick, beige-colored drink from the blender into stemmed barware.

"What is *that*?" Carter asked, sitting on his usual barstool. I kept one hand on his shoulder to prevent him from tipping over.

"Good morning," Owen said perfectly coolly, placing a tall glass on a napkin in front of him.

"That looks like shit," Carter said.

"As do you, Mr. Reid."

Carter was momentarily taken aback, but then he smiled. He pointed at Owen and drank a sip of the smoothie, followed by a larger one. "Nice," he said, taking the drink with him into the bathroom. He left the door partway open, and we could hear him peeing.

"Is that some kind of miracle cure?" I asked.

"No," Owen said. "It's a banana milkshake."

"When's the cleaning crew coming?" I asked.

"On the way." Owen checked his watch. "Here's what I recommend: Carter takes Tylenol PM, and then retires to one of the guest rooms to sleep it off," he said, "unless, of course, he'd like to wait to see his lady friend out beforehand."

"Of course he would," I said.

"I doubt that very much," Owen said snidely. His tone irked me though he was probably right.

Carter came weaving out of the bathroom, without flushing the toilet or washing his hands. He lost his balance and dropped his milkshake.

"Whoops," he said. "I want more of that," he said, pointing to the smashed glass in front of his bare feet.

"Carter," I instructed, "step away from there and sit down."

He did as I said, while Owen got out a fresh glass for Carter.

"No harm done," Owen said.

"You can sleep this off after the girl leaves," I said, taking the whole roll of paper towels over to the mess on the floor.

"Who?"

"Your . . . friend," I said. "Kimmie."

"What?" he asked.

"Just be polite to her."

"Hell no," he said. "I don't want to see anyone. I look like ass." He tried to duck under the counter and hit his head on the granite.

"Wait, wait, wait," I said. "'No, don't be that guy."

"What guy?"

"She—Kimmie, that is; she has a name—Kimmie is coming out here after she puts some clothes on, one can only hope, and I want you to say good morning and then walk her to the elevator. Please, Carter, don't be a jerk."

"The fuck is she talking about?" Carter asked Owen, who handed him a new milkshake.

"Etiquette," Owen said. "Gentlemanly behavior. Civility."

"No way."

"We are suggesting," I said, "that you treat the girl you brought home with you last night with a modicum of respect."

"Why?" Carter asked.

I closed my eyes and breathed. "Because," I said, opening my eyes again, "that's what a stand-up, decent guy would do. I'm assuming you had *sex* with her. So just sit here for another minute, drink your shake, and walk her to the goddamned elevator. It's the least you can do."

Carter shook his head at me and focused on his milkshake as Owen went to greet the three-person cleaning staff. They had a brief conference and went off in different directions. Kimmie came down the hall in Carter's white T-shirt and her miniskirt, carrying her stilettos but wobbling nonetheless. She had washed off her makeup and put her hair in a sloppy ponytail. She looked as bad off as Carter did.

"How you feeling?" I asked.

"Uch," she said.

Meanwhile, out of the corner of my eye, I saw Owen quietly direct one of the cleaning women to start in on the bedroom; she slipped by discreetly with her caddy of supplies and went down the hall. I pictured the used condoms on the carpet, the puke on the pillow, and felt really bad for her. I would make sure Owen included a huge tip for today's combat duty.

"I'm wrecked," Kimmie said. "What time is it?" She squinted around the kitchen until she spotted Carter. "Oh, hey, you!"

"Hey," he answered.

"Kimmie," I said, "would you like a banana milkshake?"

She looked at me like I was a pervert. "Do you *want* me to throw up again?"

"Tylenol?" Owen asked. "Pepto-Bismol?"

"I can't see for shit," she said.

"I'm calling you a car service," I told her. "Where do you live?"

"Jersey City."

"Naturally," Owen said quietly. "I assume you arrived here with a coat? Some form of outerwear?"

"Yeah, it's blue fur."

Owen made a face and went off to find it.

"So if you want," she said to Carter, "text me. We can hang out."

"Sure," he said, turning on the charm. "Cool."

"Last night was cray."

"Yeah."

"A ton of shots."

"I know." They both half laughed.

"So much blow."

"Right?"

"So I'll see ya."

"Yep."

"You think?" she asked.

"Sure."

"Text me, or"—she shrugged—"I don't know. If you want."

"Great. Yeah."

A whole conversation, and not one multisyllabic word was uttered. I was impressed and horrified. But I was definitely pleased when Carter actually got his butt off his barstool to walk with Kimmie over to the elevator.

———

When I got home, I decided to take Charlotte out for a nice sushi dinner; we had both earned it.

"So he was actually there?" she asked. "Like he's doing the show after all?"

"You don't want to know."

"Yes I do!" she said. "I want to know everything. And when do I get to tell Megan? She's gonna lose her shit."

"As soon as I feel like I've got things under control, which may be never."

We ate *maki* rolls, and I recounted the entire ugly scenario, minus all the truly unsavory details.

"We made retrogress today. I don't see how in the world he's going to be ready in a week. He's probably out at a club, picking up another girl as we speak."

"Gross," Charlotte said. "He's such a player."

"On the bright side, at least he's practicing safe sex."

"Oh my *god*, how do you know that?"

"Wait," I said, grabbing my phone. "I bet he's all over the tabloids today. The producers are going to go through the roof if they hear he was drunk at a club. I'm supposed to make sure he's on his best behavior."

Charlotte laughed. "You're making it sound like he's a five-year-old."

"His actions last night were decidedly adult," I said wryly.

"I was online pretty much the whole day, and I didn't see anything."

"Since when do you spend a whole day surfing the Internet?"

"Since I got into my first-choice college and I'm on vacation," she said, clearly pleased with herself.

"You've earned some leisure time, I agree." Meanwhile, I was Googling Carter, looking for anything scandalous to pop up. "Please don't let there be a picture of him doing something embarrassing. How the hell am I going to force him to get his act together by *next week*? I've got to figure out some way to keep him clean for eight straight months."

"Just be a total hard-ass, like you are with us."

"I'm a hard-ass?"

"When you have to be. Go full prison warden on him."

"But then he'll kick me out," I told her, as I scrolled. "You guys don't have the luxury of firing me, but Carter can just show me the door."

Charlotte thought about that a second. "Yeah, you're screwed," she said. "Sorry."

"Thanks."

"Hey, put your phone away during dinner," she said. "It's rude."

When we got home from the restaurant, Charlotte opened her laptop and scoured the Internet, but she couldn't find any negative mention of Carter out on the town, either. No rumors of Carter doing coke, no pictures of him leaving the club with a girl. Either the paparazzi were off on vacation, asleep at the switch, or they somehow missed the crazier parts of the evening. *People* had one picture of him on Star Tracks, but it was simply a sighting of him in L.A., along with a breakdown of the clothes he was wearing.

"Your man-whore seems to have evaded the paparazzi somehow," Charlotte said, "so you got a free pass on this one."

"Thank God."

"But I did find an old picture of him trying to stick his tongue in Miley Cyrus's ear. That guy needs to learn some manners."

"How do I teach him?" I asked.

"Don't ask me." She got up to go to bed but came across the room and gave me a hug first. "Maybe it'll go better tomorrow."

twenty

CHARLOTTE MUST HAVE THOUGHT over my predicament during the night because she was up at seven in the morning, dressed as if she were headed out for a run. "I'm ready," she said. She was wearing cropped leggings, a tank, and a hoodie.

I was drinking a cup of coffee in the kitchen before heading off to Carter's, looking at a picture that Michael had sent of Jack at the Stockyards in Fort Worth, and one that Lauren sent of her family standing together on a mountain; Megan was bright-eyed and happy, ski goggles perched up on her helmet.

"Ready? Ready for what?" I asked. "What's in the bag?"

"My workout stuff," she said. "Carter must have a kick-ass gym in his building, right?"

"I wouldn't know."

"So I want to use it."

"You can't just use his gym."

"So ask him."

"Charlotte, come on. We can't just decide it's 'bring your daughter to work day.'"

"Well, technically he hasn't even hired you yet, and 'work' isn't going too great so far, so it can't hurt to bring me along."

I felt wary, but I looked at Charlotte, smart and wholesome, standing there in her workout gear, hair pulled back in a ponytail, and wondered if she wouldn't be a good influence on him.

"I won't stick around if he doesn't want me there," she said, "but I'd like to lift some weights, use the cardio machines. And it would probably be good for him to work off his hangover."

"Okay, but if he's an asshole to you, or if he . . . you know, man-whore-propositions you—"

"Mom," she laughed, "I can handle myself."

I finished my coffee, and we put our coats on, bracing for the walk to Carter's. The wind turned Charlotte's cheeks pink as we walked south on Central Park West, and I smiled to see her pretty eyes; it had been a long time since she'd kept her face turned toward me in a conversation.

"So why are you making him do this musical if he doesn't want to?" Charlotte asked.

"It's not me making him," I explained. "He made a commitment, and now he has to follow through."

"Maybe it's just a bad play."

"It's not," I said. "You want to read it?"

"Can I?" she asked.

"Of course." We turned into the private courtyard, and I stopped her, feeling a need to give a warning. "He'll probably be in a rotten mood today because, well, he always is; it might get ugly, so just leave if he's unpleasant."

"I bet he'll be nicer with a stranger around," she said. "I'm not there to ruin his life like you are."

"I'm trying to improve his life."

"Details," she said. "He doesn't see it that way."

I waved to Jeffrey, and Charlotte and I got in the elevator. She looked nervous.

"You can still go home, you know," I said.

"No, that's okay," she said casually. "I'm curious."

We entered the penthouse, and I was surprised to find Carter up already, wearing jeans and a T-shirt. He was sitting in the living room, watching *South Park*.

"You're looking much better than yesterday," I said. "You were a little green around the gills when I saw you last."

He looked up at me and then noticed Charlotte. He shrugged and turned back to the television. "It's not my fault I was hungover as fuck."

I was tempted to argue that remark, but now wasn't the time. "This is my daughter Charlotte," I said. "She was wondering if she could use the gym. With you, if you want. Exercising would be—"

"Mom," she said, pushing her sleeves up. She was clearly annoyed. "What?"

"I can speak for myself," she said.

"Sorry." I took a step backward to give her some space.

"I just wondered what the deal is with the gym in this place," she said. "Have you checked it out?"

"You work out?" he asked, looking over at her. His eyes scanned her up and down. I took a step forward again.

"I run," she said. "Long-distance. I'm thinking of doing a marathon this spring."

"You are?" I asked. She glared at me.

"Isn't that, like, fifty miles or something?" he said.

She didn't correct him.

"So . . . ," he said, "you're fucking crazy, is that what you're saying?" He checked his phone and shrugged. "I guess I'm up for sweating a little."

"Great," she said. "Is there a pool?"

"I don't know."

She laughed. "You don't know? How can you not know?"

"What? It's not like I live here." He got up and went back to his room to get changed.

"He seems nice," she whispered.

"He's not all bad. But I wouldn't go so far as 'nice.'"

She laughed suddenly. "I can't believe I'm about to work out with Carter Reid. Who would believe it?"

I went to the kitchen and got my laptop from my bag while Charlotte wandered around looking out the windows at the view. She stopped to see the turtle. "She's so cute. Can we get one?"

"Absolutely not," I said.

Before I could explain the many problems of having red-eared sliders as pets, Owen arrived and saw Charlotte leaning over, watching Skittle. "Ah, here we go again," he muttered as he took off his coat and hung it in the hall closet. "I was expecting a quiet day."

I introduced Charlotte, and I was proud but unsurprised to see that she walked right up to him and shook his hand.

"Ah, I see," Owen said. "I apologize. I thought you were another overnight guest."

"Me? God, no."

"How is the young thespian today?" Owen asked. "Is he up and about? In need of sustenance?"

"What did he call me?" Carter asked, coming in barefoot, holding his shoes.

"Thespian," Charlotte said. "It just means you're an actor."

He looked up, offended. "I'm *not* a fucking actor."

"Okay, well, have fun, you guys! And, Carter, go easy on that knee," I said, trying to sound extra-cheery.

I knew that exercise was a perfectly good way for Carter to start his day, but as the elevator doors closed behind them, I was uneasy.

"Lovely young woman," Owen said. "The whole day seems an improvement so far."

An improvement, yes. But I wasn't sure how to accelerate the progress and actually get Carter to be productive.

I sat down with the intense schedule the stage manager had sent me, trying to figure out how I could get Carter to show up prepared to the various singing, dancing, and acting rehearsals. His life was about to kick into full gear, and I wanted both of us to be ready. I needed to allot substantial time for him to go over his lines and get into a positive frame of mind. While I waited for them to return, I made a tentative schedule for the day, booked physical therapy appointments for the week, and then, with Owen's help, discussed meals for the whole rehearsal period.

When Charlotte and Carter came back from the gym, sweaty and panting, they collapsed on the couches in the living room.

"That's the nicest gym I've ever been in," Charlotte said. "It has a lap pool with skylights."

"That pool's shit compared to the one at my house," Carter bragged.

Owen brought them water and cut-up fruit, while Carter put his feet up on the coffee table and turned the television back on. *No, no, no,* I thought. *Time to work.* Charlotte was sitting with her legs tucked under her, browsing through the book of Audubon etchings, when I came in with a copy of *Limelight.*

"Hey, Charlotte," I said. "You want to take a look at Carter's script?"

"Yeah," she said, sitting up and holding her hand out. She turned to Carter. "I mean, is that okay?"

Carter saw the script in her hand, shrugged, and flipped channels.

For the next two hours, Carter watched TV while she sat hunched over, reading *Limelight*. Every once in a while, she laughed out loud, and I noticed that Carter was watching her.

When she finished reading, she closed it and tossed it on the couch next to him. "For what it's worth," she said, sitting up and stretching her arms up over her head, "I really like it."

———

Charlotte went home to shower and change, and I took this moment alone with Carter to ask why he'd come back to New York. While he ate his lunch, he told me that he'd seen his lawyer and agent in L.A.; they'd explained the contract to him, including one part that stated his manager and agent would be entitled to their cut whether Carter did the show or not.

"I have to pay those assholes a shit ton of money no matter what," he said, "so I'll do their fucking show, but I'm gonna do only what I have to, and get the fuck out the second I'm done."

That, I supposed, was better than refusing to do the show entirely, but I knew I had my work cut out for me if the Campbells were expecting to see a hard-working, centered, enthusiastic, well-rested cast member at the first rehearsal. And I somehow didn't think Kevin Kline was going to find Carter's half-assed approach to theater acceptable, either.

He pushed his plate away and went to his room to play *Call of Duty*. I walked in after him and handed him a piece of paper, hoping to derail his obvious plan to spend the rest of the day with his Xbox.

"What?" he asked.

"Read it."

"I don't want to read shit right now."

"It's two sentences, Carter. Just read it and nod if you agree."

He threw his controller next to him on the bed and looked at my statement:

"I, Allison Brinkley, hereby work for you, Carter Reid, and it is my hope that you'll take my advice from time to time. As your personal assistant, I will be discreet and will keep your personal and professional well-being as a top priority at all times."

"Huh?"

"It means you're hiring me to be your personal assistant. Unless you don't want to."

He exhaled, thoroughly irritated. "Fine," he said.

"Fine? Really? Like it's official?"

"Jesus, are you working for me or are we getting married?"

"I'm working for you?"

"I said 'fine' already."

"Because I think I can really help you, not only get through this, but maybe even thrive, you know, like really do well—"

"Go tell that guy in the kitchen to make me a milkshake."

"You mean Owen?"

"His shakes are crack."

"Okay. And how are we going to handle salary?"

"Fuck if I know. Just talk to that lady."

"What lady?" I asked.

"I don't know. That lady who does all the money shit for me. Her number's somewhere."

So with that, I became an employee of Carter Reid. But how could I get him to listen to me? To get started? To put down the damn game controller? I had the fat script under my arm. I saw Carter's eyes fixed on the video game, and I got a sick feeling, knowing how many lines there were to memorize, how much work there was to do.

At least, for now, I'd gotten my spot in the entourage legitimized.

———

The next day Carter had an appointment with a physical therapist who came recommended by the orthopedist we'd seen. The physical therapist was going to make sure that Carter's knee had fully recovered, and he would work with him throughout the rehearsals and run of *Limelight*, if necessary. This first session was a long one, so I went with Eddie to drop him off and fill out paperwork, and then came back to the apartment.

When I got to the lobby of 15 CPW, I saw a group of young girls sitting on the couches.

"They're here for you-know-who," Jeffrey said slyly, "and they insist they're invited."

"I'll handle it," I said.

"Whoa, new boss in town," he said.

"That's right."

I walked up to the girls, noticing that they were all about Charlotte's age. "Hello," I said, pulling off my gloves and hat. "Can I help you ladies?"

No one looked happy to see a middle-aged woman encroach on their party, but I was used to this dynamic.

"Who are you?" one girl asked. In spite of the below-freezing temperatures, she was wearing a crop top that showed off her gold bellybutton ring.

"I work for Carter. What can I do for you?"

"We're hanging out with him today," she said.

"And who are you?" I asked.

"Kelsey."

"Hi, Kelsey. And you?" I asked, indicating the other girls, all in similar short skirts, silky tanks, and high-heel ankle booties.

"This is Tammy, Talia, Cindy, and Callie."

Now that I had their names, I was ready to take them on. "So nice to meet you girls. Carter's not here. And today's not a good day anyway. In fact—"

"Uh, yeah, *whatever*. He said to come over. Like, we're invited."

"Not today, Kelsey," I said.

"Who are you?" Callie asked.

"His . . . personal assistant." I had almost said babysitter. "And where did you meet Carter?"

"At a club," they said in unison.

"Uh-huh. Well, Carter, as it turns out, is starting a new job in a few days and won't have time to socialize for the next few months."

"That's not what he told us," Callie said, her voice full of attitude.

"And, more importantly," I went on, "he tested positive for strep throat this morning. So you girls should run along because he's contagious, and this is not happening."

I waited to see which would follow, compliance or rebellion. Fortunately, I got compliance, complete with sighs of disappointment and eye rolls.

"Tell Carter we hope he feels better," Talia said.

"I will," I promised.

"Everyone says he's a jerk," Kelsey said. "Like, the tabloids, I mean. 'Cause he sometimes acts, you know, like a jerk. But he's a really good guy underneath."

I liked her attitude. I was hoping she was right.

"Do you want to leave your number," I asked, "just in case he lost it or something?"

Callie entered her number in my contacts, and they waved to me as they left the building, passing Charlotte as she walked in.

Charlotte made a judgmental face. "Who were they?"

"Fans," I said.

"Oh my god. *Groupies*. Vomit. And you sent them away?"

"Obviously," I said. "We don't have time for this."

"He'll be pissed."

I smiled at her. "*Whatever*," I said, using my best teenager voice.

"Please, never say that again," Charlotte said flatly.

We took the elevator upstairs and said hello to Owen, who was doing a walk-through with a maintenance man, pointing out items that needed attention, such as the heated towel racks in the master bath that had gone cold. "Unacceptable," I heard Owen say.

"So have you figured out," Charlotte asked me as we walked into the kitchen, "how you're going to get Carter to do *anything*?"

While Charlotte sat at the kitchen island, flipping through the script, I considered her question. Kaye and Wilson had said I should take control of every aspect of Carter's life, hiring guards to keep him under constant surveillance day and night. Maybe that was the way to go, but I was doubtful it would work; wouldn't a kid like him rebel and go wild? I was leaning toward a friendlier, more familial approach, one that would involve being consistent, trustworthy, and kind. A sledgehammer doesn't work with teenagers; one needs to be smarter than that, subtler, by giving them enough room to let them make some good decisions, while ultimately controlling the situation and keeping them on the right path.

But I couldn't do it all. I couldn't be the one keeping his head on straight and also be the one to force him to learn his lines. It's like when a parent tries to teach a kid to swim, and the child does nothing but scream and cry, and yet with a swim teacher they're compliant and willing; some tasks are better left to someone else.

"He's got a ton of lines to memorize. Mom?" Charlotte was saying. "Hello?"

"Sorry, what?"

He was scared. Scared of the script, scared of the words, scared of failing, scared of embarrassing himself. I should be the one to give him confidence, to keep him focused and on a schedule. I would create a stable life for him in the apartment and make sure he ate, slept, and showed up on time.

But I needed someone else to help him with his lines, someone outside the theater, someone smart and organized. Someone nonthreatening. I glanced up at Charlotte, noting the intense look of concentration in her eyes in spite of her chunky glasses sliding down her nose.

"How would you feel about being his tutor?"

Charlotte took the *Limelight* script to make a copy at FedEx, and Eddie brought Carter home from the doctor while she was still out. Carter was feeling pretty good. "My knee's fine," he said. "Is there food?"

"Owen's got lunch ready. Oh, and some girls came by earlier. Callie and her friends."

"Who?"

"You met them at a club. They seemed nice."

"Are they coming back?"

"No," I said bluntly. "I explained that you have to hunker down now and work for the next few weeks. They were really impressed with you. And so excited about your show. They understand completely that there won't be time for hanging out or partying until the show opens."

"Pffft," he said dismissively, "sure there will."

"Maybe after you learn your lines, they can come back. But for now you're going to have to put some time in the script."

"Fuck me," he said. "This is going to suck."

"It'll be fun," I said, wishing my own enthusiasm for this project would eventually rub off on him.

He sat down at the counter, and I took the turkey-and-brie panini Owen had made out of the warming drawer and put it on a plate in front of him.

"You need a coach," I said. "A helper. It'll go faster that way. I want you to have more time to relax, so I want someone to work with you on your lines, outside of rehearsal, okay?"

"No," he said. "No fucking way."

"Yes way. You *need* someone to work with you."

"Who? *You?*"

I already knew he loathed the sound of my voice. "Not me, no," I said. "Someone else."

"I'm back," Charlotte called out. She came into the kitchen, pulled her coat off, and got the scripts out of her bag. She reached her hands up and swooped her hair up in a ponytail holder. "Hi," she said, looking serious and eager. "You ready?"

———

They went into the living room together after lunch. Carter had a baseball in his hand, and he sat back on the couch, tossing it up in the air and catching it.

"Want to work out later?" Charlotte asked.

"Nah. This shit totally kills my buzz," he said.

"We don't have to overdo it today. Let's just read through some of the big scenes. Just to get a feel for it."

"I fucking hate it," he said. He missed the ball, and it bounced off the coffee table and rolled under a chair. He left it there.

"It's not that bad," Charlotte said.

"It's stupid."

"Yeah? Stupid how?"

"My agent said there's an old guy in it, right? I mean, let's just be real for a second: who would a hot babe like Annabella Hatter wanna bone? Me or him?"

I was sitting in the kitchen on my laptop, pretending to work, but the truth is I was straight-up eavesdropping and wishing I could see the look on Charlotte's face. I had my back to them, and I angled the screen to see if I could capture their reflection.

"You mean, you or Kevin Kline?" Charlotte asked.

For me the question was easy, and not only because Carter was a teenager and of absolutely zero interest to me. No, I'd had a crush on Kevin Kline ever since *Soapdish*. No, ever since *The Big Chill*; I loved his thick brown hair, his kind eyes, even his mustache, and I wasn't normally into mustaches, but on Kevin, it looked perfect. I imagined taking Carter to the theater and meeting him. *Oh, I'm such a huge fan*, I might say. But I didn't want to sound like Kathy Bates in *Misery*. I wanted to be cool. *Gosh, Kevin, I just loved you so much in* Dave. "Gosh"? I was glad I had time to prepare for our future meeting.

"Yeah, I mean he's fucking old and all," Carter was saying. "And I'm, you know, me."

"True," Charlotte said diplomatically. "But you're not really *you* in the play, you know?"

"What?"

She paused, and I heard her turn the page of her script. "I mean, you're playing someone else. You're Neville."

"Yeah, sure, but hey, the audience is gonna be looking at me. And who's gonna believe that she'd go for the old guy when I'm standing right there?"

"People do stuff that doesn't make sense all the time. Why did my smart ex-boyfriend dump me for a friend of mine who has an IQ of four? Oh, I remember—because he's an asshole."

"Is your friend hot? Because maybe you should get in on the action. Dudes love a three-way."

I got up off my barstool. *Too much!* I was ready to yell.

"Ha," Charlotte said casually, "I wouldn't give either one of them the satisfaction."

I had to stop myself from saying *Good for you!*

"Let's start," she said. "Why don't we read that scene where Neville and Thereza have lunch together?"

"I'll just go through it on my own tonight."

Come on, Charlotte, I thought, *make him read, somehow*.

"How about we do a page or two, just so my mom will shut up about it. And then you feel like working out?"

"Maybe."

Charlotte cleared her throat. "So like Neville's first big scene? When the guy at the restaurant says, 'Table for two,' and Thereza and Neville end up being seated together, and it's awkward because they've met before, and they both know it, but she's acting like she doesn't know him, and he decides to remind her, and to make sure, I guess, but he doesn't know that moments before she pretty much proposed to Calvero, and so she's, I don't know, reluctant to be alone with him, I guess."

"What?"

"The lunch scene."

"I haven't read it," he said.

And she went over the whole thing again, more slowly this time and with fewer details. "Really it's just a guy and a girl having lunch together. But he makes her confront the fact that they have a past."

"That sounds boring. Let's start somewhere else."

Charlotte proposed six different scenes, one after the other, all of which Carter rejected. They finally got up and went to the gym.

I was beyond frustrated. It wasn't Charlotte's fault, but I wished she could have gotten him to run some actual lines given that we were running out of time. And then I realized, Charlotte had just talked him through Neville's entire role in the play.

twenty-one

MEGAN, JACK, AND MICHAEL RETURNED from their trips, and the apartment filled up quickly with noise, food, and dirty laundry. The morning after they'd all returned and emptied their various suitcases all over the apartment, Michael made coffee while I was getting ready for work, one of many reasons I was happy to have him back home.

"Natalie and Jim are going to knock out the back wall of their kitchen," he said, "so they'll have this whole new . . ." He searched for the word while using his arms to indicate the scale of the addition.

"Breakfast room?" I said, taking my coffee and the theater section of the *New York Times* to the dining room table.

"I guess. But I think Natalie called it a solarium."

"That's a little pretentious."

He sat down with me. "I was thinking, I guess I'd be willing to look at houses outside the city."

"What?" I put my coffee mug down. "Because of a solarium?"

"Because of houses in general. I forgot how much easier life is when you can spread out a bit. And I kind of miss driving around."

"What about celebrity sightings and French bistros? And the commute—"

"I'm only saying that I think you were right: it makes sense to keep the option on the table."

But I didn't have time to think about the suburban options at the moment. This morning, as the kids were enjoying their last moments of winter break, Carter would be going to his first rehearsal, a full read-through of the script with the entire cast. In spite of Charlotte's and my best efforts, he was hideously unprepared.

Jack was still sleeping, and Megan was up making breakfast when Charlotte walked into the kitchen and got a coffee mug.

Michael filled it for her, and then turned to watch Megan working away over the stovetop. "Did you tell her yet?" he asked me.

"Tell me what?" Megan asked.

"Michael!"

"What?" he said. "You're going to have to tell them all eventually."

"I already know," Charlotte said proudly in a singsong voice. "No big deal."

"Tell me what?" Megan asked again. "What does she already know?"

"Tell you . . ." I said, "that . . . we're very impressed with your new cooking skills."

"Allison."

"Just tell her, Mom," Charlotte said. "You'll totally make her day."

I took my coffee cup to the sink. "Fine," I said. "It's nothing, really. It's nothing at all. I have a new job, that's all."

"Doing what?" Megan asked suspiciously, like she thought I was going to say pole dancing.

"I am, well, this may be a little surprising, but I'm the—"

"She's the personal assistant to Carter Reid," Charlotte said.

Megan's mouth fell open, but she didn't say anything.

"Don't you people just say PA in the business?" Michael asked.

"I have to handle him regardless of what we call it."

"*Handle* him?" Michael asked.

"Gross," Charlotte said. "Say 'manage,' not 'handle.'"

"Fine, I manage him. But I'm not his manager."

Megan still didn't say anything.

"And I'm his tutor," Charlotte added. "I get to help him memorize his lines."

Megan's eyes were wide, and she looked like she had choked on something.

"Breathe, Megan," Charlotte said.

"Anyway, you'll probably meet him at some point," I said, "like backstage on opening night, maybe. If he actually makes it to opening night. That remains to be seen. But in principle, you can maybe meet him. If you want. At some point."

"Is she okay?" Michael asked.

"Megan?" I said. "Megan, your pancakes are burning."

—⟡—

I had butterflies in my stomach when I walked to Carter's, hoping his very first day of rehearsals would get off to a good start. It didn't happen. I couldn't wake him up, and when I finally did, he was slow and sluggish. I kept offering coffee and saying the kinds of things Michael always said to our kids ("Chop-chop, let's go!"). Carter scowled and barked back, "Stop rushing me!"

In spite of my nagging and prodding, we pulled up to the rehearsal studio on Thirty-Eighth Street twenty-five minutes late. I couldn't bear the thought that the director, cast, and crew were sitting there and waiting for him. I asked Eddie to wait while I took Carter into Ripley-Grier, the rehearsal studio that would house the show until they moved into the theater. We took the stairs up to the second floor and entered a spacious lobby that had a cool industrial steel and glass staircase.

We were greeted by Butch Grier, the owner of the studio. I introduced Carter who, rather than say hello or make eye contact, stuffed a piece of gum in his mouth and abruptly walked away to the bathroom.

"Sorry about that," I said.

Butch just smiled, hands in jeans pockets, clearly unfazed to have dozens of Broadway bigwigs milling about. The energy and excitement in the room were not lost on me, but for Butch this scene was part of his everyday life.

"I was wondering about security," I said, having noticed that we had simply walked right into the building, without passing any kind of doorman or guard.

"You can station anyone you need at the front door to check bags and ask where they're headed. But we've got twenty-four rooms here, so there's going to be traffic."

"Of course," I said. "I'll bring it up with"—I looked around the lobby at the dozens of people—"someone."

"I think Rob's your man," and he pointed. "Or the production assistant." He handed me his card. "My wife, Patricia, and I have been in the business about thirty years now, so call me if you need help with anything." He spotted someone over my shoulder. "Ah, look who's here," and he walked away to say hello to Melissa McCarthy. I hoped I wouldn't embarrass myself by fainting in her presence.

Carter came out of the bathroom. I walked to the door of the studio with him and stopped him before he went in. "I hope it goes really well today," I said. He ignored me.

"Do you want me to stick around? Or bring you anything?" I asked, handing him his script.

He shook his head.

"Carter," I said, a bit more quietly. "You should probably apologize for being late. It would be polite."

"They haven't even started."

It was true that people were coming in and out, but we had gotten specific instructions: *10am sharp.* "But still," I said.

I followed him in.

"Carter," I said.

"*What?*"

"They chose you, you know," I said. "Of all the singers in the world, because they know you're going to be great."

He nodded and started to walk away.

"And one more thing," I said.

"*Jesus!*"

"I was just going to say, maybe don't make any special, complicated requests today, you know? Just be easygoing. It's the first impression, so if you need something, text me instead of asking anyone here." I pulled a banana and a Fiji water out of my bag.

"I'm not taking that," he said. "They've got food in there."

"Fine. So will you spit out your gum?"

He made face at me like I'd asked him to take his pants off.

"Please?"

"Why?"

"You can't eat and meet people and read the play and chew gum at the same time."

He sighed and took his gum in his fingers, and since I didn't see a trash can nearby, I put my hand out.

"Seriously?" he said. He dropped the gum in my palm. "You're so gross."

I found an old CVS receipt in my bag and wadded the gum up in it, and with a knot in my stomach, I watched him walk away into the rehearsal space. It was like a first day of school; it never seemed to get any easier.

The rehearsal room, vast and open with large windows facing down Eighth Avenue and across Thirty-Eighth Street, was a fishbowl, so I could see the scene inside: an informal breakfast buffet was set up on one wall and people were milling about, eating bagels, mingling, and looking at posters on easels that depicted the set and costume designs. The tables were arranged in a large square with a second ring of chairs encircling the first.

Kaye Campbell turned and saw me through the window. I hoped she might wave me in, but instead she came briskly out to meet me. She stumbled in her high heels on the little step down from the rehearsal room.

"Sprung floors," she explained.

I nodded.

"Your boy's late," she said.

"I know. I'm sorry," I said. "We had some confusion—" I could tell that she wasn't interested in hearing my excuses. "It won't happen again."

"If it does, we'll dock his pay," she said. "If he starts out by disrespecting people's time, he's going to piss everyone off."

"Got it."

"At least there hasn't been any negative publicity in the past few days," she said. "How's he doing with the new diet?" Kaye asked.

"Oh, fine," I said, my voice jumping up an octave. "I've got a great team assembled. I wanted to ask about security here—"

"It's already covered. There will be two guards downstairs and one up here starting tomorrow."

I sighed with relief to know that I wouldn't have to do the hiring.

Kaye, meanwhile, surveyed my outfit, which she seemed to find lacking, even though I had put on nice black jeans and a cashmere sweater, just in case I met Kevin Kline. "Edgar expects the cast to be off book in two weeks," she said, "so give him the flaxseed oil I sent over. It's good for brain function."

"*Two* weeks?" I asked, my eyes popping wide open. "He's supposed to have *all* his lines memorized in *two* weeks?"

"Of course," said Kaye. "That's a normal pace."

"Right," I said. "I mean, that seems fast. I just didn't realize—"

"Keep him focused," she went on. "No distractions."

"Focused," I repeated, wondering if the Xbox was going to have to go. Could I break it somehow? I looked through the window into the studio and watched the cast and crew mingling. "I didn't know so many people would be here today."

"The table read," Kaye said, "is an *event*. It's all about seeing the show's potential in a bare-bones room. Nothing but the talent we paid for. Most of the producers are here for the meet-and-greet, but they'll head out in a few minutes before we get started. There's Steve Sloan," she said, nodding her chin in his direction, "the owner of the penthouse. He won't stick around once he's met the stars."

Steve Sloan, looking exactly as he did in every tabloid paper I'd ever seen him in, bloated face and shiny bald head, was talking to Carter. He laughed and put his hand on Carter's shoulder. Carter took a bite of a donut; I glanced at Kaye to see if she noticed him devouring high-fructose corn syrup. Steve then greeted Annabella Hatter, placing his hand way too low on her back as he introduced the two stars to each other.

It was thrilling to see Annabella in real life, much less makeup than on-screen and shorter than I had thought she was. But she looked so alert, well rested, and eager to start.

Carter nodded his head at Annabella but then walked away, checking his phone as he took a seat at the table.

Just on the other side of the room, I spotted the back of Kevin Kline's head and felt all the blood in my body rush to my cheeks.

"Oh my God," I said. "This is exciting, huh?"

Kaye smiled at me like I was a child. "Being part of a cast requires becoming a team player." She was watching Carter scroll through his phone, his body turned away from the group. "He's used to being a solo act, but this"—and she swept her arm toward the bustling scene in the studio—"is all about the ensemble."

I nodded, seeing that there was clearly work to do in that area.

"You're going to get an email from Jean," Kaye said, handing me a business card. "She's the new PR person. She'll be sending you dates for interviews and events, so keep a calendar and never let him be late to appointments she makes for him. And this," she said, handing me a fat manila folder, "is from the stage manager. It's everything you need to know about the coming weeks."

"Good," I said. "Not to worry. It's all under control."

She turned to go back to the breakfast, tripping again on the step up.

"Sprung floors," she said. And then she smiled at me. "I love theater, even when it makes me look bad."

I felt uneasy leaving before the reading got started, but Carter didn't want me hanging around, and Kaye hadn't invited me to stay.

———

I went from the rehearsal studio to the subway at Penn Station, taking the C to West Fourth and walking through Washington Square Park. The new semester at NYU didn't start for another two weeks, but Howard was signed up for a course called the Global Short Story and wanted to go over the syllabus with me. We met at a quiet coffee shop on MacDougal Street and went over the list of authors he would be reading, from Carlos Fuentes to Margaret Atwood to Haruki Murakami.

When we were done, he put his papers away, and I caught him up on Carter's return and decision to do the show after all. I was still revved up from my visit to the rehearsal studio and nervous about the first day. I had little confidence that Carter would make a decent impression on anyone.

"The musical takes place in the fifties," I said. "It's a love story, but it's about show business and celebrity. And it's very philosophical at times, delving into the meaning and value of life. It begins with a thwarted suicide attempt."

"Sounds heavy."

"Not really. The singing and dancing lighten the mood. I just don't know if Carter's up to the challenge."

"Maybe he needs a role model," Howard suggested. "Can he talk to someone famous who's got a good head on his shoulders? John Legend, maybe? Or Justin Timberlake? Beyoncé?"

"I wouldn't have the faintest idea how to arrange that. He's the first famous person I've ever met."

"I saw Alec Baldwin once. Where's Carter's mother?"

"She died when he was little."

Howard shook his head. "Family?"

"Not that I know of."

"He must have friends."

"He doesn't seem to have anyone. No steady girlfriend. Maybe he has friends in L.A. but he's never mentioned anyone. I think most people just take advantage of him. He's got no real support at all as far as I can tell."

"My wife always says I'm the calmest person she knows on earth, and you know why? I always say it's because I've got a rock-solid family. I don't know how people get by without it. Maybe you're going to have to be his family."

I laughed. "You saw how he is with me."

"He doesn't have to like you. He just needs to know you aren't going anywhere."

I appreciated the sentiment, but it seemed Howard was misunderstanding how little Carter valued me. "It would be so good for him to make friends in the cast, go out to dinner with Kevin Kline, maybe."

"Did you meet him?"

"Kevin Kline? Oh my god, no. I saw the back of his head this morning. If I actually came face-to-face with him, I'd probably faint or say something stupid."

"You better get prepared."

"You think?" I asked.

"Well, that depends if the kid goes through with the show."

———

To pick Carter up from rehearsal or not to pick Carter up from rehearsal? That was the question that plagued me all afternoon. Ultimately

I decided, in an effort to give Carter space when I could, not to baby him or embarrass him, to send Eddie to get him on his own.

While I waited at the apartment, I reviewed all the paperwork I'd received from the stage manager: rehearsal information, calendars, contact list, et cetera, and put the week's schedule on the refrigerator, placing the rest of the papers in a three-ring binder. Then I ransacked the office where his former personal assistant Lyle had left his mess of documents, phone numbers, scribbled notes, and random receipts. As far as I could tell, there was no organizational strategy of any kind and the worst financial record keeping I'd ever seen. But I managed to find what I needed to understand the cast of characters in Carter's professional life.

There was Simon, the manager. Or maybe the former manager. There was someone named Randy who had been his PR person. And Cindy was an accountant at a firm called Mitchell McDuffy. Someone named Jacqueline was his stylist, but she lived in L.A. Also in L.A., there was the talent agency (that employed Skip, who'd called me) and Carter's lawyer. I wrote out my own edited list and brought it to the kitchen, where I sat with Owen, drinking an espresso and trying to contact the accountant to figure out what paperwork she needed in order to put me, Eddie, and Owen on the payroll, as opposed to asking Carter monthly for a wad of cash. I wanted W-4s filled out and taxes withheld, everything legal and correct.

I figured I still had about an hour to work when Jeffrey buzzed, letting me know that Charlotte was on her way up, with Jack and Megan.

"No, no no, no! What are you doing?" I asked as the elevator opened.

"Is he here?" Jack said. "Can we meet him?"

"It's not fair that Charlotte's the only one," Megan said.

"Shoes off, beasts!" Owen said firmly.

They immediately dropped to the floor and pulled off their boots.

"These are my other children," I told Owen. "Megan and Jack."

"Are there more of them or is this all?" he asked.

"This is it," I said.

"Megan and Jack," he said, nodding at each in turn. They stood up, shook his hand, and then followed Charlotte into the living room.

Owen checked his watch. "Are they staying?" It sounded almost like a warning.

I shook my head. "Not today," and I went after them.

"Did you see all the fans outside?" Megan asked. "All waiting for Carter?"

"Those aren't fans, stupid," Charlotte said, cleaning her glasses on her Caltech sweatshirt. "They're paparazzi assholes, waiting to ambush him."

"Cool," said Jack. "No one at school will believe any of this."

"We need proof," Megan said. "We need pictures."

"Absolutely no pictures," I said.

"A turtle!" Jack said. "Can I hold him?"

"No," I said.

"Just try not to embarrass me when he walks in," Charlotte said as Jack and Megan ran to look out the windows.

"Don't touch the glass," Owen called after them.

"Shouldn't he be back by now?" Charlotte asked.

"I love your instinct to want to share the excitement," I said, pointing to Megan and Jack, who were sliding in sock feet across the hardwood floors, "but Carter doesn't want to come home to . . . *all* of this."

"This apartment is *insane*!" Megan yelled. "When's he getting here?" She ran to the powder room and checked her face in the mirror, fixing her hair. She was wearing lip gloss.

Jack played with the dimmer switch in the kitchen to turn the lights up and down; Owen came over and shooed him away with a *tsk tsk*.

"Why can't we live somewhere this nice?" Jack asked, and then he turned around and noticed the big naked boob photo in the living room. "*Awesome*. Can we get one of these?"

Charlotte turned to me. "I see your point."

"Listen up," I told them, "Carter's going to be here any minute, and this is definitely not the day to meet him. We'll do this some other time but not today."

"Okay, creeps," Charlotte said, walking to the entry and holding up their shoes. "You saw the place. Now let's go home."

"I want to stay," Jack argued. "I have to meet him."

"Not this time," she said.

"Please?" Megan asked.

"You have to be invited first," I explained. "You understand, right?"

"I guess," Jack said reluctantly.

They sat on the floor and pulled their boots back on. "Tell him I said hi when he gets here," Jack said.

I smiled. But imagining Carter walking in the door was filling me with a nervous energy, and I hustled the kids toward the elevator, stopping Charlotte before she walked out.

"You'll come back after Dad gets home, right?" I asked her. "I'm really hoping you two can run lines."

"Relax," she said, "I'm sure he did fine. All he had to do today was read. How bad could it be?"

I frowned, knowing how stressed some students get reading in front of a class.

The kids left, Owen cooked lasagna, and I sat at my computer, filling in the gaps of everything we needed to keep Carter's life on track. We didn't need to worry about Simon for the time being, now that Carter was doing the musical. Carter could hire a new manager when he returned to L.A. if he wanted. The Campbells had given Carter a PR person for the run of the show, a woman named Jean who had sent me three emails already, so I crossed Randy off the list. I sent an email to the stylist Jacqueline (who told me she had a colleague in SoHo I should contact), called the accountant to discuss salaries and payroll, and left a message for Jean. I got a solid start on making sure that appointments were being made, money was being managed, bills were being paid, looks were being created, appearances were being scheduled. Next, I created a list of important addresses to give to Eddie, so that he'd have it with him in the car whenever he needed it. I looked up and saw that it was dark out already.

I texted Eddie: *On the way?*

He texted back: *Be there in 20. fyi he needs a new phone.*

That sounded ominous. *Oh god*, I thought.

Owen went home and I waited, pacing the floors, until finally the elevator doors opened. Carter came into the apartment, bag over his shoulder, script under his arm, looking like a college student.

"Hi," I called out. "How did it go? Was it okay?"

He dropped his bag on the floor and went straight to the fridge.

"Owen made lasagna and a salad. I bet you're hungry," I said.

Carter took out a water bottle and closed the door. *Booze?* Did I smell boozy breath? I would need to have a word with Eddie about forbidding alcohol in the SUV.

"Everything okay?"

He shook his head.

"So," I said, "you want to talk about it?"

He held a hand up to silence me. I thought for sure he was going to walk out of the room and slam his bedroom door, Charlotte style. But instead, he dropped his new copy of the script onto the counter and said, "It was total bullshit. I'm not doing this. I quit."

And then he walked down the hall to his room.

"Okay," I said, following him. "So what happened? First days are always hard." I took a step into the doorway, as far as I dared to go. He sat down on the edge of his bed.

"I'm not going back there," he said. "Those assholes fucking sat there and—because I, what? I messed up a line or two. I reversed a word, I maybe mispronounced some shit—and I didn't know what 'retisen' meant?—'ratison'?—like I would ever use a word like that anyway? How the fuck would I know. I didn't know half the shit I was saying. And Annabella Hatter is such a cunt. And then that old dude, Kevin some-thing, the one who's playing the main guy? The two of them sat there and smirked at each other. I saw it, I saw them looking at each other, and at one point she leaned over and whispered to him, the asshole looks up at her and smiles. Fucking dipshits. Making me look stupid."

"I'm sure it wasn't you," I said, trying to process his story and figure out what had actually happened. "What about the director?"

"What about him? He fucking hates me. They all do. Every five sec-onds someone either laughed at me or made a face like they were pissed. So why the fuck did they want me to do this anyway?"

"Because they know you're going to be terrific. But no one's terrific right away. This was the *first* day."

"They were hating on me the whole time. Like they already knew I was going to fuck it up." He turned his anger on me. "And you're a fucking asshole for making me go. I don't know any of this shit. And then Simon called, and I threw my phone out the car window, so get me a new one tomorrow. All of you, you and Simon and— You guys totally set me up."

He was right that I'd let him go in unprepared, but I couldn't imag-ine it had gone this badly. "Look, there was a lot going on in that room today," I said. "No one knows anyone yet, everyone's trying to impress everyone else. You're probably feeling a little, you know, paranoid, and—"

"Bullshit!" he yelled. *"You weren't there."*

I leaned against the doorframe, feeling like I'd let him down. "You made it through the first—"

"They were laughing at me!" He didn't look mad like he normally did. He looked miserable. Mortified. "I hate those shitty people. I hate the play. I'm not going to work with a bunch of assholes. I'm fucking loaded anyway; I don't need this shit. *And who the fuck is Charlie Chaplin?*" he yelled.

"What?"

"Charlie. Who is that?"

I took another step into the room, shocked that his manager, his agent, someone, hadn't told him. Why hadn't *I* told him? "He's—"

"Charlie Chaplin this, Cindy Chaplin that. 'Oh, they're legends.' Whatever. *Fuck* those people."

"They're dead anyway," I said.

"Well, good! I'm glad they're dead." Carter fell back on his pillows.

I took half a step closer. "Charlie Chaplin wrote it and performed in it," I explained, "and his son Sydney was in it, too, playing Neville—"

"Simon is such a fucking liar; he told me it's a brand-new show."

"No, he's right, it's never been done as a *musical* before. He— Charlie Chaplin, that is—wrote and starred in the original movie. Did Simon mention—?"

"No one told me shit about a movie."

I shook my head. "They—Simon—or I—someone should have told you. There was a movie, an old black-and-white film from the fifties. It was also called *Limelight.*"

"How was I supposed to know all this?"

"You're not supposed to. This was way before your time. Before *my* time, even."

"I've never heard of it, either," Charlotte said.

I turned around to see that she was standing right behind me.

"Should I . . . come back later?" she asked.

"We were just talking about the movie," I said. "You guys are both *way* too young to know about it. It's good. Do you . . . do you want to watch it?"

"Is it the same story," she asked, "or did they change it?"

"It's the same in some ways, just very dated. There's a man who's this famous performer, a comedian—a clown, really—who saves a young dancer after she tries to kill herself. And the man's career is failing. And the girl, Thereza, falls in love with him."

"My part is shit," Carter said. "I barely even come in until, like, half an hour into the show. I can't believe Simon agreed to this."

"It's not entirely shitty," I said meekly. "It's actually a nice role. Neville is romantic and a great musician, just like you."

Carter kicked his shoes off. "That guy Kevin is such a dick."

"Impossible," I said, my loyal fandom revealing itself.

"How do you know?" Charlotte asked.

It was a reasonable question but irked me nonetheless. "Everything I've ever seen him in, he's always been wonderful and endearing. And theatrical. And he's playing a really decent guy in this show who on some level *wants* Thereza and Neville to be together because he knows they're perfect for each other."

"I couldn't pick him out of a lineup," Charlotte said.

"Seriously?" I said. "Because I would consider that a parenting failure if it's true."

Carter threw his arms over his face and groaned.

Charlotte came farther into the room. "Was it really that bad?"

"It was completely fucked. The director was correcting me all the time, in front of everyone, every time I opened my mouth." He put a pillow over his head.

"First days always suck," Charlotte said.

"Last day," Carter said, speaking into the pillow. "No fucking way I'm going back there. I'll just deal with whatever shit I have to to quit. I'll pay anything. *Anything.* Seriously, I don't even care. I'll sell my house."

I was desperate to get out of this negative place, to make sure he didn't give up now, before he'd even gotten started.

"Who's hungry?" I asked them.

"I want a shot of Patrón," Carter said, pulling his coat off and throwing it across the room. He pulled off his socks and put his feet back up on his bed. "I want to get drunk and forget all about this shit and go back to L.A. tomorrow."

"Now come on," I said cheerfully, and I clapped my hands together. "How about lasagna instead, okay? Let's talk over dinner."

Carter groaned.

"I hate to say it," Charlotte said to him, "but you gotta go back tomorrow. Otherwise they beat you. Trust me, my first week at school sucked so hard, and my *mother*"—she said it like it was the worst word she could think of—"kept saying"—and then she mimicked me—"*'You're just adjusting, it'll get better, give it time,'* and I was all, 'Fine, whatever.' And then after a few weeks, I met some decent kids, and it turned out it was true."

"No way this is gonna get better. The guy I'm playing isn't getting any better. He's a loser today, he'll be a loser tomorrow. Why would I want to play a loser? Do you know he fucking *cries* in the story? Twice! He cries twice!"

"So quit later, and you'll really screw them over," Charlotte said. I thought I heard a bit of desperation creeping into her voice. "But not after the first day. It makes you look bad."

"I don't give a shit," he said, completely unmoved by Charlotte's opinion. "I want out."

"Where's the thing?" Charlotte asked nonchalantly. "The script. How about I read Annabella's part and you do you. You can go in there and show 'em up tomorrow."

"No way."

"Just don't ask me to sing," she said suddenly and laughed. "Because I can't carry a tune."

"You probably can," he said.

"Yeah, right," Charlotte said. "That's easy for you to say. Next you'll be saying I can dance."

I didn't want to get my hopes up, but he seemed to be calming down.

"You probably could if you tried."

"Oh my god," Charlotte said. "You have no idea the extent to which I *suck* at dancing. I don't even want to talk about it. Where's the script?"

"I'm too tired," he said. He closed his eyes, and it looked like he had won.

"Well, I'm starving anyway," she said. "Let's eat and maybe watch the movie." She turned and went to the kitchen, and—miracle—he got up and followed her.

I served Owen's lasagna, while they got cans of Coke, took my laptop, and started to go back to Carter's bedroom. I took Charlotte by the elbow.

"*What?*" she whispered.

I wasn't even sure what to say. *No food outside the kitchen? Thank you for helping? Watch out for him? If he offers you drugs, just say no?*

"Keep the door open," I said.

Charlotte looked at me like I was crazy. "God! *Mom!*"

"Sorry," I said. "I'm confused about what's happening."

"What's happening is you're giving me your Amazon password so we can watch the movie."

———

When I went back to Carter's room to check on them a little while later, the movie was playing, and they were both sound asleep, Carter on the bed and Charlotte in the big armchair. What was it about this movie that made people pass out? I certainly hoped the musical wouldn't have this soporific effect on its audience. I sat at the foot of the bed and watched it on my own for a few minutes, wondering if Carter could play such a sensitive, earnest man. It was no wonder they were asleep; the scenes were long and philosophical, the clowning felt terribly old-fashioned. How could kids who grew up with special effects that showed explosions, 3-D space battles, and fast-paced action stay awake through an old, charming movie like this? And what in the world could Carter find to relate to? I listened to the characters talk to each other, endless speeches about life, longing, love, and disappointment that I found engaging as a middle-aged woman. But for the under-twenty crowd? The very demographic the producers expected Carter to attract? This would be a tough sell.

But the adaptation? New pop songs and the all-star cast? I wondered if all that would be enough to not only keep people from sleeping in their seats, but also have them on their feet when the curtain came down.

twenty-two

THE NEXT DAY I DID SOMETHING I had never done before: I called Charlotte's school and lied. I said that Charlotte had a doctor's appointment and would be in by eleven o'clock.

Michael thought I'd lost my mind. "You're letting her skip school?"

"I'm asking her to skip a class or two. It's an intellectual exercise," I said. "It involves reading. She can put it on her résumé: 'Celebrity tutor.'" I sat on the edge of the bed pulling my shoes on as Jasper came over and rubbed up against me.

"She's skipping school so that he won't skip rehearsal?" Michael said. "I don't get the priorities."

"It's English class she's missing, and she's already read *Great Expectations* twice. Given the senioritis that most kids get, this is a better use of her time than zoning out during a class discussion."

"But spending time with that guy? He's eighteen; she's seventeen. What if they start . . . you know . . . dating?"

"No way." I pictured Kimmie staggering into the kitchen. "If you'd met the last girl he brought home, you'd believe me. Charlotte's a totally different creature. They aren't each other's types. It's mutual."

"If you say so," Michael said. "But I don't like it."

Jack ran into the room with his shirt on inside out. "I can't find my math homework."

"It's on the floor by the television," I said.

He ran back out.

"Odd couple or no," Michael said, putting on his belt, "I just want to make sure we keep appropriate boundaries between them."

I stood up, got my bag and laptop, and checked my face in the mirror. "If Carter quits today, like he said he would last night, none of this will matter."

———

Jack, Charlotte, and I walked against a bitter wind to school, and after Jack ran inside, Charlotte and I went to Carter's, walking blithely past the paparazzi, one of whom coughed grotesquely and then spit onto the sidewalk.

"Ugh, disgusting," Charlotte hissed.

I reached in my bag and found three wrapped cough drops. I walked over, handed them to the guy, and said sweetly, "Maybe you should get out of the cold for a few hours."

"Thanks," he said, sounding truly grateful. He popped one in his mouth and smiled.

Charlotte stared at me and whispered, "You better sterilize your hands when we get upstairs."

Carter was actually up and dressed, sitting in the kitchen while Owen served him breakfast.

"Eggs?" Owen asked Charlotte.

"No thanks," she said, "but is there coffee?"

"Gross," Carter said. "Coffee gives you bad breath, you know."

"Well, unlike you, I won't be making out with Annabella Hatter today."

Carter looked up from his plate. "I make out with her?"

Charlotte was confused. "I thought you read through the whole play yesterday."

He flipped his script open.

"Didn't they read the stage directions out loud?" she asked.

"I wasn't really listening," he said.

"You and Annabella totally go at it at the end of one of your songs."

"No way," he said, trying to find the moment in the script.

As I already knew, Charlotte was brilliant.

"You know," I said, deciding to jump in on this move, "for the last part of the play, you'll be wearing a really snazzy military uniform."

He looked up at me. "So?" he said.

Jeesh. It was hard to know what young people were into.

———

There was a little over an hour before we had to leave for Ripley-Grier, so while Carter and Charlotte went into the living room to go over lines, I reluctantly ran over to the AT&T store on Fifty-Seventh and Broadway to pick up a new phone for Carter. The woman recognized me from the last time I was there, and the process was a whole lot easier. "You got your old SIM card?" she asked.

No, I most definitely did not have the SIM card. According to Eddie, the phone was smashed to pieces somewhere in the vicinity of Forty-Second Street.

She set up the new phone, and I paid her in cash.

———

I walked back into the apartment, saying, "Okay, guys, time to go."

Carter got up from the couch sluggishly and stretched.

"We've only got five minutes, okay?" I called out, handing him his new phone as he walked back to his room. His posture and expression made me worry he might be going back to bed.

Charlotte came over and whispered, "We've got a serious problem."

I took her by the hand, and we went into the office and closed the door.

"He doesn't seem to— It's like he can't hear anything he's saying. He can read okay, more or less, but he can't comprehend the words he's saying at the same time that he's reading them."

"Maybe he just needs more practice?"

"They're going to eat him alive today," she said, putting on her coat. "I wouldn't want to be him."

A few minutes later, we got in the car with Eddie. Charlotte got some notes out to study on the way.

"What's that?" I asked.

"I have a quiz fourth period."

"Oh my God, why didn't you tell me?"

"It's fine," she said. "Here," and she handed Carter a notecard on which she'd written out his act 1, scene 3, lines.

"The fuck am I supposed to do with this?" he asked.

"Carry it around all day and look at it whenever you get a chance. Like in the car or when you're getting a coffee. Or when you go to the bathroom. I once added up all the little windows of time in my day, and it came up to twenty-seven minutes. That's so much time, and why waste it, you know?"

"Wow," Carter said. "You're a serious nerd, huh?"

"I'm a nerd who's going to ace my quiz today," she said, smiling, "so you'd be wise to take my little tips."

At Ripley-Grier, Carter and I got out of the car, and Eddie drove Charlotte to school. I turned to Carter and asked, "You feeling okay?"

Carter was gripping his notecard. "Sure, whatever."

I wanted so badly to say the right thing, something encouraging but not overbearing. Given that he rarely made eye contact with me, if ever, any sentiment I wanted to express felt forced. "You'll do fine," I said anyway, and without thinking I put up my hand for a high five. He let me stand there with my hand in the air for an awkward amount of time until I finally dropped my arm. "If there's something I can do to help—" but he was already walking toward the building. His back—the hunch, shrug, and shape of it, in any kind of clothing—was something I was getting to know well.

"Ya know you don't need to bring me here," he said, over his shoulder. "I don't need a babysitter."

I watched him walk in, past the new security guards standing by the door, feeling that very specific kind of worry when your kid is about to get hurt. *You weren't there*, he'd said to me. *Well, maybe I should be*, I thought.

So I pulled my purse up on my shoulder and walked into the building after him, giving my name and showing the contents of my bag to the guards. I nodded confidently at them and walked to the stairs. On the second floor, I stopped at the front desk and was told the cast was meeting in the smaller studio that morning. It was crowded, and there were folding chairs placed in rows, all facing out the big windows overlooking Eighth Avenue. The other three walls were mirrored and had ballet bars. Dancers, dressed in tights and sweatshirts, were stretching on the floor and talking to each other. The stars were all assembled, and I gasped seeing Melissa McCarthy and Kevin Kline again, only a few feet away from me, sitting together like old friends. I wondered if they knew each other already, or had they just met yesterday? Kevin Kline was so handsome, even better-looking in real life, relaxed, comfortable, and when Melissa leaned in and said something to him, he threw his head back and let out a beautiful, booming laugh. I sighed, starstruck, and the thought popped in my head: *How the hell did I end up here?* Meanwhile, Annabella, in tights and a tank top, was talking intensely to a man wearing Adidas sweatpants and holding a clipboard; she was a little high-strung, perhaps. I felt like telling her, *It's only the second day, sweetheart. Relax.*

And then I spotted Carter. I slid into a seat in the back of the room, catty-corner to where he was sitting, just out of his line of vision. From my chair in the back, I could see him there, all alone, slouching down in his seat, scrolling through his phone. He wasn't part of the group; he wasn't even trying to be. He looked like he didn't belong.

The director, Edgar Sterling, a handsome, older man in black jeans and a white, untucked, rumpled button-down, walked to the front of the room and called over the young guy with the clipboard. They talked for a moment and then the guy in the sweatpants called out, "Let's get started, people."

Annabella went over and sat next to Kevin, who opened the notebook on his lap and took a pen out of his shirt pocket. Melissa patted him on the knee. "It's go time," she said loudly, and everyone in the room clapped, except for Carter.

Edgar stepped front and center. "In a minute or two, Rob"—here he gestured to clipboard guy—our illustrious stage manager and his assistant will go over some scheduling changes, costume appointments, dance rehearsals, and some shifts in call times. We'll be running a really tight ship, so if there are any conflicts, Rob needs to know immediately. We have rehearsals scheduled in all three studios throughout the day, every day, so check for emails from Rob at night for changes." Melissa nodded and Kevin wrote a note to himself in his notebook. Everyone was sitting up straight and listening.

Carter was looking at his phone.

Edgar, with graying hair and a stern countenance, continued: "I'd like to take a moment first, to say a few things about the show and yesterday's read-through. For the most part it went well. There's some good chemistry, lots of laughs. As we all know now, this show is an epic reimagining of sorts; we're taking a true classic and giving it fresh color. New life in a way that I believe will make a huge impact."

I didn't know what he meant by "impact," but I wondered if it would translate into Tony Awards. After all, Edgar had won two for directing, and Kevin Kline had recently won for best actor in *Present Laughter*.

"Some of you," Edgar said, and here he glanced briefly in Carter's direction, "will appreciate the notion of a new image. But as you probably all have gathered, a reinvention takes a lot of thought, a lot of time, some luck, and enormous effort. But no surprise there. Putting on a show with ambitious musical numbers and complex choreography is hard work. The script is sophisticated, funny, and touching, and it requires your attention." And here he turned to face Carter. "Honestly, I didn't foresee the amount of script work that's going to be required by some of you, but Rob and I made adjustments in the schedule yesterday to accommodate certain actors who are going to need extra time getting the lines, well—understood, frankly—and delivered comedically, artfully, and thoughtfully. I think you know who you are."

Just like that, he called Carter out in front of the whole group. As a teacher, as a mother, I couldn't fathom the insensitivity. To think that shaming him would be anything other than disastrously counterproductive was mind-bogglingly dumb. And humiliating for Carter. No wonder he hadn't wanted to come back.

And then, just as I was completely taking Carter's side, I looked over at him to see his reaction, but if Carter was even listening, I couldn't tell. No one could. He was sitting, neck craned downward, looking at his phone. His phone! Now *that* really pissed me off. I sat up in my chair and wished I had something, an empty Coke can or a tennis ball, that I could lob at Carter's head to get his attention. Or a remote-control electric zapper. *Sit up and look at your boss! Pay attention!* I wanted to yell.

Edgar saw that Carter was still looking at his phone, and he shook his head. "Didn't think I'd have to do this since we're not in high school anymore, but let me remind everyone of some of the house rules for the run of the rehearsal period: when I'm talking, put your goddamn cell phones away. I don't want to hear so much as a fucking ping once rehearsal has started."

Carter didn't budge. I had no idea if he was deliberately ignoring Edgar, or if he was actually so engrossed with *Minecraft* or Snapchat or whatever he was looking at that he didn't realize what was going on around him. From all the way across the room, my fingertips itched with the urge to smack him.

"Pardon me," Edgar said, "Mr. Reid."

Carter looked up.

They stared at each other. I sat there in the back row with my eyes wide, holding my breath like everyone else in the room. Kevin Kline looked at Annabella, and she raised her eyebrows back at him.

Edgar turned and whispered something to Rob. Rob then whispered something to his assistant, who made a note. Edgar looked back at Carter. "I'm adding an appointment to your schedule at four thirty. With me."

"I'm out at four o'clock today," Carter said.

"Not anymore you're not."

Even Melissa, who I imagined as laid-back and understanding, was sitting with arms crossed in front of her chest, likely pleased to imagine this kid getting schooled on the importance of showing respect to the institution of Theater.

This is bad, I thought. *This is really, really bad.*

Rob called out a series of instructions about dance rehearsals, including which group would go to the large studio and which was staying in the room we were in. Some of the actors began exiting through the side doors, and Carter walked out without even seeing me.

As soon as the room had mostly cleared, I got up and, in spite of feeling horribly intimidated, went straight to the director, who was talking quietly with Rob.

"Hi, can I talk to you a second?" I asked, as politely but urgently as I could.

"You're . . . ?"

"I'm Carter's assistant. I can see there are problems, and I was hoping to go over a few things with you."

Rob stepped back from me, saying, "We're not interested in hearing about Carter's extra demands right now."

"No, no, nothing like that," I said. "But I wanted to talk about how to, I don't know, how to *fix* this. Make this whole situation better, all of it."

Edgar looked at me, and maybe it was my age, maybe it was the very genuine concern I was demonstrating, but he excused Rob and took me down the hall into a smaller office space.

He pointed to a chair and sat across from me.

"I've got three minutes," he said.

Thinking an apology might be the best way to begin, I said plainly, "I'm really sorry."

"I'm going to be honest," Edgar said, in an angry whisper. "Carter's a serious pain in my ass already. If it were up to me—"

"I know," I said. "I completely understand. But he's in this now, so can we try to make this better somehow?"

"How?" he asked. "He has no respect whatsoever for me, for the cast or crew, or for this show, as far as I can tell."

Looking at the creases in Edgar's eyes, I was guessing he had more than twenty years on me. My heart was racing, and I realized I was flat-out afraid of him. "If the goal," I said, "if *your* goal, is to get an improved attitude from him, a better situation going here, I'd like to make some suggestions, share what I think will help, ways to get him in line."

"What kind of suggestions?" He looked at his watch.

"If you could start by—and I know you don't want to, and I completely get that—but if you could let him know you think he can do this, that the songs will come easily, for example. I know you're in no mood to reward his awful behavior, and it's fine if you want to lay down ground rules, I certainly would, but he's in a pretty precarious place right now, and his confidence is extremely low—hard to believe, I know—and if the goal is to get him through this—no, if the goal is to help him really kick ass in this play, then I really think your approval or even admiration of him is key."

At the end of my speech, I smiled.

"He's an asshole," Edgar said. "I don't admire him, and I don't approve of anything he's done since he walked in here yesterday."

"Right, but see, the more you think and say that he's an asshole, the bigger an asshole he's going to be." And then I added, "He thinks you hate him."

"I do hate him," he answered.

"Right."

"And it's not my job to stroke his fucking ego."

"I'm not asking you to stroke his ego. No, well, maybe a little. But as a means to an end. I want him to want to do well for you. I swear, I'll work with him at home, I'll teach him how to behave here, but if you could just try this for me, just try conveying one positive message to him today. You and I both know he's going to have to work his ass off, and he knows that, too."

"His phone's gotta go," he said.

"Done. I'll take care of it."

"I objected to this casting from the start," he said bluntly. "The guy's a train wreck. And I don't want him taking this show down with him. It's like there's the whole cast, and then there's Carter; he clearly doesn't give a shit. He isn't even trying."

"I can see what you're saying, but I'm just telling you that the way to turn this around is not to make him even more insecure and angry and isolated. He needs to feel good about being here, about being part of this."

"Insecure?" he scoffed. "He's an arrogant prick."

"I know he comes across that way, but if you get to know him a little—"

"I'm not his kindergarten teacher."

"I know," I said. His irritation seemed only to be getting more intense. "Thank you for hearing me out."

"You know he was late yesterday?"

"I'll work on that as well. I'm really going to do everything I can because it's really important to me that he succeeds. But I can't do much if he thinks that you think he sucks."

"Then maybe he shouldn't suck."

Ouch. This wasn't going as well as I'd hoped. "Things can't get much worse," I said. "So it's worth a try, right? If you say one nice thing to him today, find one thing he does well and say so. It's all I'm asking. He's singing today, so surely there's a compliment to be given about that.

Maybe you could even ask him to help out in some way, give him the responsibility of being a leader."

At that suggestion, Edgar got to his feet. "Help out? *Leader?* Are you out of your mind? He's *disengaged.*"

"I can see that," I said, standing up as well. "But I also see that he's young, and he needs some encouragement. Preferably from you."

"I've got *actual* child actors in this show, and Carter's not one of them."

"Well . . ."

"This is a job, he's a professional. And I'm late," he said and walked away.

In the hallway, I walked past a small studio window and saw Kevin Kline, running through a scene by himself, gesturing with his beautiful, expressive hands. In the adjacent room, the one we'd been in earlier, I saw a group of children working through choreography. And back by the lobby, in the big rehearsal space, I saw Carter. He was holding sheet music, and listening to the music director, who was seated at a piano. It was a minor thing, but Carter was standing slightly apart from the rest of the cast.

I didn't know much about theater, but I could see he wasn't part of the group. Maybe I could arrange a playdate with Annabella. Call up her personal assistant and plan a trip to the Museum of Natural History.

He looked up and saw me through the window. I put my hand up and gave him a little wave and then hurried away before he had time to react.

I was a nervous wreck all day. Between Edgar's low opinion of Carter and Charlotte's realization that he wasn't processing what he was reading, I decided that something new had to be done. I devised a plan I hoped would speed up the process and texted Charlotte so she would know exactly what I had in mind to turn the situation around. And then I called Howard.

Eddie drove me to the rehearsal studio at four o'clock; I wanted to be around for Carter's meeting with Edgar. I went up to the second floor and found them sitting together in the office. The door was only open half an inch, but I could hear Edgar talking. I thought about simply eavesdropping but decided against it, feeling that these men would need some help communicating with each other.

"Am I late?" I asked, coming in and taking a seat next to Carter.

"We're just getting started," Edgar said. Neither of them looked surprised to see me. And neither of them looked happy to be there. Carter, sitting in a chair with his legs out straight in front of him, arms crossed in front of his chest, was projecting an attitude of not giving a shit. Edgar's body language conveyed the opposite; he looked fed up and angry.

"How'd it go today?" I asked.

Carter shrugged.

"We started on some of the choreography," Edgar said. He looked at me and added, "Carter caught on quickly. He's a great dancer."

Carter nodded smugly.

"Wonderful," I said. "Isn't that nice to hear, Carter? And the songs?"

"He did well," Edgar said. "Really well."

"Great," I said. "And it's only the second day!"

"I want to go over some ground rules," Edgar said, clearly ready to stop with the ego stroking. "Like this morning, Carter. If you're on the phone the whole time I'm talking"—he tried to mask his anger with a laugh—"it really pisses me off."

"I was listening," Carter said defensively.

"It sure didn't look that way."

"Come on, Carter," I said. "You know that phones are a no-no during work."

"A 'no-no'?" Carter asked. "What am I, *five*?"

"You know what I mean."

"No cell phone from now on," Edgar said.

"Done," I said. "Right?"

"Fine," Carter said. He sounded sick to death of this conversation already.

"Good," Edgar said.

"And you need to get here on time every day. Our scheduling is so tight, and when you come in late, it throws off the whole day."

"That's on me," I said. It was like negotiating a treaty, and I wanted to make my own pledges. "I promise he'll get here punctually from now on."

"So tomorrow," Edgar went on, "we'll schedule some time for you to spend with Annabella to work on the first song and run lines. She might need some help with the harmonies, but let's go easy on her."

Brilliant, I thought.

"Yeah, sure," Carter said.

"But you're going to work on the lines at home, right?" he asked. "I need you off book in two weeks."

Carter didn't respond.

"Is that going to be a problem?"

"No," I said, "he can do it."

Carter sat up and shoved his chair back. "Don't talk for me," he said. I felt my face go hot.

"Carter?" Edgar asked. "What's the deal?"

He looked up at Edgar and swallowed. "It's a lot," he said. "It's more pages of stuff than I thought."

Edgar nodded. "Okay. It'll come easier once we start running the scenes. And blocking will help, too."

"This isn't the kind of shit I'm used to doing."

Edgar nodded, and he looked at Carter with understanding for the first time. "It's definitely different. So let's work really hard, see how it's going in a few days, and then talk again."

"Sure."

"Glad you said something, Carter," Edgar said.

I was impressed, both with Carter's honesty and with Edgar's measured, mature response. Maybe they hadn't needed me there after all.

But when we stepped into the elevator on our way out of the building, Carter sighed and said, "What a fucking dick. I can't believe I have to work with that asshole."

So much for my optimism.

Carter took a shower after we got back to his place. I had reminded him that he would be working with Charlotte again as soon as she could get there, and he'd gone off to his room and closed the door.

I looked at my watch. And right on the button, the door buzzed. I waited by the elevator for Howard to come up. When he walked in, we shook hands like we always did and went to the kitchen. He placed his uniform hat on the counter next to him and looked at the view, down at Columbus Circle, up at the skinny, absurdly tall Steinway Tower, and over the bare trees in Central Park.

"The city looks different from up here," he said.

"Bigger?" I asked.

"Richer."

I introduced him to Owen, who was getting Carter's dry-cleaning ready for pickup.

Carter came out of his room showered, well dressed, and with good color. I was glad he looked awake enough to keep working.

"I'm starving," he said.

It was amazing to me the way he could enter a room and ignore everyone in it. "Hi," I said. "You remember Howard?"

"Yep," he said, without even glancing in our direction.

"Howard was kind enough to offer to read lines with you and Charlotte tonight," I said.

Carter took a bite out of the baguette Owen gave him and said, with his mouth full of bread, "Nah." And before I could react, he turned his back to me, took a glass of orange juice that Owen held out to him, and went back to his room.

Howard looked at me and smiled.

"I'm so sorry," I said.

"It's fine."

"That was *so* rude."

He shrugged. "I told you he wouldn't want my help."

Owen sighed. "He was raised by wolves."

"I'll pay you anyway," I assured Howard, "obviously."

"It was worth it just to see this apartment."

I walked with him to the elevator, and we went down to the lobby together. "It's so embarrassing," I said. "He's has no manners. You should have seen how he treated his director today."

"I was pretty tough on him after the show we saw that night. I doubt he's used to that."

"Nevertheless, there's no excuse." I looked up and saw Charlotte coming through the courtyard, tall and confident in her big, black glasses, her backpack slung over one shoulder and her hair, long and loose for once, hanging down over the other. She looked like a college girl. Jeffrey held the door open for her, and she came into the lobby.

I introduced Howard to Charlotte, and, as I knew she would, she smiled and shook his hand.

"Unfortunately, Carter kind of . . . ," I started.

"He doesn't want me here," Howard explained.

Charlotte looked worried. "We really need someone to read with us."

"I'm not sure how to talk him into this," I said.

Charlotte dropped her backpack to the floor while she took off her coat and gloves.

"You have to tell him he doesn't have a choice. It's like Jack saying he doesn't want to get his teeth cleaned," she said. "It would be like me saying I don't want to get immunized."

"I'm not his mom," I reminded her.

Charlotte sighed heavily. "We *need* another person for lines," she said.

"You'll find someone," Howard said. "Someone he knows and trusts."

"Who?"

"What about him?" Howard asked, pointing to Jeffrey.

"No freakin' way," Jeffrey said.

"There's a guy at school I could ask," Charlotte said.

"I don't think it should be a boy his age," I said. "I think he'd feel insecure."

"Dad?" Charlotte asked.

"Dad can't take time off work for this."

"I'll tell you what," Howard said. "Why don't I wait here while you talk to Carter. If you need me, let me know. You're paying me for the hour anyway." He walked over to the couches and took a seat.

"I'll go up," Charlotte said. "I'll just tell him he's being stupid and stubborn."

"No," I said. "I'll tell him. It's like good cop, bad cop. I'll be the bad cop. You need to stay on good terms with him so he'll work with you."

Charlotte and I went back up to the apartment together, and I started to go back to Carter's room, when he came down the hall.

"Tell that asshole—the director or whatever—that I'm gonna take the day off tomorrow," Carter said as soon as he came in. He spotted Charlotte and said, "Hey," with a nod.

Charlotte glanced over at me.

"You mean Edgar?" I said. "That's not possible."

"I need a break," he said. "I'll just take a day, work out, maybe. Chill. Whatever."

"You can't miss rehearsal tomorrow," I said. "Where's that schedule?"

I got the copy of the week's rehearsal schedule that I'd put on the refrigerator door. "You know, you're only doing the scene in the stationery store," I said, trying to sound relaxed while all I wanted to do was start screaming, *No! You can't skip the third rehearsal!* I could imagine the call I'd get from the Campbells if he was a no-show. "And then in the afternoon, you're in a music rehearsal. You should save a skip day for something worse. Look," I said, showing him the schedule, "on Friday you're doing scenes most of the day with Kevin and then one with Annabella. Maybe skip Friday. But don't skip both because then everyone will be pissed, and they'll get on your case about it."

"Nah," Carter said, not even really listening, "I'm not feeling it. And I don't need so much dance rehearsal; I can do this shit in my sleep."

"Maybe I'll skip Friday, too," Charlotte said. "I have a physics test."

"So why don't you both take a personal day on Friday," I said, trying to sound as if the very idea wouldn't make me break out in hives. "But not tomorrow, okay?"

"Come on," Charlotte said. "We've got some time. Let's just go over the lines you have for tomorrow." She headed into the living room. "It's not much at all."

"I fucking *hate* this shit," Carter said, but he did, in fact, follow her.

About thirty seconds later, I felt my phone vibrate. I checked it and saw Charlotte had texted me: *Talk C into letting Howard help tomorrow. We need him.*

twenty-three

I WALKED TO 15 CPW FEELING UPBEAT, with a donut in my hand for Carter and a mantra in my head: *Let this be an easy day.*

I'd given him a wake-up call at seven thirty, reminded him of his schedule for the day, and then taken Jack to school, staying for half an hour with the parents to see the art show. I'd walked around with Jack through the various classrooms where lopsided ceramics and brightly colored collage projects were on display. With huge relief I'd noted that not one of Jack's creations even bordered on the inappropriate.

When I entered the apartment, I found Owen in the kitchen, frying bacon. The apartment was cheerful, and fresh flowers wrapped in paper were on the island, ready to be arranged.

"Good morning!" I said, energized by the liveliness of the scene. I handed Owen the donut bag, which he opened, sniffed, and put aside on the counter.

"Latte?" he said.

"Yes, please. Where's Carter?" I asked, watching Owen play barista.

"How should I know?" Owen asked. "He's your responsibility, not mine."

"I just assumed he'd shown some sign of life." The sun went behind the clouds suddenly, and I felt a shift. "I already talked to him this morning, so I know he's up."

I walked down the darkened hallway: *Please be reading the script, please be getting dressed.*

But, as it turned out, he wasn't even awake.

"No, no, no!" I said. "Carter, shit! Wake up."

I heard him snore lightly. His cell phone was next to him on the pillow.

"Carter, you overslept," I said, as though he gave a shit. I pulled the curtains open and stood over the bed. "Carter. Carter. CARTER!"

He grumbled and rolled over, turning his back to me.

"Carter," I said, as though it were a brand new word. "You have to get up!"

He smacked his lips, adjusted his head into a more comfortable position, and lapsed into silence.

"Good morning!" I shouted.

He turned his head back and looked up at me. "What the *fuck*?!"

"You overslept," I said again. "You have forty-five minutes to shower, dress, and get downstairs to the car."

Carter grumbled something incomprehensible.

"The last thing we want is to get off on the wrong foot with Edgar today."

"Who?"

I couldn't figure out if he was still asleep or just being stupid. "Your *boss*," I said. "Edgar. The director of the show you're in."

"Fuck," he said and closed his eyes.

I thought through my options. A bucket of ice water? A bullhorn? "Carter," I said firmly. "Get up and get in the goddamn shower. Now."

Nothing.

"Seriously!" I yelled.

Seriously? *Seriously?* Like, what was that word going to accomplish?

Carter slept on. I could hear Owen in the kitchen, being industrious, and felt like a failure. I walked up to the bed again.

"Good morning!" I said. "Rise and shine! Up and at 'em!" He didn't budge. What, I wondered, might motivate a guy like this?

"Hey, Carter, I just got a call," I lied. "It's about Annabella."

"Huh?"

"It's really bad."

"What?" he asked, rolling over to face me.

"Well, from what I understand from her PA, she's thinking of skipping rehearsal today because she's too nervous to sing in front of you. She thinks you're going to, you know, make fun of her because she's not experienced, and she feels like a fraud. She was crying about it yesterday."

"Crying?"

"Yeah. Well, sure. Poor girl is feeling very intimidated. I feel sorry for her. And I heard from Rob that Melissa complained that the choreography is too hard for her."

"It's not hard at all," he said, rubbing his eyes.

"For you, maybe. But everyone in the cast is kind of falling apart."

He sat up slowly. "What time is it?" he asked.

"It's late," I said. "You have to leave in half an hour."

"Half an hour?" he yelled. "Fuck." He threw off the covers and got out of bed, adjusting his boxer briefs. "Why didn't you wake me up? *Jesus*," he said and went into the bathroom.

"Hey, Carter," I said through the door. I waited until he finished peeing. "Don't mention any of this to Annabella or her PA. Or anyone," I said. "I think she would be even more insecure if she knew you knew."

He opened the door. "I get it," he said. "I gotta get ready." He pointed to the hallway.

Back in the kitchen, I drank my latte and tried to decide if I should be pleased with myself or ashamed for being so outrageously manipulative.

——◆——

According to the schedule, Carter was on a break from twelve to twelve thirty. I decided to communicate with him using text: *Hope it's a good day. We NEED Howard to run lines. Just try it.* I added a smiley face.

He never answered.

When Howard showed up early that evening, I expected an argument, but Carter didn't say a word about it. He was in a terrible mood and sulked in a chair that he placed slightly apart from where Howard and Charlotte were sitting.

"I'm not too good at this," Howard said. "I read the lines for Calvero?" He opened his script and put on his glasses. "We're not singing, are we?"

Howard faltered over words, missed cues, and mistakenly read all the stage directions for his characters out loud; I wondered if he was intentionally messing up to set Carter at ease. Charlotte's role was leader of the group, and Carter accepted that without challenging her in any way. She corrected them when necessary and stopped them when there was confusion.

"If I have to say 'gee whiz' or 'gosh' or 'golly' one more fucking time, I'll lose my shit," Carter said.

"Story seems dull," Howard added. "I hope it picks up a little."

"It won't be dull when it's staged," Charlotte said. "It needs to be acted."

"Neville's a limp dick," Carter said.

"What?" she said. "No, he's a perfect gentleman."

"This Calvero fellow?" Howard asked. "He's a sad case, isn't he? I don't get what she sees in him."

"You and me both," Carter said.

For a second I thought they might high-five or something, but the moment passed.

———

Over the course of that week, Carter's apartment became this lively, bustling place, nothing like the silent tomb I'd walked into a couple of months before. Eddie was coming and going, dark glasses on and car keys in hand, ready to do an errand or pickup when needed. Owen was busying about, cooking and ordering and organizing. Carter was indulging in tantrums when the vocabulary proved too challenging or when he drew a blank trying to recall a line. Howard was often sitting in the kitchen working on a homework assignment or reading through the script to get familiar with Kevin Kline's part. (I came in one morning and found him dozing upright on his barstool.) Charlotte came by before school and again after winter track. She didn't seem to mind showing up at Carter's sweaty, with hair pulled back in a braid, wiping her horn-rimmed glasses on her track pants; she had a look that was enhanced by sports.

I would return to my own apartment at the end of the day, marveling at how equally busy it was there with Jack practicing piano, Megan and Sabrina baking cookies, and Pancake, the pug from down the hall, tormenting Jasper. Michael and I had little time alone, and I imagined sending the kids off to spend weekends with my mom in Katonah, weekends when Michael and I could be by ourselves, enjoying New York, and getting a little peace and quiet.

The walk from Jack's school to Carter's apartment in the morning became my favorite time to call my mom. I would stroll down Columbus, filling her in on Carter's latest issues and finding out how her plans for the move were going.

"I'm coming up for the inspection," she said one day. "Maybe we could all go together. I'd love Michael's opinion on the house. It's not too late to pull out of this deal."

"Do you want to pull out?"

"I guess that depends on what we find in the inspection. Maybe the beams have wood rot. Maybe the attic has squirrels."

I pictured the house across the street and wondered what Michael would think of it. If Jack saw that tree swing, that sweep of front lawn, he'd probably start packing.

—————

I may have let my guard down and started to relax a little. Carter was getting to rehearsal on time, most of the time, and Edgar seemed satisfied, if not thrilled, with his progress on the script. Kevin Kline had been collegial during their rehearsals together. At one point, I had spied on them through the window as they worked through the scene where they run into each other at a bar. Edgar had looked impatient, but Kevin had smiled and put his hand on Carter's shoulder, leaning in to say something to him.

"What did he tell you?" I asked Carter later. We were in the back of the SUV while Eddie battled the midtown traffic.

"He said it's a real tough scene for him and that it might take him a while to get it right."

My crush on Kevin Kline doubled. "What did you say?"

Carter frowned. "I said every scene's a tough one for me. Edgar kept saying this shit about how the characters are all good people. Like they have honor. But that's what I hate about the play."

"What do you mean?" I asked.

"People aren't good like that in real life. People just let you down."

"There are a lot of good people in the world."

"Name one," he said.

"Michael," I answered, without even thinking.

Part Five

BETTER WORK

"You wanna Lamborghini?
Sippin' martinis? . . .
You wanna live fancy?
Live in a big mansion?
Party in France?
You better work bitch."

Britney Spears, "Work Bitch"

—

twenty-four

THE CALENDAR THE CAMPBELLS had given me was dog-eared and scribbled on. I had it with me at all times to make certain that Carter was where he needed to be, when he needed to be there. In addition to fittings and props and schedule changes to contend with, he also had publicity events for the production: appearances on morning shows, photo shoots for print ads, and interviews with every cultural outlet in New York and beyond.

In the midst of this, maybe Edgar decided that my method of getting Carter to commit and care was worthwhile after all, or maybe this was going to happen anyway: he invited Carter to attend a meeting with songwriter Max Martin to discuss some of the lyrics. Max had worked with Carter on his last album, and they were happy to collaborate again. When I went to pick Carter up that day, I walked in just as Edgar was saying to the entire cast, ". . . and thanks to Carter, we made some excellent adjustments to some of the details of the vocals. Max is a taskmaster and a perfectionist, and I have to say watching Carter work with him today was a great experience."

"Wooo, Carter," Melissa said. Kevin slow clapped.

Edgar was perhaps not as scary as I'd initially thought.

That same day, Jack and Ben had a playdate, and, since I was at Carter's, I'd asked Megan to stop by Lauren's to pick him up at five o'clock. She left without her key, and they texted to tell me they were locked out of our apartment. Carter was in a reasonable mood, so I told Megan and Jack to come meet me.

Megan was so nervous when she walked in, I thought she might collapse on the floor. "I didn't even get a chance to dress up or anything," she said.

Jack was just plain excited.

Carter was surprisingly friendly, actually saying hello to them, and it occurred to me, as I watched him make a point of looking at my kids when he talked to them, that maybe he was better with children than he was with adults. *Perhaps,* I thought, *that was a strength he could draw upon.*

"What's up?" he asked them.

Megan took that pleasantry as an actual question and told him about how her teachers were useless and that they pretty much just left you there on your own to drown but she was hoping to get into a new school that she could go to with her friend Sabrina because Sabrina's the best and knows everything about New York and they were taking a cooking class together and did he like cookies or brownies better because she'd be happy to make either for him. Or both.

"Brownies," Carter said. "And throw some pot in while you're at it."

"Now then," I said, "that's definitely not going to happen."

"And what about you, dude?" Carter asked.

"My school's awesome," Jack said.

"It is?" I asked, happy to hear him say something so positive.

"Yeah," he said, "it's great."

Carter smiled. "I never heard any kid say something 'great' about school before."

"I like mine," Jack said, shrugging.

"Well," Carter said, "then you must be getting a lot of pussy there, am I right?"

Megan and I froze for a moment in stunned silence.

"No, but we have a hamster in our class," Jack said. "My mom says you have a turtle."

"Yeah, you want to meet her?" Carter asked. "You can hold her, but you gotta wash your hands after or your mom will lose her shit."

He sat on the floor with Jack and Megan while Skittle crawled around between them, and he seemed in no hurry for the kids to leave.

After half an hour, I told them it was time to go home. Carter put Skittle in her tank, and they went to kitchen to wash their hands. Then he high-fived them and went back to his room.

"Nice to meet you," Megan called after him.

"Holy shit," Jack said. "He's so cool."

"Don't say 'shit,' Jack. Please," I said. "And actually don't ever say, you know, *any* of those other words he just said, especially at school."

I took them down to the lobby and gave Megan my key.

"Can we sign up for Blue Apron?" she asked.

"I guess so. Is it good?"

"They get all the ingredients together in a big box and you follow the recipe. If you sign us up, I'll do the cooking," Megan said.

"Then yes. Absolutely."

———

Two weeks into rehearsals, and I almost started to believe that we had gotten over some kind of hump.

In the evenings, I often waited for Carter after rehearsal, not because he wanted me there, but because I felt I should be available, in case anything ever came up; I don't know what I was anticipating, exactly, but something. When my kids took swimming lessons, I was there in the bleachers; this felt like pretty much the same thing.

There was a bench under the landing of the steel staircase, and that became my go-to hangout.

One day, when Carter was rehearsing a big scene, a dance number with the entire chorus line, one of the mothers of a child actor came storming out of the rehearsal, tight-lipped, hands in little fists.

When she saw me, sitting on the bench, answering emails on my cell phone, she planted her fists on her hips and marched over.

"Do me a favor, would you?" she asked. Without waiting for an answer she leaned in and whispered, "Your pop star in there needs to stop using the C-word, the P-word, and the F-bomb in front of my child.

And the other C-word. *And* the D-word. I guess he thinks he's very amusing, but he teased my son about"—and here she lowered her voice even further—"'cockblocking' him with the female dancers. I can't even imagine what he means; my son is only ten, and I won't have him hearing all this bad language." She was slim and dressed like a teenager, though she had to have been in her late thirties. Her outfit—skinny jeans, boots over the knee, and a down vest—made me feel frumpy. I looked down at my black jeans and suede booties and decided I would call Carter's stylist for some help.

"I'm so sorry," I said. "I'll talk to him."

"He's being a terrible example, and the moms are not going to stand for this."

"I thought all the kids sort of liked him. I know he jokes around with them . . ." Recalling Carter's choice of vocabulary with Megan and Jack, I understood exactly why she was distraught, so I didn't bother trying to finish the thought.

"Of course they like him. They worship him. And I can't have my son going into PCS this afternoon, talking about f-ing this and f-ing that."

"PCS?"

"Professional Children's School."

She didn't appreciate the blank look on my face and shook her head, swinging her chandelier earrings.

"It's a school for kids who are professional dancers or actors or competitive athletes. How did you think these kids get through school with a schedule like this?"

"I guess I thought they had tutors or something."

"Maybe Carter did, but most of the kids here go to PCS, unless they're homeschooled."

I wondered if Carter even had a high school degree; it didn't seem likely.

"You should wash that boy's mouth out with soap," she said.

"Do people actually do that?"

"Just do something," she said. "It's not too much to ask that he show a little restraint around minors, is it?"

"I'll take care of it, and thanks for telling me," I said, grateful that she hadn't gone straight to Edgar or the producers.

When I broached the topic with Carter that evening, he laughed and said, "Did that little fucker rat me out or was his mom listening?"

"Maybe she overheard. I guess you should assume all the moms are listening, all the time."

"'Cause if he ratted me out, he's a piece of shit."

"But the point here, Carter—"

"I mean, what a little dipshit. Seriously."

"But—"

"Nah, it had to be his mom."

"Carter, please, I'm trying to—"

"Freedom of speech, man. Freedom of fuckin' speech. What ever happened to that?"

I decided this wasn't a battle worth fighting.

———

Carter was getting used to his routine, and I was convinced he was starting to enjoy himself, not that he would have admitted that to me or even to Charlotte. He hadn't exactly bonded with his castmates or the director, but he seemed to like music and dance rehearsals. He was in his element there. I would overhear him singing in his room and found it immensely satisfying to think he was actually becoming invested in the show. He would come home sweaty, grumbling about period costume choices, but never about the music, never about the choreography.

"Fucking suspenders," he would say. "Who wears that shit?"

He would vent to Charlotte about Annabella Hatter's struggles to get the songs; her incompetence as a dancer and her weakness as a singer had certainly leveled the playing field.

"I just wish the guy wasn't such a loser," I heard him say, once again.

They were sitting on the floor of his room, running lines for the long scene in which he professes his love for Thereza on the steps of the brownstone.

"Who? Kevin?" Charlotte asked. She knew perfectly well who he meant, and it amused me to hear her try to distract him.

"No, Kevin Kline's really cool."

I smiled at that, wondering when I would get my introduction.

"No," he went on, "*Neville*. The fuckboy I'm playing. The douchebag."

"I don't think he's a douchebag," she said.

"He is."

"Then maybe you need to embrace your inner douchebag. Your inner Neville."

"I don't have an inner douchebag. Or an inner fuckboy."

"Of course you do. Everyone does. I do."

"Not me," he said.

I was standing in the hallway outside Carter's bedroom throughout this exchange, holding on to my laptop. I hadn't meant to eavesdrop but didn't want to interrupt them, either. So I listened.

I heard Charlotte snap a bubble with her gum.

"How are you a douchebag?" he asked.

"I'm a total Neville-style nerd," she said. "Straight-A student. I always do the right thing. My favorite people are fictional characters from books."

I decided I would hug that girl the second I could get my hands on her.

"You're smart," he said. "I didn't even do school."

"Yeah but you're *you*. And how much of the stuff I've learned am I really going to use?"

"I'm not smart. Not like you."

"You're smart enough to know that the more you get over being too cool to play this awesome geek, the better you'll do in this show. Can you imagine if you end up being the one with good reviews? And little priss Miss Annabella *Hater* gets trashed?"

"It's embarrassing."

"Why?"

"Saying that stuff. 'Say you love me, just a little!' It's so fucking *stupid*."

"'Please, don't,'" Charlotte said dramatically, taking Thereza's lines, "'it's useless!'"

"'I've tried to fight against it,'" Carter said, in a cartoonish voice, "'but I can't. You're as helpless as I am.' What a fucking douche."

"Neville's charming. And if you embrace it, like really go for it, you'll show everyone that you're totally comfortable with yourself. It shows confidence, like you're so comfortable with who you are, that you're fine with playing a character who's different from you. Embrace your inner Neville!"

"Shut up," he said. "Embrace your inner . . . ," but he couldn't come up with anything.

"Loser? Nerd? Geek? What? You don't like my glasses?" she laughed.

He must have softened, smiled or something. "Your inner you," he said.

From my hiding spot, leaning against the wall in the hallway, I froze.

"Are rehearsals going okay?" she asked. "Better, at least?"

"You should go with me."

"To rehearsal?"

"You could come, like as my coach. Or something."

I thought I heard an attentiveness in his voice, making me wonder if he was looking at her. But she answered in a way that sounded neutral, offhand: "Jesus, you've got more coaches than you know what to do with. One more person in your entourage harassing you is the last thing you need. You've already got my mom up your ass, talking at you all the time. And Owen, and Howard. You must feel completely usurped." She paused. "Overrun, taken over, whatever."

"It's okay."

"Come on," she said, "say your next line. Go."

I tiptoed down the hall to the kitchen, utterly confused by their relationship. She normally couldn't stand guys like him, and he couldn't possibly have ever met a girl like Charlotte before. A girl who coded. A girl who put brains and common sense above appearances. Frankly, she was way too good for him.

I thought of asking Charlotte later if maybe Carter was getting a little too cozy, but she'd kill me. And frankly, it seemed so unlikely, so ridiculous—Carter and Charlotte? It didn't seem possible that he would even appreciate someone like her, and the fact that he did made me like him more.

⸻

Charlotte got her fifteen minutes of fame that Sunday. It was Carter's day off, and some paparazzi guy got a long-lens shot of her and Carter in Magnolia Bakery together, holding cupcakes, his hand on the small of her back. The caption read: HAS CARTER FOUND A SWEETIE IN NYC? Her name was online soon after the picture came out. She spent the next day quashing rumors, explaining vehemently that he was "only a friend." She wasn't upset, but she wasn't basking in the fame, either: "What do I care what people think?" She joked with Carter about it, and when Carter apologized to her for the unwanted attention, she shrugged it off. "It'll blow over once everyone knows we're *obviously* not together."

I doubted Carter had ever had a girl around him who showed affection and kindness but no desire, who listened but called him on his shit. I watched them, saw an absence of chemistry, and felt relief. But then again, maybe I was misreading the situation.

"Are you sure she's not just denying it so we won't know?" Michael asked the night the Magnolia Bakery photo came out. It was late, and we were going to bed after a long day, a day during which Megan had cooked fettuccine alfredo, but then was in tears over a science project, trying to write a lab report without any discernible guidelines.

"Lauren saw the picture and asked me the same thing today," I told Michael, turning out the light on my night table. "Charlotte doesn't seem to like him that way at all. A teenage girl completely immune to his charm? Who is she?" I asked. "I sometimes feel like I don't know her."

"She's a teenager; we're not supposed to know her."

"Did I tell you she hugged me the other day? And she's so patient with Carter. I can't connect with him like she can."

"You're probably the first middle-aged woman he's ever seen up close before."

"*Middle-aged?*"

"Sorry."

"We're moving to the theater in a couple of days."

"Are *we?*" Michael teased.

"And Charlotte thinks that being on the actual stage will help him get more comfortable with some of these scenes. Do you think she's right?"

He turned out the light on his side. "There's only so much you and Charlotte can do."

"If he does well in the show, they'll extend his contract."

"What makes you think he'll want to do this for any longer than he has to? He was desperate to get out of this just a few weeks ago."

"It's just a feeling I've been getting lately, that he's having a good time now. And I'm having a good time, too. I like this job."

"You can always get another one," he said. "You could teach in the fall."

He may have been right, but the prospect of this excitement coming to an end made me want to cry. Anything would be a letdown after organizing my time around a Broadway rehearsal schedule. And how could I bring myself to take Carter's elevator key off my keychain? How could I give up the combination of order and warmth that Owen created for us every day, handing me a frothy cappuccino anytime I wanted? How could I go back to the daily grind of managing a classroom?

"Or you could teach in Westchester. When we go up for your mom's home inspection, we can take a look at some schools and houses in the area. I wouldn't mind a bit more privacy. Not have Jack barging in to use our bathroom morning and night."

"I wouldn't object to more privacy at all," I said. But all I could think was, *Please don't let this end.*

twenty-five

CARTER'S SCHEDULE GOT HEAVIER as the cast perfected the complicated choreography. He would come home and try to teach Charlotte some of the numbers, and she would allow herself to be awkward and clumsy around him; it was her chance to be the one who struggled.

Carter was still having trouble with his lines, which felt increasingly worrisome to me now that opening night was becoming more and more of a reality. I'd just received a general email from Jean, the PR person, about the opening-night party, which would be held at the Marriott Marquis ballroom. She sent the guest list of media people and celebrities, letting us all know that a host of people, including Chrissy Teigen and John Legend, had already accepted. She wrote me separately, asking me to send her names of anyone I wanted to add to the list.

Opening night was only three weeks away, and Carter was still running lines with Charlotte and Howard. Howard would calmly read the prompts, and Charlotte would patiently give hints when he needed them.

One night they kept at it for so long, I finally came in to suggest they take a break.

"You guys have impressive stamina," I said.

Howard closed his script and slid it into his bag. "I'm thinking I might take a playwriting class next semester," he said.

"That's a great idea," I said. "What about Shakespeare?"

"I'm thinking something more contemporary." Howard, protective of his time, always left promptly after their sessions were over. He said good night and went home, leaving Carter and Charlotte to keep working.

"It's been a pretty long day," I said.

"Let's keep going for another half hour," Charlotte said. "You're so close to having this scene memorized."

I went back to the kitchen with their empty glasses and the leftover chips, and sat at my computer to wait. I listened to them read the scene aloud, trying to imagine it brought to life on a grand stage.

Charlotte read one of Thereza's lines in the final scene of the play and sighed heavily.

"What?" Carter asked.

"Love triangles are so frustrating."

"You mean *hot*."

Charlotte laughed. "I mean sad. Neville loves Thereza, Thereza loves Calvero, and Calvero, well, it's tragic."

"Jesus, I didn't know you were such a fucking romantic."

"And how cool that she tells Calvero she loves him first! *She* proposes to *him*."

"What's wrong with her saying it first? Guys like a girl who's got a hard-on for them."

"God! You're so disgusting!" She laughed.

"What? It's sexy," he said.

"Yeah, well," she said, "there is a guy I like, actually."

I froze with a chip in my mouth, holding my breath.

"So . . . ," he said, "what are you going to do about it?"

"Nothing," she said. "I'm more of an all-thought, no-action kind of girl. I prefer to pine away and keep my feelings to myself. I'm no Thereza."

"Come on," he said, "you can do better than that. Make a move."

"I can't."

Carter didn't say anything for a second. And then he said, "I'm more of an all-action, no-thought kind of guy," he said.

"No you're not."

"Yes I am. All action, and I haven't gotten laid in weeks. I'm fucking dying here."

"I haven't gotten laid in . . . ever."

"*Ever?*" he asked. "Like *ever?*"

I admit I was surprised. Charlotte had been on birth control for over a year for what was purportedly "acne treatment" and I'd wondered if—no, I'd sort of *assumed* that she and Theo had had sex.

"Shut up!" she said.

"No, it's cool, I just didn't know that was even *possible*. Wait, how old are you?"

"Screw you," she said, but she was laughing.

"No, that's . . . Wow. Just don't get weird about it. Don't go taking one of those fucking Jesus pledges."

"Whatever." I heard her open the script. "Like, one out of every four New Yorkers has herpes, just so you know," she said. "So use a condom."

"Every time," he said. "Are you fucking kidding me? Always."

———

There were a few unfortunate incidents. Carter was late to rehearsal a handful of times, due to morning sluggishness and/or a bad attitude. I always called the assistant stage manager with some lame excuse: Carter has a sore throat and needs a cup of tea before we leave. Carter is a bit congested. Carter's knee is sore and we're alternating cold packs and heat wraps. Meanwhile, I was also making excuses for Charlotte to the secretary at her school: Charlotte's got terrible allergies; we're just waiting for the Zyrtec to kick in. Charlotte's got cramps this morning, but I expect she'll be better by ten.

And then there was one day when Michael and I took the kids to Charlotte's robotics competition in Hartford. It was Owen and Carter's day off, and I invited Carter to go with us, but he said he wanted to sleep in for once. While we were away a group of musicians from L.A. showed up. Apparently Diddy (or P. Diddy, or Sean Combs, or Puff Daddy, or Puffy, or whatever he's called these days) sent them a case of his top DeLeón tequila as a gift. The term "sipping tequila" isn't one that Carter or the guys seemed to know about, so they did shots all day until Carter puked in the sink on top of a pile of lime wedges and passed out. I arrived at the apartment to find the Jim Dine Venus wearing a lacy, pink bra and Carter curled up on the kitchen floor. Somehow I got him on his feet and down the hall to his bedroom. He leaned on me heavily and spoke gibberish in my ear, exhaling his vomity breath in my hair. The next morning he was too hungover to go to rehearsal. I called the stage manager and said he had food poisoning. Owen called his cleaning crew to come in for additional hours since four of Carter's visitors had stayed overnight, breaking the mirror in the entry and hurling a shoe through a TV screen. I found Carter's smashed phone in the toilet and went to AT&T to get him another new one.

"Oh, honey," the saleswoman said, shaking her head when I pulled the plastic baggie out of my purse. "How about you take two this time?"

———

A fly on the wall at the rehearsal studio, I enjoyed my state of near-invisibility. I was there in the hallway one day when a dancer ran out of a studio in tears and sobbed in a corner, telling his mother on the phone that he'd had it with the whole profession. His mom must have talked him off the cliff because ten minutes later, he went back to rehearsal.

I was in the bathroom when a girl came in and made herself throw up in the stall next to mine. I pulled my feet up and held my breath so she wouldn't know I was there. Later I offered her a banana, telling her she looked like she needed potassium.

I was there when Annabella pulled a groin muscle. She sat on the floor wincing in pain, the first time I'd ever seen her looking truly discouraged.

I was on my bench under the staircase landing when Melissa McCarthy was working on a solo, and I gasped when I heard how well she could sing.

I was peeking through the doorway when the hired drummer started playing in rehearsals, bringing new life and energy to the music. The songs were getting stuck in my head.

I was in the lobby when a delivery man dropped off a big sushi order from Nobu; Annabella's assistant came to get it and paid $300 for the food and then threw in an extra hundred for the tip.

And I was there when Carter blanked on his lines once again. I saw Edgar, elbows on the table, drop his head into his hands, the picture of pure despair. The actors kept going. Edgar's assistant brought him a cup of tea.

"Just put the script down," Edgar said, exasperated. "It's a crutch. Just try the scene without it in your hand."

Carter tried, but Rob had to feed him almost every line. I ducked out of view so he wouldn't know I'd witnessed the humiliation.

There were successes as well. The producers organized publicity events where press would be invited into the studio to watch a few numbers. Carter blew them away. I overheard one of them on his phone as he left, saying, "I can't believe I'm saying this, but Carter Reid just impressed the hell out of me. Annabella can keep up. But Carter? He's damn good." He paused. "No, like *way* better than Timberlake."

———

And then the day came when Edgar said that Carter couldn't have the script with him at all anymore in rehearsals.

"I don't want to see it in his hand again," Edgar said to me when he walked out of rehearsal.

The mood in the rehearsal space was tense; the crew was preparing to move the whole production out and into the theater. Edgar stormed away, and Rob pulled me aside.

"He means it," Rob said. "Carter's gotta get off book."

"There's still time, though, right?" I asked. "Opening night's a long way off."

"You're forgetting previews."

"Previews?" I asked, nervous about the weight he was giving that seemingly benign word.

"Allison," Rob said, like I was the worst student in class, "we're going to have a paying audience in the theater in two weeks."

I was stunned. Opening night had been on my mind as the big moment, the final deadline. "I thought 'previews' just meant . . . more important dress rehearsals or something."

Rob shook his head at me. "Can't you work with him?"

"We're working," I said. "He's working on his lines every day."

And it was true. Charlotte was making Carter follow the actual blocking while repeating the same words, over and over, with Howard reading for Calvero. They had rearranged all the living room furniture to make it match the set.

One afternoon they got hung up on this one small passage.

"After you left, she was quite ill," Carter recited.

"And then she got better?" Howard read.

"Oh yes. She's been on tour, you know."

"Great," Charlotte said. "Again."

"After she left, and then she got better."

"After *you* left. *She was quite* ill," Charlotte corrected. "You just read Calvero's line."

"Fucking fuck!" Carter shouted. "After she left, you were quite ill."

"After *you* left. *She was quite* ill," Charlotte said calmly.

And on and on. At one point Carter stopped. "I'm so *sick* of this shit."

"You're running this scene with Kevin tomorrow, so let's keep at it."

"Not me," said Howard. "I've got to get home." I checked the time; they'd gone over by an hour already.

"I'll pay you overtime," I promised Howard as he stepped into the elevator.

"I'm sorry he's not making more progress," Howard whispered.

When Charlotte and Carter finally took a break, they came into the kitchen to get a snack. Carter said, "She's not even that bad, actually."

"Annabella?" Charlotte said.

"I felt kind of sorry for her today. I was hanging out with some of the dancers this morning, and she was just off in the corner working through her routines by herself and icing her ankle."

"What happened to her ankle?" I asked.

"Twisted it. She was working with Kevin, lost her balance, and landed bad. It's, like, the third time she's gotten hurt."

"You know," Charlotte said, "the better Annabella is, the better you'll be. I think you should offer to help her." She was making a face like she was solving a calculus problem. "Why don't you stay late tomorrow and go over the choreography with her?"

"Why?"

"To be nice," she said. "Plus if you help her, she'll be grateful to you and more generous with you onstage. It's like with my robotics team— we have to work together; otherwise, we all look bad."

"Wow," I said. "That's so true."

"Also," she went on, "the audience needs to think there's good chemistry between the two of you. The closer you are in real life and the better you actually get along, the more convincing you'll be onstage. You need the audience to believe you're completely in love with her and to want you two to get together in the end; no way you can do that if you don't even try to like her as a person. You should text her. Find out if she's okay."

"No way," Carter said.

"Just say, like, *Today sucked but you did great. How's your ankle?*"

"I don't even have her number," he said.

"I do," I said, jumping up to get the cast contact list from my binder.

"She'll think I'm high," he said. "Why would I text her out of the blue?"

"Don't be weird," Charlotte said. "You're working together. It's kind of a dick move *not* to check on her."

I handed Carter the contact list, and he took his phone and went to his room.

"Charlotte," I said after he walked out. "Charlotte Brinkley."

"What?" she said. "That was just basic, sound advice," she said. "Everyone knows this stuff."

"Maybe. But you were the one smart enough to tell him." I smiled. "Thank you."

She shrugged. "Don't be weird."

twenty-six

IN MID-FEBRUARY THE CAST AND CREW moved the production of *Limelight* into the theater. It was a thrill to be there at last, right on Forty-Fourth Street in the middle of the bustling theater district. The day we arrived, I walked all around the theater, down the carpeted center aisle and upstairs into the curtained box seats, taking in the contrast of the old-fashioned gold-painted ornamentation with the high-tech lighting tracks. I sat up in the balcony seats looking down at the royal blue proscenium arch and onto the stage, where a half-dozen people were scurrying around, placing props, swapping out set pieces, and working on the front door hinges to the brownstone, the focus of the opening scene. I went down into the orchestra seating, and sat front and center, admiring the painted ceiling and chandeliers above my head.

Carter was less impressed. He took one look at the dressing room, the one he would be sharing with two other actors, and said, "What a fucking dump." He turned to me. "Are you kidding me with this shit? I want a better room."

There was no other room.

"But look how authentically *Broadway* this is," I said. "Did you know that Nathan Lane used this same vanity? Audra McDonald changed costumes in this very spot! Neil Patrick Harris sat in this chair!" I was making all of this up.

"I'm not sharing," he said. "I want my own room."

"You can commiserate with Charlotte," I said. "And as I told her, it's temporary, so just make the best of it."

We were all a little testy. Eddie hit a pothole one day, and Carter let him have it.

"I don't make the streets," Eddie said to me later. "He wants New York City to have better roads? He can bring it up with the fucking mayor."

I calmed him down and explained that Carter had yelled at me on countless occasions, and I was still here.

"You're a fabulous driver," I said. "He didn't mean it. Let's just make it to opening night."

"I can't because he fired me," he said.

I waved an imaginary wand over his head. "You're unfired."

The first preview was approaching, and although Carter was technically "off book," he was still making mistakes, and it seemed he had plateaued. No matter how many times they went over certain passages, he just couldn't seem to hold on to the lines in his brain. He was snappy with all of us, and we tiptoed around him, feeling the enormous pressure, the word "preview" hanging over our heads.

Only Charlotte wouldn't take any shit from him.

On Friday morning, before the first preview, everything felt more tense than usual. Charlotte and Carter were standing in opposite corners of the living room, while Howard, buttoned up in his uniform, was sitting at the edge of a chair positioned right between them. I was in the kitchen with Owen, listening and catching glimpses of them over my shoulder. Carter was being especially difficult, and Charlotte was losing patience with him.

"Stop being such a baby," she said.

"I'm still fucking up my lines for act two," he said. "Why shouldn't I be freaking out?"

"Because freaking out doesn't help anything."

Howard cleared his throat and said, "Let's just simmer down." Howard was never one to waste time or lose his cool. "My wife needs me home at eleven so she can get to work. Let's start at the top of act two."

"I don't even need to be doing this," Carter said. "The director was talking to the stage manager yesterday about feeding me lines through an earpiece. Anytime I go blank, someone can just prompt me."

This was the first I'd heard of it. I turned around on my barstool, trying to see if he was serious.

"That's great," Howard said. "It's like wearing a life preserver, just in case you need it."

Why hadn't I realized that there was a contingency plan for actors who just couldn't memorize text? With all the money invested, $9 million *before* opening night, I'd been told, of course there was a backup plan. I was relieved.

"And maybe you won't even need it," Howard went on, "but at least you'll feel better knowing it's there."

"That's what I was thinking," Carter said.

Charlotte dropped her script on the coffee table. "Is this for real?" she said.

"What?"

"Is anyone else going to use one?" she asked. "Annabella? Kevin?"

"I don't know. Maybe."

"Find out," she said. "I'll bet you a billion dollars they're not."

"So?" Carter asked.

"It's humiliating. The director is basically saying you can't do it. And you can. Besides, it's like cheating."

"*What?*" he said.

"You won't be as good if all you're doing is repeating words."

"Am I cheating when I dance my *ass* off?" Carter asked. "Am I cheating when I perform every goddamn song perfectly? Am I cheating when I teach Annabella the steps?"

"What's that got to do with it?"

"They can't expect me to do everything perfect," he said, raising his voice now. "I need help."

"Not that kind of help," she argued. "That's just embarrassing."

"I don't know my lines," he said slowly.

"Oh, come on," she said, sounding disgusted. "Just *learn* them."

I heard Howard sigh loudly, in irritation more than fatigue.

"What do you know about it?" Carter snapped. "You're not there. You don't know half of what I do all day."

Charlotte took that in and seemed to nod in agreement. "Maybe, but I certainly know how to study and—"

"Let's just get back to it," Howard said, trying to settle the teenagers down. "The sooner we get going, the sooner we'll be done."

"We'll never be done," Carter said, "because I can't do it."

"Wow," Charlotte said. "Nice attitude."

"Fuck off," Carter said.

"*Excuse* me?"

At that, I got up and came into the room.

"Okay, okay, okay," Howard said, "let's just everyone cool it."

"I'm going to get some Adderall," Carter said. "I know a guy. He says it makes you super-concentrated and smart. Or I'll just do some coke."

"Now hold on a sec—" I said.

"How's that going to help?" Charlotte said over me. "Don't be stupid."

"What's stupid about that?" he said. "And why do you always say stuff about me and 'stupid' in the same sentence?" he asked.

"Let's keep going," Howard tried again, opening his script up to the scene they'd been working on.

"I hate this shit," Carter said, flopping down on the couch.

"You're being a real jerk," Charlotte said. "We're here, trying to help you, so just do the fucking work."

"Okay, let's quit with the name-calling," I said. "Everyone's tired. Why don't we take a ten-minute break?"

Carter didn't throw anything, didn't break anything, but I could tell he was furious. "'Do the work'?" he said. "Fuck this shit. All I *do* is work." And he got up and went to his room.

Howard put his script down on the table with a heavy thud. Charlotte was silent.

"Hey," Carter called to me from the hallway leading to his room.

"Me?" I asked.

"Come here," he said and went back in his room.

I grabbed a Clif Bar for him and followed.

"What's up?" I asked.

"Tell everyone to get out."

"Tell—?"

"I'm not going to rehearsal today." He was texting and didn't look up at me. "It's my apartment. I want everyone out. You, everyone."

I stood in the doorway of his room, thinking, *Fuck, fuck, fuck.* What was he planning? A bender? Would he just up and leave for L.A.? Was it even safe to leave him alone? "Now, the thing is, Carter—"

"Call that dickhead. Joe or Rob or whoever, the stage manager. Call him, tell him whatever you want. Tell him I'm dead."

"Carter, I really don't think this late in the process is a good time for you to take a day off."

Carter looked up from his phone, full eye contact. I started to say something more, when he walked toward me and slammed the door to his room. I stepped back just in time to keep it from hitting me in the face.

———

Howard didn't need to be asked. He picked up his bag, put his script in it, and said, "Let me know if you need me again."

"This is quite common," Owen said, standing behind me and placing his hand on my shoulder. "Divas demand solitude from time to time, until they find out how lonely it is. Just a meltdown. Let's give him some space." He and Howard got their coats and took the elevator together, leaving me and Charlotte in the living room.

"You, too," I said.

"Me, too, what?" she asked.

"He wants everyone out."

"He said me?"

"He said *everyone.*"

Charlotte looked at me as if this were my fault. "Fine," she said and walked away in a huff.

"Don't be mad at me," I said. "Did you . . . I mean . . . did you have to come on quite so strong?"

"You're blaming *me*?" she asked. "He acts like a total asshole, and it's my fault?"

"I'm not blaming you, exactly, no. But he's skipping rehearsal now, so this fight wasn't exactly productive, was it? I just don't think you had to be quite so hard on him about the earpiece thing."

"Who wears an earpiece on *Broadway*? That is so embarrassing. Who does that?"

"Maybe lots of people," I said. "How would I know? You don't know, either."

Charlotte was looking at me like she didn't know me anymore. "How can *you* encourage something like that? Should he lip-sync while he's at it? If I said I was sneaking a cheat sheet into a test, I suppose you'd find that acceptable?"

"That's totally different," I said.

"Yeah, because I wouldn't do it."

"Not everyone is like you," I said. "Not everyone can read something and just . . . know it and understand it immediately. Things come easily to you, I know. We're all very impressed, okay?" I wished I could take the edge out of my voice or even stop talking, but in that moment I didn't seem to have that kind of control. "But maybe you could try to be a little more understanding of people who don't find it all so easy, for people who are struggling."

"Struggling or just being lazy? I work hard, too, you know. It's not like Caltech was handed to me."

If I could go back in time, I might have chosen not to escalate the situation, which is exactly what I did. "I'd rather you not come here anymore if you're going to make my job harder."

Charlotte backed away from me. "If you didn't want me here, you should have said so."

"No, I do want you here," I said, backpedaling half-heartedly. "I know Carter probably wouldn't have gone to a single rehearsal if it hadn't been for you. I just think you could try to understand that this is really stressful for him and not everyone is as smart as you are."

"Fine," she said, getting her backpack. "Tell Carter I said good luck, break a leg, whatever. I'm done here."

"I'm done, too," I said. "He kicked us *all* out, remember?"

"Take the next elevator, then," she said. "I want to be alone."

"Charlotte, I'm sorry," I called after her. "Charlotte, wait." She grabbed her coat from the hall closet and left.

When Carter came out of his room a few minutes later, he found me standing in the entry in my coat. "Don't worry, I'm leaving," I told him. "I just needed to give Charlotte a head start. She's pissed at me."

"Is there any food?" he asked.

"Sure," I said. I took a step toward him. "You want something?"

Instead of going back to his room, he surprised me by sitting down at the counter. I took my coat off again and hung it back up.

I knew Carter well enough to know better than to talk. I found what I needed in the kitchen: eggs, cheese, ham. I scrambled the eggs and found a croissant in the bread box, sliced it, and made a sandwich. Owen was so organized the whole thing was done in a matter of minutes. I slid the plate across the counter and got him a glass of juice. Then I turned my back and started cleaning up.

"I don't see what's wrong with wearing an earpiece," he mumbled.

I didn't dare turn around. "Nothing," I told him. "That's between you and the director. It's not for me or Charlotte or anyone to tell you what to do."

I looked over my shoulder and saw him nodding to himself.

"Just so you know," I said, "they're probably going to fine you for missing today."

He didn't say anything. He ate the second half of his sandwich in two bites and pushed the plate away.

"For what it's worth, Carter, we're all really proud of you. Charlotte, too. I know she may have come across as dismissive of all the work you've done, but she doesn't think that way at all, none of us do. You've worked your butt off, and all of us—Howard, Owen, Eddie—we're really proud."

"Everyone thinks I'm a dick."

"None of us think that, Carter," I said.

"Not you guys, maybe," he said. "But everyone else. I'm sick of it."

He looked up at me and handed me his phone; the screen was broken. Again. Without making a judgmental expression, I went calmly to the office, took the extra phone I'd bought out of its box, and brought it to the kitchen. I popped the SIM card out of his broken phone with the end of a paper clip and put it into the new one, sliding it across the counter to him.

"Cool," he said, turning it on. "Also can you tell someone I punched a hole in my wall? It looks like shit."

"Sure," I said, trying not to look alarmed. "Is your hand okay?"

"It's fine," he said, holding it out; his knuckles were red and swollen. I got two plastic baggies from a drawer. I filled one with ice, and I put the broken phone in the other. I handed Carter the ice bag, and he handed me his new phone.

On the screen there was an article. It was a typical celebrity hit piece on a disreputable site: it had terrible pictures of Carter with a story detailing his selfish character, sexist attitudes, disgusting behavior, and—worst of all—it predicted his failure on Broadway. It was mean-spirited, claimed to have inside sources saying that the cast hated working with him, and it declared the end of his career as a singer. The last paragraph went so far as to say he was eating his way out of his bad moods and had gained twenty-five pounds in a month; there was a distorted picture of him from the day he went to Magnolia Bakery with Charlotte that made him look bloated and pudgy.

"Well," I said indignantly, "this is just utter nonsense. It's tabloid bullshit. How can you stand it?"

Carter shrugged.

"You shouldn't read this garbage, Carter. People know that none of the stuff they print is true or verified or in any way close to reality."

"Some of it's true," he said.

"All celebrities deal with this, right? Jennifer Aniston? Ben Affleck? They fight this negative press all the time."

"Yeah, but mine is only bad. No one ever says good stuff about me."

I tried to remember if I'd ever read a positive story about Carter and couldn't think of one. I looked for a byline on this article to see who I wanted to kill. "Ignore it, or even better yet, prove them wrong."

"How? It doesn't matter what I do. They always give me shit press. That's what people think of me. I'm just a dick."

"That's not what your fans think," I said.

"No, they think it, too, but they don't care 'cause they like the music. I'm sick of it. I'm sick of everyone always thinking I'm nothing but an asshole."

"Those of us who know you don't think that. You know what Charlotte said to me the other day? I won't get this right exactly, but she said that when she was thirteen, she was a huge fan of yours and loved you as a celebrity, from a distance, but that now that she's gotten to know you, the real you, she likes you as a person."

Carter got up. "Doesn't sound like something she'd say."

I shrugged and stuck to my story. "Those weren't her exact words, but that was the sentiment."

"Tell Eddie to pick me up in half an hour."

I wanted, desperately wanted, to ask him where he was going, but I didn't dare.

"Okay, so I'll see you later? Like in the evening?"

"Nah, you don't need to come back today."

Carter left to go who knows where (A club? A brothel? California?), and I was facing a day filled with anxiety. I went home and tried to distract myself by catching up on my life. With Jasper on my lap, I went through piles of mail and paid the bills. I cleaned the cat box and vacuumed. I called Sara and made plans to have dinner with her after the show opened. Then I called Lilly to make separate plans with her.

"How's it going with Carter?" she asked.

"Great," I said, relieved she couldn't see my face as I lied. "Couldn't be better."

"I've been meaning to call you. You should let him know that if he wants to write a book, like a Broadway book or a memoir or anything, I'd be interested in talking."

I couldn't imagine Carter having the patience to write a book. "I don't know," I said. "He's not really the writerly type."

"Oh please." Lilly laughed. "Very few big celebs are. We would hire someone to work with him."

"Like a ghostwriter?"

"Someone experienced with stars, with how to shape their stories. Just keep it in mind." And then she laughed. "And by 'it,' I mean keep *me* in mind."

"Got it," I said. "And I'll see you at the opening-night party?"

"Hell yes," she said.

I kept busy and tried not to worry about where Carter was spending his day. And just as I was taking the recycling to the trash room, it occurred to me: I'd never called anyone to say that Carter was missing rehearsal. I ran back into the apartment to get my phone, but I stopped before I dialed, realizing that no one had called me, either, demanding to know his whereabouts. Was it possible Carter had gone to rehearsal after all?

I texted him: *You at rehearsal? Everything ok?*

Unsurprisingly, there was no response.

At three o'clock I bundled up and went to pick up Jack from school, talking to a few of the mothers while we waited.

"Hey, Allison." Robin, the nice, young nanny, pushing her younger ward in a stroller, walked up to me, looking even more bright-eyed than usual. "Is it true you're working with Carter Reid?" she said. She turned to see if the kids had been let out yet. "Because I love him. I mean, for real, *love* him. I've always been his biggest fan ever. Ever since I was a kid. Did you know we were born two weeks apart?"

"No, I didn't know that."

"It's true! Two weeks. I'm older." She was turning bright red.

"Listen," I said, "there's going to be a party for Carter's opening night. Would you want to come?"

She screamed. "Are you being serious?"

"Of course. I'll put your name on the invitation list."

"Oh my god!"

"You can bring a guest. Only one, though, okay?"

"Oh my god!" she said again.

This was fun. Robin was still squealing as Lauren walked up to us. "What's all the commotion?"

"Allison's letting me go to a party for Carter," Robin said. "I might *actually* die right now."

"I want to go to a party," Lauren said.

"You can both come," I promised.

Lauren looked intrigued. "Who's going to be there?"

"Oh, you know, same old same old," I joked. "Just some Broadway singers and dancers, and my pals Sarah Jessica Parker, Tina Fey, the usual crowd."

Robin screamed one more time. "Thank you so much, Allison. Thank you so so much. I'll email you." She hustled off, typing frantically into her cell phone.

"Lucky for you to have something so distracting going on in your life," Lauren said. "I can't stop obsessing about the high school decision letters. Every time I think about it I want to throw up. I had to take a Xanax last night."

"So stressful," I said. She was right, of course; my mind had been elsewhere, and I was grateful for it.

"The waiting is the worst. And I keep thinking, what if Sabrina doesn't get in anywhere? There were a bunch of kids that happened to last year."

"And then what?"

"We go into round two."

"What's round two?"

"You know what," Lauren said, shaking her hair nonchalantly. "Let's just not even go there. I'll explain it to you later, but only if it comes to that, and let's just hope it doesn't come to that. Now change the subject. Quick."

"Okay, I got you four tickets to the show on one of the dates you sent me."

"*Seriously?*" Lauren said. "Thank you! I tried every way I know how and failed."

"It was no problem," I told her. And it hadn't been. I'd called Kaye to ask about tickets, she'd put me in touch with someone at the box office. When I'd asked how much I owed, I was told they were complimentary, a major perk of the job.

"The kids are going to be so excited," Lauren said. "So how is it anyway? Is Carter amazing?"

"He's great," I said. Even with Lauren, I never said anything negative about Carter, which means I also didn't mention that at that moment I had no idea where he was, nor had I ever mentioned his partying, bratty behavior, or broken phones to her or to anyone else. As Owen had modeled for me, I was unwaveringly discreet.

"Well, I hope he breaks a leg," she said. The school doors opened and our boys came running over to us.

"Can Jack come over?" Ben asked.

"Of course!" Lauren said.

I looked at Jack, wondering if he wanted to go.

"Take my backpack home?" Jack asked me.

We arranged a pickup time, and I watched while Jack walked happily away, waving over his shoulder.

That afternoon Megan came home by herself since Charlotte had a meeting for her coding club, and the two of us went out for manicures. Later in the afternoon, we cooked chicken marsala together from a Blue Apron box that arrived in the mail. I wondered what Carter would do for dinner, where he was, who he was with. As I watched Megan, confidently chopping parsley and sautéing mushrooms, I noticed what good posture she had, her deft movements showing a new inner calm. I didn't know if it was the cooking classes, the big trip she'd taken with Sabrina, life in New York, or a temporary stabilization of her hormones, but everything about her, from her newly painted nails (an Essie shade of pink called "Ballet Slipper") to her genuine smile, looked cheerier.

We picked up Jack together, spending a few minutes with Sabrina and Lauren while Jack searched for his shoes that had gone missing in the apartment. By the time we got home, Michael was back from work, and Megan began "plating" the Blue Apron dinner on our best china. While I watched her, I texted Charlotte to find out what time she'd be home.

With Carter, she answered.

"I thought they had a fight," Michael said.

"They did. I guess they made up," I said, completely surprised. "Or else they're still going at it."

"'Going at it'?" Megan asked. "What does *that* mean?"

I didn't know. Were they fighting or working on lines or . . . what?

At his place? I asked.

We sat down to dinner. Minutes went by and she never answered.

Where are you? I texted.

The text wasn't delivered.

Michael looked worried. "Do you think she's over there?"

"I don't know," I said. "He said I didn't need to come back today."

"That was before he and our daughter decided to make plans on a Friday night. I want to know where she is."

It sounded completely reasonable when he put it like that.

After dinner I went to Carter's and found Owen there by himself. He had cooked dinner: steak, mashed potatoes, and creamed spinach.

"I didn't know if he wanted me to come back today, but I assumed he'd want dinner."

"Where are they?" I took my coat off and put my bag on the counter.

"How would I possibly know?" he said flatly.

"I mean is he here?"

Owen just looked up at me, as if to say, *Not my problem.*

I walked down the hall toward Carter's bedroom and started to open the door. I thought better of it and knocked, ear pressed up against the wood. No one answered. I opened the door and found the room empty, the bed still unmade. I turned and went back to the kitchen.

"It's a little late, isn't it?"

Owen sighed. "It's not my job to enforce his curfew."

I texted Charlotte: *Hey, honey. Where are you? On the way?*

I waited but saw that this message wasn't delivered, either.

I texted Eddie: *Where are you guys?*

The texting dots came up, the dots went away. The dots reappeared. The dots went away again. Finally, the dots came back, and I waited for the text to appear: *all ok.*

I wrote back: *??*

Eddie answered: *Got Charlotte and Carter. Home soon.*

When? I asked. *It's late.*

Don't know.

I suddenly got worried. *They're not drinking, right? No drugs?*

It's ok

I noted that he hadn't actually answered the question.

At ten thirty Owen got ready to go home, and I promised to put away the leftovers.

"Charlotte is quite a force," he said.

"She's something, anyway."

"I was impressed with her gusto this morning. I always have the suspicion she's operating on a different plane, several steps ahead of we commoners." He put on his coat. "Have some steak," he said and left.

I sat in the living room to wait. I was pissed that Charlotte wasn't getting my messages. Were they at a club? Were they at the theater, going over lines? Why was no one texting me? After another hour went by and they still didn't show up, my anger turned to worry.

No Charlotte, I texted Michael.

It's after midnight!!!! he answered.

For some reason his overuse of exclamation points irritated me. *It's fine,* I texted back. *She's entitled to a little freedom at 17.*

It was true. And thinking about how responsible she had always been, I felt terrible about our argument. She had spent countless hours making sure that no one would laugh behind Carter's back, wanting him to know the meaning of every word he spoke and understand the nuance of every joke and reference he made.

I sat and stared at the naked boob picture, which Charlotte had told Carter was an affront to all women.

"It's hot," he had said.

"It's tacky," she'd answered. "It's sexist and offensive."

"How are tits offensive?"

"It's the relentless objectification of women that's offensive," said Charlotte. "The music industry is one of the worst offenders."

"I fucking love women," he said, "and I love fucking women, so no way do I ever do whatever it is you just said I do."

Carter had nothing to do with the apartment decor, so Charlotte couldn't really blame him.

"So you must really hate the sculpture by the elevator," he said.

"Of Venus? No, I like it."

"What's the difference?"

"It's Venus!" she'd said, like that explained everything.

"She's naked. Tits," he said, indicating the photograph in front of them, "and tits," he said, pointing in the direction of the Venus. "But *you* get to decide which tits are acceptable and which ones are porn?"

"Yes."

Carter didn't say anything for a second. And then he sighed. "Well, in any case, her boobs are showing."

Charlotte laughed. "She's a goddess, a symbol of fertility, of love, and of prosperity."

"She's got a hot body."

"Well, she represents beauty, desire, and sex, so she should be hot."

"How do you know all this shit?"

"School," she said. "Eighth-grade mythology. It stuck. You should pack Venus up and take her to L.A. when you go. She'd be perfect there."

I completely agreed. I could picture Venus out by a swimming pool. In fact, she looked like she'd just come in from skinny dipping.

"Can't," he'd said. "It's not mine."

"So buy it, moneybags," Charlotte had said.

I checked my phone, played a hand of solitaire, read the headlines on my news app.

I texted Eddie again: *On the way??*

soon

I started to text him back, when Michael texted again, *Is she back?*

I didn't answer anyone. I kicked off my shoes and stretched out on the couch.

Finally, just before one, Eddie texted that he had dropped the kids off at the door: *Back. See you tomorrow.*

I quickly texted Michael to let him know.

"Sorry," said Charlotte as she walked in and kicked off her UGGs. "Terrible traffic."

"It's the middle of the night!" I said. "Where in the world were you? Why didn't you answer my texts?"

"Our phones died."

I gave Charlotte a withering look. "Eddie's got a charger in the car. You really had me worried."

"Is there food?" Carter asked.

"Kitchen."

They both looked a little clammy, nervous. "Are you guys okay?"

I saw Carter glance over at Charlotte.

"We're great," she said.

"So where'd you go? Any trouble with the paparazzi tonight?"

"Nope," Carter said.

"So where were you?"

"Rehearsal," Carter said.

"You went?" I felt the relief physically. I wouldn't have a mess to clean up tomorrow with Edgar or Rob or the Campbells or anyone.

"I'm so glad you went. Good for you," I said. But then, "And where'd you guys go tonight?"

"Nowhere," Charlotte said.

"It's past your curfew."

"Curfew?" Carter laughed. "Fuck that."

"Charlotte has a curfew," I said sternly. "And you have rehearsal tomorrow."

"We had to blow off a little steam," Charlotte said.

"What does that mean?" I asked. "What steam? You smell like beer."

"Okay," Charlotte said, "I may have had a beer."

"*A* beer?"

"Yes, I had *a* beer. And there's one other thing I did, but don't get pissed, okay? I mean, don't get all . . . you know, the way you get."

"All what?" I asked. "Pissed about what? What other thing?"

And with that Charlotte gently peeled her sweater off over her head, leaving only her tank top. She turned around and pointed to her shoulder blade. "Is this not *the* coolest thing you've ever seen?"

And there it was. Under a layer of Saran Wrap and tape, a tattoo. I held my breath, rested a hand on the granite countertop, and walked over to get a closer look.

"You didn't," I said. I turned up the lights on the dimmer switch. Under the plastic, her skin was bloody and irritated. "What is it?" I asked.

"A constellation," she said. "It's our family. There's a tiny star for each of you. Here's you and Dad together. Jack's here, and that one's Megan."

"Where are you?"

"I'm the star right in the middle."

The family connection was touching, I admit, and I couldn't help being amused: so typical, I thought, that a teenaged girl would put herself in the center of her own universe.

There were thin lines connecting the stars. "I'm leaving for college, so I thought— Oh, never mind. You hate it," she said. "I knew you were going to hate it. I knew you'd make a huge, negative thing out of it."

I studied it, realizing that, while it was true that I seriously hated it, I didn't altogether hate it. "Give me a minute to adjust," I said. "I don't know what I think." I honestly didn't. I appreciated the sentimentality of it, especially since Charlotte wasn't normally one to be sentimental. I appreciated the thought she'd put into it; she hadn't picked something stupid out of a book. And then there was the part of me that had a knee-jerk reaction against a tattoo, any tattoo.

"How do you know you didn't get hepatitis?"

"Do you know me at all?" she asked. "I did my research. I picked a place with proven safety ratings. It cost a fortune."

"When did you plan this? And how did you pay for it?" I asked. "Didn't it hurt?"

"I thought I'd die, it hurt so much. But I love it!" she said again. "I'm so happy." She ran into the powder room to get another look. "Oh, and Carter treated me to it."

I turned to face him, my eyebrows raised as far up my forehead as they could go. "So. What do you have to say for yourself," I asked him, "now that you financed the permanent defilement of my underage daughter's skin?"

"I owed her," he said, pulling his hoodie off and showing his arm. "She helped me fix it."

Also red and angry, Carter's "FUCK YOU LIE" tattoo had been altered with an overlay of fancy, gothic script, and it now read:

ROCK
YOUR INNER
NEVILLE

The letters were transformed, so you couldn't see Lyle's misspelled name anymore.

I started to say something, when Charlotte came out of the powder room. "We worked with what we had," she said, "and now it's got a positive message. It's, like, a tribute to his time on Broadway."

I looked at her and then at him, at their surprisingly expectant faces.

"Time and hard work," I said, smiling up at Carter. "I like it a lot."

I thought for a second he was about to smile back.

He turned his head away. "I'm getting a turtle tat next."

I got the plates out from the warming drawer and served their dinner.

"You should have seen what happened when Carter picked me up at school," Charlotte said, laughing. "The fledgling robotics nerds haven't had that kind of excitement since Cassini crashed into Saturn. They're naming a drone after him."

"Robotics," Carter said, shaking his head. "You're such a geek."

"Takes one to know one," said Charlotte, pushing him on his non-tattooed arm.

twenty-seven

IT WAS THE DAY before the first preview.

I opened Facebook that morning and saw a post from my friend Lilly:

So glad I got the hell out of Manhattan—great public schools in Montclair, and zero insanity! #BestDecisionEver!

And she attached an article from the *New York Post* about this being the toughest year ever for public school admissions: highest number of applicants ever for the specialized and screened high schools. The predictions were dismal for kids getting into their first-round choices.

I didn't want to think about Megan's chances for landing a spot in one of her chosen schools.

In the midst of the school and theater stress, I got a welcome distraction in the form of my mother. She had come up for her home inspection, which I realized—with tremendous guilt—I couldn't possibly go to; it was bad timing, but the first preview was the same day as the inspection, and I couldn't leave. I told Michael about the problem, and since he had already agreed to take a day off to drive up for it, he said he would take her without me. I threw my arms around him.

"Thank you," I said. "If it snows, she'll have to postpone it."

"I can drive in snow," Michael said.

"I bet it'll be so pretty up there. I'm sorry I'm not coming."

"It's no big deal," he said. "It'll be fun. Your mom and I haven't had any quality time alone together since, oh, Christmas, I remember."

"I deserve that," I said, smiling, as Jack ran past our bed to use the bathroom. I thought about Lilly's #BestDecisionEver. "Just so you know, there's a house up there that was for sale the last time I went, and it's pretty nice on the outside. If you got up there and the realtor wanted to show it to you . . ."

"Do you think there's something wrong with us?" Michael said.

"What do you mean?"

"One day you hate it here and I love it, and the next day I hate it here and you love it. And I suggest the suburbs, and now you have an actual house in mind. But neither one of us wants to leave New York."

"True. But"—and I pointed to Jack, who was now running back out of our room—"space and privacy would be really nice. And what if my mom is lonely out there?"

"Your mom fills up her calendar faster than anyone I know."

"Check out the house directly across the street from hers. I'm just saying glance at it as you're getting out of the car and tell me what you think. It's just sitting there. You were the one who said, 'Keep the suburban option on the table.' Remember?"

He kissed me. "Maybe we just love to hate it here. Or we hate to love it here."

"We should probably figure it out."

After riding with Carter to the theater, I decided to walk to MoMA, where my mom and I were meeting for lunch. I went up to Fifty-Third, looking up at the sky to get a feel for how much snow might be coming, and then headed east toward the museum. And as I approached Sixth Avenue and walked past a cart selling roasted chestnuts, the smell of which made my mouth water, I came to a dead stop at the corner: directly in front of me was a massive Jim Dine Venus de Milo statue, just like the one in Carter's apartment, only this one was four or five times larger. The surface of the sculpture was rougher, and instead of royal blue, she was verdigris, standing in a shallow pool with the hem of her garment floating on water. I felt like I knew her, like we were old friends running into each other in an unexpected place.

"Fancy seeing you here," I said out loud.

I approached the statue and tried to take a selfie by holding my phone low and angling it up to get as much of Venus in the frame as I could. The angle was unflattering to me, but I kept the picture in spite of my double chin and texted it to Carter with the words *Look who I found!*

When I got to the museum, I went into the restaurant to meet my mom. She was sitting alone in a booth, looking petite and lovely in her gray cashmere V-neck sweater and black slacks, reading a book while she waited. She had decided—once again—to follow after me and my family, willing to move all the way across the country to keep us close. It seemed selfish not to pack up and live outside the city near her. Shouldn't we move one inch to her mile? Seeing her in the booth made me feel guilty, and simultaneously elated.

"You made it," I said, giving her a hug and smelling the familiar Clinique moisturizer she'd been using her whole life. "You don't waste any time."

"I'm a jet-setter," she said, putting her book away. "Michael is so sweet to go with me tomorrow. Should I get him a bottle of wine or something?"

"He's happy to go," I said, taking off my coat and sitting across from her. "I'm sorry I can't go along."

"Don't be silly. The timing's impossible for you. How's the boy doing?"

"Pretty well, thanks to Charlotte. But . . . they got tattoos together."

I could tell she was shocked, but all she said was, "I can think of worse things."

"Seriously? That's all you're going to say about it?"

She thought for a moment and said, "Is the tattoo on her face?"

"No."

"Is it some cultish religious symbol?"

"Nope."

"Is it a skull, a Smurf, or a naked man?"

"No," I said, laughing.

"Then let's count our blessings. Charlotte is hardly a troublemaker."

"That's for sure."

"However, I saw an article in a grocery store tabloid that says Carter's in rehab as we speak. Heroin, I think it said."

"Horrible!" I said in faux outrage. "And how weird that I just dropped him off at the theater twenty minutes ago."

"Incredible, isn't it? The way they make things up about those people."

The waitress came to fill our water glasses and give us menus.

My mom thanked her and set her menu to the side. "Look at this," she said, and she got a notebook out of her bag. "I've got a list of all my furniture and I'm going to plan out the whole arrangement. I think I'll need a new rug in the living room but I have to measure first."

"Mom." I put my menu down as well. "Do you remember the house we saw? The one across the street?"

"The big one for sale? Of course."

"I was thinking Michael should take a look at it."

"And leave all this?" She pointed out the window at the sculpture garden behind me.

"That house looked so perfect, and I feel bad because you've moved for us before, and you're going to all the trouble of keeping up with us, and I was just thinking it might make you happy if we met you there, like if we moved out to the suburbs with you."

"Is that what *you* want?"

"I don't know. It depends." I looked around the restaurant, aware of how lucky I was to be having lunch in this museum at all. "I'm starting to feel at home here, but there are definitely times when I feel like we're bursting out of our apartment, and I don't know if Megan's going to get a spot in a good high school, and I imagine Charlotte visiting next year and having to share a room with her sister again, I don't know. New York isn't the easiest place to live with a big family."

My mother listened carefully, then leaned in. "Losses and gains. I'm moving to Westchester because I want to be close by, but I don't want to give up my garden and move into a tiny apartment. I never made this decision thinking that you would leave New York for me. If you decide it's too hard here, then maybe you'll need a change. But either way, I'll be making a life there. And if you stay in the city, I'll provide refuge from Manhattan when you all need a break."

"What would you do if you were me?"

"I'd take my time and let it percolate. Chaplin was right in *Limelight* that 'Time is the great author. It always writes the perfect ending.' And while you wait for time to sort things out, we'll eat lunch and go take a good look at the Pollock collection. Did you know your director is inspired by his paintings?"

"Edgar? Where'd you hear that?"

"I read his interview in *Playbill*. He said Chaplin's silent films and Pollock's paintings are the 'noisiest,' most impactful works of visual art he knows. I think that's a direct quotation or very close to it. Isn't that clever of him? He's a brilliant man."

"Yes, he is," I said, feeling a rush of excitement. It was true: *Limelight* was turning out to be impactful in more ways than I ever could have imagined.

———

It only snowed two inches during the night, and Michael was happy to be taking a drive up to Westchester, which was sure to be gorgeous.

They headed off on their trip, my kids went to school, and I went to Carter's. From the moment I walked into the apartment, he acted like a complete asshole. He was ranting and agitated and spent most of the morning in the bathroom. He asked for a shot of tequila for breakfast and called Owen "a worthless piece of shit" when he refused. Owen gritted his teeth and shot the finger behind Carter's back, with both hands; it was so out of character, I had to stifle a laugh.

There was a run-through in the morning, and after Eddie let us out in front of the theater, I felt the need to give Carter a pep talk over the noise of an ambulance and rattle of jackhammers down the street: "I hate to sound like a broken record, but I think you've taken on this entire project with incredible bravery and stamina."

"Yeah, you've said that, like, a hundred times already."

"Because I mean it," I said. "I'm proud of you, and—"

"Don't come tonight," he said abruptly.

"What?" I felt like he'd slapped me.

"Any of you. I don't want anyone I know there."

I could tell by the look on his face that he meant it, and I wondered how I would break the news to Charlotte. My shock at being uninvited must have shown.

"Look," he said, "I'm not fucking ready for anyone other than complete strangers, so don't show up. I'm not kidding, don't."

In the midst of this crushing disappointment, I tried to see the bright side: he didn't see me as a complete stranger.

"We'll pick you up at two, and you can decide then."

"I already decided," he said and walked away.

A couple of hours later, Carter came home to rest. Charlotte skipped track and went with us to the theater at his call time, even though he'd stuck with his decision to uninvite us to the show. I'd asked her to pick up Jack on her way over because Megan was at a cooking class, and Michael wasn't coming back with my mom until evening.

"You're gonna kick butt tonight," Jack said from the back row of the SUV.

"Nah," said Carter. "But tonight doesn't even count. It's just a preview, so whatever."

Jack leaned over the seat. "Aren't people gonna be there?"

I turned around to smile at him, while placing my finger over my lips.

"Not people who matter," Carter said.

I didn't argue; he was nervous enough already. We all got out of the car and walked him to the stage door, where he lingered just for a second.

"Have fun," Charlotte said, "and text me to tell me how it goes."

Carter wiped his hands on his pants. "Sure, it's no big deal."

"Why aren't we seeing the show?" Jack asked.

"We're respecting Carter's wishes and seeing it a little later," I said. "Opening night, maybe."

"You're used to singing in front of, like, five billion people or something," Jack said. "This'll be way easier, right?"

"I guess," Carter said.

Charlotte said, "You'll do great," and she hugged him. I didn't dare.

"Break a leg," I said.

"I won't see you tonight," he said, opening the door. "The cast is going out together after."

"Don't party too hard," I called after him.

"*Mom.*" Charlotte sighed.

"What? He has a show tomorrow."

We walked out the stage door and past the front entrance. Kevin Kline's picture, life-size, was framed on the wall beside the entrance. He was spinning adorable Annabella Hatter under his arm. She was wearing a graceful, vintage dress, and Kevin, in his fifties-style suit, looked dashing. On the opposite side of the door, there was Carter, posing with a fedora in his hand and looking over longingly at Annabella.

We walked into the main lobby and stopped at the will call desk, where I returned my complimentary tickets to the theater manager.

"I assume you can sell these?"

"In about two minutes," he said.

"Can I show my kids the theater?"

"Who are you again?"

Just as I started to explain, Edgar, the director himself, came out of the house, dressed elegantly for the show. I introduced him to Charlotte and Jack, and Edgar asked them if they'd like to see the set. I was surprised that he'd take the time, on this of all nights, to spend with my children.

As he walked us in, the house lights were up, the curtains were open, and we stood in the back, looking at the interior of Calvero's apartment: downstage there was a modest but cozy living room with posters of Calvero on the walls. To the right there were brightly painted folding doors that opened onto a slightly elevated bedroom, the place where Thereza would make her recovery from the brink of death.

Someone in the booth was checking the lights, and they kept clunking and changing, sending a nervous jolt through me. We watched as the light onstage would alter slightly, a little cooler and then a little warmer.

"Whoa," Jack said.

"Would you like to see the booth?" Edgar asked him.

"Yeah," he said. "Can I?"

Edgar waved over a production assistant, and Jack walked off, talking away at her as though they knew each other.

"Don't touch anything," I called after him.

He gave me an exasperated look.

"Have you seen this?" Edgar asked, and he handed me a copy of the *Playbill*; it had the bright yellow header and the word LIMELIGHT in bold, black letters. There was a silhouette of a man wearing coattails on a stage, his arms out receiving the audience's praise, with bright footlights lit up in a row across the bottom. I flipped through it, looking for Carter's bio, which I'd helped write. The first line read **CARTER REID** *is making his Broadway debut and sends his thanks to the cast and crew of* Limelight.

I had tried to get him to say "heartfelt gratitude" but he'd refused. *Good enough*, I thought. Holding the *Playbill* and spotting Carter's name in the cast list was almost as exciting as seeing his picture out in front of the theater.

"This is thrilling," I said and handed the program to Charlotte. "I hope the show does spectacularly well."

"It all came together in the end," Edgar said, "the script, the music, the cast." He smiled. "'Time is the great author,'" he said. "'It always writes the perfect ending.'"

"Act two, scene one," Charlotte said.

"Very good," he remarked, pleasantly surprised.

"That's so funny," I said. "My mother just quoted that same exact line to me the other day."

"Smart woman," he said, standing up straighter. "It's the motto of the patient, trusting optimist. Well, I'm off to a quick dinner. I won't be able to eat a thing, of course."

He took a pencil from behind his ear, gave a little nod, and walked out of the theater.

Charlotte and I walked in the other direction, down the center aisle, to get a better look at the stage.

As we got closer, I saw that two people were sitting in the very front row. Kaye turned her head and looked up at me.

"I just love an empty theater," she said.

Wilson was next to her. "I prefer the seats filled, myself."

"Touché," she said. They stood up and stepped out of the row, adjusting their evening attire.

Perhaps Edgar's "trusting optimist" attitude had rubbed off on me, but I smiled at them and said, "I'm certain the show will be everything you hoped for. A smashing success."

"Please, let's wait for reviews before we get overly enthused," Kaye said dismissively. "The audience seemed pretty rapt when they were watching the dogs last year and look how that turned out."

"At least there's still time to iron out the kinks before the reviewers come," I said.

"Reviewers are coming next week," Kaye said.

"What?" I gasped. "But we're in previews. I thought that meant—"

"The reviewers come the week before opening night," said Wilson. "But whatever you do, don't tell Carter. We don't want him hamming it up for the press."

"The reviews come out on opening night," Kaye said, "so the critics have to come before."

My stomach lurched, and I could feel Charlotte tensing up next to me. She, too, was likely imagining Carter on the receiving end of a vicious critique and longing to spare him the pain and embarrassment.

Random sounds started playing through the speakers: a doorbell, a phone ringing, a car horn, birdsong. Jack was clearly enjoying himself with the soundboard.

"I suppose Carter will be thrilled for all of this to come to an end," Wilson said. "He probably can't wait to get back to his life in California, all the parties and sunshine."

"No," I said. "He hasn't said anything about that."

"He's been a huge draw for ticket sales," Wilson said, "which is exactly what we wanted to get the show off the ground. But my guess is that he'll tire pretty quickly doing eight shows a week. You can't imagine the stamina it takes."

"He's got stamina," I assured them. "He's worked so hard for this production and kept up with the demands the whole time."

Kaye looked at me like I was nuts. "He was late to rehearsals on at least six occasions. He skipped twice, once for what was called"—and she used air quotes—"'food poisoning.' He goes up on his lines regularly, which means the assistant stage manager has had to be on book in the front row for every single rehearsal."

Both Charlotte and I visibly stiffened.

"He's come a very long way," I said.

"True," Wilson said. "Let's just hope he can maintain focus in front of an audience and keep it up for his six-month run. Then he's off the hook and can go back to his usual debauchery."

"Well," Kaye said, "Enjoy the show tonight. Let's hope he's ready."

I didn't mention that Carter had explicitly said that he wasn't ready for us to attend. Instead, Charlotte and I watched them saunter up the aisle and out of the theater.

As soon as Jack came back from the booth, we walked out to the street and got back in the car with Eddie.

"They're assholes," Charlotte said.

"Who're assholes?" Jack asked.

"The producers," I said. "And don't say 'assholes.'"

I was running Wilson's words through my head, trying to determine if he had just tipped his hand regarding Carter's future with the production.

"Did I misunderstand or was that guy basically saying that they're replacing Carter in six months?" Charlotte asked.

"That's what I'm wondering. I know his contract says there's an option to extend."

"Didn't sound to me like they want that option."

"What option?" Jack asked.

I had to agree; that was precisely what it had sounded like to me as well. "Wilson may be right, though; Carter's probably looking forward to getting back to California."

"It seems early to decide all this, doesn't it?" Charlotte asked. "Before the show's even opened?"

"I don't know how the timing of this works."

She shook her hair. "Well, let's just ask Carter."

"Ask him what?" Jack asked.

"If he wants the extension," Charlotte said.

"No, don't ask him anything yet," I said. "He needs to focus on the show right now. The press is going to be in the audience a week earlier than we thought."

"But—"

"And really," I said, "this is between Carter and Simon or whoever his manager is now. Who knows what they've got planned for him six months from now."

Jack made a frustrated huff. "Who's Simon?"

"Even if he wants to go home, it still sucks if they dump him. It's mean, don't you think? After all the work he's done?"

"Maybe he should dump them first," I said.

"Who's getting dumped?" Jack asked.

"Hey, how'd you like that sound booth?" I asked Jack.

Jack told us all about it while I looked out the window, wondering what I could do to make the world be a little kinder to Carter, what he needed to do to make people think better of him.

———

When Michael and my mom got back from Westchester, we ordered pizza, but Charlotte and I were too nervous to eat. Michael kept saying reassuring things to us: "He's a professional, a performer; he knows how to do this."

"Tell us about the house," I said, trying to focus on the other milestones in the family. "It passed inspection with flying colors?"

Michael smiled and said, "The kids are going to visit her and never come back."

My mom laughed. "I can't offer Broadway theater or celebrity sightings or cooking classes with important chefs. Seems to me you've got a pretty good thing going here. But I can offer a nice backyard and a place to store your bikes."

"It's intermission," Charlotte said, looking at her phone, "in case anyone wants to know."

"He didn't text, did he?" I asked.

She shook her head.

After dinner, I put the plates in the dishwasher, while Charlotte and Megan did homework at the dining room table. My mom sat with Jack at the piano and goofed around playing simple four-hands pieces with him. I decided to fold laundry and carry the piles of clean clothes to where they belonged. Charlotte was drumming her pencil on the table, and I kept walking back and forth past them all from the laundry closet to the girls' room, back to the laundry closet. I checked my phone again: the play was over, and the cast was taking a bow.

"Just go already," Megan said. "I can't take it; you guys are making me have an anxiety attack."

"He's not expecting us," I said.

"Who wants to come home to an empty apartment after performing on Broadway for the first time ever?" Charlotte said. "We should be there to support him."

"True," I said. "You're absolutely right."

Charlotte jumped up and put her coat on, and I threw the clothes I was holding onto the couch.

"We'll be back soon," I called, blowing kisses to them all as Charlotte and I walked out.

***

At ten o'clock we were sitting at the kitchen island at Carter's, waiting. Charlotte had texted him to find out how it went, but he hadn't answered. She had her global history book out and was trying to read. I couldn't. I was worried that Carter was going to come home upset or even worse: foul-tempered and drunk with another busted cell phone. I remembered Simon telling Carter that doing the show was his chance to turn his image around, to be taken seriously. But what were any of us doing to make that happen? To make the most of this opportunity?

"I'm going to make a call," I said.

I went to the office and sat at the desk with the list of numbers I'd written out. It was after seven o'clock in California, so I wasn't surprised that Simon didn't pick up. I left a message: "Hi, this is Allison Brinkley, Carter's PA. There are a few matters I'd like to discuss with you, so give me a call please. It's important."

I thought about the story Carter had shown me in the tabloid, how he said he never got good press. If his reviews were bad and the producers dropped him, I didn't know how he could bounce back from all that negative publicity.

As I got up to leave, Simon called back.

"How's he doing?" he asked.

"Great," I said. "Much better than the last time you saw him."

"I'm impressed he stuck it out. I was worried he was going to blow up his whole career."

I decided to get right to the point.

"The producers said something today that made me think they're not extending Carter's contract, regardless of how he does in the show. I was wondering if they told you anything."

"Not yet, but it wouldn't surprise me. They want these big stars for their names and for initial sales, but they're expensive, so they let go of them when they can. Jennifer Hudson's a perfect example. And Carter's got an additional problem because of his reputation for partying. They see him as a risk."

"If they're planning to replace him, then frankly, I'd rather he pre-empt their rejection, by announcing that he's decided to move on to bigger and better things." There was a pause. "I'm just trying to protect him, especially if they're keeping the rest of the cast."

"Does he want to extend?"

"I doubt he's given it much thought. He's been working too hard on the show to look past opening night. But either way, I don't want anyone or the media saying he got pushed out. Can you look into it? See if there's a way we can be proactive about this?"

"How's his frame of mind these days?"

"Well, that's the other reason I'm calling. I think he's open now to what you were telling him that day, about changing his image and getting people to take him seriously. There was an awful tabloid article recently, and he admitted to me that he's sick of people thinking so poorly of him. So maybe this is the time to do something about it, to use the momentum of the show to rework his image and get him some positive press for a change?"

"Hmm," Simon said. The call sounded windy, like he was talking to me from a convertible. "Let me think about all this. It would be nice to reward the kid for getting his act together."

"I agree," I said.

"I'll see what I can do. Maybe we can even make the producers sorry."

I had no idea what he meant by that, but I liked the sound of it. "Perfect."

"I'll be in touch," he said.

"I was wondering . . ." I wanted to ask if he was a decent guy or just another jerk making money off Carter, if he cared about him at all. All I could think to say was, "Are you coming to opening night?"

"I would, but I don't know if he wants me there."

"I think you should come," I said. "I think he needs people to show up for him."

"Then absolutely, I'll be there," he said and hung up.

———

Finally, at about eleven, Carter came home and seemed unsurprised to find us waiting for him. He was a little buzzed but perfectly coherent. He came in smiling, pumped about the show.

Charlotte and I practically collapsed onto the barstools in relief.

There had been a few problems, he said: a misplaced prop in one scene and a missed cue by one of the minor actors, but, he told us, it otherwise went well. And he'd loved having an audience.

"Fans," he said, "you know?"

"So when can we see it?" I asked.

"Opening night, I guess. Edgar said we're gelling as a cast, and we'll get better and better."

"Did Annabella do okay?" Charlotte asked.

"She messed up this one part at the end, and she apologized to Kevin. He said something like, 'As an ensemble, we're here to rescue each other when needed.' Or something like that. And hey," he said, elbowing Charlotte affectionately, "I barely fucked up my lines at all tonight," he said.

Barely? I wondered how exactly he defined "barely."

———

When we went home that night, I crawled into bed and told Michael that I suspected Carter's contract wouldn't be extended.

"It's starting to look like my work with Carter will be done in August," I said, trying to sound as though this news didn't upset me. "In a way it's perfect; I can line up a teaching job in September."

"Is that what you want?"

"I've got to do something since both Charlotte and Carter are abandoning me."

"We could move before the start of the school year," Michael said. "That house," he said and whistled.

I sat up in bed.

"It's still on the market? Did you go inside?"

"I didn't go in, but I may have peeked in a window and possibly trespassed into the backyard. It's gorgeous."

Careful what you ask for, I thought. "But you love it here."

"*You* love it here, too." He sat up as well. "The thing is, I'd still be in New York every day, just not here," and he indicated the room around him. "You and the kids would be giving up the city."

"And it's you who would spend hours commuting every day." I was imagining taking the pictures off the wall, putting the coffee maker in a box, rolling up the doormat. But I was also imagining having an upstairs, putting my kids on the local school bus, not having a cat litter box in my living room.

"Is that what you want?" I said.

He didn't answer.

I kissed him. "Losses and gains. How are we supposed to know which one outweighs which?"

"To move or not to move," Michael sighed, "that is the question."

Megan walked in. "We're moving?" she asked, her voice high and desperate. "Why?"

"What are you still doing up?" I said.

"I don't want to move. We just got here. And what if I get into Beacon? And what about my cooking class? And Sabrina?"

"It's just something we're considering."

"We wouldn't go far," Michael said, patting the bed, inviting her to sit. "Just north of the city. You could still see Sabrina. We could have a nice big house again, with a backyard and your very own room."

"After Charlotte goes to college, I'll have my own room anyway."

"But we could have a real kitchen," he said, "so you can do some serious cooking. Wouldn't you like that?"

Megan shrugged. "Not really."

Michael looked at me for reinforcement. I shrugged, too.

twenty-eight

MY MOM RETURNED TO DALLAS, and this time she didn't let me take her to the airport. Instead she sent me to Bloomingdale's, where I bought a new dress for opening night. And then, with money she'd insisted on giving me, I bought a dress for Megan and a cool outfit for Charlotte as well.

It was Carter's day off, before the second week of previews got underway. After I went shopping, I stopped by to bring him his opening-night suit, compliments of Ermenegildo Zegna bespoke. They were sending an expert tailor over to pin it for alterations that afternoon.

"Carter?" I said, after checking the kitchen and his bedroom and finding them empty.

"Up here," he called out.

He was upstairs in the loft, one of the few times I'd ever seen him up there. He was sitting at one end of the couch, a leg thrown over the arm, leaning on his elbow. He didn't look upset, but he was making a face I'd rarely seen him make before. Something was different. And then I realized what it was: he wasn't doing anything. He wasn't on his phone. He wasn't playing video games. He was . . . thinking.

"What's up?" I asked. "You okay?"

"Simon called," he said.

"Yeah?" I asked. "How was that?"

"Good."

"You guys made up or whatever?"

"Sure," he said. "He was right about me doing the show. I haven't hated it so much once things got going."

I smiled, unable to contain how pleased I was to hear him admit that. "So was he just checking in?" I asked.

"He wanted to talk about my future."

"Sounds serious," I said, sitting in the chair across from him.

"I'm supposed to think about my image."

"Oh yeah?"

"And like how other famous people make their fans see them a certain way. I could make something, like Sean Combs and that dope tequila. Do a brand kind of thing."

"I think George Clooney owns a tequila company, too. Does that appeal to you?" I asked. "Going into business?"

"Not really," he said. "I guess I don't know much about it. I want to learn mixed martial arts."

I wasn't sure what that had to do with anything. "Didn't Tonya Harding do mixed martial arts?" I asked. "I think it marked the end of her dismal career."

"Who?" he asked.

"No, wait, I think that was boxing." I scooted my chair a little closer. "So is that the kind of thing Simon has in mind?"

"He just said to think about my image. Like a year from now, what do I want people to say about me? Doing this musical means I can make myself seem like I'm smart. Like I'm more smart than people thought."

"You are smart."

He didn't say anything. He just rolled over so that he was lying on his back, both legs over the couch's arm. Sitting in the chair next to him, I felt like a therapist. "Anyone who has all the skills you have—" I said, "singing, dancing, acting—is plenty smart." I crossed my legs and placed my hands on my knee. "What about writing a book? Like a book about your life and career? Your time on Broadway?"

He thought about that for a moment, before concluding: "Too hard."

"You wouldn't have to write it on your own. Someone could work with you. You'd have a cool cover with your picture on it. Go to book signings."

"Maybe. Or something like watches," he said. "I could team up with Rolex or someone and make my own line."

"Oh yeah?" I said earnestly. "You like watch design?"

He didn't answer.

I was hoping he'd choose something less entrepreneurial and more thoughtful and philanthropic; something that would make people think highly of him.

"Is there a side of you that people don't know?" I asked. "Something about you that might surprise us? You could explore that, or write about it."

He looked up at the ceiling and didn't answer.

"Ricky Gervais is really into animals, for example," I said, "especially his cat."

"I hate cats."

"It doesn't have to be cats, exactly. But you could do something kind, like support an elephant sanctuary. Or retired greyhounds."

"That's so fucking random."

I tried to think of what Carter actually might like or care about and started to say turtles, but since his own was an illegal pet, I figured it might be best if he stayed quiet on that topic.

"Angelina Jolie changed her image, remember?" I said. "She was kind of wild and crazy, and then she became a UN Goodwill Ambassador to bring attention to the plight of refugees."

"No."

"Or orphans."

"Fuck that," he said.

At least he was honest. "Okay, fuck the orphans."

But I felt like I was onto something. "Is there some cause you do care about? Or could learn to care about?"

"Like what?"

"Like . . . what about prisoners?"

"What about them?" asked Carter.

"Help them in some way? With literacy or job training."

"No."

Something closer to home, I wondered. "What about music programs for children? Like donating money to public schools for musical instruments or lessons?"

"Nothing with kids," he said.

"Or arranging concerts for veterans with PTSD? Or veterans with spinal or brain injuries?"

"You're depressing as shit. I'm more into the watches idea. Or cologne, maybe. I like cologne."

"Yeah, that's true." I leaned forward, putting my elbows on my knees. "But look, Carter, I'm just thinking, based on what Simon's asking, maybe you could do something more meaningful than branding a product. You're so privileged, so fortunate. Maybe you could give back, give something to others, have them see that you're a good guy."

"I don't want to pretend anything, acting like I give a shit about a bunch of poor people. Everyone'll know I'm not into it, and the poor people will end up feeling, like, worse about themselves because they're not me."

I was offended, but I also got his point.

"Charities are for shit," he said.

"Well, wait now," I said. "I mean, not all charities, right? The Red Cross? Habitat for Humanity? Greenpeace? World Wildlife Fund? The ASPCA?"

"What's the gun one?"

"Pro-gun? Or pro–gun control?"

"Like you shouldn't just be able to get one that easy."

Thank God. "Like Gabby Giffords's organization? Or Sandy Hook Promise? You want to support one of those?" I asked.

"No. I just didn't know what they're called."

We really weren't getting anywhere. "You know, if you were to come up with your own idea, we could set up a foundation. A scholarship. Or a research fund. Whatever you like. If you think of something cool, anything that means a lot to you, that you feel a personal connection to, I have a friend who could help you figure out how to do it. The Carter Reid Foundation for . . . whatever you think is important."

"I can make up my own thing?" he asked.

"Of course. You just have to think of something you really care about, what you'd want to talk to people about."

He was still lying on his back, kicking his heels into the side of the couch. "There is one thing," he said, "but you'll probably think it's lame."

"I'm sure it's not lame at all."

He sat up and swung his legs around to the floor. "Then call your friend. I have an idea."

"Okay," I said, wary of what his idea was.

He stood up, and we started down the stairs. "Also Simon said I should get back in the studio the second I'm done here. He thinks six whole months of doing the show is enough. Max is writing some new shit for me already."

"Wonderful."

"But I don't know. If I want to, I can do the show for a couple extra months."

"You can?"

"I learned all this choreography and all the lines and shit. Seems dumb to walk away before I have to."

It clearly hadn't occurred to him the producers might not want him to stay.

—

Lilly's post on Facebook, the one in which she congratulated herself for leaving the city, got hundreds of likes from like-minded friends who were happy to have escaped the madness of Manhattan's public school placement. "Never looked back!" one mom posted from Pelham.

"Of course they say things like that," Sara told me. "It's their only way of justifying the stupidest, most boring decision they've ever made, which is to leave the city and settle for the monotony and homogenousness of the suburbs."

Sara and I were meeting for coffee at a place in her neighborhood in Brooklyn. The café served my cappuccino in a fabulously oversize cup, and we were sitting across from each other in big armchairs along an exposed brick wall. I had prefaced the topic of our discussion in an email, and I was ready to get an earful from her about everything wrong with Carter's idea. Instead she showed up with her laptop and a thick file of information.

"Don't buy into that antiurban bullshit," she said after I shared my anxiety that Lilly's post had exacerbated. "Your kid will get in some-where." Sara was looking especially stunning, sitting cross-legged in her armchair, her messy, gorgeous hair hanging over her knees, black eye-liner perfectly smudged. The barista was leaning on the bar, gazing at her, ignoring the orders that were coming in. His coworker walked by and smacked him on the head.

"It's hard not to," I said. "It's literally the only thing the moms are talking about right now. So what did you think of Carter's idea?"

"I like it," she said. "It's really interesting."

"Seriously? I never thought you'd say that."

"But is he really *behind* this?" she asked. "Or are you the one de-ciding this on his behalf? You have to be honest because he'll be a lousy spokesperson if he doesn't actually care."

"This was his idea. Entirely his."

"Well, I'm impressed. Shocked. But impressed."

"All I did was encourage him to consider the broader idea of chari-table giving over doing something more entrepreneurial. So how do we do this?" I asked. "Should it be a straight-up donation, or a yearly thing? I don't know how this works."

"We can set up a foundation that gives to specific clinics."

"In his name?"

"Absolutely. We need to work on his vision a bit."

"I know. His mission statement basically reads: 'No one should have a kid if they don't want one because that would totally suck.' "

"Well," Sara said, "I happen to agree with that mission completely. I applaud him, especially since he's including the whole spectrum of wom-en's health issues. It's a weird choice for a guy like him, right?"

"No. Yes. A little. Maybe it was all those condoms you told me to give him."

I could have told Sara that I suspected that his mom's teenaged preg-nancy and subsequent early death from a curable cancer factored into his decision, but since Carter had never said anything about her to me, it felt wrong to speculate. And it wouldn't have felt right to discuss some-thing so personal.

"It's surprising given his reputation for being a complete misogynist."

"You'll be happy to know that he's strongly pro-choice," I said, "and he'll want his name on this, for sure. Maybe something like the Carter Reid Reproductive Access Project?"

"CRRAP?" Sara asked. "I don't think so. So part of the point here is we're improving his image?"

"It's definitely about his image. Does that piss you off? I mean that part of his motivation is self-aggrandizement?"

"I'm not naive."

"Then you may as well know that I want the media to ease up on their relentless attacks on him and say something nice for once. And I want everyone who looks down on him to rethink their opinion." I was including the producers in this wish. "He and Charlotte have become friends, so he can't be all bad."

Sara sat back and nodded. "You know how to make him look really good? Have him pledge some of the money he made on the show to the cause. He can donate his salary for as long as he's on Broadway."

I smiled at her. "That's brilliant."

"I've been in the business of helping people look better than other people for years," she said. "I know all the tricks."

She wrote some notes out and then put her papers away.

"So how are things going with you?" I asked.

"I'm great. I'm dating a married couple in my building."

"Huh," I said, refusing to appear prudish or conservative, "that's . . . convenient."

"How are your brats?" she asked.

"Fine." I didn't bother her with any details. "So do you want tickets to see Carter's show?"

"Fuck no. I hate Broadway. Don't you know me at all?"

Part Six

SHOWTIME

Irene: "I do think a toast before an opening makes everything so much better. Takes away nerves and jitters and that dreadful feeling in the pit of the stomach. Don't we all feel better now, hmm?"

Moss Hart
Light Up the Sky

twenty-nine

THE LAST WEEK OF PREVIEWS CAME TO AN END, and I'd heard from Rob that the Tuesday-night and the Wednesday matinee performances had been full of press, everyone from the *New York Times* to *People* magazine.

On Friday, Sara came to the penthouse for lunch. From the second she walked in, Sara had Carter in the palm of her hand. I'd never seen him so impressed by anyone, which was hilarious to me given that he was perfectly comfortable hanging out with celebrities. When she offered her hand, her fingers covered in etched silver rings and her right wrist in thin leather strappy bracelets, he took it without prompting and made eye contact with her. I practically had to be revived.

Owen had set the table in the formal dining room, a room I'd barely ever been in since Carter always ate in the kitchen at the big granite island, and as we went in, I stepped to the side to let them sit next to each other.

"So what's your goal here, Carter?" she asked him. "And you can be straight with me, dude," she said. "I might be older than you, but I'm much more open to sexual appetite than, say, Allison here is." She leaned in to him as though that would prevent me from hearing. "I don't know how Allison ended up so uptight. She and her husband insist on this monogamy crap, and, frankly, it bores the living shit out of me."

"Hey," I objected, "I'm not uptight." They weren't paying attention to me.

Carter thought about her question. "The thing is," he said, "people get laid."

"Yes," she said, giving him her full attention, "yes, they do."

"And they should be able to without any bullshit," he said, "because . . . because sex is awesome."

"It certainly is," she said. "Better than awesome, am I right?" And she took a bite of Owen's chicken paillard.

They both nodded, reflecting on their vast experiences, I supposed. I reflected on mine; neither Sara nor Carter could possibly understand that Michael was my "better than awesome."

"But you gotta be careful," he said. "Like, you gotta be safe, you know?"

"You're a responsible guy," Sara said. "I respect that. I literally have not left my house without condoms for the past thirty years. I don't even go for a run without bringing protection."

This had to be an exaggeration.

Carter nodded. "Right, and I just want to make it like that for everyone."

"So that's it?" she asked.

"Pretty much."

"So," Sara summed up, "we're going to make it possible for adults—consenting adults, that is—even if they're poor and uninsured, to be sexually active while having access to contraception."

"Yeah," he said. "Just, like, give them shit tons of free condoms and pills and whatever. Getting pregnant when you're young, like my mom was . . . ," and he abandoned the rest of that thought. "I know I don't want a kid."

"You and me both, dude."

"And also," he said, "seems like people should get to see doctors so they don't get cancer and die for no fucking reason."

"Hell yeah," Sara said, slamming her hand on the table, making the silverware jump. "Screenings, treatment, all of that. Cancer's a fucking bitch."

"That's what I want to do," Carter said. He was smiling at her.

"I'm impressed," she told him. "An advocate for family planning? People are going to think you fucking rock." She leaned over and clapped him on the shoulder, the bangles on her left wrist making a tinny noise. He didn't flinch.

"Hey," he said, "are you coming to my show?" He turned and looked at me. "Comp her some tickets, okay?"

"Sara," I said, "of course I'll get tickets for you." I turned to Carter. "Sara just loves Broadway."

———

I had to pick up Carter's altered suit at Ermenegildo Zegna on Fifth, get my hair cut and colored, and make sure the kids were dressed and ready to go on time. To add to the craziness, our neighbor had gone out of town, and his dog Pancake was actually staying at our place for the weekend. He'd tinkled on my bathmat twice already.

At six o'clock, two hours before the curtain would go up for *Limelight*, we all met for dinner at Sardi's; it was Michael's idea to go to a New York classic for our big night on Broadway. There were the five of us plus Sara, Owen, Howard, and his wife.

At a table in the middle of the room, surrounded by red walls that were covered in framed caricatures of showbiz celebrities, we celebrated with champagne, steak tartare, and cheesecake.

"I suppose the voices of critics will be heard far and wide tonight," Owen said, which caused my anxiety to surge. He held up his glass. "Let's hope the reviews are smashing."

I clinked glasses with him.

"I'm not going to let bad reviews kill my buzz one way or the other," Charlotte said. She seemed to be coaching herself more than sharing her point of view. She had barely touched her French onion soup.

"I read that the show's completely sold out for the next three months," Michael said. "So it's a success already."

"You're right," I said. But I also knew that if Carter got panned in the press, it would be hard to keep his enthusiasm up for the duration of the run. He still had a hell of a long way to go to see this through.

At dinner I took in everything that was happening around the beautifully set table, listening to snippets of everyone's conversations.

Michael to Jack: "I'm just saying that the next time you decide to invite a dog for the weekend, you should probably ask us first."

Jack to Megan: "But if I freeze up, would you get Annabella Hatter's autograph for me?"

Megan to Howard's wife: "Carter's handsome and all, but he's definitely not my type. Not that I know what my type is yet, but it's not Carter."

Howard's wife to Howard: "How can you always stay so calm, even on a night like this? I'm about to have a heart attack, and I've never even met the boy."

Howard to Sara: "I've got those lines down backwards and forwards. I can get onstage and understudy for Kevin Kline if there's an emergency."

Sara to Owen: "Come on, you can tell me: What's the weirdest, kinkiest shit you've seen these one percenters do?"

Owen to Charlotte: "Well, if you're in Pasadena, and Carter's in L.A. . . . won't that be nice?"

Charlotte to Michael: "He won't blank on a line tonight. For sure. I know he won't. He's got this."

The sidewalk in front of the theater was crowded and chaotic, with a line of people going down the sidewalk for will call and another line for people holding tickets. It was bright and noisy; limos and cabs were pulling up and honking at each other and security guards were checking bags with flashlights and corralling people through the sets of double doors. While getting jostled by the crowd, I handed out the tickets to our group, but I couldn't go in yet. I couldn't just sit there and wait for the lights to go down. The little lobby was so packed that I went back outside to get some air. Charlotte had gone backstage, bringing Carter the flowers and cards we'd brought him, and now she came out the stage door and found me pacing.

"Calm down," she snapped. "What are you even doing out here?"

"Is he okay?"

"Sure. He smoked a little weed," she said, "but I made him stop after four or five hits and switch to blow to keep his energy up."

"Very funny," I said.

Charlotte had handed her coat to Michael before she went back-stage, and she was looking very New York chic in the short suede skirt and tall boots I'd bought her, her long legs stretching out in between.

"He's been doing this every night for weeks," she reminded me.

"I know."

"Look what I just posted," she said, handing me her phone. "See, he's relaxed, he's centered." It was an adorable picture of her backstage with Carter, with the caption, *Basking in the #Limelight*. She added the twinkly stars emoji.

"That's a lot of likes," I said. But even the adorable picture did nothing to settle my nerves. "Maybe he should have worn that Bluetooth thing in his ear, you know? Just in case."

"No." Her certainty on this topic was unwavering. "He's a profes-sional. He's a performer. He's young, and he shouldn't need a crutch like that. He'll be fine."

I nodded, took one last deep breath of winter air, and looped my arm through Charlotte's. We walked in the theater and through the lobby with the lights flashing on and off. I spotted the Campbells, who were sitting up in a box seat with a group of glitzy people and recognized the blockheaded billionaire Steve Sloan, real estate tycoon and owner of the apartment I spent so much time in. He had a girl who looked like a *Sports Illustrated* swimsuit model practically sitting in his lap.

Taking my seat and gripping my *Playbill*, I held Michael's hand and looked around at the packed house, at the 1,200 people who were gath-ered together to get caught up in the drama, to lose themselves in a story, to be entertained.

You can do this, Carter. I closed my eyes and tried to slow my racing heart. Michael leaned over and kissed my cheek.

"Break a leg," he whispered.

The lights went down and the audience started clapping.

thirty

CARTER'S PERFORMANCE WAS SURPRISING in many wonderful ways. I had been witness to bits and pieces of the show for weeks, and yet to see it all come together felt like a new experience. For instance, I had seen a dozen fifties-style men's suits hanging on the rack backstage, each with its own hat and briefcase, but seeing Carter, tall and lean, come onstage wearing his suit and his hat and carrying his briefcase, made me actually forget who he was for a moment. He was lanky and uncomfortable initially, exactly as he was supposed to be, exactly as Sydney Chaplin had been. In fact, in his opening scene, Carter looked a little like him, as he walked along with stunning, vintage black-and-white images of Greenwich Village projected onto the stage behind him. *Edgar*, I thought, *may be a director, but he's taught Carter how to act.* My opinion of Edgar soared.

I had thought I knew the music already from hearing singers behind the closed door of the rehearsal space and listening to Carter singing to himself in the apartment. But to see and hear the band onstage, tucked beside set pieces, while the whole cast was dancing in sync and Kevin Kline crooned, had me unintentionally tapping my feet, nodding my head, and smiling embarrassingly wide.

Kevin was hilarious, especially in the opening scene when Calvero drunkenly stumbles past the children playing on the street and into the apartment building where he saves Thereza from the gas she's turned on in the oven. And yet he was so convincingly brokenhearted when he realizes that his first comeback performance was a career-ending failure.

There was one scene in which Annabella inconspicuously fed Carter a line that he missed; I saw the flash of gratitude in his eyes and the relief as they moved into the dance that followed. As that moment unfolded, Charlotte, sitting on my left, grabbed her armrests and strangled them. I looked down the row at Howard to make sure he wasn't having a stroke.

Edgar had directed the final moment of the musical, the tragic and unexpected death of Calvero, in such a way that the audience mourned him, and yet welcomed—with a collective "Ahhh"—the gesture when Neville offers his arm to Thereza, to comfort her.

The woman next to me had tears running down her face.

During the curtain calls, I alone forgot to clap because I was too busy watching Carter's face, slightly sweaty and full of joy, while he took his bow. Once I started clapping, I did so until my hands smarted.

The house lights came up, and I found myself exhausted and weepy. It felt as though I'd been holding my breath for the whole two hours. Charlotte, Howard, and I hugged, and then I had to sit back down to keep from hyperventilating. *Carter was good*, I thought. *He was really astonishingly good.*

Finally, I stood up again, kissed my program, and put it in my bag. Michael and I worked our way slowly up the aisle and outside, catching up to the rest of our group outside the theater. Michael got everyone in cabs to go to the party, but I waited in the SUV with Eddie and Charlotte right in front of the stage door. A big and rowdy crowd had gathered, mostly young girls waiting for autographs and selfies. When Carter finally came out, he looked ecstatically happy and very distinguished in the perfectly fitted new suit. We watched while he engaged with his fans, shaking hands and signing programs. I glanced over at Charlotte, picked up her hand, and squeezed it. "Thank you," I said.

"What for?" She was following Carter's every move and smiling.

"You got him through this." I let her hand go and patted her knee.

"It was fun," she said. "Not the way I thought my senior year was going to go."

"He did good?" Eddie asked from the front seat.

I leaned forward, so he could hear me. "He was fabulous. He was funny and charming and . . . so attractive."

"Gross," Charlotte said.

"I don't mean to me!" I said. "I mean to all of them," and I pointed out the window at the teenaged girls fawning all over him.

We watched Carter as he came in and out of view, soaking in the adoration, knowing, it seemed, that he had pulled it off; he had stepped onto a Broadway stage and held his own, and he'd been his very own version of the nerdy, earnest composer.

And then Annabella came out of the stage door, smiling, waving. She looked darling, her hair in ringlets over the shoulders of her belted camel-colored coat. Carter smiled at her, and they shared a laugh as she walked up to him. He slipped his arm around her waist. She leaned away from him to sign a few autographs, and then she stood back up with her back to him. He twirled her around and dipped her gracefully. She turned her face toward him, and—not for the first time, by the way it looked, anyway—they kissed.

The cameramen went crazy, snapping photos, yelling, shoving each other to find a better position. The celebrity couple posed for them and then kissed again, Carter moving his hand up to hold the side of Annabella's face. Then, to my complete shock, they walked hand in hand out to the curb, hopped in Annabella's limo, and drove away together, leaving us behind.

——

"So I guess we're going on without him?" Eddie asked.

I was too stunned to answer.

He pulled the car away from the curb and started driving toward the Marriott Marquis. Once we got about a block away from the theater, I finally found my voice.

"Sorry if I'm old-fashioned and always the last to know everything, but . . . *what the fuck was that?*"

"I don't know," Charlotte said, looking calmly out the window. "I guess he's hooking up with Annabella."

"Hooking up," I said. "Like for real? Or do you mean like making out?"

"I'm not discussing this with you," she said, laughing mildly.

I tried to read the expression on her face. "Are you upset?"

She turned to me. "Why would I be upset?"

"Did you know about this?" I asked.

"No."

"Did you, Eddie?"

"Sorry?" he said, as though he hadn't even heard us.

"I said, did you know about this?"

He looked at me in the rearview mirror. "I just drive the car."

"But you've driven her around before?" I asked.

Instead of answering, he pointed out the window. "We're here already, but it's gonna take a minute to pull up to the entrance. Unless you want to walk from here."

"When did this start?" I asked Charlotte, not ready to move on from what was for me a major, new development. "I thought he only barely liked her."

"He doesn't have to tell us everything," Charlotte said. "And the last couple of weeks it seemed to me like he's been enjoying her company."

"I thought—" I lowered my voice so Eddie wouldn't hear me. "I thought you might . . . I thought maybe you might feel, I don't know, let down or something. Or jealous."

"Jealous?" She laughed. "Why would I be jealous? I'm seeing someone else."

"You are?" I said, hurt that she would keep this from me. "Who?"

"There's this guy who goes to my school. He's really nice."

"Well, great. That's great. I'm just . . ." I looked at her, knowing we'd had all the relevant talks. Saying more seemed unnecessary at this point.

"What's his name?" was all I asked.

"Adam."

"Adam. Okay, then. I'd love to meet him. Will you bring him over?"

"Oh my god, relax, sure," she said. "It's not serious. I just really like him."

"So you never wished that you and Carter, you know . . . ?"

"God, *Mom*," she said. "Carter's awesome, and we're friends, but he's, like, a total player. We don't really have much in common. Don't you know me?"

"Yes," I said. "I know you. And I'm happy for you. Adam, right? I'm trying to keep up here."

"Well, stop trying and just enjoy yourself."

Eddie pulled in front of the Marriott, where the largest pool of paparazzi we'd attracted so far was swarming the entrance. It never failed to amaze me how fast news can travel. We walked into the hotel and were directed toward the ballroom full of flowers, elegantly set tables, and glamorous guests. There was a backdrop of an old-fashioned theater marquis with the word *Limelight* in actual lights. People were standing under it, posing for pictures.

I immediately recognized Simon when he walked in the room, looking very suave in a dark suit and shiny, baby-blue tie. He walked right up and shook my hand, seeming genuinely happy to see me.

"And you must be Charlotte," he said, turning to face her. "Carter's mentioned you on the phone, says you've been a big help to him." He shook her hand. He looked relaxed and happy compared to the last time I'd seen him, when he was standing in the living room just before Carter smashed his first phone.

"What did you think?" Charlotte asked.

"I'm blown away," he said, "to be perfectly frank. I was hoping he could pull it off, but I had my doubts, especially after that bad spell he had last fall. I wasn't sure he'd be able to handle the pressure or the work. You think he can keep this up? Through the whole run?"

Given that we had six months to go, I wasn't in the least bit sure. However, I saw no advantage to sharing my concerns at the opening-night party. "Absolutely," I said.

"And what did you think of our little stunt?" He was smiling slyly.

"What stunt?"

"You didn't see it? We arranged a little romantic interlude between Carter and Annabella at the stage door. I'm sorry you missed it."

"No, we saw it, but we didn't . . ." I shook my head. "Wait, that was a *stunt*?"

Simon laughed. "Genius, right?"

"I don't get it," I said.

"I talked to Annabella's people and told them I thought it would be great for publicity."

Charlotte's mind was grasping the point of this "stunt" faster than mine. "Oooh, smart."

Simon turned to me. "We thought we'd make the onstage romance between them a little more believable. Annabella loved the idea. And I liked the thought of trolling the producers."

"So Kaye and Wilson . . . ?" I asked, trying to figure out where this was going.

"The Campbells are going to be sorry they've decided to separate Broadway's most popular, adorable celebrity couple."

"That's brilliant!" Charlotte laughed.

"And when the reviews come out tonight," he said, "maybe they'll be even more sorry. We'll have to wait and see what kind of press he gets."

I was still stuck on the word "separate." "So no matter what the reviews say," I said, "they won't renew? They made their decision?"

He unbuttoned his suit jacket and put his hands in his pockets. "Nothing's been announced, but I heard it from a friend of mine who's a manager. They've already cast his replacement."

"Wow," I said. "Well, I guess that's that."

"Does he know?" Charlotte asked.

"*No one* knows, so don't say anything. We'll get a press release out to announce that he's recording a new album starting immediately after his initial contract expires. He'll save face that way, and he never even has to know they'd already decided. He'll be too busy to give it another thought. He's working with Max Martin on some new music, and he'll go on tour as soon as the album's done. James Corden's even letting him reshoot *Carpool Karaoke*."

Simon had solved the problem perfectly, but for me the clock had just started counting down Carter's remaining days in New York.

"He and Annabella should keep up the pretense of a romance for at least a couple of months, if he wants to show a sweeter side of his personality. You can coordinate with Annabella's publicist to schedule dinners at high-profile restaurants, make sure they're seen around town. Their fans are going to love them together."

Having seen them kissing, I couldn't help but wonder if there was more to it than just a PR move. Maybe I was naive, but what if he'd fallen for her? And now some other guy was going to swoop in and take his place onstage? It seemed cruel. Maybe it would be for the best if it was all an act.

"Who did they cast in his part?" I asked.

"This is top secret," and he whispered, "Sam Smith. He'll be great. Know him?"

Charlotte nodded. I shook my head.

"Let's talk next week to go over the plans for the next few months." He remembered something and pointed at me. "And Carter mentioned the possibility of writing a Broadway memoir. Something about finding his 'inner douchebag.' I didn't get it, but he said if he does it, he wants to work with a publisher you recommended."

Charlotte laughed.

I was shocked. "He did?"

"Yeah, he said you suggested it."

I threw my hands up in wonder. "Yeah, I have a friend who wants to work with him. And she'll find him a cowriter."

Simon checked his phone. "We can work through all that after he's back in L.A."

"Eventually we'll need to get him a new PA out there," I said, knowing someone was going to swoop in and take my place, too. "Do you know anyone? Not a jerk, not a crook, not a bad influence. A really decent person, preferably middle-aged. Is there someone you recommend?"

"I'll send you some résumés," he said. "Carter says you've never been a PA before," Simon said. "Is that true?"

"Never," I said.

"She's been my PA twenty-four-seven since I was born," Charlotte said, smiling at me. "She's pretty good at it."

At eleven o'clock the party was going strong. Eddie drove Megan and Jack home, and Charlotte was out on the dance floor with an actor she'd met from the cast of *Hamilton*. The guest list was a who's who of the entertainment world, and Michael and I were standing near the dance floor watching the celebrities. I spotted Lauren and her husband, Bill, coming across the room.

"Amazing party," she said. "So much more fun than the boring charity events we go to."

"This isn't our usual social set, either," Michael said, shaking Bill's hand.

Lauren took me by the shoulders. "Well?"

"Well what?" I asked.

"What's the news?" she said.

"I don't think the reviews came out yet—"

"Not the reviews, silly. The school decisions."

I had completely forgotten.

I grabbed my phone out of my clutch and turned it on, waiting while it powered back up.

"What about Sabrina?" I asked. "Where's she going?"

"She didn't get into Beacon or LaGuardia," Lauren said, "but it's fine—she got her third choice. It's much smaller, which I think is better for her anyway. And the location is great."

"Congratulations," I said, wishing my phone would hurry up.

Michael looked over my shoulder while I opened my email, and there it was, the letter from the school counselor at Orbis. I clicked on it and opened the attached document from the Department of Education.

"I'm too nervous," I said and handed my phone to Michael.

He read through it, smiled, and said, "She got into Eleanor Roosevelt."

Lauren let out a squeal. "Oh my god, don't you just love it when things work out? I knew they'd end up together."

"Honestly, Lauren, thank you for helping me figure all this out."

"Sabrina's going to go crazy when I tell her," she said, starting to get her own phone out.

"Tell her later," Bill said, taking her hand and leading her to the dance floor.

Michael handed my phone back to me. "So what do we think? Are we staying in New York?" he said, slipping his hand around my waist. "Are we city people now?"

I looked around the ballroom and considered the splendid evening, the unpredictable, exciting life we were building, unthinkable anywhere other than here. "I think we're staying," I said. "Right? Or do you really want the backyard?"

"I've been trying to talk myself into a backyard because I thought it would be better for all of you."

"I want to stay," I said, feeling sure for the first time that it was what I really wanted, what was best for everyone. "I definitely want to stay."

He kissed me. "In that case, I'll go get us some champagne." He went off to the bar and when I turned around to watch the dancing, I came face-to-face with Kevin Kline.

"Hello," he said.

God, he was handsome. That sincere smile. Those gorgeous eyes. I tried to speak, but nothing came out.

"I've seen you around quite a bit," Kevin said. "You work with Carter, don't you?"

I nodded.

"I'm Kevin," he said.

"Yes, I know, I'm . . . I'm . . . I'm your number-one fan," I said. *Shit, just like Annie Wilkes. Damn it.*

He smiled, and gave a little laugh. "And do you have a name?"

"Allison," I said, blushing and putting my hand out to shake his. "Sorry, my name's Allison."

He took my hand, turned it over, and kissed it, just like Dr. Rod Randall in *Soapdish*. "Pleasure to meet you. I'm off to find Phoebe. I know she's here somewhere."

"You are— You were— I thought you were completely wonderful tonight," I said.

"Thank you." He placed his elegant hand on his chest and nodded graciously. "And you did very well with Carter." He winked at me, and walked away.

Part Seven

THE PRESS

"As I waltzed in . . . I exclaimed, 'Weren't the reviews wonderful?!'
He raised a warning finger and said, 'Never read your reviews. If they
praise your work, they will only serve to make you self-conscious. If
they criticize you, which most of them usually do, they can cause you
real harm.' Of course he was right."

Helen Hayes
My Life in Three Acts

thirty-one

OK! magazine:

HELLA CARBELLA!
Talk about unstoppable chemistry! The news of a romance between co-stars Annabella Hatter and Carter Reid has absolutely lit up Broadway! New York City fans were quick to note the electricity and passion between the rom-com sweetheart and her bad-boy crooner. A friend of Annabella's told us, "They just can't keep their hands off each other! It started out as a really lovely friendship, but it quickly became much, much more." And a close buddy of Carter's confessed, "I've never seen Carter like this before—he's clearly gaga." Theatergoers are flocking to get tickets to see the lovebirds together as they star in the hot Broadway production of *Limelight*, a fab reimagining of the classic fifties Charlie Chaplin flick. But if you're holding your breath for seats, you might just run out of air. This show is the hottest ticket in town.

People magazine:

POWER PLAY!
New York's cutest twosome Carter Reid and Annabella Hatter were spotted dining at the latest Tribeca restaurant-invention of celebrity chef and winner of this season's *Knockout*, Brock Manzini. And on a double date no less! *Carbella* was spotted out on the town dining with *Kimye*, out on a sans-kids date night. We can't get enough of these two hot Broadway superstars, who appeared last week in the Bravo Clubhouse with *WWHL*'s Andy Cohen. There was a special kiss-cam just for the occasion. Meanwhile, Carter is out on the town bringing awareness about issues of reproductive health care access for women, a cause his new sweetheart is also passionate about.

TMZ.com:

PUBLICITY STUNT OR BANGIN' BODS?
Rumors are flying about Carter and Annabella with some cynics saying they're duping fans with a phony relationship. But TMZ has the real scoop, and it's hot, hot, hot! A sexy video of the pair went viral today, showing Carter in a SoHo Victoria's Secret fitting room, serenading Annabella while she models this spring's hottest thong. The lucky viewer sees a shake of her booty, a shimmy of side tit, and hips that definitely don't lie. May we hear a hallelujah! The couple was none too happy about their naughty encounter going public, but hey, people, haven't you ever heard of security camera footage? Because we have!

Huffington Post:

UNEXPECTED VOICES: CARTER REID BECOMES A
SPOKESPERSON FOR PLANNED PARENTHOOD
Playboy misogynist or a modern-day feminist? Carter Reid has shocked the nation by becoming one of the leading voices for access to reproductive health care. His strong stance on free birth control, regular cancer screenings, and even abortion rights has made him a champion of women, young and old. Lena Dunham wrote, "It's about fucking time a man saw the need to join the fight for reproductive freedom." Cecile Richards went

on record saying, "We welcome Carter Reid's support and the support of all men who understand the vital role Planned Parenthood plays in their lives." And Annabella Hatter was quoted as saying, "Carter is one of the first guys ever to remind the nation publicly that this is a human rights issue. He's telling men to stand up and support family planning."

When asked about his cause on *Real Time with Bill Maher*, Carter said, "Well, for one thing, I like fucking as much as the next guy, you know? So I'm confused that people keep asking me why this would matter to me. Of course it matters to me. How could it *not* matter to me? Like my boy Usher said in 'Confessions,' 'I ain't ready for no kid.' And another thing, my mom was only sixteen when she had me, and she died from this totally curable cancer. If she'd had one of those tests, one of those pap things, she'd still be alive today. And I really coulda used a mother, you know?"

REVIEWS FOR LIMELIGHT

"A rocking, rollicking good time." —*Variety*

"Kevin Kline is a marvel. He brings his craft and presence to what will likely be known as the performance of his lifetime, paying a touching tribute to one of Chaplin's most poignant films. Just as he did in *Present Laughter*, he displays a talent for physical comedy that few actors possess. He is, however, saddled with a cast of incompetent 'stars' who lack the very skills that Kline exemplifies. In the hands of an ensemble of outstanding actors, the play would soar. Unfortunately, Carter Reid and Annabella Hatter are not those actors." —*The New Yorker*

"We knew Kevin Kline would kill it in this monumental role. But who would have ever predicted a multidimensional performance coming from the likes of Carter Reid? He plays the role of Neville, a character with depth and sensitivity, brilliantly! Totally unexpected. And Melissa McCarthy's cameo appearance? Delightful!" —*TimeOut*

"Carter is cartoonish when we wish he were real, unconvincing when we desperately need to believe in him. And the only thing more disappointing than the supporting cast is the abomination of a script. And to replace Chaplin's award-winning music with commercial pop?—

What a travesty. Fortunately for director Edgar Sterling, who has sold his soul to make this vomitous, infuriating, commercial mess, Kevin Kline is there to save the day, salvaging a fragment of dignity that this iconic show deserves." —*The New York Times*

"It's not deep, but it's entertaining as hell! And the music? A perfect ten." —*USA Today*

"This show combines the best of modern-day pop, thanks to Max Martin, with the sweet innocence of the past, ultimately revealing that showbiz is a heartless, fickle enterprise. It makes one nostalgic for simpler times when optimism and true passion prevailed." —*Wall Street Journal*

"Like Jennifer Hudson did in *The Color Purple*, Carter Reid has successfully made the leap from musical talent to Broadway stardom, wowing fans with his hilarious, genuine performance as the charming, impoverished underdog in the hottest new show in town. Costar and significant other Annabella Hatter also shows that the film-to-stage transition is not only doable, it's meant to be! Melissa McCarthy brings her genius for comedic timing. And Kevin Kline! Just as he did in the eighties and nineties (think hit movies *A Fish Called Wanda* and *Soapdish*), he delivers a brilliant performance!" —*Vanity Fair*

"How anyone could have expected more out of Carter Reid, a playboy who is known to be childish, moronic, and superficial, is a mystery. Broadway is devolving before our very eyes. They have handed over the keys of serious theater to juvenile delinquents and talentless hacks. What was Kline thinking when he attached his cart to that ass? What a pity." —*The Guardian*

"Can't get tickets to *Hamilton*? Fuck it! Go see *Limelight*."—Seth MacFarlane

"Carter Reid fans, prepare to have your world rocked!" —*New York Magazine*

Part Eight

CLOSING

"I'm gonna swing from the chandelier, from the chandelier
I'm gonna live like tomorrow doesn't exist . . .
Keep my glass full until morning light, 'cos I'm just holding
on for tonight . . .
One, two, three, one, two, three, drink."

Sia, "Chandelier"

thirty-two

SIX MONTHS LATER IN THE MIDDLE OF AUGUST, I stand looking out at the city from the penthouse windows of 15 CPW. Charlotte, her boyfriend Adam, Howard, and Eddie are watching Carter in his 190th and final performance of *Limelight*, and I'm with Michael and Owen, getting ready for the goodbye party we're throwing for Carter. He will be leaving New York—for good—the next day. I'm betting he'll have a brutal hangover on the plane.

In two weeks, Charlotte will leave me as well.

I'm happy for them, I swear.

But I admit I feel sorry for myself: I'm losing two jobs.

Looking out at New York from this spectacular vantage point, I feel forlorn. I can't imagine my life in New York without Carter and Charlotte in it, without the excitement and drama.

Everyone, it seems, is moving forward, except me.

Charlotte has been spending less time with Carter; she has her boyfriend and an internship at Columbia. She has one foot out the door anyway, chatting with her new Caltech classmates on Facebook. She still acts like a teenager, but she rarely takes her stress and moods out on me anymore; she's affectionate, and I'm still surprised every time she hugs me out of the blue. She has already packed some of her things and purchased her bedding online; it will be waiting for her when we fly her out to school.

Carter's busy as well, performing eight shows a week and frequently going out with Annabella. I've stopped trying to figure out if their relationship is real, imaginary, or something in between. Sometimes I think it's nothing, but I've come over in the morning on occasion to discover she spent the night. I don't get it, but I don't have to; that comes as a relief.

Owen has been hired by Steve Sloan's wife, who has left her fat, philandering husband and will be moving into the apartment—legally hers as soon as the divorce is settled—in October. She wants the floors refinished and the bathrooms and kitchen remodeled, and she's already hired a decorator who has come over to take measurements. She's getting rid of everything; she told Owen she wants absolutely no memory of her husband or any of the women he has housed there in the past. She wants the place emptied and sterilized, the furniture tossed out and the artwork sold off.

Eddie has been hired by Sam Smith, on Carter's recommendation.

Howard took a playwriting class during the NYU summer session, and he's taking an advanced seminar on Ibsen and Beckett in the fall. He doesn't need me anymore but insists that we keep meeting. I think he's worried that I'll fall apart if I lose three jobs at the same time.

I don't expect that Carter and I will stay in touch after he leaves tomorrow, green-faced and queasy from tequila. He'll replace me as soon as he gets to L.A. with a woman I interviewed and hired on the phone. He'll move on without me. As he should.

"You've been good for him," Michael says, offering me a tissue as I stand looking out at the brightly lit skyline.

I shrug.

"It's true," he says. "You're leaving the campsite better than you found it."

"I don't know why I'm feeling so emotional," I say, trying to shake it off. "This is a party. We're supposed to be celebrating, but I just feel like everyone and everything is going away."

"'Nothing's gone. There are only changes.'"

I smile. "Act two, scene three."

"And for what it's worth, you've planned a fabulous party to mark this change."

And as if on cue, the elevator opens. I rush off to greet the rest of the caterer's staff, and then I review the official guest list for the security team I've hired. In addition to the entire cast and crew and celebrity friends of Carter's, I've invited a few people of my own: my mother, of course, who took the train in from her new home, and Lauren and her husband. Howard and his wife. Robin the nanny and Jack's teacher Carolyn Hendrick. Lilly and her husband. And Sara, who says she won't show up. "A dressy, upper-class party on Central Park West?" she asked. "Why the fuck would I want to do that?"

I keep busy, placing one tall flower arrangement on the table in the entry and two shorter ones in the dining room, and then getting Michael to help me move Skittle's tank into Carter's bedroom. I go to the kitchen to see if Owen needs anything. *Keep moving*, I think. *Don't slow down. Don't think.*

I look at my watch. It's act 2, scene 7, the last musical number before the finale.

"Forty minutes until people start to arrive," I tell Owen and Michael. "And I need to figure out what to do with the rest of my life."

"Now?" he asks.

"At some point."

Michael looks at me like he's afraid of saying the wrong thing. "But for now, how about a glass of wine?"

"Or champagne," Owen suggests. He hands me a flute. I take a huge sip, and he refills it right away.

"Here's to . . ." I can't finish the sentence.

"To Carter," Owen says. "I never would have thought he'd make it through this project so swimmingly."

The intercom buzzes, and the night doorman Bernard announces that someone is waiting for me downstairs. The missing member of the bartending staff, I assume. "Send him up," I say.

Bernard answers, "You need to come down here."

"Why?"

"I'm not sending *this* guy up."

I'm grateful to have something new to distract me. I hug Michael.

"Everything okay?" he asks.

"Sure," I say. "Just handling details." Champagne in hand, I take the elevator downstairs, and walk up to the desk in the lobby.

"Look." The doorman nods his chin toward the driveway outside. "It's that clown."

I see who he's looking at, but I don't recognize him. "You know him?"

"Sure, he used to hang around here all the time. Drove Carter around sometimes. Brought girls over. He's a real sleazebag."

He certainly looks like one. He's wearing a leather vest, shiny jeans, and dark glasses; he looks like a male escort. And he's leaning against a black BMW.

"He asked for you specifically," Bernard tells me.

"Lyle?" I ask.

He snaps his fingers. "That's him."

I walk outside, marveling at the balmy weather, and watch my step as I carefully place my stiletto heels over a grate in the courtyard.

"Let me guess. I busted your mirror, didn't I?" I ask him as I approach the curb. "That was practically a year ago."

Lyle pats the roof of his BMW, the car that catapulted me into my life in the city. The door still has a deep scratch from my careless driving. "I was out of the country," he says. "I've had this baby in storage."

"Vacationing on Carter's dime?" I ask.

He looks offended. "No way," he says. "I've been working for a different guy, a jazz singer. I got him through his European tour. Twenty-five cities."

"Carter could probably sue you for embezzlement," I tell him. "You charged him an obscene amount of money, and you kept incredibly shabby records."

"I never took one penny more than he agreed to."

"You took advantage of an underage kid for years. And you abandoned him when he really needed you."

"Oh, boo-hoo," he says. "I did everything for Carter. I'm expensive, sure, but he was a lot of trouble. You gotta pay me to clean up that level of shit. Whatever he's paid you, I bet you earned it."

"He's not so bad."

"Is that right?" He smiles at me. "By the way, if you've had enough of Carter, I've got a client for you. I just dumped her. She's a real piece of work. I walked out on her this morning. Maybe you want to give her a try."

"Me?"

"You seem to have kept Carter's shit together. This girl is an even bigger challenge. Way bigger."

"Who is she?"

"Bailey Woodrow."

"The ice skater?" I say. The kids and I had watched her performance in the US Olympic trials; she had no grace whatsoever, but that girl could stick the landing of every triple Lutz, Salchow, and toe loop, always wearing costumes that had far too many sequins and not nearly enough fabric.

"*Former* skater. Very hot. She was headed to the Olympics, everyone said, but she went through puberty and doesn't exactly have the skater *physique* anymore, if you know what I mean." And he uses his hands to indicate just exactly what he means. "She did great on *Dancing with the Stars* and now she's breaking into film with a small part and started shooting with Channing Tatum and Rooney Mara yesterday. They fucking hate her."

"Already? What happened?" At the end of each skating program, I would watch her picking up stuffed animals and flowers off the ice with a big smile and then sitting next to her coach awaiting scores with a sour, sulky expression.

"She was jacked up on coke and threw a fit on set, said Rooney was trying to mess up her scene. The director says he can't work with her. Should I give her agent your number? He's desperate for a handler. I could put in a word."

"And why would you do that?"

"People say you handled Carter pretty good, that he never skipped a performance. You've got a reputation now. And to be truthful, I can't deal with the ones under twenty. I'm not exactly the father-figure type as you probably figured out. Plus me and Bailey hooked up one night, and now she's all testy with me, saying I led her on."

"Shame on you," I say.

"I think it coulda worked if she was here short term, but she's only seventeen and needs a lot of attention and handling." He smirks.

"Seventeen? Where are her parents?" I ask. "Why aren't they looking after her?"

"They have a bunch of other kids," he says, "all breaking into show business in L.A."

A girl. I wonder how my kids would deal with a girl. Could I get her to listen to me?

"I'll tell you what," he says, getting his phone out. "I'll send you her contact information—"

I cut him off abruptly, saying, "No, thanks, I'm looking for a high school teaching job." I'm trying out the sound of it, and it falls flat, even to my ears.

Lyle looks up from his phone. "Teaching. *Teaching?* You're used to the fast lane now, lady. You won't like regular work anymore."

"I'm not a fast lane kind of person."

"Really?" he asks. "You sure look it to me."

Standing there in the courtyard of 15 CPW, holding my champagne flute and decked out in a Diane Von Furstenberg silk wrap dress with Phillip Lim shoes, all ready for a party I've planned, I can see how I might make that impression.

"I'm only acting the part," I say.

"Whatever you say. Here's my information." He hands me a glossy black card with white-and-red writing. "Email your insurance shit when you get a chance."

"Fine." I look out to the sidewalk and see the paparazzi herding together, cameras around their necks, ready to make misery.

"Good luck," Lyle says.

He gets in the car, revs the engine, and looks at himself in his rearview mirror. His side mirror, meanwhile, dangles down on the door of the car, holding on for dear life.

"Wait," I call out.

———

Hours later the party is in full swing; there's live music (friends of Carter's in from L.A.) and a wild crowd. The rich are here, as are the famous and the powerful, and yet I walk around like I'm the belle of the ball. Alcohol helps. People are dancing and laughing and spilling things. I roam from room to room making sure everything is running smoothly.

My mother, who has been spending much more time in the city after volunteering at the Caramoor Summer Music Festival, has arrived on Edgar's arm, her lovely green sheath dress adorned by clunky reading glasses that she wears on a chain around her neck. Edgar, who is in the middle of rehearsals for a new show, looks tired as he chats with the cast and crew, and I see him get my mom's attention, tap his watch, and point to the door hopefully. With a boyish grin, he helps her with her silk shawl, lightly kissing her cheek, and they head to my place together to look after Jack, Megan, and Sabrina. The night I introduced them, they bonded over their mutual appreciation of Jackson Pollock.

I'm surprised when I spot Sara across the room, because she specifically said she wasn't coming. I run over and hug her.

"Who's that hottie over there?" she asks, pointing to Robin, who has become a regular at Carter's parties.

"She's too young for you."

"Speak for yourself."

A waiter comes by with a tray of shots. We drink them down, and I'm thinking I should probably eat something. Trays with minisliders and shrimp skewers pass by me just out of reach.

Sara, weaving through the crowd to congratulate Lilly on the book deal she signed with Carter, inadvertently catches the attention of Rob, the stage manager. I see him tap her on the shoulder and introduce himself.

"Make out with me later," Michael says to me in passing.

"Of course! When? Where?"

He kisses me. "Anytime, anywhere."

The music is pounding, and over the vocals, I hear a glass break in the kitchen. I decide to ignore it.

Carter and Annabella are dancing with the city skyline behind them. Sam Smith is talking to Kevin Kline and Phoebe Cates in the center of the living room. Kevin, who won a Tony for his role as Calvero, is intense and animated, telling a story or giving advice, maybe, and Sam is hanging on his every word and nodding, like he wishes he had paper and pen to write it all down. He looks nervous, and I smile, knowing that he now has Carter's shoes to fill. Carter's understudy, who never once got the chance to even try to fill Carter's shoes, is also here, sulking in the corner.

Lauren dances over to me, in an embarrassing white-lady way, snapping her fingers and circling her wrists. She's sloppy drunk and hugs me. "I'm so glad we're friends!" She holds up her champagne. "Here's to more New York madness."

More shots. More champagne.

"I prepared you a plate," Owen says. "Come to the kitchen and eat something."

When I go in, I'm surprised to see Michael sitting there with Carter.

"You'll be happy to get back?" he's asking.

"Sure," Carter says. "California's the best."

"And what are you going to miss about New York?"

Carter takes a sip of beer and shrugs. "Nothing much."

I hide my hurt feelings by disregarding him in return. "You know what I'm going to miss?" I say. "That bright blue Venus lady. I've gotten very used to seeing her every day, and I'll tell you what I like most about her—"

"Oh fuck," Carter says. "Here we go."

"I like her," I say, joining them at the kitchen island, "because she's a grand dame with her feet planted smack on the ground. She's grounded, is what she is. She's steady, even though she's lost her head." I dig into the food Owen has given me. Sliced filet of beef on pieces of baguette. Tiny stuffed button mushrooms. Cherry tomatoes speared on a toothpick with buffalo mozzarella and basil. I close my eyes and savor every bite.

"Do you get high?" I hear the click of a lighter, the bubbles of a bong.

"Not since the nineties," Michael says, laughing.

"Want some?" Carter asks.

"No," I whine, "it's bad for your brain. Please put that away."

"Even when she's drunk, I get a lecture," Carter says. "No way, not tonight. I did everything you told me to do for months. I finished my run. I can get a little high now if I want. I'm going to L.A. and cutting loose," Carter says, with a whoop in his voice. It sounds like a threat.

I put my head down on the cool granite counter in defeat.

I hear Michael pat Carter on the back. "You're lucky to have her looking out for you. And when you head out tomorrow, keep in mind that Allison and I are here for you if you ever need anything."

I'm smiling in my state of tipsiness. Or at least I think I am. I love my husband for saying that.

"Upsy-daisy." I feel Michael's arm around my waist, pulling me up. The music is playing, the floor is shaking, the champagne is flowing. I don't want to go home just yet.

I wake up with a headache. I'm wearing Diane von Furstenberg in bed. I picture shrimp dumplings and Charlotte in a blue strapless dress. Sara making out with Carolyn Hendrick.

Carter! I suddenly sit up and look around. I'm home. Michael is asleep next to me.

"What happened?" I ask, pressing my palms into my temples.

Michael rolls over to face me. "Nothing," he says. "You got a little drunk. We took a cab."

"Oh my God."

"It's fine. It was a great party."

"I have to go." I try to get up. "I have to say goodbye to Carter."

He checks his phone. "It's only six. Go back to sleep. You have plenty of time."

I lie back down, and Michael hugs me.

"We were in the living room. How did I—?"

"Carter helped me get you down to the lobby."

"No, no!" I groan.

"He said you helped get his 'drunk ass' where he needed to be. I thought that was fair enough."

"Oh god."

"What?"

"I'm mortified."

"Why? It was a great night. You gave a terrific speech."

"*What?!* I did not."

"You clinked your glass and everything."

I get a vague flashback: *Yoo-hoo! Can I have everyone's attention, please?*

"Oh no." I put my pillow over my face.

"It was really good. Very heartfelt and personal. I think he actually appreciated it."

My big moment with Carter, and I can barely remember it.

"Are you still glad we're staying in the city?" Michael asks. "Even with Charlotte and Carter leaving?"

"Yes," I say. "The gains outweigh the losses. I'm sure of it. Are you?"

"Yes, I'm embracing the filth. The sewage. The pushy crowds."

"The expense, and the construction, and the hot, sweaty subway. I love it all," I tell him. "How weird is that?" And I fall back to sleep.

———

A few hours later I ride in the SUV with Carter to Teterboro airport. Carter chooses to sit up front with Eddie. I sit in the back with Skittle next to me in her travel tank. As we swerve and hit potholes, I realize how close I actually am to getting sick.

I lean my forehead against the car window.

We drive through the Lincoln Tunnel into New Jersey, listening to music from Carter's iPhone through the car speakers. I like it and ask Carter for the name of the band. He hands me his phone, which says "Hiatus Kaiyote," a grotesque misspelling, I assume, but the music is terrific. I look more closely and notice a crack in Carter's screen. I feel a sharp pain in my heart, knowing that I won't be the one to replace it.

Eddie parks the car and goes ahead of us with Carter's bags, leaving us alone.

"So good luck," I say and hand him Skittle in her box. "I'll be keeping an eye on you from afar." I can tell that sounds creepy, and without warning, I start crying.

"Seriously?" Carter asks. "What the fuck?"

"Sorry," I tell him, wiping my eyes on my sleeve. "I can't help it."

He puts on his sunglasses. "All that shit you said last night. Was that for real?"

Parts of my epic speech have come back to me in the last few hours.

"Of course. I think you're an amazing person, Carter, and I'm so proud of you—"

He shakes his head at me. "That's not what I'm talking about."

Shit.

"Later on. You were obsessing about Thanksgiving. You were wrecked so maybe you were just bullshitting, but you said all of this stuff, like you wouldn't shut the fuck up about Thanksgiving."

I have no memory of this whatsoever. "Well, no, I wasn't bullshitting." I take a guess: "You want to come to New York for Thanksgiving?" It seems like the wrong question. "You're always welcome."

"What? No," he says.

"No?"

"You said it's too far for Charlotte to go back to New York. So you're going to fly out to California to, like, cook a turkey at my place or something."

"Oh, that," I say. I may have been drunk, but I really like my thinking. "Yes, absolutely, we're going to L.A., for sure. That's the plan. So let's spend Thanksgiving together."

"Yeah?"

"Yeah, definitely, I'm in. I'm totally in." He's looking away at the plane I've chartered for him. It's sleek and fast-looking; the sight of it makes me nauseous. "How come you aren't hungover?" I ask, realizing what a complete reversal this is. "Did you have fun last night? It was a good party, right?"

"It completely kicked ass," he says and checks his phone. "So I'll see you in a few months, then."

"Yeah, I'm looking forward to it," I answer. "Keep in touch, okay?" I want to hug him, I need to hug him, but instead I watch him walk away. I wonder if he'll turn and wave.

"Hey, Carter," I yell across the tarmac. "Have a good flight."

He doesn't hear me and climbs on board the jet.

———

Eddie and I drive back to the city, this time over the George Washington Bridge. Through my dark glasses, I watch a cruise ship on the Hudson, wondering who's on it, where it's going. How surprising to find myself at home in a place I'd thought was dead set on rejecting me. I'm living here. I might even be thriving.

Eddie drops me off in front of Carter's, and I hug him goodbye.

With the key in my hand I take the elevator back up to the penthouse. Going up, up, up for the last time to the lofty life I've been enjoying. New York is so strange in its verticality. The rich, the poor. The penthouse, the basement. Everyone simultaneously rising and falling.

In spite of the wild party, the apartment is as quiet and spotless as the first time I was there, smelling faintly like cigarette smoke, cologne, and Windex. I lay the key on the table in the entry and then walk through the apartment one last time, stopping in the kitchen to lay my hands on the granite island.

Before calling the elevator to take me back down to street level, I stop in front of Venus and put down my bag. There's a stepstool in the hall closet that I place right next to the pedestal. Using the wall to steady myself, I climb up so that Venus and I are finally the same height, and I air kiss her where her cheek is supposed to be. Maybe I'm still drunk, but I wrap one arm around her waist and take a selfie of the two of us with the view of New York in the background. I send it to Carter with the caption: *Going to miss this lady! I'll miss you, too, Carter. I wish you all the best. xo.*

And then a week later, the doorbell rings: Venus has arrived at our apartment. For a second, baffled to see her standing on my doormat in the carpeted hallway, I think that my mind has conjured this absurdly oversize, headless blue goddess outside our door. "What is *she* doing here?" I cry out, and then I laugh until I can barely breathe. Several strong men move her inside on a dolly, and she assumes her pose, taking up way more than her share of space in our little living room. She looms regally over the upright piano and Charlotte's stuffed duffel bags, and Jasper creeps over to pay homage, reaching up to rub his chin against her foot. She looks ridiculous here. She looks spectacular. I hope the floor can support her.

After the men leave, I stand there marveling at her, this woman from another place and time who makes herself at home wherever she lands, taking the stage in our storied, starlit city.

Then I see the note taped to the pedestal:

Want u to have her. CU in LA. —Carter

ACKNOWLEDGMENTS

I'm so grateful to Emily Bestler at Emily Bestler Books and to the Atria/ Simon & Schuster team, including Lara Jones, Stephanie Mendoza, Jackie Jou, and Albert Tang, for everything they have done to get *Limelight* ready for showtime. I am so proud to have that little fox on the spine of my books.

My heartfelt thanks to my wonderful agent, Linda Chester. I appreciate her guidance, care, and friendship more than I can say. And thanks so much to the lovely Laurie Fox and Gary Jaffe as well. And a big thank you to Kathleen Carter at Kathleen Carter Communications.

And to my editor Anika Streitfeld: as I was searching for classic films to stage on fictional Broadway, it was Anika who said, "What about Charlie Chaplin's *Limelight*?" I am so grateful for her great ideas, knowledge, humor, high expectations, clever insights, and incredibly good instincts. I look forward to our projects ahead.

I have the most wonderful family. Sending so much gratitude and love to David and to my sons Alex, Andrew, and Luke. And a million thanks to my dear sisters, Wendy O'Sullivan and Laurie Mitchell, and to my dad (and best early reader ever), Jere Mitchell.

So many wonderful friends offered inspiration and concrete help with this book on topics ranging from Broadway production schedules to NYC public school admissions, to Manhattan real estate. For their expertise and wisdom, thank you to Tony Shalhoub, Hilton Als, David Youse, Roger Horchow, Fiona Davis, Linda Powell, Butch Grier (of Ripley Grier studios), Elissa Bassist, Dawn Charles, Michael Holland, Joanne Douglas, Lynda Forsha, Lindsay Ratowski, Benjamin Binstock, Megan O'Sullivan, Maddie Woods, George Kryder, Julie Klam, Jamie Brenner, Emilie Clark, and Michelle Ganon.

Thank you also to my supportive friends and family who keep me afloat and functioning in so many ways: Brent Woods, April Benasich, Jamie Melcher, Felice Kaufmann, Candy Moss, Ana Blohm, Keith Sigel, Anna Salajegheh, Brett Burns, Sabrina Khan, Dacel Casey, Amy White, Maria White, Heidi Dolan, Ashley Cooper Bianchi, Theo Theoharis, Kristin Harman, Liz King, Donna James, Amy Weinberg,

Norbert Hornstein, Emily Homonoff, Robin Kall, Tracey Tisler, Honore Comfort, John Kim, Julie Kutner, Andrea Peskind-Katz, Peter Mitchell, Mathew and Chloe O'Sullivan, Sophie Woods, Calvin Woods, Julie Blohm, Lili D'Huc, and my lovely Venezuelan and German family members.

And big hugs to the amazing community of writers I have been lucky enough to meet: the writers of the 2017 Deb Ball, Crystal King, Lynn Hall, Tiffany Jackson, and Jenni Walsh, and of the Brooklyn Writers' Salon, Georgia Clark, and (to name a few) M. Elizabeth Lee, Sara Goudarzi, Jess Rowland, Julie Pennell, Laurie Lico Albanese, Laura Brown, Charity Shumway, Brian Platzer, Marina Budhos, Suzanne Rindell, and Rebecca Schuh.

And thanks to Tucker, my sidekick.